MW01505230

THE CARTOGRAPHER OF SANDS

Green City Books

©2025 by Jason Buchholz

All rights reserved. No part of this book may be used or reproduced in any manner whatsoever without written permission, except in the case of brief quotations in critical articles or reviews.

For more information, contact Green City Books:

editors@greencitybooks.com

Published 2025

Published in the United States of America

ISBN: 978-1-963101-11-9

FIRST EDITION

designed by Isaac Peterson

cover art by Isaac Peterson

Library of Congress Cataloging-in-Publication Data has been applied for.

Also by Jason Buchholz

A Paper Son (Tyrus Books, 2016)

The Cartographer of Sands

by

Jason Buchholz

GREEN CITY
BOOKS

For Roseland, California, and its people,
especially Jennifer Buchholz and John Buchholz

La urraca

I am not a bird. I cannot fly. I know how to stand still, though, and standing still while everything around you moves is much the same as flight. You become a center. A heart.

My name is Maria, but I am known as *La urraca*—The Magpie. I was given that name by those who do not understand the way traveling works in the desert, by those who think of the desert as immobile, something made of solid surfaces, of rocks and sand and the hard shells and *espinas* of cactuses.

Not everybody understands the desert as I do—a place of openness, of spaces full of shifting life, of animals and plants whose vitality flows easily from one corner to another, from one time to another, upon the winds that cross the sky and fill the spaces between grains of sand.

The *espiritu* is much the same as the desert, and healing is much like traveling. You enter and you wait and you pay close attention. The things that do not need you will drift around and past and away from you. The things that need you, though, will find you.

Part I: Diverge

Chapter 1

For this first part, you have to pay close attention. There's a lot to cover, and for now, you can trust everything I'm telling you. By this time next week, though, I may not be a very reliable narrator. That's a term I learned from Mr. Harris, my Honors English teacher, but I won't be attending his class anymore. Or anyone else's. Graduation is in just a couple of weeks, and the teachers are done teaching. That's fine, because I've got other things to do.

Right now I'm walking to Ayla's house. I've walked this route hundreds of times before, but never at three in the morning. The streets are still and silent. The moon hangs over the bay, and next to it a single cloud, stretched thin like a blade, fringed with silver. On most nights, only a handful of stars pierce the city's glow, but a brief shower came through this afternoon and cleaned all the dust and pollen out of the air. Far below, the glitter on the bay is as clear as if I were holding it in the palm of my hand. I can stare at the view from up here for hours, but I don't have time right now. They're all waiting for me at Ayla's.

In a few hours, my parents will be up and they'll discover my empty bedroom and the note I left for them, and then they'll see that I left my phone on my dresser. It could be either of them who first goes in there. My dad is an early riser but my mom's schedule is all over the place. Even sneaking out of the house at three in the morning I was worried I'd run into her. But I'm gone now, walking fast down the hill, and this whole thing only moves in one direction now. I don't know when I'll be going back, or what will happen when I do.

Most of us will be riding in this old van that appeared somehow, but I'll be riding with Forrest in his VW camper, thankfully. Forrest has been one of my two best friends since middle school and there's no way I could be doing this without him. I'll be able to trust him, even when I can't trust myself anymore. His brother Preston will be riding with us and helping with the driving. The two of them are already in college, and they live together by themselves, so it will be a while before anyone realizes they're gone. I don't love Preston, but I trust him enough. I would have preferred if our friend Carlos could have been with us, but he skipped second grade, and he won't be eighteen until next year. A missing minor would fuck this whole thing up.

It's harder to explain about the *centella*. I can tell you how I have it stored in two dark glass jars, both of which are packed in bubble wrap and secure in a shoebox that barely fits into my backpack. One jar contains the stems and leaves, dried and crushed. In the other jar the flowers are intact, their black-and-red petals still as vivid as when I collected them two winters ago. You don't crush those until the last minute. I can tell you how I make the tea, and how I learned the recipe when I was at my grandfather's place in the desert, when we discovered he was gone, but that's a whole other story, and it's going to have to wait because it's long and kind of strange and I don't have far to go to Ayla's.

There's a lot I can tell you about the *centella*, but as for what it does, exactly—the nature of *el regreso*—there's no way to explain it with words. Not with metaphors, not with poetry. How do you describe what lies beyond language? And there aren't any stories or accounts I can point you to anywhere else. My grandfather, Rogelio Gonzalez, *invented* it. How do you invent a flower? Apparently you become an ethnobotanist and then spend your career traveling all over the world, back and forth between your fieldwork and universities, and barely have time for your daughter or your son-in-law or your grandkids, and then I guess you wander into the desert and disappear.

Now that Rogelio is gone, I might be the only person in the world who knows the workings of the *centella del desierto*. I will tell you how I learned about it, and you probably won't believe me, but that's fine. I don't know if I fully believe it either, and I'm the one with a backpack full of it, walking to my best friend's house in the dead of night.

The trees at the bottom of our street are tall and thick with leaves and as I descend to the intersection they block out the bay and the city and then the moon, encasing me in shadow. I turn left. Two more blocks.

Wisps of doubts drift back and forth as I walk. I'm not too sure I'm ready for all this. I mean, I've done everything I can do on my own—I'm just not sure what comes next. And it's weird to have this other crew involved now. I knew early on that this thing was going to grow beyond me, but I'm surprised at how quickly it's happening. And their dedication, with their matching tattoos and all. I was not expecting disciples. I wonder what my brothers would think about all this.

The road curves to the right as it descends and I can't see Ayla's quite yet but I feel the energy of its contents, a point of vibrating heat in a little hollow of this warm spring night. Another hundred yards and the curve brings me within view of Forrest's camper, and there behind it is the van. It's big, old, and beat up, like the ones that pull up outside Gilman and spit out touring punk bands. It's real. They're here. We're underway. The road descends more steeply here, and against my back presses not just the weight of my backpack but the gathered momentum of my grandfather and his mother and everyone who came before them.

Chapter 2

From his seat in the leather armchair just inside the open window of his father's study, the bay far below looks to Gabriel like a piece of aquamarine, placid in its repose. In the middle distance, the springtime crowns of the trees that blanket the long slope stand motionless in the still morning. Beneath his window and a story below, the driveway has been recently swept clean. But his mother's garden, which stands next to it, has grown wild. If he couldn't already hear her playing, the weeds alone would tell him that she is rehearsing for an important performance.

Though Peoria's studio is two floors below him and half-buried in the hillside, the repeated sieges on her massive piano send fusillades of notes up through the house's walls. She's attacking a passage he's heard before, something Spanish, fast and insistent, and she's playing it over and over again. Redland projects his own waves of agitation, sitting behind his oversized desk, scribbling across a notepad. Tension emanates from his shoulders, the angle of his neck, his jaw. The engineer, who is almost as renowned in his field as his wife is in hers, is known for his meticulous, painstaking work. Today, though, he's full of twitches, and deep lines crease his brow. Peoria sends up another volley from down below, gets it wrong, slams her hands on the keys, starts

4

again. At this rate, Gabriel figures, it's just a matter of time before the vibrations from these two shake loose all the framing, and the Percival home collapses in upon itself.

Gabriel stands, pivots the leather armchair a few more degrees toward the open window, and sits back down. He returns his gaze to the scene outside his father's window and resumes his wait for Leonardo, who is now five minutes late. Another torrential uprising of notes, faster than before, and a silver Audi makes a fast turn into the bottom of the lane. A small screech from the tires pierces the music.

Chapter 3

Leonardo grimaces as his parents' driveway takes another swipe out of his undercarriage. He can only make it unscathed with total concentration and a little luck, and today his mind is in a dozen other places: a stack of final papers he has to grade; grant applications and publication deadlines; Yvette's increasing weirdness. And as for luck, how much of it can he expect to have on a day that began with a cryptic phone call, insisting he drop everything and come to his parents' house, right then?

"You're aware it's a weekday," he'd said to his father. "Not possible."

"It'll take fifteen minutes. Pick the time."

"It takes me fifteen minutes to get there."

"No it doesn't. Choose when."

"Maybe around eleven?"

"I'll see you at eleven, then."

"I said 'maybe.'" But Redland had already hung up.

Through the window of his father's study he can see his brother, sitting in one of the leather chairs, watching Leo's approach. Interesting. So the information is pressing enough to require his presence, as well. Is Lenore here too, or is she in homeroom, where she's supposed to be?

How about Peoria? He kills the engine and hears her at her piano. No Peoria, then.

Upstairs he walks through the open door of the study to find his father at his desk, writing in a pad, his jaw tight. There's no sign of Lenore. Gabriel gives him the slightest of shrugs and Leo claps his brother on the shoulder and sits down in the other chair, right on its edge, his elbows planted on his thighs, like a basketball player during a time-out. It's the way people sit when they know they'll be getting up seventy-five seconds later to get on with the real work.

Redland sets his pad and pencil aside and folds his hands upon his blotter. "Your sister is gone," he says, his voice small, his eyes on a spot somewhere between the two brothers. "She needs you to find her."

"Gone," Gabriel repeats. Not a question, just an echo.

"Gone? Since when?" Leonardo asks.

"Since about thirty-six hours ago, we think," Redland says.

"Night before last," Gabriel says.

"We discovered it yesterday morning."

"She's just at a friend's house," Leo says. His phone buzzes in his pocket and he digs it out, wondering why he bothered to put it away in the first place. There are a half-dozen texts from four different people.

Redland unfolds his hands, pulls opens a drawer, and produces a key fob. "Go look in her room," he says, "but don't touch anything. Anything at all." He places the fob on his desk and covers it with his hand, as though trying to protect it. "Touch nothing. And then come back here."

The brothers glance at one another, not moving, and then look back to their father.

"Please," Redland says.

Leo stands, pocketing his phone, unable to prevent an eye roll. Gabriel rises too, and together they exit their father's office.

"What's your guess?" Leonardo asks, as they shuffle down the hallway. "Mini meth lab? Headless chicken voodoo rituals?"

"No idea."

Sometimes Leonardo finds his brother's humorlessness to be painful, but he lets it go. Gabriel has thrown so many things away; let him keep his precious gravitas. Leonardo pushes through the door and together they step into the room to find that their sister has stripped it bare of the photographs, drawings, and memorabilia that have covered her walls for years. Thousands of pushpin holes dot the empty white expanses. She'd made the bed, and left a plain white bedspread draped over it.

"Okay. I don't get it," Leonardo says. His phone is buzzing in his pocket constantly now. He pulls it out, glances at a screen littered with notifications, and imagines throwing it out the window.

Gabriel steps past him and walks over to the bed, where he bends down and squints at the pillow. "Look," he says, pointing at a small square of paper.

Leo follows his brother and reads the note:

I'm okay.

"What do you make of that?" Gabriel asks.

"I guess she's okay?" Leonardo turns to his brother. "I really need to get out of here, okay, man? I've got like twelve piles of shit to deal with at work. I know Dad's all worked up, but Lenore's just flexing her new eighteen-year-old status, and Mom's acting like it's any other day, so I don't know what the hell's going on here. Help me, yeah?"

"Mom would be playing like that if the house were on fire. You know that."

"Fine. I'll go back and talk to Dad," Leonardo says, heading back through the doorway, "but I think I've got about five minutes of this left in me."

They walk back to Redland's office. Downstairs the music stops and restarts, stops and restarts. They find their father standing behind his desk now, the fob lying before him, flanked by a pair of envelopes. "I know you both have a lot of responsibilities," he says, "but this family—we need your sister found. There's a Jeep in the street. Each envelope contains a bankcard for travel expenses and a sheet with a little more information. Not much, but we tried to think of anything that might help."

The other pressures upon Leo pause in their advances. "You rented a car and set up bankcards for this?"

"That's right. I've had a busy morning."

"What about her note?" Gabriel asks. "She says she's okay."

"Yes. Well, I'd like a second opinion."

Leo reaches out, picks up the fob, and looks at it, not quite believing its existence or purpose.

Gabriel points at the envelope. "More information, you said. What information?"

"It may help you. It may not. I don't know."

"The police?" Leo asks. "You tried the police?"

"It wouldn't be the priority that it needs to be."

"So us, then?" Gabriel says.

"You."

"Is that it?" Leonardo says, taking the envelope, though his mind is already disconnecting from all this and tracking back to work.

"Isn't that enough?" Redland says. The music stops again, but does not resume. Into the fragile silence falls the whistle of a freight train making its way along the distant waterfront, miles away.

9

Chapter 4

P eoria sits at her piano, her hands folded in her lap, and listens to the voices, the doors opening and closing upstairs, the movements of her sons. She can track them upstairs as clearly as if she were watching them. She knows them by the sounds of their feet; she has been able to discern the energies and temperaments behind their footfalls ever since they first thumped against the inside of her womb. Leo, always in a hurry, moving constantly from one thing to another and back, trying to keep too many plates in the air. Gabriel, meandering, scrutinizing, but to what end? An artist in search of a medium.

They will be digesting Red's report now, and considering his request. They will be discussing Lenore, and perhaps having feelings about their mother's absence from the meeting. She could go to them, of course. There are things she could tell them. But there is too much and they will have many questions and if she starts answering them it will be three days before she's finished. Besides, these are things they must learn for themselves. She will fill in the gaps but only once they have begun to create their own versions of the story.

The footfalls grow louder as her sons descend the stairs from Redland's office and alight in the hallway, just above her head. Leo heads straight outside, his steps quieting as he descends from the entryway and into the driveway. Gabriel wanders into the kitchen. Water hisses through the pipes in the walls. Leonardo's voice comes to her now. She can't hear his words but she can feel them: clipped, agitated. Probably he's already done thinking about his sister. For now.

Redland had wanted to bring the police in right away, but she'd prevailed upon him to do things this way. Even after thirty-five years of marriage, there was still more for him to learn about the family he'd married into. But perhaps that was true of her, too. Lenore's disappearance had caught her off guard. Peoria figured it would be a few more years before her daughter started chafing at her suburban constraints.

With law enforcement off the table, they'd agreed to turn to their sons. The Jeep and bank accounts were a little ornate, she felt, but she hadn't tried to discourage Redland from his need to do all he felt he could do. If the boys are going to help out with this it wouldn't be for a car or bank accounts. They'd each have to find their own reasons.

The muscles in her wrists and fingers revolt at the stillness—they are impatient to return to their battle with Albéniz. Her arms rise; her hands find their way back to the piano keys. This morning she has been grappling with the middle part of the opening section of *Asturias*, those alternating chords and runs that require the hands to fly outwards and back in the blink of an eye. No one has ever played it the way it's supposed to sound, fluidly, at tempo. She's not even convinced that Albéniz himself could play it. Her theory is that he was issuing a challenge he thought to be impossible, just to fuck with everybody. She's almost there, but time is running out.

There are just twelve days left before the grand opening of The Golden Gate Center for the Arts and its centerpiece, Calafia Hall. The $80-million renovation will give the University of California a concert hall to rival any other in the world, and chosen to inaugurate its stage was not a man, not a European, not one of the darlings of New York or London, but she, a Gonzalez, *una hija de Califas*. The entire world will be scrutinizing her every note, and many of them—those who are more comfortable thinking of brown women as housekeepers, or nannies—will be cheering for her to fail. And that's fine with her. She will take their spotlights and their headlines and make them her own, just as she always has, just as she is claiming the works of these old dead European men, none of whom could anticipate what might befall their precious tidy compositions in the hands of someone like her.

She taps her metronome back into action and tries to fix the first phrase in her mind, but her thoughts flip back to her vanished daughter and her sons and all they don't know about the lineage that stretches back through their grandfather and their great-grandmother. Lenore, at least, had seen Rogelio's house, his lab, his supplies. She'd been able to glimpse the composition of his world: meticulous organization and deliberate methodology, surrounded by an endless wildness. Lenore carries the same combination of factors, but in her they are inverted—a fierce and feral soul brought up in a picturesque suburb, with a financial privilege that she had never been able to wear with much comfort. And what of the changes that had come over her these last eighteen months, ever since her grandfather had made his final expedition into the desert? These, at least, she should perhaps relay to Leonardo and Gabriel, but again, any one observation could lead to a thousand questions. Neither of them would know what to do with such clues, anyway. An appreciation of change requires attention over time, and neither of her sons has that capacity, each for their own reasons. Perhaps that will shift now.

She slaps her hand over the oscillating pendulum and her movements echo in the Bechstein; the cavernous instrument admonishes her to bring it back to life. Upstairs, Gabriel's steps are quiet, aimless, arrhythmic as he shuffles around the kitchen. A memory from his boyhood sneaks up unseen and falls over her all at once: a wounded, dying crow Gabriel had found somewhere in the hills above their house. He had scooped it up and carried it all the way home, blood drying on his arm. She was outside in her garden when he came walking down, and she stood up to see the crow's sleek head draped over his arm. It looked at her, and though it was resigned to its death, which would come that night, its eyes held faith and peace. She wants some arms now to come pick them all up like that. She wants a crook inside someone's elbow where her daughter can rest, a warm safe place for this whole family, where they can gather and face their various condemnations together.

Perhaps this is what she can tell them. Perhaps she can rise from her piano and climb the stairs and tell her sons that she knows how it feels to envy a doomed crow, and that's how she knows it's all going to be okay. Upstairs the water comes on a couple more times. Gabriel leaves the kitchen, treads down the hallway, returns, and then finally follows his brother out the front door. Peoria sits in silence for some time before she flicks the metronome back into motion.

Chapter 5

G abriel walks down to the kitchen out of habit. The descent of the stairs, the half-traverse of the hallway, and the left turn are a motor program so practiced he could find his way, even headless, to the heart of their home. It is where they gathered after school, scattering backpacks and schoolwork and lunchboxes, to exchange gossip and news, to squabble and to plan, to unwrap snacks and Band-Aids, which were kept in the same cabinet.

He scans the contents of the refrigerator and then fills a glass with water from the faucet. Leonardo's voice, barking into his phone, carries in through the open windows from the driveway. Problems at Cal, apparently. At the time of Gabriel's sentencing, Leo had been nearing the end of his Ph.D program. His pursuit of biology had struck Gabriel as somewhat strange—growing up, Leo had been mostly indifferent to forms of life that weren't himself. But graduate school gave Leo a structure and a trajectory, which Gabriel hadn't bothered to create for himself, and now here they are, the professor and the parolee, at opposite ends of the status spectrum. Gabriel can only relate to his brother's work travails in theory, really—it has been five, almost six years since his last job, and the greatest drama from that nine-month stint as a fresh-out-of-college mattress salesman was a spilled root beer on a showroom model.

Now, as a job seeker with a prison record in an uncertain economy, his prospects seem laughable. It is a morbid fascination to him every time he encounters the question *Have you ever been convicted of a felony?* on a job application, with its casual yes/no response boxes a half-inch apart, suggesting that this division among people might be as mundane as the division between those who want cheese on that, and those who do not. Even more fascinating to Gabriel is the follow-up question, *If yes, please explain*, and the single inch of white space allotted for an entire wayward memoir. In appreciation of the absurdity of that one inch, Gabriel composed a haiku entitled "Slippery Fingers," which reads: "Protecting a girl / I hit the wrong guy's forehead / Bad aim—my real crime." After all, he suspects anything past that *yes* checkbox serves only to provide some mid-level manager with water-cooler gossip, and Gabriel figures his efforts might as well furnish someone with a story.

The lost years, the vanishing friendships, the unemployability—it had all been deserved. When Everett Baker's eye socket absorbed the impact of the Jack Daniel's bottle, Gabriel had been doing little more than selling mattresses and rotating through the local bars afterwards. The finale of this particular evening found Gabriel in custody and Everett in the hospital, unconscious. When Gabriel sobered up and learned the situation he became so nauseous he couldn't stand up straight. He curled into a ball on his bunk and stayed like that for days, and when his parents offered him bail, and then the services of a high-priced defense attorney, he refused. Everett made a full recovery, save for a scar alongside his eye, but that had no effect on Gabriel's assessment of his own decisions, or the consequences he felt should befall him. He quietly entered a guilty plea and headed for prison, and that was the last time he'd felt a real sense of mission.

But now this. He isn't too concerned about Lenore's absence from her home or her school, from the life her parents or teachers would have her lead. She'd always been a kid of great intention, and he's sure this is no different. But she did have a tendency to get in over her head now and then.

He is refilling his glass when he remembers the envelope, and he pulls it from his back pocket. Inside he finds the bankcard and a sheet of paper which he unfolds to find a typewritten note from Redland. It's a list of observations—clues, perhaps—delivered without editorializing, without emotion, as dispassionate as a police report. He lists her usual hangouts and her friends, some of whom Gabriel knows, some he does not. Redland reports her declining grades, her absences from school. She'd lost weight, fainted twice—but, Gabriel wonders, what high-schooler hasn't had at least a couple of misadventures in their early experiments with blood-alcohol content?

He swallows the last of the water, washes and dries the glass, and when he's crossing the floor to return it to the cabinet a photograph on the refrigerator stops him—a snapshot of Lenore and her long-time best friend, Ayla, lying together on a beach, smiling. Lenore's hair is pink in this one and she is wearing her black sweatshirt, the one with arm bones running down the sleeves. He pulls the photo from the refrigerator. In his absence, Ayla has also changed from a twelve-year-old to an eighteen-year-old, it would seem. He returns the photograph to the refrigerator, pulls open the garage door and sees his sister's Toyota in its place. So she'd left on foot. To Ayla's?

He heads outside, into the driveway, where his brother is typing into his phone. "Hey man," Gabriel says, "I think we should split up." Leo gives him a blank look, his thoughts clearly elsewhere. "To look for Lenore, I mean."

Annoyance crosses Leo's face. "She'll show up on her own. I have to go back to campus, so yeah, we're splitting up. Here." He tosses the Jeep's fob; Gabriel catches it and throws it back.

"I still don't have a license," Gabriel says. "I'll find a different way."

"Fine. You want a ride down the hill?" Leo's phone buzzes and his attention returns to the screen.

"No. I'm going to walk over to Ayla's."

Leo grunts as he begins typing.

"See you later, then?"

"Yeah," says Leo, not looking up.

The piano in its underground chamber had gone silent, but now the music rises and swells again.

Chapter 6

Leo hangs up and shoves his phone back into his pocket, trying to figure out how to get his day back on track now that half of it has been pulled out from under him. But first things first. He looks down the slope of the driveway and imagines the slam and scrape of the Audi clattering into the street. One day this stupid driveway will rip his muffler right off. He digs into his pocket and his hand closes around the Jeep fob instead of his own keys. Good. Might as well make use of Redland's planning. He leaves the Audi where it is and heads out to the street, where he climbs into the Jeep. The street is too narrow for a U-turn but he guns it and drives up and over the sidewalk, exulting in the novelty of clearance. It's a short-lived victory—after muscling the giant vehicle down the hill and back to campus, he finds Clifford Baumgardner waiting at the door of his office.

"I'm sure I made myself clear over the phone," Leo says, unlocking the door. "I don't have any more time for this."

Clifford follows him inside. "That was the phone," he says. "Look me in the eyes. Look me in the eyes and tell me."

To somebody else, this might be intimidating. Clifford is a six-foot-four, 300-lb. mass of strength and mobility. As an undergraduate at USC, he'd started all four years at left tackle and helped the Trojans through several deep playoff runs. He'd been named All-American three times and won the Outland Trophy his senior year; scouts from a dozen NFL teams had come to woo him. He made national headlines when he opted for graduate school instead—apparently, he was the first person in history who'd chosen to use his head for science rather than as a battering ram.

As a fledgling biologist Clifford has proven to be a quick study, conscientious and hard-working. But he isn't brilliant. He will not innovate. There will be no Baumgardner's Law. Nobody will ever refer to anything as Baumgardnerian. Worse, he hasn't figured out the human part of it yet. He isn't getting the politics or the traditions. His perception of his own importance is grossly inflated, a misconception particularly unusual in a lineman.

Leo drops his bag onto the floor beside his chair and sits down; Clifford takes the chair opposite him. He wears a red flannel and a leather-brimmed baseball cap with a picture of a duck on it. His freckles blaze. Leo looks his student directly in the eyes and holds his gaze an extra beat before speaking. "Your contributions to the egret project have been valuable," he says. "Your work is organized and competent and we are grateful for it. But it doesn't merit authorship."

"That's bullshit," Clifford says, evenly, calmly. "I worked twice as hard on that paper as you did."

"It's fascinating that you presume you're in a position to assess my efforts, but let's go ahead and pretend like you're right anyway. Heavy lifting doesn't merit authorship. Rockefeller never bolted any pipelines together, did he?" It is a line one of his own mentors delivered to him, once when he was sitting in a chair like Clifford's.

Clifford sits back. "That's the most classist, out-of-touch comparison I've heard in my whole life." He digs a toothpick out of his front pocket and wedges it between a canine and an incisor. "Last chance—put my name on it. I deserve it."

"'Last chance'? You're issuing threats? Office hours are over. Get out."

Now Clifford smiles. He hoists his massive feet from the floor and crosses them on the edge of Leo's desk, which creaks under the heavy load. His boots are not clean. "I got another call from the Steelers. Few too many sacks last season." He removes the toothpick, studies its end, replaces it. "They've got this restaurant out there where you can get pastrami and cheese with fries and cole slaw right inside the fucking sandwiches. Doesn't that sound amazing?"

Leo leans over and shoves Clifford's feet off his desk, not bothering to wipe his hands clean. Biologists are always prepared to get a little dirty. "Yes, well, science isn't for everybody. But I hear you can make a good living at football for oh, say, five or six years. And then you'll only have to figure out what to do with the remaining three-quarters of your life, with whatever remains of your body and your IQ. I'm sure you'll be able to parlay your fame into a car dealership or a strip-mall pizza place. The kids get really excited over linemen, right? Now get out."

Clifford smiles. "Yes, having an eight-figure bank account and endless free time sounds really rough. I'm sure I'll be sitting around in retirement at the age of thirty-three, wishing I had to beg strangers for money in order to demonstrate my relevance." He shrugs and then leans forward suddenly, serious now. "Not that you give a shit, but I'll tell you why I'm going. The football field is a place of zero bullshit. You always know exactly where you stand. Causes have predictable effects, and people are straight with you. But this place here . . ." He plants a finger on Leo's desk, damning the faux oak surface, the surrounding office, the department and the university, all of academia, its past and future. "This is a place of infinite bullshit." Now he draws a circle in the air, encompassing Leo and his desk and chair. "Particularly right in this area." He stands. "Nice knowing you, Professor. Best of luck with everything." He takes out the toothpick and flicks it onto Leo's desk, where it leaves a wet swipe. He does not close the door behind him.

Leo removes the offending projectile and its skid mark with a tissue, working to keep his personal anger separate from the professional reality of the matter. Clifford was not a crucial part of the system here—he was expendable, like an appendix, and his departure will amount to about the same as the removal of one: stiffness, a few sleepless nights, and within a few weeks Leo will forget about him entirely.

His desk adequately tidied, he pulls out his laptop, flips it open. He clicks on a folder marked "Egrets_Audubon" to assess his new to-do list. An empty rectangle springs open. Zero items, declares the message at the bottom of the window. Heat floods into his chest. He opens a nearby folder—"Ospreys_Rottnest"—and finds it populated as normal. He opens the search function and tries a string of entries, none of which produce the egret files. Strange, but not the end of the world. He logs in to his online storage account and finds the folder empty there, too. Heat flashes across his brow. There must be some reason why the software isn't displaying the folder images. The data are there, certainly; the files just aren't showing themselves. Does that happen? He reaches next for his desk drawer, where he keeps a couple of external hard drives, trying to remember the last time he plugged in to them—the raw data, at least, should be in there. He might have to redo the numbers, and there would be a stack of all-nighters while he rewrites his paper, if it comes to that. Which it won't—it's all in there; he just needs to reboot, or clear some memory, or something.

But then he slides the drawer open and it's strangely weightless, and inside he finds not his drives but a framed portrait: the smiling face of Richard M. Nixon against the red and white background of a drooping flag. Leo stares at the photograph for several seconds. Dread comes like a flood. His vision blurs as the room climbs to a thousand degrees. He jumps from his desk, flings his window open, leans out, and scans the courtyard below, but Clifford is gone.

Chapter 7

Ayla's front door isn't latched, so Gabriel's knocks cause it to swing open. Inside, the living room is empty but for a low white leather couch and an empty credenza. The pale hardwood floors gleam; the white walls are empty. Through a doorway he can see the dining room, equally sparse: an empty table and two chairs, nothing else.

"In here," a woman's voice calls. Her words echo off the barren walls; she is everywhere in the house at once, an omnipresence. Gabriel walks through the empty rooms, seeing nobody. The kitchen, too, is empty. Any window coverings have been removed, revealing clear views of the surrounding trees and houses and far below the last remnants of fog over the shoreline.

"Getting warmer," the disembodied voice says.

He walks down the hallway, his steps echoing past closed doors, to the backmost bedroom, where he finds Ayla. She sits cross-legged, a few inches off the floor on a low wooden bench, in a blue kimono. Her brown hair hangs down on either side of her face, a strand on each side twisting into a loose spiral. She is folding a small sheet of paper on a table just slightly higher than her bench. The windows are wide open, admitting an intermittent breeze. Before her in a straight row stands a long line of origami animals.

"Holy shit," Ayla says, her eyes flicking up to him and then back to her work. "The middle child."

"Hello, Ayla. Moving out?"

"No. I just don't like clutter."

"Your moms approve?"

"The Christines are operating out of Stockholm this quarter." She shrugs. "I don't talk to them much these days. I have a policy against boring conversations."

"And no school today?"

"I'm homeschooling myself," she says, continuing to fold. Gabriel watches in silence as a head emerges, and then the neck of a giraffe. "Gabriel?" she asks, going to work on the legs.

"Yeah."

"Did you think about me at all when you were in prison?"

"You were twelve."

"I'm not anymore."

"I can see that," he says.

A gust of wind pushes through the window. The paper animals should tumble over and slide off the table, but they do not. As if hearing his question, she holds up the completed giraffe for him to see, sticks out her tongue, licks its feet, and sets it in the row. She pulls another sheet of paper from the stack, this one with a pale blue back, and creases it corner-to-corner. "What was San Quentin like?" she asks. "Lonely?"

"There were people everywhere."

She looks him in the eye. "Sounds lonely to me."

"I'm looking for Lenore, Ayla."

"Of course you are. Daddy send you?"

"I'm her brother. I don't need to be sent."

"Yes, you sure are." In her hands the paper is collapsing into a stack of triangles.

"So where is she? What is she doing?"

"You Percivals are just so adorable, you know that? I've always been envious of Lenore. Brilliant parents and strong, charming brothers. She's a lucky girl."

Gabriel fights a sigh. "What do you know, Ayla? Is Lenore okay? What is she doing?"

"What do you mean by 'okay,' exactly?"

"I mean is she fucking okay."

She is silent while she folds, unfolds, creases again. "Your sister is in a place of her choosing, with company of her choosing."

"What does that mean? Where is she?"

"I don't know."

"You know something."

"I know a lot of things. But not your sister's exact whereabouts."

"Approximate, then."

She makes a final fold and then holds up a sleek fish. "Do you trust me, Gabriel?"

Gabriel considers this. In his experience, the only people who ask this question are those who are worried about being trusted, and the only people worried about being trusted are those whose trustworthiness is in question. But this isn't San Quentin anymore. This is his little sister's best friend, who, truth be told, he has always liked—even when she was twelve. So what is she worried about? "I don't know," Gabriel answers. "Should I?"

"Come here," she says. She offers the fish, pinched between two fingers. Gabriel steps forward and reaches out to receive it, but instead of the fish she slips her empty hand into his. "This is all I have," she says, showing him the fish, rotating it. "*Una carpa.* A carp. There's a tattoo shop on Telegraph called The Iron Quill, and there's an artist there named Ángel. No, wait." She closes her eyes. "What day is it?"

"Wednesday."

"Sacramento. He's in Sacramento now. The shop is called Capricorn Rising. Take this to him." She removes her hand from his and replaces it with the little fish.

Gabriel opens his mouth to ask the first of a hundred questions, but she shakes her head. "You have to find Ángel now. This is how it works."

"How what works?"

She pulls another sheet from the stack. "You're all lucky to have each other. You know that?" She folds the sheet, unfolds, folds again. "I'll see you later."

Chapter 8

Leo fails to uncover Clifford in any of his usual haunts, but in tracking him he discovers the saboteur is scheduled to start his bartending shift at five at Raleigh's. At 4:45 he props the portrait of Nixon on the bar, takes a seat, and orders two shots of Gray Goose.

"My guess is he would have been more of a whiskey man," says the bartender, a skinny frat-boy type, while frowning at the photo, "but if you're buying, I suppose it's up to you."

Leo ignores him. He takes down the shots in quick succession, one-two, and orders a third. This one he does not drink; instead he places it alongside Nixon and glares at various things while the vodka works through him.

Clifford walks in three minutes early. Leo drains the final glass and then stands. "Breaking and entering," he says. "Trespassing and theft."

Clifford is unperturbed as he lifts the bar's hinged leaf and side-steps through the opening. "Evening, Nick," he says. The men bump fists.

"You know this guy?" Nick asks.

"Thirty-seventh president of the United States," Clifford says, with a glance at the photo. "He used to be a crook, but now he's just dead."

Leo backhands his empty shot glass onto the floor behind the bar. Instead of shattering it bounces off the rubber mats and deflects into a refrigerator door.

"And his unhappy little buddy?" Nick asks.

"Funny, I didn't even notice him sitting there."

Nick snickers and plunges a scoop into a sink of ice. Clifford comes as near to Leo as the bar's width will allow, stepping on the shot glass as he approaches. It breaks with the sound of a heavy branch cracking. He plants his hands on the wood and glares at Leo. "What's he had, Nicky?"

"Three shots of Goose."

"Pour me another, Nicky," Leo says. "That will be four."

Clifford shakes his head. "You're cut off."

"Give me my data, Clifford. Now."

Clifford's expression doesn't change.

"This is some very serious territory you've entered here," Leo says.

Clifford takes a rag and drags it in circles across the bar's clean surface. "No idea what you're talking about."

"So how does this play out? What do you want?"

"I want you to leave my bar."

"Give me my fucking data, Clifford."

Clifford hoists a fist the size of a cinder block into the space between them. Leo can taste the blood in his throat already; he wonders if after a punch to the face from this man there will be anything left of himself to retaliate, to do even a symbolic bit of damage. But instead of chambering his punch, Clifford extends a single middle digit.

"Here's your data," he says. "Now get out, or get thrown out."

Leo snatches the framed photograph from the bar, steps backward, and hurls it like an axe, aiming for the center of Clifford's face. Clifford dodges it and Nixon veers by him, hurtling toward a wall of bottles. Clifford lunges across the bar, but Leo is halfway to the door by then, his pounding steps disappearing beneath an explosion of shattering glass.

Chapter 9

I t takes Gabriel a half-hour to hitch a ride. He chases the decelerating Mitsubishi up the onramp, draws even with it, and finds the passenger door locked. He taps on the glass with a fingertip, but it is the driver's door that swings open. A man steps out, so tall that most of his torso rises above the car's roofline as he straightens. His sunglasses have lenses tinted the color of smoke and his thick gray hair rises straight up from his hairline, making him look even taller. "Stories!" he says. "I would need some stories. You game?" His smile is slight. "Stories?" Gabriel says.

"That's my offer." He slaps an open palm onto the roof. "Conveyance for entertainment. You tell me things, I'll drive you wherever the hell you want. You got enough to say I'll take you to Key goddamn West, buy you gas station hot dogs all the way out."

A change of wind fills their noses with the scent of horseshit from the racetrack. "Tell you what kinds of things?"

"Stories, son!" the driver says, slapping the roof again. "Real ones. I've read all the books and all the plays, seen all the movies and all the TV shows. Got bored of that so now I'm out here, looking for real stories, and my question for you is: Do you have any to share or not?"

"Would you want to hear about my runaway sister, or San Quentin?"

The driver studies him, and when he speaks, his voice is half an octave lower. "I hope you've got a ways to go, son." He sinks out of sight and slams his door behind him. The passenger lock clicks open. "Names, then," he says, once Gabriel is seated, and they're accelerating up the ramp. His seat is all the way back and even though it's reclined his hair still scrapes the headliner. He presses a button on a small digital recorder and jams the butt end of it between the warped slats of one of the dashboard heater vents. "Mine's Rourke. Yours? Give me a fake one if you want, but make it a good one. Mind if I record?"

"No. Gabriel."

"Like the angel. And your destination and purpose, if indeed you have either?"

"Sacramento. I'm on my way to deliver a paper fish to a guy at a tattoo shop."

Rourke looks at him sideways, and then at the road ahead. "Proceed, my friend."

Gabriel describes the mandate from Ayla and then walks backwards through the story to describe the meeting with his father and his brother, his missing sister, his theories about her whereabouts. After a few initial questions Rourke falls into silence, barely seeming to attend to the road, never changing out of the right lane. Beyond the slight adjustments of his hands on the wheel his only movement is a head nod, a constant motion that oscillates to the story's rhythm. Gabriel doesn't remember anybody ever listening to him like this. When he has covered the events of the day he figures he'll work backward to San Quentin, but Rourke stops him.

"Wait a minute," he says. "So you're on your way to get this tattoo, because she asked you to?"

"No, I'm just taking this fish there." He holds it up in the open palm of his hand, where it vibrates along with the car.

"I'm pretty sure you're getting a tattoo. Got any other ones?"

"I think I'm just delivering a message."

Rourke reaches up and gives his chin a slow stroke. "Forgive me, but maybe you're being a little naïve. There are plenty of ways to send secret messages these days. But only one reason to go see a tattooer in person."

"She didn't say anything about a tattoo."

"She said, 'That's how it works.' Right?"

"Yes."

"So maybe?" Rourke slows through the curve that takes them onto the Carquinez Bridge. The ground falls away beneath the road and the metallic hum of the bridge rises around them. The sugar factory sweeps past; beneath them the bay shines with the light of the midday sun.

"Maybe," Gabriel says.

Rourke nods. "Good. What about prison, then?"

Gabriel is quiet until they're through the toll plaza, and then he picks back up with the story of that decisive night at the Starry Plough and the drunken, decisive swing of the whiskey bottle that connected with the orbital of Everett Baker, an optometry grad student, rather than its intended target, the skull of some asshole who'd stalked in that night with the obvious goal of making every woman in the bar feel as uncomfortable as possible. He tells Rourke about the laughing teenager in the arraignment queue before him, who'd stolen two police cars in one night, and a cellmate named Ludwig who'd committed a string of robberies, always targeting barbershops because he liked the way they smelled.

In Fairfield the traffic loosens and accelerates, but Rourke makes no move to leave the right lane. They drop out of the hills, trading sweeping turns for straight roads through farmland. Gabriel tells San Quentin stories through another couple of towns, but then finds himself running out. There had been a handful of noteworthy events; the rest was just boredom and routine. Rourke's nodding slows. Gabriel finds an item from his teenage years and brings it forth—the story of a neighbor who'd been leading a double life, and was discovered to have a second family an hour away. It had riveted him for weeks, but now he finds himself out of details in just a few minutes, searching his memory.

"What about the rest of your family?" Rourke asks. "You've got some jail time behind you, and now you've got a sister on the loose. Sounds like a lively bunch. What else you got in that department?"

"There's a streak of. . . I don't know what you'd call it," Gabriel says, thinking about his great-grandmother, who was said to have near-supernatural powers, and about his grandfather, who might have been an actual mad scientist.

"Always is. What's it with you all?"

Gabriel had been open enough earlier, telling Rourke about Lenore's flight and Redland's request, but now it feels impossible to say anything further. There's so much of it he wouldn't be able to put into words, so little of it in the conscious realm.

"I'm not really sure." Gabriel tries to find something concrete to land on. "My mom is a world-class concert pianist."

"No shit? A line of creatives?"

"I guess you could say that." They are passing through the Suisun Marsh now. In the haze ahead of them the skyline of the state's capital appears. He catches movement in the air over the edge of a small green island and turns to see a diving bird disappear into the blue water.

Chapter 10

Leo hits the sidewalk at full speed, sprints to the corner, and wheels off of Telegraph Ave, throwing a glance over his shoulder to find no one in pursuit. He slows to a fast walk and heads for his parking place, his mind flipping back and forth from the catastrophe of the stolen data to the image of Clifford's face imploding behind the Nixon missile, as if the clarity of his imagination might re-aim his throw. A new wave of fury hits him when he sees that someone has stolen his Audi and someone else has shoved some gigantic Jeep in his spot, but then he remembers his morning.

He drives down University, not thinking, feeling wobbly from the vodka, and heads eastbound on I-80. When he exits and heads toward the Richmond-San Rafael bridge he realizes where he's going—to Marin, to Audubon Canyon and his subjects, the egrets. It isn't that he can actually accomplish any work. The stolen data had been collected over the course of a full year, the analysis and drafting of the article accomplished over months. But he needs quiet now, and a bit of familiar space where he can catch his breath and let the anger subside enough to get his frontal lobe working again.

Once he's on Highway 1 running out to the coast, he is reminded of all the reasons he bought the Audi. The Jeep handles like a bathtub.

Passing is unthinkable. So the drive won't have its usual therapeutic effects, but there will still be the canyon and the birds at the end of it, and it's a perfect spring afternoon, and the usual fogbank is not yet threatening.

When he is nearly out to the water he gets a call. It's from Yvette. "The police were just here," she says. She sounds giddy, exhilarated. "It was a blast. They said you smashed up Raleigh's. Is that true?"

"It's a long story."

She laughs. "You were supposed to be lecturing undergrads, and instead you went on a rampage. It would have to be a long story."

"It wasn't a rampage. It was an isolated incident."

"Smashing occurred, though?"

"One of my grad students stole all my data. Everything from the egrets. I don't know what he wants, but I went to find him."

"And my friends said dating an academic would be boring."

"Not a joke. It's a major fucking problem."

"You'll figure it out in like five minutes. You always do. You're just catastrophizing again."

"I'm not catastrophizing. What did you tell the police?"

"I was dazzling," she says. "Mark was just here to get photos for his portfolio, so I was in a floor-length red sequined gown, white gloves past my elbows, and Cindy was here too, so my hair and makeup were *insane*. The whole concept was like act-three *Ghostbusters* Sigourney Weaver. So these two cops show up, and they're kind of young, and one of them is kind of hot, and they get me at the door, looking like that. Are you with me so far?"

Leo is feeling lightheaded. The vodka, the stolen data, the task of driving this stupid truck. He grunts at Yvette as he steers the car back to the middle of the lane.

"So they said their thing, about needing to talk to you, and I told them they'd never take you alive."

"You can't be serious."

"By the time they left I don't think they even remembered why they were here. So where are you, anyway? What the hell happened?"

"Driving, in Marin." He pulls up behind a slow-moving plumber's truck. The road here is narrow and winding, no passing allowed. "It wasn't a big deal. I just threw something at his stupid fat face. He dodged it and it hit some bottles instead. Nobody cares."

"The cops said you smashed over a thousand dollars' worth of booze. It could be charged as a felony."

A pang hits Leo in the ribcage. "Shit. Okay. I'll deal with it later. I'm heading to Audubon Canyon to think for a while. I'm about to lose reception."

At the entrance of the canyon the gate across the mouth of the service road has already been shut and locked, the wooden *CLOSED* sign in place. Leonardo dumps the Jeep on the highway's gravel shoulder, climbs the gate, and makes his way up the road. He veers left onto a trail that ascends the canyon's northern side to the viewing platform. He hasn't been here in a season, but he knows every twist of the trail, every turn, every exposed root, each bay and oak on the way up. Once at the platform he leans his forearms on the railing, looks out over the canopy, and right away picks out four egrets in the center of the largest tree, their impossible whiteness shining out like searchlights across dark water.

He has spent hundreds, maybe thousands of hours of staring at these creatures, and that color still shocks him every time he comes across it. It's what drew him to birds in the first place. There is nothing like it anywhere else in the natural world—not in the newest flower, not in the cleanest field of snow. Those surfaces can only reflect available light, but the luminescence of egret white seems to come from elsewhere, as if the birds are peepholes into an unseen world where there are twelve suns and no shadows. They are rifts in the spectrum, gaps in the dirt and flaws that encase all the rest of the world. In Leo's headier days as a grad student—not all that long ago, in a strict count of months, but an eon ago in terms of the trajectory of his career—he had seen the egrets and their immaculate feathers as beacons, indications of bright and possible futures, proof of the existence of perfection. And then, as if that otherworldly radiance wasn't captivating enough on its own, someone had taken it and placed it in the sky and given it movement: the soar, the swoop and the glide, the climb and the dive. What must it be like to have that third dimension always available, to have no boundaries, no sense of heights, no ability to fall, not even a concept of what it means to fall?

It was here on this platform where he'd first decided to make a career in biology. He'd been here as an undergrad, blissfully direction-less, going through the motions on a paper for an ornithology class he hadn't wanted to take in the first place, when he'd found himself dumbstruck by the sight of dozens of the immaculate birds, scattered throughout the canopy. He'd watched them until they'd kicked him out, and by the time he left he vowed to return, to make himself into someone who belonged here, at eye level with these captivating beings. It had taken him several years—an extra year for his BA because he suddenly needed more classes, a year as a barely paid intern/barista, and then grad school at Cornell, and studies elsewhere, on ospreys, sandpipers, terns, even pigeons, learning how to navigate entry-level academia—before he hit on some findings that were just significant enough to convince the hiring committee at Cal to give him a shot. The egret study was—*is*, he corrects himself—his first big opportunity there.

"I thought I recognized that lone figure, striding through the brush," a voice says. Leo jumps and whirls to see Steve Pendergrass, a former instructor of his and now one of the preserve's stewards, climbing onto the platform. He has grown a thick beard, a mass of bristling white and black, since the last time Leo saw him.

Leo grins. "I'll bring you a razor or two from the big city next time. We've got electric ones now."

Steve laughs, twists the cap off a flask, and hands it over. It's Scotch, so full of peat and smoke it makes Leo shudder.

"Goddamn. That tastes like a campfire."

Steve laughs again. "Exactly. Who doesn't love a campfire?" He nods toward the highway. "What happened to the Audi? Don't tell me you've got car seats in the back of that thing?"

"God, no," Leo says, equally horrified by the thought of Yvette as a mother as himself as a father. "I'll leave the parenting to the grown-ups."

"I don't think they hand out those professorships to children," Steve says with a smile. Steve had lost his own professorship years earlier, when he suddenly vacated campus in the middle of a semester. Leo had been a senior then, and as an undergraduate he'd only known third-hand rumors about Professor Pendergrass's "nervous break-down." Years later, when Leo first found himself reunited with his former professor in Audubon Canyon, this time as a professor himself, he'd still not been able to bring himself to ask for the details. There had been times, though, sitting with him out there on the platform, watching and waiting, amid quiet conversation, when Steve would say something—not much, perhaps a half-sentence—or stare out into the treetops, and it was clear to Leo that his friend was somewhere else. At times, he seemed more like one of the birds. It would pass, though, leaving him just as he is now: perfectly at home here, his familiar fond-ness for the canyon evident as he looks out over the treetops. He tips the flask toward the nesting egrets. "So what brings you back to Eden?"

Leo shakes his head. "Remember my assistant? The big one?"

"Sure."

"He stole all my data. All my files. Sabotaged everything."

Steve's eyes open wide. "Jesus," he says, promptly handing the flask back. Leo accepts it and drinks. It goes down more easily this time, and maybe he gets a little more than he'd intended. He passes it back.

"So I tracked him down at his workplace and a few things broke and now the cops want to know what happened."

Steve swigs, shakes his head. "But that's the end of his own career, isn't it? That's the academic equivalent of a goddamn suicide vest. What's his endgame?"

"He's making what I think they call a lateral move."

"I wouldn't think he'd have much choice at this point."

"The NFL. O-line."

"You're joking."

"Passed up the draft for grad school. And now seems to have changed his mind."

Steve shakes his head. "'You were not formed to live like brutes, but to follow virtue and knowledge.' That's from Dante. *The Divine Comedy*."

"Emphasis on *comedy*."

Steve chuckles. "Fair enough."

Together the men look out through the treetops, where the egrets seem to grow brighter amid the gathering shadows of the late afternoon. Small, isolated breezes enter the canyon, ruffling treetops with their slow passages. To the west the lagoon is full of the low sun's reflected fire.

Steve caps the flask and sets it on the railing. "This isn't a regular thing for me," he says, softly, pointing at it, startling Leo. Had drinking been a part of that episode, too?

Leo isn't sure how to respond. "Not really my business," he mutters, in a way he hopes sounds deferential, not dismissive.

"Sure it is," Steve says, smiling out over the canyon. "We're all connected. We all affect one another. Helps me to talk about it now, anyway." He looks Leo square in the eye. "This place, this is much more my style." He points at the flask again. "Actually, I was expecting a special occasion. Let me rephrase that—a different special occasion. Max has been up here a lot, and he just became a grandfather."

"Max Abramov?" Leo asks, a set of memories twitching and organizing themselves inside him. Steve is talking about diapers but it doesn't matter anymore. Leo lets out a shout. "Steve, Max!" He claps his friend on the shoulder. "I'll call you!" he shouts, already running. He doesn't bother dialing the number until he reaches the road—there has never been any reception in the canyon.

"Leo! Are you here in Gainesville, too?" Max says, when he answers the call.

"No. God no. Where?" Leo yanks open the Jeep's door, which he hadn't bothered to lock.

"Florida State. The rain forest conference. You're still a bird guy, aren't you?"

"Listen Max—you know those boxes I loaned you a little while back, for the survey?"

"Of course. They have been invaluable."

"I think there might be a couple of thumb drives in there I badly need. Where are they?"

"My office. But I'm here until Monday."

"I have to get in there today. Tell me how that gets done."

"Well, Mary's around. She might be able to let you in if it's that important."

"It is. Congratulations on the grandkid, by the way."

"Grandkids. Twins! And thanks."

The Jeep slides through gravel as it churns back onto the road. If Max has those drives, Leo would be able to reconstruct nearly everything he needs. He'd be weeks behind, but he'd be able to salvage the study. He tries to make a place inside himself for some hope as he turns inland. On small farms tucked between hills, white barns turn gray in the dusk; cows on hillsides turn their heads to watch him pass. Windows glow in the falling darkness. Before him and high above the gibbous moon is an opal fixed in silver.

Chapter 11

Capricorn Rising is clean and bright, with the usual displays of tattoo artwork, and home to a dozen verdant houseplants, some taller than Gabriel. Over the buzz of a single tattoo machine comes the sound of NPR, and a report on a longshoremen's strike in Long Beach. A kid who can't be more than a couple of years out of high school sits on a stool at a wooden reception counter, tattooed down to his fingertips, stooping over a tiny drawing. His hair is carefully oiled, his white t-shirt spotless. Two teenage girls in the waiting area flip through a tattoo magazine, whispering, their eyes flicking over occasionally to the boy. A single station is in use. A meaty, shirtless, middle-aged man lies on his back on a padded table, his head turned toward the window, his body tense and his eyes glassy. A tattooer, all hair and beard and mustache and glasses, squints down at his client's chest.

"Hiya," says the receptionist, looking up from his drawing. "What can I do for you?"

"I'm looking for Ángel," Gabriel says. "I have something for him."

The receptionist leans back and folds his arms. "That sounds a little sketchy."

The girls stop leafing through the albums and sit still, listening.

42

"Sorry, no. It's harmless. It's origami."

"You're bringing him origami?"

"Yes."

The receptionist shrugs. He points to a fabric partition that hides the shop's back corner from view. "Back there. Shake the curtain a little before you go through."

"Shake the curtain?"

"So he'll know that you're there."

Gabriel heads for the partition. The bearded tattooer's eyes do not leave his work—a grizzly bear, in profile.

Gabriel takes a hold of the edge of the curtain and gives it a couple shakes before pulling it aside. Ángel is sitting on a backless stool at his station, his spine straight, reading a book. He wears a black t-shirt and black horn-rimmed glasses. A desk lamp on his table illuminates an empty chair. He looks up.

"Um, sorry to bother you. Ayla sent me here?" Gabriel says.

Behind him the buzz of the tattoo machine stops. "He can't hear," the bearded artist calls. "Can't hear, can't talk." The buzz resumes.

Gabriel turns back to Ángel, whose eyes are open now, magnified by his thick lenses. "She sent me with this." He offers the fish; Ángel plucks it from his open palm and rotates it, examining each elevation. He sets it on his table, looks up at Gabriel, and points at the chair. Gabriel hesitates, but only for a second.

It takes fifteen minutes. When Ángel is done the fish rests in flat profile against the inside of Gabriel's wrist, its creases and colors reproduced perfectly. Ángel pulls off his gloves and drops them into a garbage can. He plucks the paper fish from the table and eats it, his eyes fixed on Gabriel's wrist. When he has swallowed it he pulls a sticky note from the stack on his table, writes a few words in small, precise lettering, and holds it up. It's a Fresno address, and beneath it are the words *mañana a las diez de la tarde*. Tomorrow, ten p.m. When

Gabriel reaches for the slip, though, Ángel withdraws it. He shakes his head. With his free hand he taps the sheet and then he reaches out and places his fingertip against Gabriel's temple. For a moment he holds them together, the conductor of his body linking the appointment to Gabriel's head, and then he lets the connection go and eats the slip, too.

Chapter 12

When the water's boiling I pour in the powdered stems, using a small brush to sweep out the little glass bowl, and then I hit the button on my stopwatch. The crushed leaves will go in next, but not until the stems have softened, and the water cools off a little. The petals, still intact and bright, sit in an even layer on the bottom of my *molcajete*. They'll go in last, when the water cools a little more. It's best if I crush them at the last possible minute.

I'm brewing the tea on a lopsided table in an Econo Lodge just off Highway 101, in Rohnert Park. It's not so different from doing it on my dresser at home—it's the same camp stove, the same pot. But now I don't have to wait until the dead of night, and worry about my mom walking in on me here, even though I maybe secretly hoped she would sometimes, those nights at home when I was working on the *centella*, struggling to make sense of my grandfather's notebooks.

His drawings rest on the table just beyond my ingredients and equipment. Not the originals—the actual notebooks are hidden in Ayla's closet. I made multiple sets of photocopies for this trip. One of the drawings is a half-page, and looks a bit like an Aztec calendar that someone broke apart and tried to put back together while blindfolded. In the corner just below it, there's a little six-pointed star. It's lopsided, but it's drawn with precision, like everything else in his notebooks. The other is a descending line that divides into branches that split again and again, like in taxonomy. One set of pathways, running through the center, is darker than the others. At its nodes are small symbols I don't recognize. These drawings are the only things in his notebooks that aren't clearly labeled, that don't have some obvious connection to the *centella*. I'm missing something here.

Forrest is in the shower. Preston is staying with us in this room too, but he's out with the others, getting things ready for tonight. Our circle will be right on the Sonoma State campus, I'm told, in the basement of some building or another. Preston explained how it was secure, but I wasn't really listening. That's someone else's department.

We'll have twelve *viajeros* tonight. After we drink the tea they'll lie in a circle, with their heads in the middle. It won't take long for the *centella* to start peeling away their language. Free of the rigid constraints of words, their thoughts, memories, and hopes will begin moving again, breaking free of their borders, splitting and spilling into one another, twisting and diving away like fish from grasping hands. I'll sit in the center of the circle and sing the song that will guide our travelers through their journeys. I don't know why it works. I don't know how the song ends up in my throat. I've still got a lot to learn. This will be twice as many travelers as I've ever conducted before. I think I'll be able to manage it, though. I think I've figured out that part of it.

The first time I tried the *centella* I didn't know what to expect, and I didn't know what to make of my grandfather's scattered references to music. All my words fell away, and when I forgot my own name, the fear set in. It felt like I'd lost my center, like I'd scattered into a million pieces and I was seeing every fragment from the perspective of every other fragment, all at once. I curled up on my bed and rode it out, alone in the dark. Finally, my name came back to me, and soon after that the rest of my words: the books I'd read, the song lyrics

I'd memorized, all the stories. But they all felt a little different now. Lighter, airier. Moveable. A massive hunger came over me, a desire to ingest the sun, and I tiptoed downstairs and filled a bowl with fruit and raw vegetables and came back to my room where I ate it all slowly, savoring each bite. The next time I tried it I wore headphones and put a simple drumbeat on a loop, and that kept me from flying apart. I anchored myself to the rhythm and held on as the memories and images came pouring over me. Sometime later I heard the song. A wordless melody that seemed to be coming from the sky. It gave me a place to stand, a bit of solidity among the motion. It took some time before I recognized my own voice.

I worked on the recipe alone for a few weeks, and then I shared it with Ayla. When it was time, I could feel her there with me, and I could feel what she needed, and a different song arose—one that carried us both. And then when Paolo joined us, it was the same thing again. I had to find the balancing point, and listen for what we needed together.

Paolo Benedetti, aka Uncle Paolo—he's the one who launched all of this into high gear. I'd been hearing about him here and there from Ayla for years. He was a therapist and a researcher who used psychedelics in his practice, and he'd studied them all: psilocybin, ayahuasca, San Pedro, peyote, you name it. After Ayla experienced the *centella* she said I had to share it with him, and that we could totally trust him, and I said okay so first we went to go talk to him at his office, and then one night soon after that he came to Ayla's to try it himself. He'd worn a white button-down shirt that was a little too big for him, and had an extra button unbuttoned, and his sleeves rolled up. Black stubble, black eyeglass frames, black hair receding but no gray. His curiosity was so powerful he was vibrating but he was respectful throughout, even reverent. No talking down to us, no treating us like we were kids. No trying to pry any secrets out of me. He'd given himself straight over to the journey and then three days later he came back and told me that it was unlike anything he'd ever experienced before. "Life-changing," he said. He told me he had money and connections all over the state and could pull together help from among his network of postgrads, so that I could begin to share it. "The world needs this," he said to me, looking me straight in the eyes, his hope evident. A grown man, accomplished and successful, pleading with somebody my age. We talked. He asked questions, and I told him what I could. I told him about the song, and the way it had come out of some overlap between the three of us. I told him I didn't understand it, and he taught me an expression: *In Lak'ech A'la K'in.* It was Mayan, he told me, and it meant "I am you, and you are me." I figured he was going to try to explain it to me, because that's what people his age do to people my age, but he didn't. He was done. He just sat back and waited for me.

"Okay," I said. "Let's get started."

He tried about a hundred times to get me to wait until I was finished with high school, but I had already made up my mind. This was already in motion. Next thing you know, I was meeting Emilio and the others, and taking them through *el regreso*, and then a van appeared, and now we're here.

My timer sounds and I twist the stove knob to Off. Now I just have to wait. I had tuned out the TV, but now it's blaring a noisy ad for paper towels. I reach over to the bed, grab the remote, and start flipping through channels. I don't understand why the temperature is so important—that information must be in a different notebook. I just know that if I don't do it this way, it doesn't work very well. Maybe someday I'll figure these things out.

Knocks fall on the door and I get up to let Preston in, but instead of Preston standing there, it's Emilio. "Oh, hey," I say. "What's up?"

"Hey," he says, with a smile. "Everything's all set up. How's it going here?" He's clutching something dark and soft in front of himself, and that's where my eyes go. It's a knit cap. Isn't there some old saying about holding your hat in your hands?

"Fine," I say. "Getting close."

"Right on." He peers past me, over my shoulder. "Can I . . . Do you mind if I take a look? Can I see what it looks like?" I haven't really had a chance to take a close look at him yet. He's tall and wiry, with blue eyes, and the kind of blond hair that always looks like he just got out of the ocean and toweled off. It's a warm night, but he's wearing a light blue sweater that looks like his aunt made it. I don't remember much about him from when he first came to take the *centella*, or the other brief chat I had with him, when we were planning. I guess I'd say he seems excitable. He's pretty enthusiastic about all this, anyway.

"Sure, come in," I say, stepping back, and shutting the door behind him. He and his friends are going to great lengths to help make this happen, after all—it's only natural he'd be curious. I take my seat and he sits down on the bed's edge, studying the contents of the table.

"You're cooking it right now?" he asks.

"Kind of. I have to let it cool off a bit before the next step."

Emilio nods. "Those are the petals?"

"Yes," I say. He leans forward to peer into the *molcajete*, and I'm hoping he won't reach out. I don't think he's supposed to touch them. "Here, take a look," I say, reaching into the backpack on the floor. I pull out both glass jars, hand them over, and he squints, trying to peer through the dark amber glass.

"And this is all from the same plant?" he says. "Where does it come from?"

"Yes. Hang on a sec." I take a temperature reading, but it's not quite time for the leaves yet. I've never made a batch this big, and it's throwing off my timing. "Sorry," I say. "I have to concentrate a bit. What did you say?"

"No worries!" he says. "I asked where it comes from."

"The desert. The Sonoran Desert. I don't know where all it grows, but this is from down near the Mexican border."

"So this is like some family thing? The recipe?"

"I'm not really sure, actually."

He points at the drawings. "What about those? What are those?"

"Pages from my grandfather's notebooks." I hand him the photocopies. "I'm still trying to . . ." I trail off, not sure how I should phrase it. Hoping something else will distract him. But he's studying the drawings, rapt, waiting for an answer. "Hold on," I say, and take another temperature reading. This one gives me the number I was looking for and I dump in the leaves. He watches all the while.

"Those are the leaves? What do they do?" he asks.

"I don't know, actually," I say, circling a spoon through the mixture. "I just know it's how I'm supposed to do it."

"How did you learn all this?" he says.

How indeed? I still haven't answered that for myself. "It's complicated," I say. I could give him a short version, but I need to keep an eye on this pot, and it feels strange to be talking to him about it when my own brothers don't even know yet. "Can I have those drawings back?" I ask him.

"Yeah, of course!" he says, thrusting them at me. When they're back on the table he hands me the jars as well, and I return them to the backpack. "I didn't mean to bother you," he says.

"You're not." I give the pot another stir. "The timing can just be a little tricky."

"Gotcha."

I measure the temperature again. This is where the volume of the mixture is going to throw me off. I think it's time to start mashing the petals. I should probably make sure I work fast.

"I'll get out of your hair," Emilio says, standing. "Thanks for showing me all this. I'm just really interested."

"It's pretty amazing, isn't it?"

"Hell yes."

I lock the door behind him, take up the pestle, and begin grinding the petals into powder. The black and red smear, mix, and become burgundy. After another reading I dump in the powder and the water turns deep red. The scent—like spice and rain—rises into the room. I hit the start button on a small digital timer and circle the spoon through the mixture, once, twice. Five more minutes, and then I'll strain it.

I sit back, close my eyes. Voices in the adjacent room, car engines in the parking lot down below. A laugh from somewhere far away, maybe the sidewalk. Forrest emerges from the bathroom, dressed, his hair still damp. "Almost there?" he asks. I nod.

Chapter 13

Peoria rinses the last of the suds from the bowls and sets them in the dish drainer. Redland had offered to do the dishes, but she'd insisted. Her hands needed a task. She has decided to eschew the dishwasher again—with just the two of them here now, it's easier to just wash them by hand.

In other times, a few quiet minutes with the dishes and some warm water would often give her mind a place to rest, but that isn't going to happen tonight. Not with her children all scattered and unknowable. Not with the way she's been struggling to make the connection between the Lenore of previous years and the Lenore who left the note and slipped out. Something had clearly happened, there in Rogelio's house, or in the surrounding desert.

The two of them had driven down when Rogelio failed to materialize for their customary Sunday-night phone call, and a welfare check from sheriff deputies discovered him gone, with all the windows and doors thrown wide open. Lenore had driven much of the way, quiet in the concentration of a newly licensed driver, while Peoria had stared out the window, silent with her thoughts and memories as they coursed through the Central Valley, which lay fallow in its December quietude. She had never been to her father's place. He had always been the one to come and visit her, taking breaks from his ongoing and constant migrations, and this was a home he'd only settled into over the final few years of his life, once he'd finally retired. Or claimed to, anyway.

They'd made their way down I-5, clear down through San Diego before turning inland, driving along the border, heading for the heart of the desert. After ten hours of driving they found his dirt road and followed it into a small hollow, just large enough for his house. Lenore pulled up in the small clearing next to his dusty truck.

The front door was wide open, and they entered to find thin drifts of sand curving across the clean wooden floor. Peoria knew immediately that Rogelio was gone, and these were the first of the billions of grains her father had invited in, to swallow the house and all its contents and grind them into dust.

She knew the grief would swell and tower and crash, but not yet. Now, the contents of her father's last home came into sharp focus, and she began drifting through his rooms. He'd left his home like a museum: his bed made, everything put away, couch cushions in order, woven blankets perfectly folded and stacked. His shelves and bookcases were dusty but perfectly organized, their shelves lined with bright fabrics and full of figurines carved from stone or wood, framed photographs, a bundle of carved flutes tied together with a leather cord.

She found a key hanging from a nail and a sliding door on the side of the house that opened to a converted shipping container, wedged between the house and the base of the hill, where he'd built a laboratory. Among his equipment were shelves of notebooks and several racks of jars filled with botanical specimens, each labeled in Spanish and Latin with Rogelio's meticulous handwriting in black ink on white graph paper. Of course there had been no retirement.

Back in the house she called for Lenore but heard no response. The kitchen sat in the back of the house and there she found another doorway standing open. Beyond it, footprints led to the crest of a nearby dune. Rogelio had once told her that when it was time, he'd simply walk into the desert and disappear. He had a habit of speaking in metaphors she didn't quite understand, and she assumed this was one of those. But perhaps, after a lifetime spent studying deserts, he'd found his way into chambers so remote there was no way back.

Suddenly she was parched. At the sink she bent down and drank straight from the tap. Next to it, a dish drainer held a single earthenware mug. She flipped it over and stuck her nose inside it and detected a faint mix of spice and flowers. The unplugged refrigerator was empty but for an open box of baking soda. She sat down at the table in a daze, uncoupled from her sense of time.

Sometime later Lenore reappeared on the threshold, backlit by the setting sun. A change had come over her. Peoria had always been aware of the clear echoes between her father and her daughter: mannerisms, gestures, handwriting, the way they liked to arrange their things. And now Lenore was seeing them, too. She moved around that strange property as if she had always lived there.

Peoria rinses the last of the soap from the knives, sets them in the drainer, and shuts off the faucet. Upon turning, though, she sees the dirty cutting board she'd forgotten about. "Damn," she says. She does not reach for it right away. Instead, she leans on the counter and thinks about how strange it is not to know where any of her children are.

Chapter 14

Once in Petaluma Leo finds his way downtown and then to Max's house, where a light is blazing in the front room. He knocks but nobody comes so he knocks again, harder, and after waiting without hearing anything he knocks on the window, hard enough to rattle its casing, but that effort proves to be similarly futile. He calls Max again. In the background there is laughter and music. Sit tight, Max tells him, a slight slur in his voice—he'd call Mary and then get back to him. Leo sits down on the step and watches the last of the light fall upon the street, where a couple of boys are riding their bikes while their kid sister swings the end of a jump rope through some dandelions.

A few minutes later his phone rings.

"She's out," Max says. "Went with some of her girlfriends into the city. Said she wouldn't be back until late."

"Got a spare key hidden somewhere?"

"Nope, sorry pal. You're going to have to sit tight."

"An open window?"

"Ha! She would have had to shut all the windows to set the alarm. It'll have to be tomorrow."

"Anybody else here have a key?"

"Tomorrow, Leo. I'm sorry I'll miss you. Come back up sometime soon, would you?"

Leo returns to the Jeep and sinks into his seat. He sits for a minute, trying to think, but the kids keep staring at him, and now their mom is out there too, clearly wondering why he's there, so he heads back toward the freeway and finds a place to have a cheeseburger and a beer. Afterwards he heads back to Max's, where the driveway is still empty. Leo parks and reclines the seat a little and jabs at the radio buttons, finding nothing. He tries to reach Yvette but she does not answer and he doesn't leave a message. He reclines the seat farther, opens the moon roof, and watches the stars. His mind flips back and forth from the work in front of him to murderous fantasies about Clifford.

He awakens with a jump that slams his leg into the steering wheel. His phone tells him it's 1:30 in the morning. A car has appeared in the driveway; the lights in the house are out. He drives back to the freeway, checks into a hotel, and dreams he is eating bees.

Chapter 15

Gabriel walks slowly across the city, his bloodstream buzzing with the endorphins kicked up by the tattoo machine. Every few steps he glances down at the fish on his wrist, which is sealed in a wrap of ointment and cellophane and tape. He stops at a drugstore and buys a bottle of water and continues on, rehearsing the Fresno address in his head.

It is with a strange sense of detachment that Gabriel accepts the direction laid out before him by the inscrutable combination of Ayla and Ángel. Some great purpose seems to be hiding just behind them—he had just watched a man eat a Post-It and an origami fish, after all. Part of him wonders if he should have pressed Ayla harder, but he tries to dismiss that. He'd asked his questions, and she'd said what she said. If she'd told him what his afternoon had in store for him, he wouldn't have believed her anyway. So he'll find out what's in Fresno when he gets there.

He arrives at the Greyhound station just before dusk. The next southbound bus is not scheduled to depart until 3:45 in the morning, a time so bleak he has to ask the agent to repeat it. He walks back outside and surveys the neighborhood, his home for the next several hours. Across the street, a discount furniture store and a restaurant supply wholesaler occupy adjacent warehouses. On the next block down sits the police department headquarters, a taco truck parked at its corner. Gabriel crosses a wide boulevard and gets in line at the truck behind a trio of uniformed officers.

The eastern half of the sky is darkening now. The truck emanates light, steam, the smells of grilled meat and onions and chiles. The officers order and stand by, waiting, laughing over a traffic stop involving a minivan, crystal meth, and live chickens. Gabriel orders tacos and steps aside. A female officer about his age, dirty blond hair pulled into a short, tight ponytail, draws up to the counter next. She orders a chicken burrito and digs through her pockets, growing flustered as one pocket after another yields nothing. She is about to cancel her order when Gabriel steps forward and pushes a ten-dollar bill through the window.

"Oh, I can't let you do that, sir," she says.

"It's already done." He nods at the cashier, who counts out the change.

She drops her arms to her sides, gives him an embarrassed smile. "Thank you." Johansen, says her nametag. "My desk and my wallet are on the top floor, but I can be back in three minutes."

He shakes his head. "I'll disappear."

"Without your tacos?"

"I'm trying to lose weight."

She laughs. "Interesting diet."

They stand on the edge of the pool of light, chatting while they wait. She's on graveyard that night—fueling up before her shift, then paperwork, and then on patrol until six the following morning. Gabriel wonders where he'll be then. His tacos emerge on a paper plate, topped with carrots, peppers, onions, radish slices, lime wedges. Officer Johansen thanks him again. He nods, tells her to be safe out there, and walks slowly up the street, heading nowhere in particular, eating, the sting of pickled jalapeños spreading through his mouth.

The last of the blue drains from the sky. The roads are quiet. He finishes eating and tosses his plate, along with its squeezed-out lime wedges and jalapeño stems, in a trash can at the edge of a motel parking lot. He turns a corner and suddenly the river is there in front of him, silhouettes of trees lining its far bank. The air here is cool and smells of water, and all the other scents the river has carried in on its back. There is a bike trail along the water's edge; Gabriel turns and follows it. Clusters of trees stand along the bank and from within them come the sounds of voices and the unsteady lights of weak lanterns and the orange dots of lit cigarettes. At first Gabriel thinks of teenagers hiding with cases of cheap beer but then a pair of voices bursts from a thick clump of trees with a raspy cackle and he realizes he's skirting a homeless encampment that stretches along the river bank. He peers into the trees, which now line both sides of the path, and finds dim orbs of light hidden throughout. The smells of food and propane and piss reach him. He walks beyond the encampment, alert, and comes upon a sandy flat with a pair of benches and no one else around. Once he sinks down he realizes that he has been on his feet ever since rising from the tattooer's chair. He tears the plastic wrap and tape from his wrist and brings the fish close to his eyes, trying to study it, to figure out where it came from. He grows accustomed to the darkness and after a time he realizes that before him lies not one but a pair of rivers. Two glittering channels of reflected moonlight run from out of the north and converge right in front of him, continuing down through the valley as one. He thinks about this confluence, wondering what it would be like to be a great river, and to flow suddenly into another.

Now stars emerge, fighting through the city's light and the pollen-filled spring sky. He lies down on the bench and searches for shapes, making up his own constellations, and the next thing he knows there is a burst of pink and a hand on his shoulder, shaking him. He sits up, disoriented, to find her before him, her flashlight beam now on the ground between them. His throbbing tattoo brings the day back to him.

"Hey," she says. "It's me. Your dinner date."

All up and down the river bank are clusters of flashlights, their beams bobbing with movement. Shouting, the clatter of equipment, curses, an irate woman screaming somewhere in the distance.

"You don't look like an illegal camper," she says.

He rises to his feet. She looks sad and weary, or maybe that's the darkness.

"That's what they're called?" he says.

She's backpedaling, heading for a nearby cluster of trees, where a confrontation is escalating. "There are lots of seats in the waiting room," she tells him. "Have a safe trip." He walks back to the bus station, buys a ticket from an automated machine, and dozes off in a molded gray plastic chair under florescent lights that tinge everything blue.

Chapter 16

Leo pushes through the door of Max Abramov's office at Sonoma State University early the next morning. Text messages back and forth to Gainesville had secured the placement of a key in an envelope beneath Max's doormat at home; Leo picked it up at sunrise and sped to campus through lifting mists. His boxes sit next to each other on the far edge of a counter in Max's office, against a wall. On top of them stands a large circular plastic tray filled with gravel, and in the gravel are eight or nine species of cacti in small terra cotta pots. The tray is too flimsy to hold its shape under the combined weight of stone and succulents, but Leo does not realize this until after he has attempted to lift the tray by its edges. He curses, folds the whole assemblage in half like a taco, and dumps it on an empty spot on the counter, remembering with some irritation the anxious request he'd received a few weeks ago and the drive he'd made with the boxes to hand them off to Max at some strip-mall coffee shop in San Rafael by the freeway. Max had said he'd needed them for some meta-analysis one of his grad students was leading.

Leo pulls off the lids and digs through notebooks and loose stacks of papers, searching for thumb drives. There are several, and he doesn't know what's on most of them—he uses them rarely these days, but he does remember making a number of back-ups just before bringing the boxes to Max. When he has gathered them all he heads to the desk, where he finds himself correct in his assumption that Max would not be the type to password-protect his computer.

One by one he plugs them in, touring years of projects: hyenas, mice, beetles, and then birds—birds, but nothing recent, no egrets. As the possibilities diminish he feels the floor opening beneath him, a draft of hot displaced air blowing upward as the pieces of his career— his paper, his funding, his standing in the department—plummet into it.

It all disintegrates and the maw coughs up alternate futures for him, powdery and fragmented: a teaching position at a community college in North Dakota or somewhere, perhaps a middle management position at some dump of a zoo. In these scenarios Yvette will not be present; she has made that clear. For her a move would have to be LA or New York City. Chicago or Boston, maybe, if large amounts of money are involved, which looks to be a decreasing likelihood. No. Instead he'll be on staff at a theme park in Texas, looking after a flock of mangy penguins, married to a sea lion trainer who will love football and bear him children who will worship people like Clifford Baumgardner. He slams his fists on Max's desk, stands up, and stalks out of the office.

He needs coffee, maybe some eggs and bacon. Two buildings over he finds a snack bar with a basket of red apples and bananas on offer, and another basket of cream cheese bagel sandwiches wrapped in cellophane. There is a pot of what smells like cheap coffee on a burner, but it's full, so maybe it isn't too old. Although there is no cooktop in sight a small chalkboard advertises English muffin sandwiches with egg and ham and cheese, and because it is the only hot item available he orders two, along with a large coffee. Unwilling to bear witness to the microwaving of his eggs, he takes his coffee and heads outside.

It is still early, still quiet. He takes a sip of coffee, and even though it is as bad as he predicted the bitter heat sweeps down into his chest and manages to impart a bit of calmness. He resists the urge to run through his mental list of personal catastrophes again and instead works to pull his mind backwards, out of the mess, to see his situation from a broader perspective. This doesn't make sense, he tells himself. It's impossible that a single grad student could wreak this much damage. There must be something he isn't remembering. Junior researchers have overestimated their contributions since the dawn of scholarship, since the birth of science. But who could name Einstein's assistant, or Darwin's sidekick, or Newton's telescope polisher? Nobody, because that's how it works. You pay your dues and you wait, and if you run out of patience or brains or luck you go elsewhere. In all his years, in all the faculty meetings, all the water-cooler gossip, over all the drinks at conferences, holiday parties, and everywhere else, he's never heard of somebody being so indignant at the way things worked that he'd been this vindictive. It can't be possible.

The kid at the counter inside is calling to him, so he collects his food and walks past another couple of buildings to a courtyard where he finds a bench in the sunlight. He unwraps the first sandwich and bites into it. It has a uniform sponginess to it, but it's full of salt and fat and heat and it barely needs chewing so he works his way through it quickly. As he eats he surveys the courtyard, still quiet at this early hour. Various halls sit along each of the courtyard's four sides, a pastiche of architecture. It's strangely flat, but it's greener than Berkeley, and the air tastes better, despite the occasional whiff of cow dung. His second sandwich has gone lukewarm, and after the first bite he doubts his ability to stomach it. He sips his coffee and takes another uninterested nibble, thinking about how next he'll have to head home and answer for the scene at Raleigh's.

While chewing he notices a black lump of cloth lying along one of the courtyard's pathways, a familiar strip of broken white running through it. A knot forms inside him; he leaves his food on the bench and walks over to it and the pattern of bones that runs along either sleeve comes into focus. He picks up the sweatshirt and shakes the dew from it, and when its scent hits his brain he knows he doesn't even have to check the tag, where he'll find his sister's initials written in his father's handwriting, just as his own initials appeared on every garment he owned when he lived under that roof.

The heat has gone out of the sweatshirt; it's been sitting here awhile but he whirls, scanning the perimeter of the courtyard and peering along pathways as if she might have just dropped it. What would Lenore have been doing here? Partying? Why would you leave Berkeley to party in fucking Rohnert Park? A boyfriend? Maybe that was it. Someone older, someone she met in high school who'd come up here, or a friend of a friend, or someone's older brother. But why the games, the running away, the cryptic note? It isn't like Redland and Peoria would care—

Someone is watching him. There are three students, young men, rounding the corner of a nearby building, and one of them is watching him just a little too carefully. There is a slight falter in his step, as if he might like to turn back. He steadies his gait, and now is very pointedly looking the other way—at an empty wall. All this transpires in just a second, in the smallest of movements, but it's enough to impel Leonardo. He drapes the sweatshirt over his arm, pulls out his phone, and finds a photo of Lenore from Easter break as he approaches them. He enlarges it so her face fills the screen. "Hey guys, quick question," he says, stepping in front of them. "Have any of you seen this girl around?" He turns the screen toward them.

All three sets of eyes fly open and before Leo can react two of the boys turn and bolt. He drops the coffee and sweatshirt and lunges for the third, grabbing fistfuls of shirt and a backpack strap, static erupting in his head. He holds the boy at arm's length, his body braced for an attack, his attention flashing back and forth between the two running boys, now disappearing around a corner, and the one in his grasp. He turns to the remaining young man—who has him beat by two or three inches, and twenty or thirty pounds—with wide eyes.

Leo pockets his phone and doubles his grip, adrenaline rocketing. But his would-be combatant does nothing. He's calm, almost strangely so—his body angled away, soundless, his eyes in the distance. Through the sudden haze of stress Leo tries to fit the pieces together but nothing coheres; instead, his mind offers up only an overpowering sense of danger. He presses forward, delivering a stiff shake to his quarry. "Why did they run?" he yells.

There's still no reaction, and this triggers another surge of adrenaline. Leo shakes him again. "Why did they run?"

"I don't know," the boy says.

"Bullshit. Why?!"

"I don't know," he says again, his tone unchanged. Without pulling back he circles—not quickly, but insistently.

Worst-case scenarios flood Leo's mind and he lifts a hand and cups it around the back of the boy's neck. "Where is she, you fuck?"

The boy recoils and stiffens under Leo's hold; his eyes widen. He opens his mouth but then closes it again.

"Where!?" Leo roars, shaking him.

"Chico," the boy says, trying to twist away.

Leo tightens both grips, formulating his next question, but over the boy's shoulder there is fast movement, shouting. Three or four men, closing in. Leo lets go and runs.

Chapter 17

Gabriel awakens, lifts his head on stiff neck muscles, and peers through the grimy bus window. The sun has just climbed above the hills and steam is rising from the fields of the valley's floor. He unbuckles and stretches as best he can. At some point in the night the seat just across the aisle had collected a passenger. His neighbor wears a red ball cap pulled low across his face, thick black hair curving out from beneath it. Even in sleep his arms hug a shoebox against the front of a round belly, which is wrapped in a gray t-shirt and bulging from between the open flaps of a thin faded sweatshirt.

Gabriel turns back to the window and watches the fields rumble past, the climbing sun outlining farmhouses and the dust clouds of tractors. Canneries arise, skeletal structures with silos and conveyor belts, tanker cars parked on railway spurs. A cluster of warehouses rolls past, and then a subdivision of blocky houses. The driver announces their upcoming stop in Merced, long enough for onward passengers to climb off, use the bathroom, and buy some food.

Gabriel disembarks, stretches, heads into the station, and ten minutes later reboards with an empty bladder, a cup of tea, and a bagel and a banana in a paper bag. He sits and eats as they roll through town. The business district turns to neighborhoods and trailer parks, and then to canneries and farmland again. He stares through the window as the bus pulls him through the valley, past field after field, an occasional town.

An hour later the fields give way to greater and greater swaths of cement and metal—more warehouses, parking lots, scrapyards—and Gabriel hears a faint scratching sound over the road noise. At first he assumes it's a tire, or pebbles hitting the undercarriage, but as it persists he realizes the scratches are too close, too regular. His neighbor stirs, lifts his head, and takes the cover off of his shoebox. He reaches in and strokes something, murmurs a few words. He replaces the lid and gives Gabriel a bleary smile.

"*Lagartijas*," he says.

Gabriel slides over to the aisle seat and the man removes the lid again. A pair of brown lizards, their backs netted with tiny black diamonds, crouch on a bed of dry leaves. They are both looking at Gabriel.

"Your pets?"

The man laughs. "Not pets. *Compañeros*." His eyes are bright; his round stomach and his red hat and the twinkle in his eye make Gabriel think of Santa Claus.

"Where are you taking them?"

"Back to their home. *En el desierto*."

"Which desert?"

The man shrugs. "*No importa*. Any one. They are all connected. Like the oceans."

The sun is higher now and its beams are able to find their way through the dusty tinted windows and into the shoebox. The two little faces glow; Gabriel is sure they are smiling.

"But where will you take them? When will you get off the bus?"

The man shrugs again. "Whenever they are ready."

Gabriel might have left it at that but the man is smiling, clearly eager for the follow-up question. "And how will you know they are ready?" Gabriel asks, unable to resist returning the smile.

"They will tell me."

"How?"

"Oh, they tell me many things. They told me where I should sit."

"They told you to sit here?"

"They say they know you," he says.

"They like me?" Gabriel says, thinking the man misspoke.

"I think they like you, yes, but they didn't say that. They said they *know* you." He shrugs. "They know your family."

Gabriel laughs. "My family? Who?" But immediately his grandfather comes to mind. When he thinks of Peoria's father he is always struck by how little he knew and understood the man. Even now he still finds it startling to remember that Rogelio is dead. The transition had been a subtle one—even in life his grandfather had an otherworldly presence. Gabriel remembers that he and his brother and sister could walk into a room and play for half an hour before they realized he was sitting in the corner, reading. His gaze was not like a man's; it was like being watched by a deer or a mountain. The stories of Rogelio's mother, a legendary *curandera* of the Sonoran, made her sound even stranger.

The sprawl of Fresno has drawn them in as they talked, and now the bus exits and rumbles down an overpass into the city's heart. Gabriel's companion replaces the lid of the box and folds his hands atop it. "All your family," he says. "They say they know you all." He shrugs. "They say *adios* to you. They are looking forward to your visit."

"My visit?"

"To the desert."

"I'm not going to the desert."

The man shrugs. "Sometimes they're wrong," he says, chuckling, "but not very often."

Chapter 18

I n Chico, Leo sits in the Grand Cherokee on the edge of campus, watching the foot traffic, the motor running and the air conditioner on high against the Central Valley heat. It took the whole three-hour drive from Rohnert Park for a theory to coalesce, but once it came together its truth was self-evident. Lenore must be running party drugs to college kids up and down the state. It explains everything: her disappearance, the kids' reaction at Sonoma State, Redland's refusal to include the police. He'd fled the scene in Rohnert Park and driven northward with his nervous system on overdrive, his adrenaline churning after the strange encounter with the boys, trying to think. His cortisol-flooded brain conjured thoughts of prostitution, kiddie porn, ritualistic Satanic cult murders. But as he made his way over to I-5 and up through the miles of quiet farmland, the stress ebbed and his perspective returned. By the time he was halfway there, he began to realize he'd overreacted. This was just some ill-timed, inconsiderate, teenage bullshit. A low-level disgust moved in, displacing his fears about Lenore and clearing some mental space for his other problems to come rushing back in. He wasn't driving to Chico to rescue her from some pressing danger; he was simply putting off the messes he'd left behind in Berkeley.

And now he's sitting here on an amateur stakeout in a rented Jeep with no real plan other than hoping he'll happen upon his delinquent sister, and then at least he will have managed some bit of productivity over these two days. He resigns himself to his watch and refocuses on the scene before him. It's a busy intersection, with a movie theater on one corner, a restaurant on another, a sports bar across the street. It's the sort of intersection you'd inevitably pass through if you were a visiting eighteen-year-old from out of town. Students flow through the streets with their backpacks and water bottles, winding down their own semester, or quarter, or whatever they do up here. Pickup trucks, either meticulously polished or dirty from actual farm work, roll through the green lights, blaring country music. Passersby barely take notice.

The foot traffic thins. In the sports bar a big-screen television is tuned to a monster truck rally, where a back-flipping truck snares Leo's attention briefly before the broadcast switches over to ads. First up is a Dove shampoo ad; Leo laughs out loud when he sees it's Yvette's. He picks up his phone and sees he's down to the end of his battery, but he's got just enough juice to send her a text. *Just saw the Dove ad*, he tells her. *In Chico. Long story.* He hits send; his phone confirms delivery.

A wave of affection for his girlfriend washes over him, and in a flash he remembers the way she had appeared next to him in the lobby of the George R. Brown Convention Center in Houston, where he'd been sent to represent the department at a biodiversity conference. He hadn't been enjoying himself much—he'd found the food bad, the city uninteresting, and the conference programming a regurgitation of information any self-respecting biologist would know already. During a break he'd been trapped in a conversation with a sweaty herpetologist when suddenly she was there, elegant in a black mini-dress and a colorful scarf, looping her arm through his, a monarch butterfly above the city dump.

They'd only had a few dates at that point. He hadn't even thought the first one had gone all that well—she'd let him go after a brief hug, which all his experience told him was a dismissal, but then she'd called two days later, wanting to see him again. A second date went only slightly better, or so he thought, but she gave him a kiss full of electricity and heat before marching off into the night. On their third date he began to get a sense of her rhythms, her quirks, her oblique sense of humor. She kissed him again, for only a little longer, and then she vanished just as quickly. Two days later he flew out from San Francisco for Houston and she appeared on day two. After pulling him away from his suddenly tongue-tied interlocutor, she told him she had come for brisket and him, in that order.

They were inseparable for weeks, forsaking sleep for conversation, having constant sex, going to all-night diners for eggs and bacon afterwards, eating with their legs entangled under the table. And then things settled, evolved. They reclaimed their individuality. They withdrew their overextensions, gave up the things they'd pretended to like for the other's sake. They allowed their exasperations more space. They fought. They decided which fights would recur. They made secret lists in their minds of the traits and proclivities they'd always wanted in their partners, and did not now have. They discovered how to hurt each other.

Their on-again, off-again relationship is stumbling into its third year, and though there are days of harmony, even passion, the majority of their interactions have become what feel like negotiations between opposing parties who speak different languages. The process of deciding what restaurant they should go to for dinner can sometimes leave him depleted.

But with his professional and family lives in flames, it is Yvette to whom his thoughts and heart track. He wishes she could be here with him, right at this stupid intersection. They could sit at a table in the corner of the sports bar and drink beer and eat chicken wings and watch the monster trucks destroy themselves. He picks up his phone to text her again, but a second after the screen flashes on it goes black. With a sigh he heaves it into the passenger seat and when he looks back up, he can't remember what he's doing here.

Chapter 19

At noon, oppressed by hot cow-shit-scented breezes, Gabriel stands in the alcove of an abandoned storefront, directly across the street from the address Ángel gave him. It's a two-story building, its wooden planks in need of a new coat of white paint. On the ground floor is a discount shoe store, where a pair of languid customers circulate, and a variety store that doesn't look like it's been open in a long time. Between the storefronts is a windowless door, painted purple, with brass numerals above it that match Ángel's note. It's unmarked and seems to lead up to the rooms on the second floor, where high windows reveal only the ceiling inside.

This block sits at the edge of the city's central district, not far from the freeway. Within his view are long-empty storefronts, a liquor store, a *panadería*, a palm reader. Down the block sits a boarded-up one-screen movie theater that looks as though it went through two or three afterlives before running out of purpose. Even with the swelter there is foot traffic: women with vinyl shopping bags, clumps of idle men, everyone seemingly oblivious to the heat. Farther south the road stretches on into a sector of warehouses.

A short old man, his skin leathered by the sun, walks by just then, chewing on a toothpick. He aims a curious look into the alcove and

Gabriel is reminded of himself, his unlikely surroundings and his mission. He is newly tattooed and in Fresno, conditions he could not have foreseen a day and a half earlier.

It is not unusual, however, to feel himself pulled through the world like this by the gravity of Lenore's being. It began even before her birth, when the swelling of his mother's belly had been like the formation of a new moon, his attention a tide that rose to it. He had insisted on learning how to change her diapers and often when she cried in the dead of night he would get there before his parents. Later, when they played hide-and-seek, Gabriel was often able to peel away from the tree or the corner where he'd been counting with his eyes closed and head almost directly to her hiding place. She often gave up after two or three rounds, accusing him of cheating. He would proclaim his innocence, and tell her that it was only because he was her brother, and he knew how her brain worked, but when his mind was quiet and he really thought about it, he wondered if there might be more to it. He imagined sometimes he could see the trails she left through the world—little pale blue cloudlets, like a jet's contrails after the wind has begun pulling them apart.

Once when she was about six or seven they all traveled into San Francisco to Golden Gate Park for an Easter picnic and afterwards he and Leo and Lenore had plunged into Children's Playground, a sprawling sand pit of jungle gyms, ramps, and tunnels, a trio of long concrete slides snaking down a steep hillside. The three of them stuck together for a few minutes before dispersing through the teeming playground—Leo and Gabriel to the slides and Lenore toward the sand, where several girls her age were at work building cities. After a few circuits on the slides Gabriel was struck with a sudden need to check on his sister. He rushed off the hillside and soon found her on the tire swing, sitting with another pair of girls. A couple of boys, probably closer to his own age, were spinning it wildly. The two other girls were shrieking with pleasure but in brief flashes he saw Lenore's face—frozen, mortified. He stepped in, stopped the swing, and pulled her free, and once in his arms she burst into tears. He held her until she was quiet.

It has been some time since he's thought of that connection, but he still trusts the bond. He has a thousand questions but his interactions with Ayla and Ángel, though strange, did not suggest danger. She must be all right, or close enough to it. Regardless of what might be slated to happen here tonight at this address, he is confident of that much. The answers to the other mysteries before him will reveal themselves in time if he can just stay on her trail.

A tanker truck turns the corner, shuddering through a downshift, and creeps up the street, reflecting in its side a curved funhouse version of the storefronts and sidewalks. When it passes, Gabriel is startled to see only half of himself appear—the alcove sits in deep shadow, and in the reflected image that darkness has eaten one side of him. He steps out into the light, but the truck has already passed.

Chapter 20

t is late afternoon by the time Leo decides to pick up a new charger and resuscitate his phone. His notifications explode to life, but before he can read anything the ringer goes off. It's Yvette.

"Have you seen the news?" she asks. It's her voice, but he barely recognizes her tone. "Do you know?"

"Know what? What's going on?"

"Are you still in Chico?" The sound of the road behind her.

"Yes. Why? What's going on?"

"Where, exactly? In your car? On foot?" Her words are slow and clear, like she's talking to a group of kindergarteners.

"Why does it matter? Why are you talking like that?"

"I'm in Chico. I just got here. I'm going to pick you up, but I need to know where you are and what the area is like. Is it busy?"

"You came here?" he says, remembering his earlier wish.

"Actually, I'm pulling over right here. You come to me. It's a furniture warehouse called Dougherty's. The street is uh . . . Park. Park Avenue. Where are you, exactly, right now?"

"By campus. What was in the news? Why are you here?"

"I'll explain when you get here. Just drive for now."

Five minutes later, as Leo rounds a corner and the warehouse's big yellow sign comes into sight, his phone rings again. "I'm almost there," he says. "I can see it."

"Do you see the street right across from it? Go down there instead. Drive a half-block and then park, okay?"

"What the hell is going on?" But she has already hung up. He follows the instructions and steps out of the Jeep when someone yells at him from the half-open window of a beat-up Nissan Sentra. She looks like Yvette, but she's a shade too pale—no, it is Yvette.

"Whose car is that?" he says, and points to the Jeep. "Let's take this instead."

"It has to be this one. Get in quick."

Leo drops toward the passenger seat, sweeping a sweatshirt and a ball cap aside to make room for himself. "Yvette, what the—"

"I'll tell it all to you in one minute," she says, accelerating before he's able to pull the door shut.

"Jesus," he mutters, turning to say something else, but the angle of her jaw and the tension in her forehead stop his words. She takes a left, barely slipping through a gap in oncoming traffic.

"We have to do one thing, and then I'll explain," she says. "But first, you need to put on that sweatshirt and that hat, and pull the brim low."

"A sweatshirt? In this weather?"

"Yes. Just for a minute. There's a gas station in a block. I'm going to park on the street, and you need to go in and get as much cash as you can out of the ATM. And then come straight back to the car. Put the hat and sweatshirt on."

"You're kidding. What the hell is this? Is this a rehearsal or some shit?"

"No, it's not a rehearsal, Leo. I'll explain when you get back in the car. Please."

"No. I've had enough. Tell me what this is about or let me the hell out of this piece of shit. Whose car even *is* this?"

"Leo. Baby," she says, her voice breaking on the words as she pulls over into a spot against the curb, just short of the gas station's first driveway. "Please. I'm begging you. Please just get the money."

A pang hits Leo's stomach; heat slaps his face. He grabs the hat, pulls the brim low, and seizes the door handle.

"Wait. Let me see your phone for a sec."

"Why?"

"I just need to check something really fast. You don't even need to unlock it."

Leo climbs from the car and drops his phone onto the seat before darting for the ATM.

"Don't run," she calls after him.

He withdraws two hundred dollars and returns and as before, she is pulling into traffic before he pulls his leg in. "Leo," she says. "I'm sorry. It's the kid. It's Adam, the Sonoma State kid." Her eyes dart from mirror to mirror as she accelerates.

"Who the hell is Adam? I don't know an Adam. What kid?"

"From Sonoma State this morning! The boy you were fighting." She takes a sharp right, banking hard, and glances over at him before her eyes dart back to the mirrors. "His name is Adam. His dad is an assemblyman, whose whole thing is law enforcement. Every cop in the state loves him."

The edges of Leo's vision have begun to go gray, and he doesn't know how to fit the information together—what about this assemblyman? "I wasn't—we weren't fighting. How do you even know about that?"

Yvette turns left and dives down the onramp, heading north, and when she speaks her words are competing with tears. And she never cries. "He's in a coma, honey. He hit his head and had a seizure. I know there's an explanation for it all, but you have to understand—Adam, he's autistic, spectrum, whatever they call it now. And there's video of you shoving him and knocking him over. Video that's all over the news, that every cop in the state has seen, all these cops who love this kid's dad, and his whole family." Her voice cracks again and she sets her eyes on the road as she settles in the fast lane, her eyes still scanning the mirrors.

Leo's head feels airless now, a balloon released from a child's grip. "I didn't push him. I don't—" the words tangle, and his mouth has gone too dry for him to untangle them.

"There's video, honey. They're looking for you. All of them."

Leo closes his eyes and tries to draw in a deep breath. It hurts; it's as if his lungs are packed in broken glass. "Where's my phone?" he manages to ask. His voice sounds as if it's coming from far away, from vocal cords made of paper ribbon.

She reaches into the compartment in her door and then tosses his empty phone case into his lap. "When you were at the ATM I drove over it a few times. They would have used it to track you." She pats the wheel. "I borrowed this car because it's pre-GPS."

A gigantic billboard rises on the side of the highway: a towering white cross on a canary background, with *Psalm 23* written in black letters twice the height of a man. Crows line its top, evenly spaced, perhaps two dozen of them.

"What now," he says.

"I know a place," she says.

Chapter 21

At a quarter to ten Gabriel is back in the alcove, across from the appointed address. The block is desolate now; streetlights illuminate nothing but litter and the listless flight patterns of horseflies. A cigarette dangles from his fingers. He is not a smoker but he picked up a pack that afternoon, figuring it might look suspicious to be standing out on a dark sidewalk by himself without even that much to do. Now that he is here he finds the cigarettes serve another purpose, as well—at least one person has pissed in the alcove since his noontime visit, and the burning tobacco helps to mask the odor. He'd anticipated some nerves, but now more than anything else he's struck by the dream-like peculiarity of his circumstances. Light bisects him again, this time from the streetlamps, and when he lifts the cigarette to his lips the tattooed fish rises from out of the shadows. He drops his arm and it dives back into darkness. The shadow is the surface of the water and the fish leaps and dives, leaps and dives; the smoke is sea foam, wind-driven from the crests of waves.

He leans forward and scans the road one way and then the other, sees nothing, and leans back into the semi-darkness. He takes another drag and tries to exhale as if he smokes right here, just like this, every night. There are still no lights in the windows above the shoe store. He checks the time on his phone—ten minutes to go. He expected the battery to be dead by now, but there it is, a slight bar of red clinging to the edge of the meter. He leans forward again.

On the other side of the street a man and a woman are approaching, walking unhurriedly but with purpose, talking quietly. They look to be in their mid-twenties. Gabriel is unsure whether to make his presence known or to conceal himself. It's too early to emerge, he decides. He'll wait and see. He recedes into the shadows of the alcove. The woman produces keys and they enter the purple doorway. After a few seconds a dim light appears behind the second-floor windows.

A few minutes later a car turns the corner, moving slowly. Gabriel stamps out his cigarette and presses himself into the back corner of the alcove. The car crawls by; the faces of all three occupants, washed in phone glow, crane to look at the doorway as they pass. None of them are Lenore. Although there is ample street parking they accelerate and turn and disappear around the next corner. The engine falls silent. Doors open and close, and the three of them—two boys and a girl—reappear at the corner, walking quickly, not speaking. One of them pushes open the door and peeks up the stairway, and then the three of them head through.

Over the next ten minutes, this process repeats itself several times. Nobody parks on the immediate block. Nobody speaks much. Nobody is his sister. At 9:58, Gabriel decides to join them.

He is halfway across the street when he hears feet on the stairs, and he stops. The door swings open, and everyone emerges again, no longer furtive, disappointment in their overlapping conversations. A few of them glance briefly in his direction before turning onto the sidewalk.

Gabriel does not hear them approach but suddenly they are there, right in front of him—a trio of young men, grim looks on their faces. The one in the middle is taller, blond hair sticking out from beneath a knit cap. He's carrying a steel flashlight on his shoulder, the length of a police baton. To either side and a half-step behind him is another pair of men, who are looking around, clearly uncomfortable. They're all about Gabriel's age, or maybe a few years younger.

"Who are you, and why are you here?" the blond one asks. The flashlight kicks on, and Gabriel squints and lifts his arm to block the glare. Blinded, he imagines the steel cylinder crashing into his forearm.

"What the fuck?" one of them whispers.

"Where did you get that tattoo?" the blond snaps, before Gabriel can respond to the first set of questions.

"In Sacramento. From Ángel."

"When?" he asks.

"This is bullshit," says one of the others.

Gabriel still can't see, can't tell who's talking. "Yesterday," he says. The flashlight beam drops to his knees, relieving his eyes.

"Who sent you there?" the blond asks.

"This timing is too fucked up," says one of his henchmen.

"But this is how it's supposed to work, remember?" the blond says.

"None of this is how it's supposed to work," says the third. "We need to divert, right now." He turns and walks away.

"I'm looking for Lenore," Gabriel tells the blond, in as friendly a voice as he can manage, given his adrenaline.

"No shit. Walk in front of us."

Gabriel follows the first man, who is moving quickly. They turn down a side street, keeping their formation, their pace just short of a jog. There is a white van parked halfway up the block, and they pile through the rear doors. The interior lights reveal scattered mounds of foam mats and inflatable camping mattresses, pillows, suitcases, and bags. There's a wall of seat backs beyond it, too high for him to see how many others might be inside. The doors slam shut behind him and the light cuts out. Gabriel barely has time to sit, his back braced against the wall, before the van pulls out, fast. The flashlight beam snaps back on but it's wrapped in a red shirt now, its light dim. "Who sent you to Ángel?"

Gabriel's mind churns with threat assessments, with questions about who these people are, and what his sister's role is in all this. For now, he doesn't see much choice but to cooperate. "Ayla," he says.

He turns his head toward the front of the van. "Hey Eddie," he calls. "Make sure we aren't being followed." He turns back to Gabriel. "Where were you this morning?"

The van veers around a corner, pressing Gabriel into the wall, and then begins climbing. There are no windows in the rear; he can see none of the outside world. The engine echoes in the van's cabin as they accelerate to freeway speed.

"The bus left Sacramento at 3:45. I was on the way here."

"You got a bus ticket you can show me?"

"On my phone." He pulls it out and hits a button, but the screen stays black. "Which is dead. If you have a charger, I can show you."

"It's okay. You wouldn't happen to know anything about some recent events, would you?"

"What events?"

"Never mind. Eddie!" he calls again. "Is there anyone behind us?"

"Yeah. It could just be the traffic, though."

He pulls the shirt off the flashlight and shines it at Gabriel's feet. "Show us your wrist, please."

Gabriel extends his wrist and the beam falls upon the tattoo, which feels suddenly sore and tender. His interrogator extends his own arm, showing the origami crane on the inside of his wrist. The others reach in as well: a fox and a rabbit.

The questions resume then. "*El regreso*. Tell us about your experience."

"Hey Emilio, I don't like the look of this guy," Eddie calls. "He's kinda on my ass."

"Change lanes and haul ass for a little while."

The engine grows louder and the van veers and accelerates. "Yeah, he followed me over!" Eddie says. "What should I do?"

The flashlight leaps back up to Gabriel's face. "I came alone!" he says. "I'm by myself." The beam drops.

"Keep driving fast for another minute, and then change back," Emilio says. They all fall silent as the van hurtles down the freeway. Triangular shadows wheel through the interior, light and dark. Gabriel shifts around, trying to get more comfortable on the floor, imagining what would happen to four unbuckled bodies in a cargo van in a high-speed wreck. Eddie changes lanes again and slows down. "He's going past us," he says. "It's someone's company truck."

"Get off at the next exit," Emilio says. "Let's be sure." He wraps the shirt back around the flashlight and looks at Gabriel. "So, the *centella*. What was it like for you?"

"The what?"

"Do you know who we are? What we're doing?"

"I just wanted to find Lenore," Gabriel says. He can't figure out if revealing his relationship to her will help or hinder his cause, so he decides to keep his secret for the time.

"Yeah, you said that," the man says. "I'd ask why, but I don't think I'd believe your answer now."

They're pulling off the freeway, climbing onto an overpass. They come to a stop, turn, and descend. "Nobody behind us," Eddie says. The streetlights fall away; the red t-shirt glows like embers.

"I'm sorry if this wasn't the reception you were led to believe you'd have here," Emilio says, sounding sincere. "Things are in rapid transition, and I'm afraid we have to part ways for now. I apologize for the inconvenience, but we don't have a choice." He lifts his voice and tells Eddie to pull over.

"Wait," Gabriel says, but Emilio cuts him off.

"Our paths will cross again," he says, "and when they do, if you are who you say you are, we'll answer all your questions, and welcome you."

There is gravel beneath the van's wheels now.

"I don't know who I'm saying I am," Gabriel says.

"That's probably a good place for you to start, then."

The van comes to a stop and the back door swings open.

"What about Lenore?" Gabriel says. "She's missing."

They're stirring now, as if to close in on him. There's movement in the front of the van, too. Gabriel heads for the doorway.

"Nobody is missing. We'll see you again."

Gabriel's legs unfold; his feet touch the ground. "Who the hell are you people?"

"It depends on who you are. *Hasta luego, carpa.*" The doors close and the van pulls away. It circles around and heads back toward the freeway, leaving him alone amid endless fields of blackness, crickets, the smell of hot earth.

Chapter 22

We already have problems. I should have another dozen *viajeros* arrayed around me right now, but instead we're back in the camper. Outside closed warehouses speed past and their blue security lights color the night sky. The tea is in its Thermos in my backpack, going to waste. Also I can't find my favorite sweatshirt. I shouldn't have brought it.

I'm not sure what happened, exactly. Everything went fine at Sonoma State. Twelve participants, guided out and back. It was challenging to balance it all with a dozen starting points, but in the end, all I had to do was feel into everything, like before. It's like tuning a piano. You listen for the dissonance, and then you go fix it. So that was fine. But then the next morning, one of the participants got attacked and ended up in a coma. Everybody got spooked when they found out so we cancelled Fresno and now we're heading farther south. I feel terrible for the guy—I think his name is Adam—but I don't get what it has to do with us. What am I missing here? Once again, I wish I could have a conversation with my grandfather.

He's dead, but he seems to have ways around that. I learned this last winter when my mom and I drove down to check on him. We both knew he was gone as soon as we stepped into his living room. I called his name out anyway. Mom stopped right there, in the middle of the room, staring at nothing. Remembering, maybe. We'd been driving all day and I was stiff as I moved through the house slowly, studying details. The late afternoon sun on a bookcase of old photographs, warped wooden floorboards. In the kitchen I opened the back door and found a trail that climbed out of the little valley and up to the ridge. Once above the house I looked back and saw how in time the hills would close like jaws upon it. My feet kicked up dust clouds, orange in the golden hour. To my left was another valley and then a second, higher ridge. To the right the desert went on, endless into the haze: low stony ridges, shrubs, grasses, a tinge of green from recent rains. The trail dropped from the ridge, wove through some boulders, and stopped at the rim of a shallow bowl. Filling the stone-bound circle was a dense, low carpet of short-stemmed plants. I bent one gently. Caressed a spray of small heart-shaped leaves. And then I thought I heard my name. A whisper, on a slight breeze that was there and then just as quickly gone. A hint of movement along the edge of an outcropping. "Are you here?" I asked. Another breeze, this one silent. I sat on a rock, took a deep breath, stared into the circle of seedlings, and shut my eyes. Took another deep breath. The little plants swayed and stretched upward. They formed tiny buds and then small red flowers bloomed, their petals streaked with black. More and more erupted, until the bowl was full of red and black. The whirring of my heart like the wingbeats of a hummingbird.

"I don't understand," I said.

I closed my eyes to listen but what came next were not sounds but images: the shed behind the house, where I'd find his laboratory. A pair of amber glass specimen jars on one of the racks. A set of notebooks on one of its shelves. When I opened my eyes the flowers were gone and the tiny seedlings were back, folding back in on themselves in the fading light.

Forrest takes us onto the interstate and the city falls away. Preston's phone chimes with notifications and whatever he's reading he relays to Forrest in quiet, clipped sentences. Something about a new guy who'd appeared with a tattoo of an origami carp. I didn't know they were sending more people—I wonder who he is, and why he's here. We're outside the city now, where empty darkness swallows us.

Chapter 23

It's past midnight, and Peoria has given up on sleeping. It's muggy and she's already thrown off the blankets; now she tosses aside the lone remaining sheet and she sits up. It's too bright. The moon is nearly full and they've neglected to close the curtains all the way. She rises and walks to the windows, drawing them open instead, and letting the light wash over her and pour into the room. Redland does not stir. Her husband is asleep on his back, his face turned toward the far side of the room, his breaths soundless. His jaw looks to be made of marble in the slanting moonlight. Peoria has always been envious of the way he has been able to relegate his fears and anxieties to the daylight hours. Whatever was happening in their lives, he managed deep, unbroken, dreamless sleep. She is grateful for this. It keeps him steady and strong through the day, and without this reliable presence in her life, who knows how she might become untethered.

She closes the curtains and the room goes black, but she does not need light to find her way to her robe or the door. When it closes on her husband, the emptiness of the rest of her home knifes into her. She permits herself only the briefest of sighs and heads downstairs. A warm silver light fills the entry, and instead of heading for the kitchen, which had been her loose plan, Peoria reaches for the doorknob and steps outside.

After being confined in the muggy bedroom, Peoria feels herself expanding into the night, pieces of her loosening like dandelion seeds into an updraft. It's finally cooling down, and though there is no breeze she can taste the ocean in the air. It's a fogless night and the lights of the city far below waver as the land gives up its heat. It's the same view Lenore would have seen spread out before her the last time she'd descended these stairs, her destination some unknown fold in the panorama below.

Peoria takes the stairs into the driveway; the cement is rough and warm on her bare feet. She crosses over to the edge of her neglected garden, which covers the bottom corner of their property. Part flowers, part vegetables, part weeds—normally at this time of year she would be here for hours, tending to a young crop, but it wasn't every spring that the full attention of her entire world swung in her direction, and she'd had to make sacrifices. Perhaps too many.

She extends a leg and feels the soil with the ball of her foot and the bottoms of her toes and immediately she can feel the life flowing up and into her. It's a faint warm tingling that shoots up her ankle, across her calf and knee, and up her thigh. She sinks her weight onto her foot and then brings the other one alongside it, feeling the earth contour beneath the curves of her soles, and then suddenly her ear brings her the tone of her grandmother's flute.

It was a small clay ocarina, painted black and white and brown and red, which her grandmother kept in one of the many secret compartments hidden in her colorful skits. Once every couple of years, Rogelio had taken her back to the *casita* where he'd grown up, in the hills above Hermosillo. It sat on a small rise, all by itself, so in Peoria's memories, the whole neighborhood is just that small white concrete house, the palm-studded hillsides, and Maria, and it all sounds like that flute, which seemed to carry the voice of the desert in the hollow of its small chamber. Maria had songs for dawn, noon, dusk, and midnight. She had songs for each of the four directions, for the sky and the earth and for the surrounding hillsides. She had songs for each room of her home, depending on the time of day and the quality of light. She had played them all for her granddaughter, who listened intently. Some of them were simple repeating themes, others more complex, linear. There was one song in particular Maria would always play before heading out to check on her patients. It was a slow, rising melody and she'd play it while standing just outside her open doorway, her bare feet planted in the dirt, guiding the notes into the rising morning. *Para despertar los espíritus.* "To wake up the spirits," Maria would tell her captivated granddaughter, with a smile.

And now, with her bare feet planted in the soil and her robe hanging from her shoulders, an ache pierces Peoria's center, for she finds that her ear has forgotten that song. It had once been fixed in her mind, but she hasn't thought about it in years, and somewhere along the line it got pushed out. How could she have let this happen? There's movement, a silent gray streak overhead—an owl? Peoria closes her eyes and pictures her grandmother standing in the doorway of that little house, silhouetted against the sun-drenched desert. She sees the prints on her voluminous clothing, the silver on her fingers, and the leather barrettes that held her black-and-silver braids out of her wrinkled face. She sees the flute but the song will not come back to her.

Chapter 24

Leo awakens and an unfamiliar ceiling of knotty pine appears above him, leaving him wondering if he has fallen into a new layer of an anxiety dream but his disorientation passes and reality reassembles itself around him, one painful recollection at a time.

When he has remembered all he cares to, he tosses off the old afghan and swings his feet to the floor, coming to a seat on the edge of the bare mattress. The movement starts a ringing in his ears, and the taste in his mouth reminds him of the fifth of Jack Daniel's that had accompanied him on the last hour of the car ride. With effort he rises to his feet and steps to the window, which he vaguely remembers prying open the night before. The clearing still rests in shadow; the day's first rays are just hitting the tops of the trees. Pine needles and wood infuse the thin air.

He and Yvette had arrived just after sunset after a long climb on a one-lane strip of asphalt. By then he'd had nearly half the bottle and was all but comatose in the passenger seat. When they pulled into the wide gravel clearing with the big two-story cabin hulking in its center, the sense of strangeness that had been accumulating for the previous two days crashed down upon him with such a force that it sent him sideways.

"Leonardo," Yvette said, interrupting his confused stupor, "come inside." Somehow she'd gotten out of the car, and was holding a flashlight.

He followed her up the steps and stumbled through the open doorway and into a front room that smelled a hundred years old. She chuckled when he tried the light switch. His next memory was awakening in a bed somewhere, beneath the afghan, pain like a javelin through the center of his head. Yvette was asleep next to him, sleeping on her side, curled in a ball. Leo moved closer to share the blanket with her and the scent that arose from the back of her neck eased his headache. He awoke again still later and found himself alone this time, in the center of a boundless silence. The sky was bright; he walked to the window to find the clearing full of moonlight, illuminating the empty space where her car had been parked. He sank back onto the bed, where he felt like he was plummeting into a bottomless pit.

Now he turns away from the window and descends the creaking stairs, trying to remember what Yvette had said about this house. It had belonged to the deceased parents of someone she knew; she'd come up here a few times years earlier. There was some reason why it couldn't go on the market now, and the inheritor, whoever he was, was too busy elsewhere to deal with it. So here it sat, vacant and neglected.

In the kitchen Leo finds a note on the counter. *Back in a couple of days. It's going to be okay, baby boy. I love you.* He grabs a bottle of water and a packet of peanut butter crackers and heads for the front porch. He sits in the cool air with his feet planted wide, his elbows heavy on his knees. He drinks and he eats and he waits. When the sun rises above the treetops the brightness renews his headache but the rays are as thick and warm as a hot shower and he shuts his eyes and lets the heat fall over him.

When he opens them again the whole clearing rests in bright sunlight. Before him, Yvette's tire treads form the loop that had brought them here and then taken her away. His urge to call her reminds him that his phone is in a thousand pieces in a gutter back in Chico. He wonders when she'll be back. Does a "couple" really mean two? He wonders what time it is, and without thinking he pats his pocket for his phone, which is still not there. His headache is waning, though, and so is the taste of last night's whiskey, so he rises to inspect his quarters.

The house is furnished, but barely; only the largest pieces remain, as if someone had moved out with only a station wagon. In the living room a loveseat, couch, and recliner huddle in a semi-circle around an empty credenza, its surface discolored where a television had once stood. Through the living room lies the kitchen, his meager gas-station groceries laid out on the counter. Until Yvette returns he'll be subsisting on peanutbutter crackers and beef jerky, dried apricots, a bunch of spotted bananas, and few green apples. The refrigerator is unplugged but he looks in it anyway, standing well to the side in case something horrible tumbles out. The interior is empty and clean. Down the back hallway are an empty closet and a waterless bathroom. On the wall hangs a depiction of a pine tree in orange woven yarn, stitched into burlap. He plods back upstairs where the house is warming in the sun. The smell of wood. He finds two other bedrooms besides the one he'd slept in. One of them is empty, the other contains only a single small dresser, which lists to the side over a broken foot.

He heads back downstairs, grabs an apple, walks outside, and sits back down on the top step. He chews and stares into the wall of trees, chews and stares until the details fall away and the clearing becomes three broad strips: the bright sun across the gray gravel, the darkness of the trees and their shade, and the pale sky, with its small scattered clouds thin as spider webs.

He is nearing the end of his apple when his profound isolation rushes in and seizes him. Not only is he stranded in the woods, he is beyond the reach of all the systems that organize the rest of the world, that govern its rhythms and connections. Business hours, shipping schedules, traffic patterns, commerce—everywhere else, people are affecting one another. How many first kisses, how many punches thrown and landed in the hour he's been awake? But for Leo, sitting there on those steps, it makes no difference whatsoever what he does. There isn't a single thing he can do that would matter to anybody.

From somewhere in the darkness of the trees comes the sound of a ruffed grouse's drumming display, its wing beats buffeting the air. It's a sound that always seemed to come from a different realm, from an underworld that is just out of sight but always nearby.

Chapter 25

In the bean field Gabriel sleeps and dreams he is the zookeeper of a menagerie of origami animals. It is a daunting responsibility—he does not know what to feed them, or how to shield them from rain, and their flammability is a constant concern. He awakens and finds himself curled in a ball against the cold. The sky is a pale wash of blue, ready to receive the sun. Without rising he stretches his limbs, pressing them into the dry dirt to absorb its warmth, working the feeling into his hands and feet, gazing upward all the while. He senses movement nearby and he sits up quickly to find a coyote sitting motionless, staring straight at him. She is expressionless, and so still that he wonders if he is actually seeing her before him, but then a gentle breeze arises, rustles the surrounding bean plants, and then ruffles the coyote's fur. Gabriel crosses his legs and places his hands in his lap. Three hundred yards away, truckers groan through the valley. Above the freeway, mist clings to the tops of hills. The coyote still does not move. She does not avert her gaze. Gabriel considers speaking to her, but he doesn't know what to say, so eventually he rises. The coyote's head does not move but her eyes track his movement. They regard each other for another minute and then he turns and walks away from her.

Nearby lies a dirt road he hadn't noticed the night before, curving toward the end of a stand of cottonwoods. He heads for it, squinting into the clearing darkness to try to see its course. Now that he is in motion again, last night's encounter jostles back into his thoughts, coming in fragments—the smell of a hot van full of bodies, the Spanish name they'd called him, some experience he was supposed to have had. His night in the bean field did nothing to knit these pieces together. Where is Lenore, and what is this odd cadre that has appeared on the pathway to her? Who are they, and what do they know?

The dirt road reaches an intersection, where a left turn heads back to the highway. He'll hitch a southbound ride, but what then? A search for a single van somewhere in the bottom half of California: Bakersfield, Los Angeles, San Bernardino, Orange County, San Diego, plus thousands of communities in between, packed throughout the valleys and ranges and deserts, his only tools a dead phone and an ATM card and a tattoo. He checks the fish on his wrist and finds it inflamed and painful. Ángel had given him no advice on how to care for it, but a night in a Greyhound seat and then another in a bean field do not seem like the recommended procedure.

The road is hard-packed, but covered in a thin layer of red dust that cushions his footsteps. The sun is rising above the hills on the far side of the valley now, the rays driving the cold from his muscles. He swings his arms and stretches his shoulders, working the feeling back through them. After a few minutes of walking there is a rumble from somewhere well behind him and Gabriel turns to find an old green pickup truck approaching. The driver slows and pulls up alongside him, matching his pace, and the men regard each other. The farmer is old, his narrow, clean-shaven face lined with deep wrinkles, his skin dark and sun-hardened. His eyes are gunmetal gray. Gabriel stops, and so does the truck.

"This is private land," the farmer says. His tone is neutral, even quiet.

"I'm sorry. Last night didn't go as planned. Can I please have some water?"

The farmer looks Gabriel up and down and then nods back toward his truck bed. Gabriel jumps in and the truck accelerates, an orange cloud of dust rising behind them and thinning over the plants. The farmer veers right, away from the freeway. Another turn brings them alongside a culvert. A steel bridge carries them over a narrow strip of water and toward the next bean field which they circle, heading toward a small grove. A white Victorian sits in its center like an aging matron in a recliner, weathered and worn but completely at home in its horseshoe of trees. The truck comes to a stop at the bottom of its steps; a skirt of dust settles around them. The farmer beckons Gabriel to follow him up the stairs onto a wide shaded patio, where a wrought-iron table and a pair of chairs sit. He points at the table and disappears into the house.

Gabriel sits down, suddenly aware of the extent of his thirst and his hunger, his exhaustion. From where he sits he can see clear down a long dirt driveway that extends from the front of the house through the opening in the trees to a frontage road alongside the highway, perhaps a quarter-mile away. Cars stream by, reflections of the rising sun flashing on their windshields, their rhythm and hum hypnotic. He heard it in his sleep all the fitful night, that constant rumble of traffic, coursing endlessly through the valley, like lifeblood. He closes his eyes and listens: slight variations in the traffic, wakening bugs, the movements of cottonwood branches against one another.

His head tips; he is on the brink of dozing when the squeak of the screen door cuts through the silence. The farmer emerges with a tray and unloads a large mug of coffee with sugar and cream on the side, a pitcher of ice water, and a pint glass. He walks back into the house and emerges a few minutes later with a large stoneware plate and a matching bowl, which he slides across the table to Gabriel. On the plate, the food—a thick slice of ham, baked beans, a brick of cornbread, and a glob of butter the size of a golf ball—is so plentiful it had to be piled in layers. The bowl contains a green salad, already dressed. His host pulls from his pocket a fork and knife bundled in a red linen napkin and sets that alongside the plate. Gabriel looks up in astonishment.

"The ham's cold," the farmer says. "Microwave dries it out, and I didn't want to keep you waiting." He raises a hand to wave away Gabriel's response and then turns to leave Gabriel alone with his food and his thoughts and the climbing sun. The meal disappears as quickly as a coin in a magic act. He is about to doze off again when the door squeaks back open and his host re-emerges. Another plate appears on the table, a smaller one, holding a trio of chocolate-chip cookies.

"I couldn't," Gabriel says. "You've already been extraordinarily generous."

"You must. I'm not permitted to return to the kitchen with uneaten food, and Carolyn will know if I help, somehow." He settles into the seat next to Gabriel and sets his own coffee mug on the table. Gabriel reaches for a cookie.

"Not my style to ask a lot of questions," the farmer says, "but let me know if you've got any injuries or anything of the kind needing attention."

Gabriel chews, swallows. There is a trace of mint hiding inside the chocolate. "No, sir."

"And do you have the means to get wherever it is you're going?"

"Yes, sir."

"Well, I suppose that's all I really need to bug you about."

Gabriel collects a second cookie. With the coffee the combination of flavors makes him think of Christmas. "When I woke up this morning," he says, "there was a coyote staring at me. She watched me until I got up and moved."

The farmer swings his hand lazily at a fly, as if he does not really care whether it shoos or not. "It's their land first. Theirs and the native weeds, though God knows I do my best to give 'em hell. Carolyn and I and our crops are just guests." He reaches out and breaks off half the remaining cookie. "And you, too," he says, when he's finished his bite. He chases it with a swallow of coffee. "You can leave the dishes right there," he says. "I'll give you a ride into town." He pushes himself to his feet and leads the way back down the peeling wooden steps to the dirt. Puffs of dust rise from his footfalls and drift away.

Chapter 26

Francisco Velasquez attempts to transfer his weight to his right foot, but his foot does not land where it is supposed to and he falls hard onto his back, his chest compressing under the full but lesser weight of Masanori Sensei, who buries a shoulder into his chest, rolls easily across him, and springs back to his feet. Velasquez stands and turns to face his instructor, who wears a smirk as he yanks his *judogi* back into place. "Too many donuts, Sergeant Bosco," he says.

The insult is compact, devious, and multi-faceted, just like the man who uttered it. For one, Velasquez's nickname is not Bosco—it's Vasco. An instructor at the academy had given him the name, which then followed him from department to agency to agency. It's the name of a lawman. Bosco, on the other hand, is the name of a third-rate chocolate syrup. Vasco has no proof that his sensei's accented mispronunciation is deliberate, but he has strong suspicions. Second, he has not been a sergeant in seven years, not since his days with the Berkeley Police Department, well before he'd joined the feds. And finally: Vasco hasn't eaten a single donut since childhood.

Vasco gets his feet under him and the men circle each other. His sensei takes a grip on his sleeve, and then his lapel, and before Vasco can find a grip he is upended again.

"Too tense," Masanori says. "Relax." He gives Vasco a light slap across the cheek. "Change partners," he says, and moves on to torment someone else. Vasco finds himself confronted by Gil, a systems administrator with stubble as coarse as 24-grit sandpaper and a grip like a drowning ironworker's.

"Morning, Vasco," says Gil.

"Morning, Gilly," says Vasco. They engage.

After the morning session he heads for his office in Oakland, stopping at the Sunrise Market to grab a six-dollar cup of yogurt, fruit, and granola and a four-dollar bottle of pomegranate juice.

Just as he pulls into the parking garage, his phone chirps with a text from his boss: *come see me.* He parks, finds his way to Garza's office, and steps through the open door, scraping the last of the yogurt from the sides of his cup.

"I don't know how that stuff keeps you running for more than twenty minutes," says Anthony Garza, shaking his head. Chief Garza leans toward bacon and eggs.

"It keeps my arteries running, anyway."

Garza reaches beneath his desk and then extends a small recycling bin. "Have a seat, would you?"

Vasco discards his cup and spoon and takes a seat across from his boss. The chief is unassuming, black hair and black eyes, Italianate. He could be any mid-level businessman but for his arms, which are covered to the wrist in blurring tattoos: flags, eagles, battleships, daggers, angels. A résumé of service to his country and his religion. He's off today though. He's rattled.

"What are we looking at, sir?" Vasco asks.

"I just got a call from the University PD chief up in Rohnert Park."

Vasco's breath catches in his chest. It was heartbreaking, what happened to the assemblyman's kid. Heartbreaking and bizarre—a student at one university attacked by a professor from another. His social media feeds had been full of someone's shaky video, shot from behind the poor kid, with a perfect view of the impact as he was shoved over, headfirst into the edge of a cement planter. What did it have to do with the DEA, though?

Garza continues. "Walt's kid and his two roommates seem to have been involved in something the previous night. Take a look." He pivots his computer monitor into Vasco's view, revealing a video feed from a supermarket surveillance camera, overlooking shelves and bins of produce. A dozen or so bodies, college-age kids from the look of them, are scattered around the frame. Garza restarts the video and the bodies disappear, only to reappear a second later, streaming in together. They fan out, heading for various fruits and vegetables.

Vasco sits forward. There's something off here. The kids are all moving with a languor that also appears purposeful somehow, but that isn't it. It's their interactions, or rather, their lack of them. A dozen twenty-year-olds would normally be in groups, pairs, threes and fours, talking, gesticulating, calling to one another, joking and laughing. But these kids seem oblivious to each other. They're all in their own worlds as they hunt down their supplies. And then several of them simply begin to eat.

"I don't know about you, Special Agent Velasquez, but when I think about the munchies, I think about fries and milkshakes. Look at this darn fella right here." He taps the screen where a tall young man in pajama bottoms is taking a big bite out of a bell pepper. Garza's cadence and diction are all cop, but his vocabulary was fixed during a pious boyhood in Provo. "And here's our guy Adam," Garza says, his voice a few notes lower. Adam Yeager is farther to the back, in sweat pants and a hoodie, running his hands over heads of lettuce.

"I don't get it. What's with the salad bar?"

"Local PD got a call from the store manager. These kids, they took their veggies to the register, but then they could hardly put words together. 'Like they'd just come from some other planet,' one of the cashiers said. Someone managed to come up with some cash, though, and they all left and scattered. Police came a bit too late, but managed to come across one of them on the street a few blocks away, popping cherry tomatoes. Seemed a bit dazed, but pupils were fine, eyes clear. He consented to a pat-down but nothing—no pills, not even weed or tobacco, nothing."

"So what's the story?"

The video ends; Garza swings his monitor back around. "Heck if I know. That's where you come in. But there's more. The professor. Bank and cellphone records put him in Chico yesterday afternoon. Nothing out of the ordinary. But then all of a sudden there's a big cash withdrawal and then nothing." Garza opens his hands, as if releasing birds. "Gone."

Vasco frowns. His cases don't typically bring him big surprises—they're usually full of the sorts of characters you'd expect to be in DEA investigations. Professors and vegetarians are not the sorts he comes across often. He isn't sure what to think of any of this.

"I've got a couple of appointments lined up for you this afternoon," Garza says. He hits play on the video again and the kids make their entrance. He points to the bell pepper-eater and then to a figure farther to the back, who's peeling an orange. "These two are Adam's roommates. They were with him yesterday morning, too, when Percival confronted him. Take a look." He clicks his mouse a few times and a different CCTV feed fills the screen. Three boys make their way down a breezeway when Percival approaches from the bottom corner of the frame, a sweatshirt dangling from his arm, phone extended, his back to the camera. Two of the boys turn and bolt and then Percival grabs a hold of Adam's shirt. He drives him backward, seeming to yell, and then they circle into place. With a twist in his gut Vasco visualizes what's to come. The men tangle and then running figures enter the frame. They push and then the bodies come apart—one sprinting, the other tumbling toward the edge of the cement planter that would dent his skull.

Mercifully, Garza hits pause before the impact. "Today you're going up to join University PD for a chat with the roommates. Also in attendance will be the assemblyman himself and what I assume will be a couple dozen lawyers, so I don't expect you'll get anything concrete. Right now we're just looking for a situation report and an idea of where to start looking next." Garza swivels the monitor back in his own direction and folds his hands on his desktop. "This one is delicate, obviously. The incident is barely twenty-four hours old. We've got a significant public figure here, and all the accompanying media attention. If the press finds out the DEA is sniffing around here, this whole thing takes on a life of its own. Everyone knows that Walt Yeager loves the boys in blue, but us—we're the men in black. And these kids up there—I'm guessing they're not being real open with their families about whatever led to their shopping expedition the other night, or the confrontation yesterday. Don't expect a very warm welcome."

"I never do. What's the other appointment?"

"This professor. His family's local." He pushes a file across his desk. "Berkeley PD called on them yesterday but I'd like you to head back up and make some new friends."

Vasco retrieves the file and flips it open, rifles through papers and finds bios and headshots printed out from websites. The father, Redland, is an engineer, professor emeritus, endowed this-and-that. His gaze into the camera is even, steady. The mother, Peoria, is a world-class classical pianist. Vasco's own musical tastes tend more toward soul and hip-hop, so he hasn't heard of her. In her photo she is looking off to the side, as if in another world.

"I'll be right here in this chair until late tonight," Garza says, interrupting Vasco's thoughts. "Come find me when you get back."

Chapter 27

It is easily a hundred degrees in Bakersfield and the edges of Gabriel's mind are blistering and warping, both with the heat and with the overwhelming possibilities before him. His visit to Ayla's had put him on a single pathway toward Lenore; even out of the bean field there had been one road, one single direction. Javier had pulled over his lettuce truck almost immediately after Gabriel put up his thumb. He wore a t-shirt from a radio station pledge drive and a too-small red ball cap which sat atop the dome of his voluminous black hair like a robin on a hilltop. "You like *lucha libre*? Pro wrestling?" he asked, even before Gabriel had buckled himself in. From the rearview mirror hung a gold crucifix and a photo of a little girl in a pink dress in a plastic frame. Gospel music came from the radio. While they traveled Gabriel scanned the gas stations and motel parking lots for the van, for a glimpse of a tattooed wrist. At that point he still felt he was approaching something, that there was purpose to his movement. But as Bakersfield gradually drew in the creaking truck the options before him multiplied, increasing a thousandfold each time they passed an exit. The city unfurled, rushing in a dense uncontrollable mass to the edges of the valley like cement floodwaters.

Now as the truck pulls away and the sting of Javier's exuberant handshake fades from his palm, the heat drops down over him like a heavy blanket and he finds himself beset by uncertainty. "Shit," Gabriel says, and then he says it a second time, differently, to capture more of its meaning. He spins around, slowly, and takes in his surroundings. He's at an intersection of six-lane roads. On two of the opposing corners a Chevron and a Shell station eye each other along one diagonal; along the other a Wendy's and a Burger King emanate fumes of beef and grease. Anemic shade trees stand uselessly in giant black parking lots. A Target looms in the background, the size of a soccer stadium, its red logo wavering in the heat. Just down the road a Super 8 motel advertises HBO and a pool.

Gabriel checks into a room and then heads across the street to buy a pair of jeans, a pair of shorts, multi-packs of t-shirts, boxer shorts, and socks. He picks out a cheap backpack to keep it all in, and then adds a notepad and some ball-point pens, a toothbrush and toothpaste, a razor and shaving cream. He finds a phone charger and a paperback biography of Cesar Chavez and then returns to his hotel room. After hand-washing his stinking clothes in the bathtub with hotel shampoo and hanging them up to dry, he changes into his new shorts and heads for the pool, both for the respite from the heat and for the novelty—he hasn't been in a pool since his release from San Quentin. The water is tinted the color of phlegm and just barely cooler than the air, but it feels good to move his limbs. After a few minutes the tastes of salt and grease and diesel exhaust surface through the chlorine, along with a bitter chemical tang that makes him think of the crop dusters he'd seen swooping over the fields just outside the city. He climbs out of the water, returns to his room, and showers. Still naked he pulls down the covers, reads for about five minutes, and then falls asleep.

It is mid-afternoon when he surfaces through the layers of a dream, the shaking of rattlesnake tails transforming into the gravelly whine of his room's air conditioner. He rises and puts on his new shorts and pulls the door open. The cold air at his back and the hot air before him collide and spiral around him. His second-floor balcony looks out over the road, just up from the intersection where Javier had left him that morning. Beneath him traffic fills all six lanes of the road but it is strangely quiet, as if its sounds are unwilling to move in such heat. In the sharp sunlight even the dustiest cars manage to gleam.

Gabriel leaves the door open and takes a step out, and then another, feeling the cold behind him lose its strength. None of the cars gliding past are white vans—at least, not the one that matters, and none of them will be. Somehow he knows this the same way he knew Lenore needed him at the playground all those years ago. He has as strong a sense for her absence as he does for her presence—even during those years in his cell across the bay he thought he could tell when she was out of town, somehow reading clues about her proximity through the cement.

He looks up the street, then down it, and sees no ends; an infinity of traffic lights stretches in either direction, blurring finally into the distant heat, and again he has that sense of the impossible multiplicity of options before him. A direction will present itself eventually, though, he knows. It has to. Nothing stands still.

Beneath him a knot of cars rolls through the stoplight. A semi appears from up the street, purple flames waving across its hood, the towering structure of a folded-up carnival ride balanced on its flatbed trailer.

"You look like you're thinking about somebody," a voice says, from over his shoulder.

She stands in the adjacent doorway, her toes just across the threshold. There is a black smear across the chest of her white t-shirt, which is threadbare, discolored in random places. Her hair, black and shot through with the purple traces of an expired dye job, reaches down just over her ears, or doesn't—it looks like it was recently cut by an overzealous amateur. Her eyes are red and puffy, and seem to focus on a point somewhere between Gabriel and the rest of the world beyond the balcony. A wine bottle dangles from her fingertips.

"Aren't we all?" Gabriel says.

"I was. But once I step through this doorway, I'm going to stop, and that's going to be that." She holds up the bottle, checks the level, takes a swallow, and lets her arm drop. Gabriel is sure the bottle will slide from her hand and smash against the floor, but somehow her fingers manage to keep their hold. She takes the promised step. "There," she says.

The semi stops just beneath the balcony. The sideways image of a clown with a lightbulb for a nose leers at them through a tangle of steelwork.

"I fucking hate clowns," she says. "They're even worse than the person I'm no longer thinking about." She takes another swallow of wine and offers the bottle to Gabriel. "I'm not hitting on you, so don't get all weirded out and start feeling guilty about your wife and babies or whatever."

Gabriel accepts the bottle and watches her as he drinks.

"Not that I can't see how somebody might find you pretty goddamn appealing," she says. "But I'm a fan of the fairer sex, if you know what I'm saying."

When he passes the bottle back to her, she holds it aloft. "So here's to the ladies, all except one of them," she says. She takes another swig and passes the bottle back to him again.

"To the ladies," Gabriel says, "particularly one of them." But the bottle is empty now. He swallows the last few drops for the ceremony of it, and then sets the bottle on the railing between them. She grabs it and with an abrupt underhand motion hurls it backwards, through her open doorway. It thuds into some forgiving surface.

"Now that we got that out of the way," she says, "let me ask you something. Are you heading to LA?"

"I don't know, actually. I was just trying to figure that out."

She watches him, trying to decipher his response. Another piece of the carnival's caravan slides into the space beneath them, this one bearing stacks of roller-coaster track. Two shiny aliens aim fifties-era ray guns at them from an airbrushed sign. Gabriel imagines the electric leap and crack. He and his new friend would be reduced to mounds of cinders, lumps of molten tissue. In the afternoon heat it's not much of a stretch.

"If you are, I'll take you there," she says. "Or rather, you can take me." She tips her head back to indicate the discarded bottle. "You hitchhiked here. I saw you come in. Well, I'm too drunk to drive and I want to get the fuck out of here. So I'm offering you a free trip to LA and a place to crash tonight if you'll drive. Unless you want to admire the view some more." The truck bearing the aliens and their roller coaster vomits a cloud of black smoke that washes over them like a toxic net.

He doesn't mention his lack of a license, and she is asleep before they are free of the city. On either side of them the fields waver in the heat. In a bleached sky the sun is unforgiving.

Chapter 28

The afternoon sun presses down on the flanks of Mount Shasta like a cloak. Leonardo does not know what elevation he and Yvette climbed to the previous night, but it must be considerable—there's little in the way of atmosphere to slow the thick fall of photons, which beat the movement out of the trees and pin sound to the ground. The cabin is an oven. Leonardo sits on the top step, in the same place where he ate his meager breakfast. An overhang above the entryway provides some shade, and opening both the front and back doors of the house has created a slight cross breeze that brushes his bare back intermittently. He spent much of the previous hour doing calisthenics—it was the only productive activity available to him. He pushed himself until he was weary and covered in sweat, and only when he began thinking about a shower did he remember that his only water was in the bottles from the gas station. He stripped off his clothes, stood in the sun, and used as little as he could to clean himself off. And then, because there was no reason to put his clothes back on, he left them off and sat back down on the step where he now remains, quickly drying.

Without a computer or a phone, without neighbors, without a sound from the distant road, with no other hint of humanity beyond the items left here by the absent owners of this house, the still and empty afternoon becomes a vacuum. It threatens to pull the air from his lungs and he grows lightheaded. He plants his hands on the step and takes a series of deep breaths, but the air is hot and thin as a wire. Okay, he tells himself. Think.

But his mind will show him nothing of the future; instead it bends backward and lands upon the image of Adam's face. A coma? He tries to remember the encounter, the tangle with Adam, the bystanders shouting and running. He had let go and turned and run. A coma? How? There was a video, Yvette told him. Why hadn't she shown it to him? Had she? It strikes him that his bizarre circumstances are entirely the result of one person's account, which he'd accepted without asking for corroboration, for any kind of proof. Why had he allowed himself to be banished like this? But no—how else would she have known about it? There had been news, so something had to have happened. And Lenore—what the hell was she doing? Why were people sprinting away from the sight of her sweatshirt? As his mind darts back over the last couple of days it alights on Clifford and his stolen data, a set of problems that now seem as distant as a story he might have heard a year ago. His thoughts stretch back still farther, and next alight upon the other actor in all this—his brother.

It strikes him that he should have called Gabriel after that business down at Sonoma State. They are in this together, after all, aren't they? And Gabriel is probably devoted to searching for Lenore, anyway. Chasing down her friends or searching her hangouts or whatever. What else would he have to do?

They have always had their differences. Gabriel is the quieter one, and his reluctance to speak, to weigh in on family discussions, always made it seem like he didn't have much to say. Every now and then, though, he'd deliver an observation, or recount a memory, or draw a startling connection between things that revealed flashes of a wholly different type of insight. Leonardo, who was always at the top of his classes and fancies himself someone who knows a few things about brains, finds his brother's intellect maddening. Gabriel could answer math problems in his homework with no idea how he'd arrived at the solution, and no interest in figuring it out. Redland would simply shrug and describe it as intuition, and Leonardo came to understand that he didn't much care for intuition.

Gabriel had always been closer to Lenore. Leo assumed that their proximity in age gave them more overlap, but when Lenore's own strange intelligence began to crystallize and make itself known to the world, he realized that perhaps it had more to do with the quirky wiring they share. They communicate in languages he never learned. Gabriel will be the one to find her, Leonardo realizes. He'll be there for her whenever she re-surfaces. He always has been.

There had never been any overt animosity between the brothers, but at some point they had simply diverged, and then eventually lost sight of each other, and then suddenly one of them was a professor and the other was a prisoner and the differences between them were so momentous they occluded all similarities. But now there's another man in another hospital, and the distance Leo assumed would always separate him from his brother is quickly vanishing.

What had it all been like, for Gabriel? Leo was in grad school at Cornell at the time of his brother's arrest—thousands of miles away, both literally and figuratively. He remembers the call from their father, but there was nothing he could do, so he did not try. His contribution to the drama was to stay the hell out of it. He'd read some of the coverage online, and then there had been the plea and the sentencing and then Gabriel had a mailing address at San Quentin. Now he wishes he'd paid a little more attention. Such circumstances might not be as foreign to him as he'd once thought, it would seem.

A flurry of wings sounds above him somewhere, out of sight. An ache opens up inside of Leo, a longing for his brother and his sister, and the effortless, braided coexistence they once shared. He hasn't felt this way in years.

He's dry now, and the wooden steps are getting hot, and the shifting sun is about to take away his shade. He'll have to move somewhere else soon.

Chapter 29

On the burgundy couch that stretches along the back wall of her studio, Peoria dreams. She is dreaming of the desert, as she often does, though she has never lived there herself—she knows it only from stories and from the visits she's made. This is the extent of her familiarity with most of her father's geographies. She has had brief acquaintances with various jungles, a number of South American capitals, scattered university towns across the Southwest and Mexico, and a handful of out-of-the-way places where he was engaged in field work. She'd always tried to visit at least once or twice before he was summoned elsewhere as a recipient of some fellowship or another, a consultant attached to some team or project or expedition.

It had not always been like this. For her first sixteen years she'd had a fairly conventional childhood, growing up in a single home, in a single place—a white Victorian on a quiet street in the Oakland foothills. Her father and mother taught and she went to school and went to her piano lessons and ran around the neighborhood with her friends until one spring Saturday when her mother, while driving on one of the redwood-lined boulevards that run along the city's ridges, simply left the road, hit a tree, and died. It was inexplicable. There had been no other cars around, no witnesses. It was a bright afternoon, a dry road. She hadn't been speeding. The autopsy revealed no heart attack, no stroke, no aneurysm. She had braked but too late.

Flora's sudden absence was maddening, cacophonous, and Peoria and Rogelio fled from it in the same way—by hurling themselves into their work with obsessive fervor. For Rogelio it was his research, but for Peoria, it was the piano. As a younger student she'd been largely indifferent to the instrument, to practicing, to her own talents. But with her mother gone she fell upon her piano as if determined to consume it, to possess everything it could ever be. She and Rogelio, similarly occupied in their respective ends of the house, would sometimes startle each other in the kitchen and freeze, paralyzed, the whole tableau a blinding reminder of what had been lost. Her father had never had much use for words, and with Flora gone he spoke even less, but the embraces he wrapped his grieving daughter in were all she needed. She remembers the strength of his arms, the stubble on his neck, the smells of a thousand herbs and trees and flowers. Eighteen months later she auditioned at Juilliard and was awarded multiple scholarships. Rogelio sold the Oakland house and disappeared into South America, and whenever she saw him after that, it was in a different place and under different circumstances, but his hugs were always the same. They were what was left of her home.

Now they're gone, too, and in their place she has these dreams of the desert, which always carry the sense of her father's presence. Sometimes she finds him in the form of a lizard, or even, once in a while, himself. But today she cannot feel him anywhere—instead, she dreams that her three children are here, which does not seem right. They are not of this place, and there are so few hiding places if you do not know where to look. And there is something else out there, too—a figure making its way through the dry brush. She cannot see who it is and cannot sense what it wants, but she knows she needs to find her children.

Redland's soft knocks cut through her sleep, and by the time he comes in and sets the plate of food on the end table, the dream has faded and her eyes are opening. He frowns. "I didn't mean to wake you," he says. She tries to remember the dream, but the waking world has broken it apart and scattered the pieces, a stone tossed into the reflection on a pond's surface. She stretches and glances up at his gift. It's a Caprese sandwich with tortilla chips, and the sight of it reminds her that she has not eaten since breakfast. "I thought you might be hungry," he says.

"You were right."

She does not sit up yet, though, so Redland seats himself at the far end of the couch and drapes a hand over her feet. His eyes are unfocused, and he looks like he could use a nap of his own. Such a swell of gratitude rises in her that she can feel it in the hairs on her arms, in the corners of her eyes. Where would she be without this man? Where would any of them be? His constancy, his evenness and patience. As the years have gone by she has come to appreciate him more and more, and now she cannot help but marvel at her own wisdom in choosing him, and at a time, all those decades ago, when she was far more likely to make bad choices than good ones. There had been some knowledge in her body, some counsel from her ancestors or from her future that managed to reach her heart, her brain, her womb, and it's a fortunate thing it did, because without him now, there would be nothing to keep her and her children from hurtling into space. She might be the family's flaming heart, but he is the quiet, tireless rhythm that governs its contractions. A metronome. "It's all going to be okay, Red," she says.

Chapter 30

The meeting in Rohnert Park proves informative not because of what is said but because of what is not said, and as Vasco drives back to the city he thinks about the Percival file and the raid on the produce section and tries to figure out what they might say about all the missing information. It had been a crowded meeting: Adam's housemates, parents and lawyers, local PD, Assemblyman Yeager, Special Agent Velasquez. A dozen sets of secrets, and all of them haunted by the specter of a friend, a son, fighting for his life in the hospital. Such heartaches were not new to Vasco. In his years with Border Patrol, tragedies like this one unfolded weekly. The desert and the border had a thousand ways of ripping families apart, and a father's grief and anxiety were the same whether he was a state senator or a migrant. Something was there, just out of reach, and though Vasco searched beneath the conversation and emotions for some kind of direction, no lead surfaced. Maybe his next visit would reveal a direction.

The Percival home sits high in the Berkeley Hills. Vasco weaves through the grid of streets in the flats and into the hills' winding mazes, still trying to grasp the scope of the situation before him. All of this would be odd enough without the events of the day prior, when Leonardo Percival had used a framed portrait of Richard Nixon to wreak twenty-five hundred dollars of damage to a student bar. Or the brother who was only weeks out of San Quentin. Each of these events was hard enough to make sense of by itself, and he had no theories at all about the connections between them. In his years in law enforcement he'd seen a lot of tragedy, but there were patterns, templates. Variations on themes. This was a combination of elements he'd never seen before.

The road climbs and the homes get larger and more opulent, carrying Vasco into yet another novel element—the upper class. His GPS takes him through a half-dozen more turns before the Percival home appears, just beneath the ridge. It's Spanish-style, with walls of stucco and a roof of terra cotta tiles. He parks in the street and walks down a long driveway, past a flowerbed that needs some tending and a silver Audi coupe. Far below the bay glitters in the sunlight of a cloudless afternoon.

He rings the doorbell and after a second or two there are footfalls and then the door swings open to reveal a woman a foot shorter than he is. She's in a red flowered skirt and a loose white blouse and a pair of silver barrettes just manage to keep the wide curls of her wavy black-and-gray hair under control.

"Good afternoon, ma'am. I'm Special Agent Velasquez with the DEA. Are you Mrs. Percival?"

"How is Adam?"

"I haven't been made aware of any changes in his condition."

She gives the smallest of nods and then looks him over carefully before her eyes track back to his face. "I'd invite you inside, but I've been inside for days, and I need some fresh air. Would you care for a drink?"

"No thank you, but that's kind of you."

"I'll be right back." She shuts the door behind her, the footfalls recede, and a minute later she reappears, carrying a tall glass of lemonade and a bottle of water. "For later," she says, handing him the bottle. She gestures to the step where he is standing, and together they sit, looking west, out toward the edge of the continent. "So what does the DEA want with us?"

Vasco sets the bottle on the step next to his feet. "To be perfectly honest, ma'am, I'm not sure. I was hoping you could help me out with that."

"They don't just hand out cases to you gentlemen for no reason." Her voice is even, her eyes stare into the distance.

"That's true."

"So why are we sitting here?"

"There was an unusual incident two nights ago, in Rohnert Park. The night before the altercation. Certain aspects of it appear to have been drug-related. I'm wondering if there's a connection."

"What sort of incident, Mr. Velasquez?"

"It's an active investigation, so I'm not at liberty to discuss those details just yet," he says.

"I don't need details. What I need is for you to understand that I'm a mother who is trying to make sense of all this."

"Then we want the same thing. We can work together."

Peoria closes her eyes and takes a deep breath. She takes a sip of her lemonade. "Think back to when you were a boy, Señor Velasquez. A time when you were sick, lying in bed. Do you remember?"

She sips her lemonade. He declines a response. Waits.

"Your *mamá* is in the kitchen, making you *medicina*," she continues. "Imagine the scent in the air. Wood, spices, leaves, smells that would linger in the house for days. Remember it?"

Vasco is transported. Her short description conjures the clearest memory of the small house he shared with his parents in Roseville. He can see the way the light fell on the walls, hear the sounds of the massive switching yard just two blocks away. And the smells of the *medicina*, wafting through the house. "No," he says quietly. "It was *mi padre* in the kitchen."

She nods. "I can still smell it." She rises to her feet and Vasco follows suit. He's lost his line of questioning.

"Nobody wants to see the *pinche federales* come knocking," she says. It takes him a beat to realize she's referring to him. "But if it had to be someone, I'm glad it's you," she says.

He has no response. His thoughts are still back in his childhood home where he's resting in his bed with a fever or a cold, while his dad prepares tea and herbal compresses in the kitchen.

"I'll pass your information to our lawyer," Peoria says. "Now do me a favor, and don't forget what your *papá* taught you."

Chapter 31

Gabriel drives the ancient Monte Carlo ninety easy minutes before he hits a nasty snarl of traffic, which brings him to a halt. It's just as well—he doesn't know where they're going yet, and he doesn't want to wake his companion, who reclines in the passenger seat, snoring lightly, her hands draped loosely across her belly. After twenty minutes of stop-and-go she finally stirs, groans, forces her eyes open, and gasps, as though coming up for air. Gabriel glances over, nods. She studies him for a long time before speaking.

"It looks like we're heading to LA," she says.

"Wasn't that the arrangement?"

"I don't remember, to be honest." Her crossed arms are a protective cage over her chest; she shifts herself to the far edge of the seat, against the door. The Monte Carlo inches down another choked section of freeway. "Could I ask you to remind me what the arrangement was?" she says.

"You provide the car, I provide the driver."

"That's it?"

"That's it."

"That's all I said?"

Gabriel glances over. She's trying to sound relaxed, but she isn't. She needs real answers. "Regarding the arrangement, yes," he says. "But you did propose a toast to all of womankind. With one exception, you said."

Her arms unfold and rise up over her scalp until her face is buried. "One big exception," she says, her voice muffled. Her hands fall back into her lap. "Did I give you a name?"

"No," he says. "I'm Gabriel."

"I'm Serena. It's nice to re-meet you."

He nods and smiles. "Likewise."

The traffic loosens a bit and they roll forward. She ratchets her backrest up, re-centers her ass in the seat, and looks out the window, across an endless field of low crops. Cabbages, maybe. "Did I say anything else to embarrass myself?" she asks, after a time.

"Hard to tell. Some of it was kind of garbled. And most of it was in Latin."

She keeps her head turned away from him, but he can see from the way her cheek bulges that she's smiling.

"Latin, huh?" Her laugh is not audible; he feels it instead.

A pickup truck behind them roars its engine, leaps out of their lane and into the next one, surges forward, and then immediately has to brake to avoid rear-ending a minivan. Serena scrutinizes its driver.

"Did you already tell me why you're going to LA?" she asks.

"I'm looking for my sister. She ran off a few days ago. I hitchhiked into Bakersfield and we met at the hotel. You offered to get me to LA if I drove." He shrugs. "Here we are."

"How old is she?" Serena asks.

"Just turned eighteen," he says.

"I hope you find her. Unless she doesn't want to be found."

"Me too," Gabriel says, though he's unsure what he's agreeing to.

The back of her sedan holds overstuffed canvas-sided suitcases, two tied-off plastic bags, a box of pots and pans, a guitar in a case, a banjo not in a case, a potted cactus. Gabriel imagines the trunk holds more of the same.

"Where are you coming from, anyway?" Gabriel asks.

"The desert."

"Which one?"

"The sandy boring one."

"Which part of it?"

"It doesn't matter. Every part is the same as every other part."

The pickup truck rides the minivan's bumper forward a few feet and then wedges itself into a tiny slot in front of the Monte Carlo.

"My grandfather disappeared into a desert," Gabriel says, with a tip of his head toward her. "So that's one difference. There's the part where he was supposed to be, and the part where he really was, and all the parts where he wasn't supposed to be, where he might have been."

The pickup leaps sideways again, cutting off the minivan, drawing a honk.

"Okay," she says. "But you don't know which is which, right?"

Gabriel shakes his head.

"Then there isn't a piece of that desert that doesn't have a piece of your grandfather in it. Do you know what a hologram is?"

"Kind of."

"Every little piece of it contains all of it. So go out to the desert and pick up a handful of sand. That's your grandfather."

She's looking into the distance again, out across the farmland. The lane next to them comes to a halt and they rumble slowly past the pickup, which squeals and lurches into the spot behind them, exactly where it started.

"Where am I taking you, anyway?" Gabriel asks.

"My friend's place. You'll be able to crash there, too, if I didn't already mention it."

"Don't worry about me. I'm good."

She looks him up and down. "Bullshit. I know a fucking stray when I see one."

Chapter 32

A lot of this is going to be just waiting, I think. Waiting to get places. Waiting for places to become available, and for people to gather. Last night everybody wanted to get far from Fresno so we drove for an hour before pulling over to sleep for a while. After a little food we drove out here to the coast, and now we have a whole day to kill so we're at the museum in Morro Bay, learning about whales. The museum sits right on the water, with decks and picture windows that look toward the ocean.

I don't know much else about the guy in the coma, or the guy who showed up with the wrist tattoo. Either way, we're back on track. Tonight I'll conduct our second journey, this time near Cal Poly. I think the plan afterward is to drive all night, somewhere far up north. I'll be in the camper's bed, sleeping off the *centella*, so fine. Drive wherever you want.

An exhibit on birds' feathers. There are many types: remiges, rectrices, coverts. Semiplumes and filoplumes. Down and bristle. Seven types of feathers. Who knew? Names within names. Forrest is at the window, looking at his phone. I drift toward him and he puts it away. When I lean on him he circles his arm around my shoulders. The sky is cloudless, the ocean a blue so deep it's almost purple. At the mouth of the bay the great round dome of Morro Rock sits, like a guardian before the ocean. A stone island amid moving sand.

"Everything okay?" I ask him.

"Yeah," he says. "We had to move a few dates around."

"How come?"

"It'll work out better like this. You doing okay?"

"We're on track, right?"

"Yes, but what about you?"

"No problems here," I tell him. I just want to get underway.

"Good." He releases my shoulders. "I'll be right back," he says, and then he's gone.

Now here's a map of California, and all its biomes. Patches of color, with more and more names. In the corner, that little star, the compass rose. It strikes me—my grandfather's drawing, with its little star. Could it be a map? But his star has six points. He might have been able to create new flowers, but I don't think he created new directions. I close my eyes and fix his drawing in my mind, with that asymmetrical star. North, south, east, and west. And then what? I need to go study it some more. I turn to look for Forrest and there before me is a stuffed mountain lion, lying on a rock, looking through me.

Chapter 33

When the sun sinks into the tops of the trees, their trunks thin and dark like prison bars around the clearing, it occurs to Leonardo that he has just passed the quietest, most solitary day of his entire existence. He'd never been one for camping alone, or even hiking alone. Even on his longest, most remote research trips, he'd always been with a team, or at least an assistant. He'd never even driven more than a few hours by himself, and even then there had been music, podcasts.

He had done everything he could to distract his mind from the day's excruciating void. He'd reached for his nonexistent phone fifty times before the automation of that circuitry finally began to disintegrate. He'd made another, more careful examination of the house, which yielded one wire hanger and one paper clip, both of which he'd placed in the kitchen, alongside his meager store of gas-station food. He threw rocks, paced, stretched, and walked a hundred yards down the long driveway before his fear of being seen drove him back to the clearing. He thought about a graphic he'd seen online not too long ago, charting the amount of time we spend alone through different stages of life. Family and friends become scarcer through the twenties and thirties; our children grow up and move out when we're in our forties and fifties. Coworkers vanish with retirement in our fifties and sixties, and then our partners die. A vast solitude is waiting to take us all in our final years, biding its time, watching as those we love fall away, one after the other. If the painful emptiness of this day is portentous, then Leo will have some work to do to prepare himself.

Sundown finally brings respite from the heat and he puts his shirt back on, not because he needs its warmth but because it feels strange to be sitting in his underwear with the darkness coming on. Bright planets and dim stars appear and then, just as the sun disappears from one edge of the sky, a full moon rises from the other edge to replace it. It's a sight he's seen before, but not like this, not when the transition into evening is perhaps the only significant event in his entire day.

And then he remembers that he hasn't used his voice all day, so he greets the moon, and introduces himself by name. His voice sounds small and foreign, but in the emptiness it reaches up and fills the sky.

Chapter 34

Gabriel awakens early and descends to the lobby of the Matador Arms, a seventies-era apartment complex in West Covina, just off the San Bernardino Freeway. By himself in the quiet morning light, he sees details he'd missed the previous night: the stained orange rug in the hallway, a panel of worn mailboxes, a bulletin board stratified with a thousand faded fliers. He heads outside into a hazy morning, propping the door open with a beat-up cardboard box full of junk mail. Across the street is a low concrete wall, and then eight lanes of freeway. The traffic is thick but moves quickly, a dense school of fish. The noise it makes is thick, solid, undifferentiated, except when the groan of a semi or the whine of a motorcycle passes down the nearest lane.

The grocery store is a block away, its air conditioning already cranking against the day's coming heat. He buys a dozen eggs, a pound of bacon, potatoes, a pound of coffee, sugar and cream, and a half-dozen *pan dulces*. When he returns the apartment is still quiet inside. Just as Gabriel finishes cooking his hosts emerge from a bedroom, coming through the farthest of several doors that crowd a long hallway. Watson, with a wide, loose afro and a faded *Free Leonard* t-shirt, is in the lead, followed by his girlfriend Naomi, several inches taller than he is, whose gaze, Gabriel had noticed the night before, tends toward the middle distance. He'd met the young couple briefly the previous evening, but he'd felt like the encounter had been less a welcome, and more a cursory threat assessment. Who knows what Serena had texted them about the random guy she was bringing in? The exchange had only comprised a few words before Watson and Naomi sequestered themselves in the back bedroom, shifting their attention to their heartbroken friend, who was presumably still asleep back there.

Now they stop at the kitchen's threshold, where the stained carpet gives way to beige linoleum, as if in respect for Gabriel's new claim upon the kitchen. They discover the extent of the impromptu buffet and wonderment falls upon their awakening faces.

"It usually doesn't smell like this in here," Naomi says.

"Please," Gabriel says, sweeping an upturned hand over the platters.

Watson, impressed, heads for the plates. "Where did Serena find you, again?"

"At a Super 8 in Bakersfield."

"And tell me your name again? Gabe, was it?"

"Yes. Or Gabriel."

"Gabriel," he repeats, nodding. "Nice. Many thanks for this bounty." He scoops scrambled eggs onto a chipped stoneware plate.

Naomi picks up a piece of bacon, smells it, returns it to the plate, and reaches for the coffee pot with a smile. "You can stay on the couch forever," she says. Her shoulders are bare, revealing tattoos of stars and a moon and symbols Gabriel doesn't recognize.

"Thank you. I'm still trying to figure out my plan."

Down the hallway a door opens and closes, and then another. The murmur of voices arises from behind the walls. He wonders how many other souls are tucked away back there.

Naomi turns from the counter, a mug of coffee in one hand, the strip of bacon now retrieved. She takes a small bite and chews slowly, her eyes on Gabriel now. After a sip of coffee, she says, "We understand you're searching for a beautiful, bejeweled needle in this big stinking haystack?"

"That's right." The previous morning, he would have said that the odds of finding the van were infinitesimal. He knows they still are, scientifically speaking. But what had happened yesterday, at the Super 8? As soon as he'd lost his direction, a new one had appeared. He's here for a reason. He just needs to keep moving, and to watch and listen, and he'll come across a signpost eventually.

After breakfast his hosts direct him to a bus stop, just in front of the grocery store. His instinct was to head for the heart of Los Angeles, but when he asked his hosts where it was, they looked at one another and shrugged. "There are many," Naomi said. So he boards a bus heading vaguely westward and lets it carry him into the city's momentum, a stick thrown into a river. The bus rolls through the sprawl, its passage smooth and effortless and unhurried, as though the driver has driven the route ten thousand times. Miles go by, boulevards and intersections and churches and parks and schools and shopping centers, repeating themselves in an endless loop, slight variations on a theme. The sun climbs higher; the waft of air each time the bus stops and opens its doors grows hotter.

An hour or so later he is passing through a tidy, featureless neighborhood when a storefront catches his eye—a tattoo shop called Age of Aquarius. He jumps off the bus at the next stop, backtracks two blocks to the shop, and pushes through the door. It's bright, clean, and sparse, leaning more toward Scandinavian modernism than hippy kitsch. A single lava lamp with a brushed aluminum base is the only nod to its sixties namesake. There's one station in use, where a female tattooer with her back to the door works on a fiftysomething woman's ankle while a teenage girl looks on. Mother and daughter look over as Gabriel enters and then return their attention to the work in progress.

Gabriel steps to the counter and opens a binder of photos, looking for origami fish, unsure what he'll do if he finds one. He flips through dragons on shoulders, octopi on calves, sharks on forearms, birds on chests, and then a door in the back of the shop opens and man of about seventy emerges, wiping his hands on his jeans. A pair of gray braids stretch from just behind his ears and hang down over the front of his plain black t-shirt. His eyes are large and blue and they light up when he sees Gabriel. He approaches the counter and takes a seat on a stool. He doesn't have a single visible tattoo.

"Good morning, young man," he says. "I'm Zeke. How may I help you?"

"Just browsing," Gabriel says, taking pains to keep his healing fish in view. Zeke takes the bait.

"That looks like a fresh one. May I see it?"

"Sure," Gabriel says, extending it across the counter.

Zeke reaches under his counter, dons a pair of latex gloves, and then cradles Gabriel's arm. He studies it for several seconds, long enough for Gabriel to suspect that he knows about its origins and meaning. A flare of hope lights inside him. Finally Zeke releases the arm with a nod. "Lovely. There are some pretty interesting details in there."

"Thanks."

"Where'd you get it done?" Zeke asks, as Gabriel hoped he would.

"Capricorn Rising, in Sacramento," Gabriel says, watching Zeke's face closely for a reaction.

Zeke laughs. "My astrological sister shop!"

"You know the place?" Gabriel asks, trying to sound casual.

"Never heard of it. But I'm happy to see they're doing the zodiac proud." He reaches under the counter and produces a bottle of lotion. "Now let me help you out with that," he says, nodding at the tattoo. "It's looking a little dry."

Gabriel thanks him, trying not to let his deflation show. "Do you know anyone who specializes in this sort of thing?" he asks, as Zeke works the lotion into the tattoo.

"Sure. Hundreds of them."

Chapter 35

I went to Spain on a school trip once. Madrid was loud and hot and dirty but then I'd walk into a cathedral—soaring ceilings, cool silence, filtered light. That's how this redwood grove feels. I'm wrapped in a blanket, lying on a camping pad on a picnic table, staring at the treetops.

We've been waiting at this rest area since mid-morning, somewhere outside Eureka. Preston is here reading and Forrest is walking. In the forest. The others took the van somewhere. Getting food I think, but I don't think I'm hungry. Am I? We have a place we can stay the next couple of nights, with someone Paolo knows. A friend. And tomorrow we're going to conduct *el regreso* right there, in her house. But she's not available until later this afternoon, so we're waiting.

Everything at the last stop went fine. Twelve *viajeros*, twelve journeys. While I was doing my work I tried to think about my grandfather's drawing, the one that might be a map. Nothing came of it. But when it was all over there was no weirdness, no fights, nobody in a coma. Just twelve people, coming back from a long deep journey through the wordless parts of their brains, with sudden cravings for plants.

In the late afternoon the color is draining out of the sky and the branches and needles frame a thousand jagged shapes that flex and shift as the trunks sway. The woods are silent but for the birds, or an occasional motorcycle whine.

The *centella* has run its course but I'm feeling tired and fuzzy, like my head is full of cotton. I've never done two journeys over three nights. I wonder how I'd be feeling if we hadn't cancelled Fresno, and we were coming off three nights in a row. If that would have even been the plan. I'm glad I can rest tonight.

A breeze I can't feel starts the trees swaying, a soft clatter of limbs in the forest canopy. I try to find the nodes where the branches are knocking into one another. It sounds like they're talking. The real conversation is underground, though. Did you know that? Messages rippling through webs of mycelium, the trees in constant communication with one another, and with everything around them. Hidden languages. I wonder what they would say about me.

Chapter 36

Yvette returns in the late afternoon on the third day. When she pulls up Leonardo is sitting on the steps in the sun, eating pistachios, flicking their shells toward a circle he has drawn with a stick in the gravel, several paces away. He has thought of her often during these three days, whether because she is his lifeline to the world, or for some other reason, he doesn't know.

He's been thinking of the winter morning he met her, at the DMV in Oakland, where they found themselves, both without appointments, waiting next to each other on plastic chairs contoured to fit nobody in particular, at the mercy of a flu-decimated staff. They exchanged first-date information during the first hour—he learned she was a bartender from Tennessee, who moonlighted as an instructor for a kickboxing-themed exercise class. During the second hour their conversation deepened to include second-date information—she'd run away from home at seventeen and she was self-conscious about her knees. By the time she was finally called to the counter, they'd exchanged phone numbers. He called her right away and in the coming weeks they devoured whole swaths of the city, tireless in their mutual infatuation, their sudden need to share with the other every restaurant, every bar, every out-of-the-way movie theater they'd ever known. He sleepwalked through his workdays, fueled with caffeine and dopamine. As a bartender she was already nocturnal and could sleep through the days after evenings when they'd stay out until the bars closed, returning afterwards to one or the other's place for more drinks, and then sex until they collapsed.

That era spun down; she started modeling and his teaching schedule intensified. Her work hours changed and expanded and there was less time for each other. The late nights became rare. It was soon after that when he began suspecting her of an affair. He had no evidence of this whatsoever—his suspicions were based on statistics. Relationships simply did not last. And now that she was modeling, she spent every day looking some variety of stunning, slinking through a constantly shifting landscape of photographers, editors, and designers, many of whom seemed to be males with names like Timber or Bison or Ranger. "Ranger?" Leonardo had asked her that time, interrupting her story. "That's the name of a grown man? You're sure he's not a golden retriever?" She had laughed with him, but not as much as she should have. So infidelity was just a matter of probability and time. She was cheating on him, statistically. But they'd made it through a year. Her trajectory in modeling turned out not to be as dizzying as it once seemed it might—it was her auburn volumes of hair that seemed responsible for the majority of her contracts, and the recognition and money that would have carried her to LA or New York for good did not appear, and that was fine with him. They made it through another year, their rhythms and routines evolving and settling.

And now she has come to be the only person in his immediate world, and the thrill that jolts him when he sees her drive around the bend of the gravel drive is so strong he almost chokes on a pistachio. The tires of her borrowed car smash into his pile of shells and she emerges like Artemis from her chariot. She does not embrace him at first, but keeps one hand on his shoulder, her bent arm between them, holding the distance so she can look at him. The fingernails of her other hand trace lines down his cheek like the paths of skiers; tingles spread across his face like the cold spray of powder.

"Oh, my beautiful baby boy," she says. "It's going to be okay." She looks, he thinks, a bit too concerned for somebody who is in the process of issuing such an assurance, but then she encircles him with her arms, guiding her nose into his ear and her lips to his neck, and his misgivings evaporate. She makes love to him right there on the steps, and though he knows there's a threat of splinters in his bare ass, he does not care. His face disappears into the mahogany shroud of her vaunted hair; darts of sunlight find openings and flare in the shadowed enclosure. When he comes, fireworks explode across the underside of his scalp.

Later, when he has eaten the still-a-little-warm cheeseburger she has brought for him, and they are sitting on the step in the sun, she produces a manila folder filled with news articles she'd printed out for him, from over the last three days. He scans through them, following the focus as it shifts from the confrontation at Sonoma State and the manhunt to the disappearance of Lenore. Once she appears in the timeline, the assemblyman and his lawyer suddenly decide they need privacy from the press. Yvette is quoted two or three times, always pulling the story back to consternation over Lenore. There's a small mention of the incident at Raleigh's at one point, but it's no more than a footnote. By the timestamp on the most recent article, from just that morning, the focus has shifted from Leonardo's villainy to a litany of unanswered questions. He closes the file and passes it back to her, wondering anew at her capabilities.

"I faked a call from you yesterday," she says, splaying a hand over the top of Leonardo's thigh. "I had someone call me from a pay phone in Gilroy, and I showed the call history to the cops. I told them you were concerned about Adam and remorseful over your heat-of-the-moment actions, but nonetheless still quite suspicious of him, and, above all, distraught over your sister. You aren't coming in yet because then you'd be helpless, and your sister needs you. You extended an apology to the hard-working men and women of law enforcement, but you've decided that your role as a brother and your duties to your family are the most important things at this time, and when that's no longer the case you'll come forward."

Leonardo studies the tops of the trees, the jagged line they make against the immaculate sky. He feels like crying, but he isn't sure why. He can't remember the last time a lump took over his throat like this.

She stays with him that night. They haul the mattress outside and toss it down in the clearing and make love beneath the rising moon, this time slower, pausing whole minutes, still connected, to kiss and to breathe together and to feel the night against them. Afterward, they lie on their backs, still naked, naming the constellations they know and inventing names for those they don't.

"Let's be quiet for a minute and see if we can hear the Lemurians," she says, when they have finished cataloging the sky.

"That would be Madagascar. I don't think you brought me that far."

She chuckles. "Not lemurs. Lemurians. Descendants of the lost continent of Lemuria, which sank into the ocean. A graceful, agile species, far more developed than we are spiritually, and less encumbered by weighty intellect."

Leo laughs. "I see. Friends of Bigfoot?"

"They wear white robes and live in jeweled caverns inside this mountain." She rolls onto her side and places a hand on his chest. "Maybe, if you can make contact, we can come back when this is all over and learn their ways and live all the rest of our days in peace and grace."

The next morning she unpacks the trunk: sheets and a blanket, cases of water and canned soup, a camping stove with spare propane canisters and a pot, a crate of apples and oranges, bags of dried fruit and nuts, a loaf of bread, four salamis, mustard, dehydrated eggs, boxes of crackers, a radio, sunscreen, a notepad and a pen, and a whole grocery bag full of used paperbacks.

"Don't freak out," she says, pulling the books out of the bag and stacking them on the kitchen counter. "I just don't know exactly when I'll be able to come back up. I wanted you to have options."

"Thanks," he says, trying not to let her see how much he is freaking out. "What's next?"

"You'll continue roaming the state, trying to find your sister, checking in occasionally."

He nods.

She gives him a long kiss and a tight hug. When the sound of the car finishes its long dwindle the silence leaves him fighting to breathe.

Chapter 37

Vasco runs through the turn at the pergola, completing his first lap around Lake Merritt and embarking on his second. A check of his watch tells him his pace is a little slower than normal, but that's okay. He's not pushing himself today. There's too much to think about. The warren of mysteries before him now includes a high-school runaway and her two-word note, as well as the appearance of the professor's girlfriend, who has apparently nominated herself the spokesperson for the family's troubles. She's been effective, too. In just a couple of days, the professor has gone from rampaging villain to distraught brother. She could have a hell of a career in crisis management when the modeling thing winds down, if she wants. There hadn't been any real developments the day before, and now the news cycle is ready to shift its focus elsewhere, which suits Vasco fine. It's easier to do his work without scrutiny, and he needs all the help he can get. The connections between the Percivals, Adam Yeager, and his own father's homemade *medicina* are as clear as the urban lake's notorious waters.

He passes the glass cathedral and jogs down the lake's west side, weaving around leashed dogs and strollers, thinking about that phone call. It had been brief, and had come in from a payphone in Gilroy. The professor, if the girlfriend could be believed, was full of remorse and condolences, and on a brotherly mission to find his sister. Media fodder. What Vasco cared about was whether or not he'd been caught on camera. Was he alone? Was he in a vehicle? If so, what kind? Using his watch, he dictates a short text for Garza: *Anything from Gilroy?*

He's passing the amphitheater when a notification comes back, but it isn't Garza. It's Nicole, and her message is terse: *Final offer.* They've been working to find a suitable afternoon for her to introduce him to rock climbing. Or at least, she's been working—though he accepted the invitation, he hasn't held up his end of the arrangement in the scheduling department. She'd brought it up a second time, and now this. It's not that he doesn't like her. It's just the opposite, and that's the problem.

They met at the gym where he goes for the occasional yoga class. He's never attended class regularly enough to make any true progress, but it helps him stay limber, which helps him recover from the abuse he takes elsewhere. Two weeks earlier, he and Nicole, both running late, had arrived at the doorway simultaneously to find there was only one spot left in the class.

"Please," Vasco said, stepping back, gesturing toward the empty spot on the floor. "Take it."

"Are you sure?" She looked him over, as if searching for some hidden clause of body language. Wisps of blond hair, which had escaped from her ponytail, rose from her brow like sun flares.

"Yes. It was either this or go eat a whole pizza by myself. So I've got Plan B all figured out."

She laughed. "I'll tell you what." She dug into the small bag she was carrying. "I'll accept your offer, because I really need this after the morning I've had. But here." She held out a card. "I teach rock climbing here. I'd like to give you a free intro lesson to say thanks."

"You don't have to do that. It's really not a big deal. But thank you!"

"I know I don't have to," she said, watching him closely. "I want to." She extended the card another inch.

"It's really not necessary. Just enjoy yourself, and the next time I see you heading this way I'll just walk a little faster."

She smiled, but only with her mouth. "Zoom out."

"What?"

"Zoom out. Like in the movies. See that lady on the far side of the room, in the yellow shirt? Imagine she's watching this interaction."

"Okay?"

"Does she want to see you accept this offering, or does she want to see me have to put it back into my bag?"

Vasco held out his palm and watched the card fall into it.

"Enjoy your pizza," she said, turning.

He encountered her again a week or so later. He was on his way into the gym; she was on her way out. It was early evening, a busy time, and there was a stream of people going in both directions, so she reached out and took his arm and steered him down the sidewalk, out of the traffic. He didn't recognize her at first—she'd traded the gym clothes and cross trainers for a black dress and strappy sandals. Dabs of silver circled her wrists and neck. Her hair was down, and she wore hints of makeup so slight he could not be sure they were actually there. Her grip was firm, and did not leave his arm. For a moment he considered the possibility he was being accosted by some other agency. She didn't look much like a fed, though. CIA, maybe?

Only when she turned and smiled did he recognize her. "That climbing lesson," she said. "What do you say?" All her weight on one foot, a hand on her stuck-out hip, a curve in her back.

"Let's do it," he said. "I'm guessing this isn't a good time, though."

She looked down at herself and smiled. "I'm meeting my dad for dinner. I should probably get your number." But she was empty-handed, without so much as a phone or a set of keys.

"You're traveling light. Why don't you give me yours?"

"Tried that already." A family of four, tourists, were just then wandering by; a teenaged son held a guide book in one hand, a pen in the other. Nicole turned and touched him on the arm, and his eyes bulged. "Can I please borrow your pen?" she asked.

"Where are your things?" Vasco said. "You're allowed to go places without your phone?"

"Left them with my dad, down the street. I had to run back here to drop something off. Any other questions?" She pulled up the skirt of her dress three inches, exposing the top of her thigh.

"Yes . . . what are you doing?"

"Taking care of business. Now give me that number." When she was finished writing his number on her leg she replaced her skirt and returned the pen to its wide-eyed owner. "Thanks," she told him. "Enjoy your visit to our fine city." She turned back to Vasco. "Hope you have a good class. Now get on in there before some other girl has to bribe you for the last slot." She gave his arm a squeeze and merged into the sidewalk's traffic.

Now as he runs up the lake's eastern shore he considers her two-word ultimatum. This would have all been very exciting for a younger version of himself. It's not that he has grown immune to the charms of a striking woman—far from it. He can feel the heat in the circuitry that links his brain and his dick and the spot on his arm that still carries the memory of her hand's pressure. The chemicals are all still there. But they're tempered with the awareness that the men and women in his profession have a tendency to burden their loved ones a good deal more than average. Every one of his colleagues' wives and husbands, even the most supportive, spends at least some of their time hating aspects of their spouse's job. And Vasco is even more absorbed in his work than many of them—without a family waiting for him at home, he can put in hours of guilt-free overtime and chase down leads that other agents might deem too unimportant to warrant attention. And when he's not working on cases he's at the range, or at the gym, or at the dojo, or doing laps around this lake. It has gotten to the point that the more Vasco likes a woman, the worse he feels about the prospect of asking her to like him back. He hasn't quite figured out where this will lead him, but he isn't losing sleep over it, either. He's got other things to think about. And while Nicole had only proposed an hour-long bouldering lesson, Vasco has learned that the best time to stop something is before it begins. A deal is a deal, though, regardless of whether or not he entered into it under the imaginary pressure of the lady in the yellow shirt, across the room. He sends her a text back: *Tomorrow afternoon?*

He rounds a curve and the pergola, his finish line, comes into view. His pace has slipped even further. It's interesting—some of his best times have come on days when he felt like crap. Today he felt fine, but his legs aren't moving like they should be. Too many thoughts dragging him down. He accelerates and finishes the last few hundred yards as fast as he can. While he's pacing on the lawn, trying to catch his breath, a pair of one-word texts comes in. Garza's says *No*. Nicole's says *Yes*.

Chapter 38

Leo sits on the porch for another hour after Yvette's departure, feeling sorry for himself. It is bizarre, this complete absence of purpose—never before has he experienced such inaccessibility, such a split from the components he thought his existence comprised. There were always places to go: his office, his lectures, department meetings, dinners, conferences, the gym, outings with Yvette. When he was lecturing he thought about his research; when he was researching he thought about his lectures. He watched television with his laptop open and he pondered data while he worked out.

A full bladder finally gets him up and he shuffles across the gravel clearing, unzipping, heading to the spot he'd randomly selected his first evening there. Before he reaches the woods though he catches the scent of the previous day's piss, and realizes that he'll have to be methodical about this, now that his residency status has been upgraded to semi-permanent. He veers, continues into the woods for another thirty or forty feet, and picks a spot.

Birdsong comes to him then, thick as a sudden fall of rain, and he wonders why he hasn't noticed its extent already. The scientist in him awakens and now he can parse their voices: finches, jays, warblers, the lilting call of a lone chickadee, other songs he can't identify. And then the forest canopy above him comes to life; what had been a quietly shifting mass of leaves now becomes an ecosystem, a unique biome in a complex system of overlapping habitats, migration patterns, and interdependencies.

Without ever having meant to, he'd spent most of his career among shorebirds. He wonders about that now. Perhaps growing up in Berkeley, with that great bay resting always just outside his bedroom window, he'd been susceptible to the call of the water. Or perhaps it was just a case of gravity, holding him at sea level simply because it never occurred to him to expend the energy to fight it. The birds are easy to spot down there—large and slow and noisy, their nests on the ground, little in the way of cover or camouflage. Here, though, he thinks, squinting into the trees and seeing nothing, is an entirely different habitat. The birds are smaller, lighter, agile. Despite the chorus around him, it takes him a minute or two before he actually sees one: a quick movement on a branch, the turn of a small head, and then an arrow's flight from one treetop to another, or beyond—he can't tell; a wind-driven shrug of leaves masks the movement and the little bird disappears into the forest. But then there is another, and another, visible only through their movements. He thinks again about the egrets and their sublime, pristine stillness, the shining white holes they punch through the landscape. These, though, are birds who seem to have no colors, no forms, who exist only as motion, like wind, like shooting stars.

Leonardo returns to the house, fills a shopping bag with food and bottles of water, and retrieves the notebook and pen from the kitchen counter. He steps back outside, feeling both elated and sheepish, and he crosses to the back of the clearing and plunges into the woods. At this altitude the undergrowth is sparse, and it's easy going between fir trees on a bed of fallen needles. He records the first couple of birds he sees but then quickly puts the notebook away, choosing instead to just wander and watch. Every hundred yards or so he turns around and checks the trail behind him, making sure he knows the way back to the clearing, searching the area for distinctive landmarks: stone outcroppings, a burnt snag, a patch of wildflowers. His heart rate climbs; the movement and the exertion provide him with some relief from his mental torments. It's a hot afternoon and soon he's sweating. He peels his shirt off and stuffs it in his bag, then downs a half a bottle of water.

His route takes him up to the top of a small, open butte, which affords him a clear view of the mountain towering above him, its higher elevations streaked with snow. Gradual slopes lead down the butte's backside, descending toward the mouths of a pair of adjacent valleys, which tilt steeply toward the summit. He turns and studies the landscape beneath him, the series of ridges that fade into the west and disappear into the ocean.

He sits on a fallen log and eats some peanut butter crackers and drinks a little water and then plunges down the butte's backside, studying the mountain before him, considering which valley to explore. The slope to his left offers an easier climb so he veers that way, moving even faster now with gravity helping him, the dirt and fir needles cushioning his footsteps. It's a short descent, and soon he's climbing again, alongside a dry creek bed. At the valley's high end he blazes a trail of switchbacks to reach the next ridge, halting briefly to take in the expanding view. There's still plenty of sunlight. He continues his climb, but finds the mountain steepening here, forcing him to move laterally, circling to the north. After climbing up to the top of another butte he hears the sound of water. He hurries down the embankment and finds in the bottom of a shallow grassy vale a clear stream, its waters tumbling easily over flat, smooth rocks. He peels his clothes off without slowing down, dumps them on the bank, and plunges straight in. The water is bracing, miraculous, and the sudden cold sends a cleansing shock through him that makes his eyes go blurry. In the middle of the stream the water level rises to just above his knees. He squats, gasping as his ass hits the surface, and submerges, and when he plunges his head in he can feel the grease and grime and sweat sloughing not only from his brow and his hair but also from inside his throat, from his arteries. Once he's shivering he scrambles back onto the bank, shakes himself off, and puts his clothes back on. There's a flat stretch of granite alongside the creek, just big enough for him. He stretches out in the sun, beneath photons plump and bright as ripe oranges, and shuts his eyes for a few minutes. When he is dry he rises, collects his bag, and begins the walk back. As he approaches the top of the first butte, he notices that the colors are wrong—the shadows aren't in the right places, the greens are too dark, and the yellows have gone to gold. From the vantage point atop the butte the ridges to the west reappear, the sun hanging just above them. His stomach twists. He's been out far too long—had he fallen asleep? It's two hours back to the cabin, he estimates, but the sun will be down in half that time.

He continues, accelerating, heading back at almost a jog now, racing the sun. After circling along the mountain's flank, he lets gravity carry him downward. Across the valley, the sun is also sinking, dipping behind the horizon. He'll have just enough light to get back to the cabin. He squints at the terrain below him, searching for the route he blazed on the way up, through the switchbacks. Striated with deep shadows now, though, the terrain resists recognition, and he can't remember what had come before the switchbacks. The view doesn't seem right, either—he can't remember being able to see this far to the north from here. Probably he'd just been focused on his feet the first time he passed through. He plunges down the hillside and into the woods, which wrap him in shadows. After another half-hour of descending, he reaches the edge of a massive gulch that was definitely not here before, and his mistake becomes clear—he'd abandoned his traverse too early, and descended the wrong part of the mountain. The last of the day's light reveals his options: head back up the way he'd come, or continue downward, and hope to find a place where he could descend into the gulch. But then what?

Feeling numb, he hoists his lunch bag, testing its weight. Two bottles of water remaining, a single packet of peanut butter crackers. At this elevation, maybe the creek water would be safe to drink. But what about food? Warmth? He hadn't even brought his sweatshirt. At least the coming night is still holding onto the day's warmth.

"Fuck," he says, and plants himself on a fallen log. He twists the cap off one of his remaining waters and allows himself a tiny sip. All around him, the spaces between the trees fill up with darkness.

Chapter 39

After a few hard days we've found a haven. The house is huge, hidden in the woods above Arcata. It reminds me of a party house you'd see in a 1970s movie. There are houseplants everywhere, and through the picture windows the views are nothing but trees. It's dark now, though, and instead of the trees it's our reflections out there. The furniture is a mishmash of styles, and in the living room it's all been piled up along the walls. The floor is covered in blankets, where a dozen *viajeros* are now resting, splayed like the spokes on a wheel, taking deep breaths as the *centella* begins its work. I've got a room all to myself and that's where I am now, working on my own cupful. Our hostess, Paolo's friend, is like someone's fairy godmother. She's buzzing with excitement from whatever he told her about it. The other participants are her friends and some of their grad students. They're probably all nice enough people. I can't spend much time with them, outside of the journey. It would drain me too much. Small talk was always hard, but after learning of the *centella* it became excruciating.

I'm at a small wooden desk, with my grandfather's drawings spread out in front of me. They look the same as always, no matter how I spin them around, change angles, squint. There's a mug on the desk with shells glued all around its rim and it's holding some pens and pencils. I take a pencil and bring its tip to hover over the simplest drawing, the forking path. Where would he have started? The center? The top left? I pick a spot and begin tracing, trying to feel where my grandfather's hand would have been. How it moved, the bend and twist of his wrist, the curve of his fingers. The shape of his thoughts.

Emilio is here, watching me. When did he come in? Did I let him in? Was the door open? The words are falling away, winking out. He takes my arm. We walk. Now the drums, and the thrum of a dozen churning souls.

Chapter 40

t's already well after sunset by the time Gabriel boards an eastbound bus, heading out of Long Beach toward Anaheim, where he plans to switch over to an express bus heading back north toward the Matador Arms and his temporary roommates. For two full days now, he has been traveling by bus, cris-crossing the urbanscape, watching for white vans, wrist tattoos, anything that might point to his sister. He'd climbed down and lingered in the arts districts, near universities, in neighborhoods where tattoo shops and twentysomethings seemed to congregate, and when each one yielded nothing, he'd moved on to the next. On the first day he'd ridden all the way west to Santa Monica before turning around and making his way back. Today he'd worked his way southward, and now it's time to flip around again and head back. Tomorrow he isn't sure what he'll do.

The previous night he'd arrived back at the apartment to find Watson, Naomi, and Serena on the couch, arranged around a coffee table that held a couple of bottles of wine and various elaborate contraptions for smoking weed. They'd welcomed him and invited him to join them, which he had, though he'd stuck with herbal tea. They asked him about his search for Lenore, and they listened when he answered. Nobody told him it was hopeless, or questioned his methods. They wished him success, and they told him stories about their own siblings. They told him about the apartment's other inhabitants: a young couple who shared another of the bedrooms, and a recent divorcee whom nobody ever saw. They turned then to the subject of Serena's break-up. It was, after all, the event that had brought them all together. At one point, when she was sitting next to Gabriel on the couch, she broke down into tears, and he put a hand on her back. Naomi and Watson soon joined him, and they sat together for a time, surrounding her, each with a hand on her. Later that evening, Naomi brought him a handmade bracelet of hemp cord with a black stone cube tied into its center. She tied it around the wrist that did not have the healing tattoo. "Because you're a luminous being," she told him. Watson was tuning his guitar by then, and Naomi pulled a basket of small percussion instruments out from under the coffee table. A banjo appeared—Gabriel recognized it from the pile of things in the back of Serena's car. He didn't know how to play but he reached for it. Watson showed him three notes to focus on, and Gabriel managed not to ruin "Blackbird," a song that made him think of his mom.

Sitting on the bus he's tired now, stiff from sitting all day, his brain fatigued after his peripatetic vigil. He's far from the Matador Arms, and even farther from his little apartment in Berkeley, which itself barely feels like a home. There is inside him a longing to be somewhere else—but where, he's not sure. The city expands as the bus travels eastward, refusing to allow him any familiarity. It spins out into fractal patterns, repeating endlessly its iterations of shapes, signs, intersections, whole five-mile boulevard stretches. No sign of the van or its inhabitants appears. When he finally reaches Anaheim it's after midnight, and he finds that the bus line he was planning to catch back north has shut down for the day. He could pay for an exorbitant taxi ride back to West Covina, but he decides to take this as a sign, and he books a room at a cheap motel near the freeway. He lies on top of the lumpy bed and turns on the TV, which is the size of a computer monitor, bolted crooked to the wall. There's a monster truck rally on. A column of dead pixels runs down one edge. There's a loud bang into the wall behind him, and the couple in the next room starts fucking loudly. All around him the city hums with the sounds of the wrong people.

Chapter 41

The first tinge of light in the sky fills Leo with relief. It had been a torturous night, curled on the ground against a fallen tree, trying to sleep, tracking the gibbous moon's slow progress to the west. Just before the light had vanished completely, he'd found some sticks and bigleaf maple leaves, and was able to craft a rudimentary shelter by leaning the sticks against the fallen tree and covering them with enough leaves to trap a little heat inside. He'd taken his food and his last bottle of water out of the plastic grocery bag and used the bag to make a head covering of sorts and he'd lain there, thinking about his days in the field, and all the discomfort he'd endured to build the foundations of a career—a career that was in danger of imploding because of the actions of a single vengeful grad student, somehow. The causality here is utterly elusive. One day last week he'd risen early, gone to the gym, showered, and driven to campus, just as he did all the time. He'd just made it to his desk when his phone had buzzed with his father's text, and now he's sleeping in the dirt, hundreds of miles from home, wanted for questioning. A series of events link the former scenario with the latter, but he's not sure how. There are gaps in the narrative, missing explanations.

And in the midst of it, somehow, Lenore has flown the coop. He can't figure out why—it's not like she had a tough life in her beautiful home on the hill, with the endless freedoms Redland and Peoria afforded her, and the lightest of senior-year schedules. He initially suspected she'd run off with some new boyfriend, but she wasn't really the type to get infatuated with someone like that. She'd always had too much of her own shit going on. It strikes him that now, he's also missing. No phone, no way to contact anyone. What had Yvette told his parents? Anything? Were they in on this? Or were they wondering about him now, too? At least Lenore had left a note. Leo had confronted Clifford, and then that kid at Sonoma State, and then he'd vanished, for all they knew, leaving a rental SUV somewhere in the outskirts of Chico, which felt like a thousand miles away, a different lifetime. None of it made any sense, and now, he just wants to go home.

There's just enough light to navigate the mountainside now, and he pulls the bag from his head and wriggles out from under his shelter of leaves. The cool empty air hits him, surprising him with how well his makeshift bivouac had worked. His muscles ache from the hard ground as he takes a piss and then walks over to collect his trash, which he'd stashed in a crotch in a fir tree fifty paces away so as to reduce his chances of waking up with a bear in his lap.

A single bottle of water is all that's left of his inventory. He takes one big sip, replaces the cap, and starts climbing, trying to remember what he can about the route he'd taken to get down here the day before, and thinking about the coffee he's not brewing.

The earth lightens; the soreness in his muscles loosens. After an hour of climbing he reaches the traverse where he'd made the premature turn, and he turns to work his way back to the south. Far across the valley now there's gold on the highest peaks; as he walks in Shasta's shadow he watches the sunlight grow and drip down into those distant valleys like butter melting. Just the sight of it warms him. His thirst is growing, though—he takes a few more sips, taking the bottle down to half. A gurgle in his stomach reminds him of the couple of meals he's missed. The thought brings on a bout of lightheadedness, but he tells himself it's psychosomatic. He takes another small sip, and then a couple of deep breaths, and plods onward.

He crests a small rise and the next ridge comes into view, its trees glowing in the morning sunlight, and he accelerates, eager for the sun. Just as he's nearing the shoulder there's a movement in the forest canopy he can't make sense of—something big and black, changing shape. His eyes dart toward the spot but the movement stops. There could be a patch of darkness there, but maybe it's a shadow, or an empty spot among the leaves. But then, just as he steps into the light, the movement appears again, and a huge bird emerges. It flaps its broad wings twice, three times, banking in an arc that brings it right over Leo's head. He gasps when he sees the white stripes on its underwings—it's a full-grown California condor, a species that had been taken to the brink of extinction in the eighties, when only twenty-seven remained. He turns and watches the bird glide into the mountain's shadow, its nine-foot wingspan wide as the horizon. It's hundreds of miles away from where it's supposed to be. The colony at Pinnacles National Park is half the state away, the long way.

The condor flaps its wings, circles, and heads back. Leo freezes and watches it glide over him, its feathers splayed against the deepening blue sky. It banks and descends the slope now, in the direction of the cabin, and Leo hurries after it.

If it had been known that condors lived this far north, he would have heard about it, many times over. This must be a brand-new arrival. And condors form long-term mating pairs, so if there's one mature bird here, there's likely another. Why come this far by yourself? He could get funding for this. There would probably be some conservation group or another in on the research, but that would be fine. This is plenty big.

The condor stays with him all morning, either following him or leading him down through the valley, and then up and over the butte. It disappears for stretches but never fails to reappear, and as Leo steps into the cabin's clearing, it's flying right overhead. It circles over him once, seeming to look down on him, and then it crosses over the cabin, banks slightly left, and disappears.

Chapter 42

"That was actually pretty impressive," Nicole says, smiling. "Are you sure you've never done this before? Maybe as a kid?"

"I'm Mexican. When I was a kid, recreation was soccer and barbecues." He points up at the climbing wall that towers over them, its holds dusted white with the remnants of chalk powder. "Stuff like this wasn't on our radar."

"Well, you're a natural." She extricates her foot from a climbing shoe and flexes her foot. Her toenails are the color of key lime pie. "Most beginners, especially men, try to do it all with upper-body strength. With their shoulders. They do the equivalent of thirty pullups in the first ten minutes and then they're done." She reaches down to unlace her other shoe.

Nicole isn't flattering him. She isn't the type who would, but also, as their hour-long lesson had progressed, it became clear he was beyond the beginner's curriculum. He had impressed himself, actually, taking readily to the sport, quickly grasping the concepts and movements. He'd noticed the similarities to judo on his third or fourth ascent of the wall: Hang on tight, befriend gravity, move with economy. Be creative. Adapt. Relax.

The lesson had also been a nice reprieve from his frustration. Another twenty-four hours, and still no movement at all with the Yeager/Percival case. Adam's still in his coma; the professor and his sister are still MIA. Even the girlfriend, who has been speaking to every reporter in the Bay Area for days, has gone quiet. He continues to pore over the memory of his conversation with Peoria, there on her stoop. Her implication that Lenore is simply a precocious *curandera* failed to account for a few too many factors: the produce-section raid, the assault. The coma. The fact that she's a suburban kid in the Bay Area, rather than a *tía* in Sonora. Was Peoria trying to divert him? Something would arise. These were not the type of people who could simply vanish. In the meantime, he had plenty of other cases to occupy his time. Mules and *sicarios* running all manner of poison up through Bakersfield and Fresno. He had cartel activity to investigate, so why had he been spending all this time on a runaway teenager with no known connection to any controlled substances? He'd have to think about that some other time.

Beyond the break from his cases, the climbing lesson brought him other diversions as well. He hadn't been expecting to feel quite so drawn to Nicole, and it's with a touch of discomfort that he hears himself being uncharacteristically witty and charming. His jokes are landing. She's at ease and engaged. It's unsettling.

Vasco reaches down and pulls off his own shoes, liberating his foot bones. "Honestly, the hardest part was getting my feet in these things," he says. "I think I'll be ready for ballet next."

"That would be a sight," she says. "Let me see your hands."

"My hands?"

"Those things," she says, pointing.

He hesitates but then lifts his hands into the air between them. She seizes the closer of the two and makes an inspection of his fingers, handling them as if looking for defects.

"The other one," she says, and he swaps, twisting a few degrees to present it, wondering. She repeats the inspection and then releases him, turning her attention to reconfiguring her ponytail. Vasco is left feeling simultaneously relieved and disappointed that he has run out of hands. "No blisters, even," she says. "I get these office workers in here with their fingertips falling off. I take it you don't have a desk job."

"I have a desk, sort of," he says, lamely, but alarm bells are going off with this shift in conversation. He has to steer it elsewhere. "So how long before I'm as good as you are?" he asks, pointing back up at the wall.

She laughs. "Take a look at me. What do you see?"

He weighs flirtatious responses, and then decides on safety. "My rock-climbing instructor?"

"Long limbs and a light core. Now take a look at yourself. What do you see?"

Vasco smiles. "The opposite."

"Right," she says, returning his smile. "So never. Not even if you get yourself a fabulous climbing instructor. Which you already have."

She stuffs her climbing shoes into her bag and slips on her flip-flops and then there is no further reason for them to be sitting together on the bench. It's time for somebody to mention a next time. Instead of volunteering, Vasco reaches into his bag and pulls out his phone. There is a single text from Garza: *Call now. Lopez and Ochoa.* They had been working for months to uncover a suspected connection between the Salvadoran minister and the Stockton businessman. This could be the breakthrough they'd been waiting for.

"I have to run," Vasco tells Nicole. "Work stuff."

"Back to your sort-of desk for the afternoon?"

"More or less. Thanks so much for the lesson." She nods. Her smile does not quite reach her eyes. "Can I call you?" he hears himself saying.

"Of course," she says.

He nods and hurries away, dialing.

Chapter 43

think the waitress might be asking if I'm okay. Her body is shaped like an *S*, her hip curving one way and her head the other. They have her and the others wearing light-blue aprons with frills, white shirts underneath. Her nametag says Diana. We were in the middle of ordering dinner when I realized that I didn't know where we are, and then I tried to remember where we were last night, and I couldn't, and that threw me off even more.

"Sorry?" I say.

"I hope you don't mind me saying it but you don't look so great," she says. Her eyes dart from Forrest to Preston and back to me. "Are you feeling okay, young lady?"

"She's just been having trouble sleeping," Preston says. Mumbling.

"Is that so?" She gives him a sideways look.

I'm seeing myself through her eyes now, and I look exhausted. But we can't have a scene. I have to say something. "It's finals. They're kicking my butt." It seems like the sort of thing a normal teenager would say.

"Finals?" Diana asks. The *S* of her body tightens a bit. *S* for skeptical. She gives Forrest and Preston another glance.

"Mr. Hoffman is the worst," I say, looking her in the eyes. I don't have a teacher named Mr. Hoffman. I did in middle school, and he was the best. But Diana's S looks a little looser now. "I'm worried I'm going to fail mythology," I say, though I don't even know if Berkeley High offers that. But her name is Diana, so why not? "Aren't you one of those goddesses?"

She smiles. "Something like that," she says, and at least we're not talking about me anymore. "You sure a side salad is all you need, hon? You look like you can use some fries, or maybe a shake."

"Great idea. Both. With some ranch dressing, please. A chocolate shake." They both sound much too heavy, but the situation seems to call for them. Diana scribbles in her pad, nodding, satisfied, and walks away.

"Where are we again?" I whisper to them.

"Modesto," Forrest says. "We still have hours to go."

I don't know where we'll be after all those hours, but it doesn't much matter. I'm not really sure where Modesto is, either, but that also doesn't matter.

"Where's everybody else?"

"We'll meet them later. Oh, that reminds me. Emilio asked me to ask you if he could take some photos of the notebook pages."

"Photos? Why does he want them?"

Forrest shrugs. "Just interested I guess."

"I don't get why."

"Say no then."

When Diana comes back with the food I give her a big smile but the one she returns to me is tight and flat. She sets my dishes on the table and I'm struck by the sight of my milkshake. There's a little plastic tube in it. I know how to use it. I've used them millions of times. But I can't remember what they're called. Through the window a stripe of orange sits across the bottom of the sky. I take a bite of my salad and try to remember if it's sunrise or sunset.

Chapter 44

F our days to go and Peoria is nearly ready. There are a few spots she still has to work out—rhythms askew in the Granados, a lump in the de Falla, and, as always, Albéniz's challenges. It'll all come together, though. It's time for her to start letting go of it, to give it a little time to move from her mind and into her bone marrow, which is where it has to be if she is to perform it correctly. She needed to get away from her piano for a while so she has come to the ocean to plant her bare feet in the cold sand. The seaward edge of Point Reyes sweeps into the Pacific like the curve of a giant question mark, and today there is a bank of fog pressing upon the coast so thick that she'd needed to walk down to within ten feet of the waterline before she could see the waves. The last mile of the drive had been a little precarious, but after having driven ninety minutes to get here, she wasn't going to turn back. She'd slowed to a few miles an hour and felt her way into the parking lot, where the gray shapes of a half-dozen other cars huddled, drained of their colors. After pulling a heavy woolen shawl over her head and shoulders and kicking off her sandals, she'd climbed the bunchgrass-covered dunes. At the top the sound of the waves enveloped her and she dropped the shawl from her head to free her ears. The fog closed in, damp and swirling, and by the time she reached the water's edge and turned to walk along it, beads of water had begun to form on the looser strands of her black hair.

Now as she walks she can see only fifteen or twenty feet in any direction. Waves roll in from an unseen ocean, crash just beyond the reach of her eyes, and send flat aprons of water briefly sliding across the bottom of the little dome that travels with her up the coast. She has no idea where the drivers of the other cars might be—she could come across one at any time, hidden in the fog, but with miles of shoreline stretching in either direction, it's more likely that they are elsewhere, cocooned in their own little domes. Above her gulls cry out, looking for one another, and occasionally one or two circle near enough for her to see them. A phalanx of wide dark shapes appear briefly in the mist, directly overhead, their passage like a shudder. Pelicans, she figures. Coils of giant kelp briefly darken against the lighter sand as she passes, and then fade into white again behind her.

With her feet in the sand, her mind can slow down. It can stop tumbling all over itself, like it normally does when she isn't trying to find her way through a piece of music. The repetitious thoughts get a little quieter, a little less assertive. Spaces open. She walks for whole minutes thinking of nothing but the way the grains of sand compress and tighten and then shift with each of her steps.

The elk appear directly in front of her, and Peoria stops. There are two of them: a mother and a calf about half her size, whose side still shows a spray of white flecks. They're watching her with turned heads but their bodies face the sea, as if they'd been studying the waves before she had burst in on them. Unmoving, they regard her with steady gazes, their eyes black and shining in the dimness. A thick swirl of fog briefly envelops them, obscuring their faces, and just then, Peoria remembers that she had dreamed of her grandmother's flute that morning.

It had been hidden away in its secret pocket in Maria's skirts, but Peoria had known how to reach down and through its folds to find the small cloth-wrapped bundle. She'd unwrapped it, but still could not remember its music. She had awakened then.

"Do you remember my grandmother's song?" she asks the elk. Her words sound strange, cushioned in all that fog. "They called her *la urraca*. The Magpie."

She and the elk continue to watch each other, motionless, while all around them the water washes across the land and churns through the air. After a minute the mother lets out a puff of air and together, the two of them turn and walk away, immediately vanishing.

Chapter 45

Replenished on food, water, and sleep, Leo reloads the grocery bag with food and water and heads into the woods in the direction the condor had flown the day before. The hill slopes gently downward for a half-mile and meets a creek, wider and swifter than the one he'd found on his last expedition. The waters tumble through a wide, shallow valley that affords him flat ground, and he follows the creek down the mountain. In places the valley narrows or steepens but the land continues to provide easy pathways, cushioned with a layer of fir and pine needles. He knows the statistics are against him coming across the condor again—they can have huge territories, flying hundreds of miles in a day. But his gut tells him it's around. Shasta is an ideal habitat—trees for roosting, caves for nesting. Water year-round. The whole state was part of their historical home, after all. In an era not too far back, their range had stretched from Canada to Mexico.

Leo descends for an hour or so and then the sound of children's voices comes to him. He freezes and then darts into a stand of firs. With his heartbeat echoing in his ears he tiptoes through the trunks until he can just see through their boughs to a lawn, where a pair of girls are playing on a swing set in their backyard.

Neighbors! It isn't as if he can come borrow a cup of sugar, but their presence is a solace, a reminder that he still belongs to the world. Are there other homes here? He backtracks up the creek and then climbs out of the valley, walking a wide semicircle around the property's perimeter through gentle hills, scanning all the while for homes below. The woods thicken as the land flattens out and he slips into their cover, breathing quietly, listening. Before long he finds a dirt road running through the forest, and he falls into a course parallel to the road, far enough away that he can hide behind a tree if a car appears. After a few hundred yards he comes upon an intersection—there is another dirt road cutting across his path, with a cluster of weathered mailboxes at their junction.

Keeping hidden, his ears straining for the sound of an approaching engine, he approaches the intersection, drawn to this small outcropping of humanity. When he's convinced he's alone he steps out of the woods and walks down the line of mailboxes. They're a mish-mash of shapes and sizes and ages, some bolted firmly in place and others barely clinging to their perches.

Drawing in front of them he thrills to discover that each is labeled with its owner's name, and he walks slowly down the line, reading: Harris, Jorgenson, Blankenship, Camallo, Silva, and then, improbably, Percival. Leo halts, transfixed. The mailbox to which his family's name is affixed is new, the classic metal design, and small. After a glance in either direction Leo pulls its door open to find a small stack of letters, with a postcard on top, which he pulls into the light. It's a tropical scene, a wide beach with palm trees. He flips it over and finds that it is addressed to "La familia Percival." He scans the text, registering only a couple of keywords: snorkeling, ceviche, hangover. Who could these Percivals be? Parents, children, young, old? Two brothers and a sister, perhaps.

In his mind he is transported back to another home on another mountainside, in another time, when they all lived together, the five of them, he and Gabriel tumbling through the hallways amid clouds of muffled piano music, Lenore toddling after them. He wonders who is in that home now. Perhaps Lenore has returned. Gabriel? Standing in the dusty roadway now with the sun pressing down on him, cut off from everyone and only a slight idea of where he is, he struggles again to discern the continuity between the life that was and the life that is. When would they find themselves together again, beneath that roof?

The distant growl of a truck engine pierces his reverie and Leo shoves the postcard back in the box, slams the door shut, and runs back into the woods. He climbs up the mountain the way he'd come, still thinking about these Percivals. Perhaps they're the family with the swing set and two daughters who play on their patch of lawn on the precipice of this vast wilderness. He wonders if they know about the abandoned house a few miles up the slope, in a wide clearing which the plant life is slowly reclaiming.

Leo climbs up the creek bed and hikes back through the sloping forest toward the cabin, where the sight of the open door stops him in his tracks. Had he left it standing open? But then he sees that the angles don't look right. There are lines and spaces where there shouldn't be and then his brain registers the explanation. The door has been smashed in. His first thoughts are of the police, but he quickly discards that—the clearing is empty of cars. It's someone on foot, someone big enough to smash through a door, like an NFL lineman. No, that's absurd; how could—

The big round brown head appears in the doorway, sniffs the air, and turns her gaze directly to Leo. There's no alarm, no concern on the bear's face. She looks perfectly content, in fact, so at least Leo hasn't wandered between her and her cubs. With a hammering heart,

172

he stoops and collects several stones the size of golf balls, all the while watching the bear, and then he retreats back into the cover of the trees.

He waits. The bear takes a slow step forward, and then another, half-emerging from the cabin as if to assert her dominion over both interior and exterior. Her claws curl over the top step. It isn't the first time Leo has come in contact with a bear. He's had encounters with them, usually from afar, and in passing—a glimpse through trees, a crash in the undergrowth, a shape on a distant hillside, wary but calm. This is as close as he's ever gotten, and it's the largest one he's ever seen. Black bears can run thirty miles an hour and climb trees—if she decides she really wants to come see what he's up to, his stone-throwing will be laughable. There's nothing for him to do but wait.

The bear sniffs the air again, lets out a big yawn, shakes her head as if clearing it, and then trots down the wooden stairway, which groans and splinters under the weight. At the bottom of the stairs she makes a sharp turn and heads for the opposite end of the clearing, throwing one last glance Leo's way as if to make sure he isn't giving chase, and lumbers away.

Leo enters the house to find his cache of food has been decimated. The floor is a chaos of masticated packaging, cracker crumbs, smashed fruit, and half-inch curls of dried ramen noodles. The last couple inches of a salami sits among the mess—Leo picks it up, brushes some crumbs from it, and returns it to the counter, feeling suddenly light-headed. He drops to a knee and collects from out of the jumble several nuts, some apples, a few slices of stepped-on bread. Content with easy plastic-wrapped calories, the intruder had left the cans of soup and corn alone, fortunately. But eighty percent of his supply is gone. He'll run out of food long before Yvette thinks he will.

Has he ever been truly hungry? There had been times in the course of his fieldwork when he'd skipped a meal or two, or had to settle for scanty rations, but he'd never had to worry about running out.

What would he do? He salvages everything he can and arranges it all across the counter, the extent of his vulnerability sinking deep into his stomach. Bears are smart. They remember things, and that one would get hungry again, and there's no longer a front door. "Fuck," he says, under his breath, surveying his paltry stores. He'll have to figure out how to hang them from a high branch. A wave of dizziness washes over him and he plants his hands on the counter. His cache of water, fortunately, avoided the bear's rampage, and he pulls a bottle from the case, unscrews the cap, and chugs half of it. He needs to lie down a bit—he'll head upstairs, maybe escape into a book and rest a little while, and let himself figure all this out later. He grabs a paperback at random from the stack and climbs up the stairs. Right at the top of the stairway, perfectly centered like a museum piece on a pedestal, sits a giant seed-flecked turd. Nausea churns through his gut.

In the bedroom he discovers the bear's second crime scene. The mattress is shredded. Its previous form is unrecognizable; it's now a pile of tattered cloth and stuffing, much of it wet. Springs protrude comically from the mess, setting off cartoonish *boing* sounds in his mind. A pile of batting sits in the corner like a snowdrift. A breeze picks up and pushes through the window. Bits of cotton and thread swirl and drift across the floor. The sharp scent of urine rises out of the destruction.

Leo turns and leaves the room, steps back over the mound of shit, descends the stairs, and sits down on the top step, just outside the shattered front door. He hurls the book hard; it flies through the sunlight and collapses to the gravel like a gunned-down duck. He stares at the crumpled form for a long time.

Chapter 46

Gabriel, Watson, Naomi, and Serena lie on the roof, on their backs, their heads at the hub of the cross their bodies make, each lying along one of the compass's ordinal directions. Naomi had insisted upon the arrangement. Gabriel picked southwest. To his right the last of the light is diving for the horizon, an orange smear. Directly above their faces is an orderly line, four points of light, stars like sentries guarding the boundary between day and night.

"I think I'll head onward tomorrow," he says. He's given it two more days beyond his unplanned stop in Anaheim—two more day-long circuits around the metro area, scanning and listening, to no avail. He'd had no luck finding any clues that might point to Lenore, but there had been small amusements: a cup of coffee so rich he could taste it in his scalp; an overheard job interview in a café between a pornography producer and an aspiring actor, an appreciation for that moment in the late afternoon each day when the sun loses its intensity and it goes from being too hot to perfectly comfortable.

Naomi is the first to speak after Gabriel announces his impending departure. "We'll have to revert to a triangular configuration," she says, from her spot in the northwest.

In the southeast Serena stirs. Around them are scattered wine cups, a box of crackers, three cheeses on a warped wooden cutting board, a wooden pipe, and a tin of weed and matches. A thrum of music seeps up through the rooftop, bass-heavy and repetitive.

"Where will you go?" Watson asks, from the northeast.

"I sort of like the way I'm pointing," he says.

"Into the ocean, then," Serena says.

"He's right," Watson says. "It's evolution. We shall follow the dolphins, and feast upon whatever fishes are left when the ice caps melt. It's the only way to survive."

"Tell me more, honey," Naomi says, the tone of her voice like a kindergarten teacher's, though she must be six or seven years younger than he is. "Your sister?"

"Maybe I need to put my back into the corner of the country," Gabriel says. "That way, I'll know she's in front of me."

Nobody speaks for a time. The traffic churns past, relentless and monotonous. The setting sun drags more light out of the sky; stars push forward now, singularly or in pairs.

"We ought to have a toast, then," Watson says, at length.

Naomi lifts her cup. From Gabriel's viewpoint it looks as though she is reaching into the sky to gather in the stars. *"Que su guía aparece,"* she says.

"What's that?" Gabriel asks.

"She wants extra guacamole," Serena says.

"It's a toast from her family," Watson says.

Serena pushes herself to her feet. "The southeast is rising, by the way," she says, "but it will be back in a couple of minutes."

He feels the vibrations of her footfalls in his backbone as she walks back over to the fire escape. She steps over the edge, and the steel whines against its anchors as it gathers her weight.

"She's okay, I think," Naomi says, after a minute, addressing the sky.

"Serena?" Watson asks. "That's debatable."

"I mean Lenore. His sister. She's somewhere safe, I feel, and the people she's with are caring for her."

"I hope so," Gabriel says.

"You should continue hoping," she says. "It always helps."

There is the squeak of metal again and Serena calls from the edge of the roof. "Come here, Watson. I want you."

He sighs. "We are always being summoned," he says. But he rises and goes to her.

"I don't think you'll find her for a while," Naomi says. She has turned her head toward him; her mouth is only a few inches from his ear and he can feel her breath on his temple. "I'm sorry to have to tell you that."

"Okay," Gabriel says, to what he isn't sure.

The others reappear, looming over them. Serena is holding the banjo. She places it on Gabriel's stomach. "To keep you company on your travels," she says, and then she and Watson resume their positions, completing the eastern half of their compass rose.

Part II: Splay

Chapter 47

The train is new and clean and glides easily through the morning, carrying commuters out of the heart of Los Angeles and through the changing faces of its southern expanses: suburbs, industrial zones, beach towns, and ocean. Gabriel has a window seat; next to him a twentysomething in a suit sits with a huge pair of headphones, playing a game on a laptop in which tanks stalk one another within a wooded landscape. His username appears in the corner: RommelMcDonald. In the pair of facing seats sit a young mother and a daughter of about ten, both of them snoozing. The younger wears a woven necklace with beads that spell out the name Anastasia. Her mother is unlabeled.

Gabriel is heading for San Diego. There's a park there—he has seen it on maps and in pictures. It's called Friendship Park, and its defining feature is a tall steel fence that runs right down the US-Mexican border and into the sea. When Gabriel gets there he'll walk down to where the fence intersects with the shoreline, and then he'll turn around so that the whole expanse of the lower forty-eight will fit into the center of his field of vision, and then, when he takes his first step, he'll know he's heading toward Lenore. He'll fix that feeling in his bones, and he'll keep moving.

The train rumbles into a suburb; on both sides low sound walls separate the tracks from the backyards of large pastel-colored stucco homes. He wonders which side of the tracks is the wrong side. When the sight of the houses becomes monotonous he returns his attention to the train's interior, where he finds that Anastasia is looking at him. He smiles and nods at her. She nods back without smiling, her eyes steady. Her mother continues sleeping.

"Do you have a penny?" Anastasia asks. Her voice is low, slightly hoarse.

He does. He still likes to use cash for small purchases. Gabriel digs in his pocket, finds one, and sets it in her open palm.

"Watch," she says. She closes her fingers around it and holds the resulting fist in the air between them, rotating it back and forth, as if showing Gabriel the punch he is about to receive. Her eyes remain locked on his. She uncurls her fingers and reveals instead of the penny a tiny key. Its appearance is such a shock that Gabriel flinches. He looks to RommelMcDonald for help, but his neighbor is hurriedly tapping out messages in a chat window as his tank rumbles on autopilot through a grove of pixelated pine trees.

Anastasia extends the key and Gabriel accepts it, studying it as if it might reveal its origins.

"Another one?" Anastasia asks.

Gabriel, having purchased coffee, a magazine, and a bottle of water, all from different vendors, is grateful to have a pocketful of change. He hands her another penny.

"You're watching?" she asks.

"Yes."

"Carefully?"

He nods. The hand closes, rises, rotates, and opens, and she hands him a tiny plastic horse.

"Do you see?" she asks.

"No. That's amazing."

"Not really. Another one?"

The penny disappears into her fist, rises. "You have to do a better job," she says. "Tell me when."

"When what?"

"When you're ready to do a better job."

He scans the area around her, searches her mother's sleeping figure, the air conditioning nozzle and the lamp aiming down toward her from the ceiling. Ice-plant-covered hills slide by outside. He studies her face—the freckled patches at her temples, a tiny cleft in her chin, her tangle of black hair, her pale blue eyes which do not blink or waver. "Okay," he says.

She opens her hand; in the center of her palm sits a tiny metal shoe.

"Do you see?" she asks.

He shakes his head and hands her a nickel. She produces a small purple die, and then a pink rubber ball, a plastic coat button, a glass unicorn, and a small eraser with a picture of a pot of gold on it, all of which she places into Gabriel's bowled hands.

Anastasia's mother stirs, shifts in her seat, and opens her eyes. She checks on her daughter, who pretends she has been looking out the window. "You okay, Annie?" she asks. Anastasia nods without shifting her gaze. Her mother reaches out, gives her arm a little squeeze, and lets go.

She glances over at Gabriel and notices the trinkets in his cupped hands. Gabriel is not certain but perhaps her eyes widen a fraction, and perhaps she goes still. It is hard to tell; she was already sitting still. Her eyes meet his and he nods, but she does not reciprocate. Perhaps she didn't see his greeting—she is looking at the collection again. He has the sense he's doing something wrong, that he's holding two handfuls of contraband, but he'll wait and see. A fireball erupts on RommelMcDonald's laptop screen and he punches one hand into the other—whether in frustration or victory, Gabriel cannot tell. Anastasia's mother shuts her eyes and sags back into the seat. Her breathing settles and slows and after a few minutes Anastasia returns her attention to Gabriel.

"Do you want to know how I did it?" she asks.

Gabriel glances down at the assortment. "I thought magicians weren't supposed to give away their secrets."

"I'm not a magician, and I didn't say I was going to tell you."

"You just asked me if I wanted to know."

"Yes. I want to know if you're the type of person who would want to know or the type of person who wouldn't."

"Are you the type of magician who would tell?"

"I told you, I'm not a magician. And I asked first."

"I guess it would depend on the situation."

Anastasia opens her hands, palms up. "This is the situation."

"Then no. I don't want to know." Does his restraint please her? He can't read her change of expression. She folds her hands in her lap.

They have entered the outskirts of an approaching town. A liquor store, a surf shop, and a bar & grill form a loose gathering around a quiet intersection. Broad gravel shoulders instead of sidewalks line the roads. At a gas station a woman is pumping fuel into a battered SUV with plastic and duct tape where its rear window is supposed to be.

"What are you going to do with those?" Anastasia asks, pointing to the contents of his hands.

"What do people usually do with them?"

"I don't know."

"Maybe I'll give them to my sister."

She shrugs. Outside the town comes together—its buildings fall into line; pedestrians traverse paved sidewalks. "We're getting out here," Anastasia says, her eyes back on the scenery. "Do you know where we are?"

"No."

"Escondido. It means 'hidden,' or 'secret.' What do you think about that?"

"Is it hidden?"

"Did you know about it before?"

"No."

"Then I guess it is. Where do you live?" she asks.

"Berkeley."

"What does that mean?"

"I'm not sure. I think it was some guy."

"You should find out. Names matter."

"You're right, I should." He takes the trinkets and drops them into his backpack. "Can I ask you a favor? Can you help this banjo find a new owner?"

She looks at the banjo and then back at him. "Sure."

"Thanks." He passes it over and she settles it on her lap and then plucks each of the strings slowly, listening.

The train lurches and decelerates. Anastasia nudges her mother, who stirs and straightens. She covers a yawn with her hands and then her eyes flick open to find the banjo on her daughter's lap.

"Whose is that?" she asks, sitting up straighter.

"I don't know yet," Anastasia says.

Her mother turns to Gabriel. "This isn't yours?"

"No, ma'am."

"Well, it should go to lost and found, then," she says to Anastasia.

"Nobody lost it, ma'am," Gabriel says. He nods at Anastasia. "She offered to help."

The train continues to slow. Outside the village has formed itself around them. The station draws them in.

"Did I ever tell you that your dad played banjo?"

"Yes," Anastasia says. "But you can tell me again."

Together they regard the instrument in silence, different versions of the same thought visible on their faces. The train stops and they rise and nod to Gabriel in synchrony. "Have a blessed day," the mother says, and then they turn and depart.

It isn't much farther to downtown San Diego, the train's terminus, and over the loudspeaker the conductor reminds the passengers they must all disembark. Gabriel wonders whom this announcement is for—are there passengers who bought tickets for San Diego, while privately hoping the train had some farther, secret destination? He himself is happy for the finality—it's one fewer option he has to consider.

Outside the station the streets are quiet in the late-morning lull between rush hour and lunch. Gabriel has never been here before but it's strangely familiar, as if it's the setting for some recurring dream. He walks, heading west, waiting for the sense of recognition to fade out, but the landmarks continue to fall into place where he expects them: a small park, the waterfront, wide piers, a ferry terminal. And then looming before him is the USS *Midway*, an aircraft carrier-turned-museum, and Gabriel remembers Martín, and laughs.

They had only been cellmates for a few months, but the San Diego native was Gabriel's favorite—always smiling, always buoyant, a bit of light amid the tedium. Martín had been an automotive connoisseur with a particular fondness for German engineering. A storyteller, he described the feeling of careening in a stolen Porsche through the canyons and foothills that lay east of his city with such detail and emotion that he seemed more artist than felon. Martín didn't care about money—he could have made suitcases of it from the city's chop shops but he chose instead to drive his stolen property for a few hours and then abandon it on the edge of the city somewhere, minus a few stripes of paint. He'd been caught at a gas station, pumping air into the tires of an M5 he'd stolen with a fob swiped out of a valet stand. "I finally scored an M," he'd explained to Gabriel, "and the *cabrón* didn't even know how to take care of it. He should be the one in this cell!"

When he wasn't talking about his joyrides he talked about the San Diego waterfront and the restaurant his family owned, which sat two blocks southeast of the *Midway*. In prison he'd had stacks of photos which he augmented with detailed descriptions, repeatedly, like an evangelical promising the hereafter. Now as Gabriel continues southward along the waterfront he finds that Martín's presentations had been complete and accurate, and he walks to Celia's, Martín's family's restaurant, as if he's been there a dozen times before.

He approaches to find a woman about his age opening the door for lunch. A single black clip keeps her short hair out of her face. As he passes she nods at him with only the smallest flicker of a welcome in her eyes, which are framed by thick eyeliner. It's a nice place—clean white stucco walls accented with grids of Talavera tiles, dark wooden furniture, a full bar, nice lighting. Behind the bar is a framed antique photo of a dozen *bandidos* in giant sombreros, bristling with revolvers, posing in front of a train. *Corridos* are playing over a sound system, but not too loudly. Gabriel can hear sounds coming from the back, but nobody else is visible until the woman from the front door overtakes him and circles around to her spot behind the hostess stand.

"One?" she says, picking up a menu.

Gabriel nods. "Also, I'm looking for Martín?"

She puts the menu down. "And why's that?"

"I'm an old friend of his."

She folds her hands atop the stack of menus. "He has a lot of old friends." Her voice is flat, her face unreadable while she waits for his response.

"He's a likeable guy," Gabriel says, at length. "I'm not surprised."

"And most of them are *pendejos*." No vehemence, no smile. She looks bored.

"I don't represent the *pendejos*. I'm just here for the tamales. Martín told me all about them."

"Yeah? When was this?"

"We used to be roommates. Up in Marin."

"Martín's never lived . . . oh." She reaches up, adjusts her clip, and returns her hand to the stack.

"You must be Isabella," he says.

She looks away, to a point over his shoulder, considering responses. None of them prove quite adequate, though, and she turns suddenly and darts away, shoving through a swinging door. Over the stereo a horn section comes to a crescendo, drops off, and gives way to a warbly alto. Voices rise in the kitchen, and then Martín bursts through the swinging door, a grin stretching from one side of his face to the other. He claps twice and throws his arms open. "Percy! You remembered!" He's grown a mustache, which bends comically downward around the corners of his mouth and disappears somewhere under his chin. His hug smells like *masa* and onions.

He points to a generously upholstered stool at the bar and circles around to the other side. "I ain't even going to talk to you yet," he says, pulling a bottle from a knee-high shelf in the refrigerator. He pops the cap and sets the Modelo down in front of Gabriel. "Lunch first." He heads back to the kitchen.

The beer is sharp and clear and cold. A cluster of people has appeared at the hostess stand and Martín's sister is at work, ushering them to their tables. She is only slightly more welcoming to the other patrons than she was to Gabriel. There's an animated conversation in the kitchen, broken by frequent laughter. Car doors slam in the parking lot; the glare of the midday sun dims as more customers fill the doorway. Gabriel takes another sip and then Martín re-emerges with a huge tray and proceeds to unload dish after dish. When the tray is empty he pulls a bottle of hot sauce from his pocket and adds it to the array.

"Welcome to Celia's, my man," he says, laughing at Gabriel's wide eyes.

"This is one of your dishes?"

"Nah, homie. It's all our dishes! A little bit of everything." He places another open beer on the counter, though Gabriel is only two sips into his first, and then he points to each of the items, quickly naming them. On the menu is some of every Mexican dish Gabriel has ever heard of, and several he hasn't. "Pace yourself, okay?" he says. "I gotta go do some shit, but don't go nowhere till I come back out." Gabriel lifts his fork and bends his head, surveying the spread like a determined general over a map of enemy territory.

The restaurant fills for lunch; a happy clamor rises. Servers and bussers whirl around the restaurant, carrying out their tasks with practiced efficiency. They trade jokes, communicate with glances and gestures, navigate crowded spaces with the selflessness of honeybees. They are their own nation; behind the food and décor and customer interactions there is a language, a culture. Gabriel envies them their effortless coexistence, their superstructure. He thinks about his own father, working at his desk with his pads of graph paper, and his mother at her piano with her endless charts. Each of them immersed in their own world. Leonardo and Lenore could be anywhere on the planet right now. He takes out his phone to reach out with texts but he'd neglected to plug it in the night before and it's dead again. He tells himself to remember to check in later.

Martín emerges from the kitchen and points a finger at Gabriel. "What you need, *hermano*? More tortillas?"

"Another stomach?"

"You try those enchiladas yet?"

189

Gabriel nods.

"Good. You ain't even got to say how good it is because I already know. Hey, what are you doing down here anyway?" But there is a crash in the kitchen and Martín is gone and Gabriel's attention returns to his plate and the restaurant's heartbeat.

But isn't he here because of his family, too? Wasn't his pathway to this place as determined by his sister's actions as Isabella's sidestep is, when she has to navigate around a cousin behind the bar? After all, the same quantitative logic governs both his parents' concerns, with their sheets and their symbols and their codes, manipulating matter and proportion, seeking elegance and grace. Maybe on some unseen level there is an equally deterministic system governing the migrations of his own family. Perhaps it is just a matter of distance, of scale. If Martín and his family are molecules, bouncing and colliding, always seeking stasis, then Gabriel and his family are their own solar system, their movements and gravity invisible but every bit as interlocked, asserting their influence over one another across distances more celestial than atomic. The music of the spheres.

A half-hour later Gabriel is picking through the last bites of his food, sipping occasionally on the second beer. There is a lull in the lunch rush and Martín re-emerges from the kitchen, his chef's tunic now splattered, sweat on his brow. He grabs his own Modelo from a cooler, pops the cap off, and touches it to the neck of Gabriel's bottle. "To motherfucking freedom," he says.

"And to Celia's," Gabriel adds, hoisting the glass. "I can see how torturous that chow hall must have been."

"Fucking-a, *carnal*." The men drink. Isabella emerges from the doorway with a rack of clean bar glasses and goes to work wiping them down and replenishing the shelves. "Never again," says Martín, after gulping half the bottle down. "I don't hardly ever steal cars anymore," he says. "Just when they deserve it."

Isabella shakes her head.

Martín ignores her. "Like if I find a Ferrari? I'm gonna redistribute that shit. It's political resistance. For *la raza*."

"Joyriding isn't redistribution, *tonto*."

"Bullshit. I redistribute it to myself for a while. I'm starting a charity. 1-877-Cars for *Cholos*." He slaps the bar and then offers his bottle for another clink, a toast to his own joke. "I'm a *pinche* Mexican Robin Hood."

She shakes her head. "You're a Mexican dumbass."

"Love you too, sis," he says, toasting her. He turns back to Gabriel. "So what brings you to San Diego, homey?"

"Friendship Park."

Isabella fumbles a slippery glass; it caroms off the edge of a counter and bounces to the floor, where a thick rubber mat prevents it from shattering. Martín raises an eyebrow and turns back to Gabriel. "What do you want with that place? If you want to lay eyes on the motherland, they'll just let you right into Tijuana, you know."

"The motherland?" Isabella asks, her hand on her hip, the dropped glass forgotten.

Martín chuckles. "She thinks you're *puro gringo*, homey. Tell her! She might like you more."

Isabella rolls her eyes, but he has her attention now.

"My mom's Mexican," Gabriel says. "My grandpa is from Sonora. He used to live down here, somewhere out in the desert."

"See? Only half-gringo," Martín says. "Maybe he likes his sugar brown, just like his old man."

"It doesn't matter what he is," Isabella says. And then to Gabriel: "Why do you want to go to Friendship Park?"

"It's kind of a long story."

"Most of them are. You want to know about the border? That's why you came here? Not the zoo, not the beach, not that stupid costume party? Not because my brother owes you money or some shit?"

"Costume party?"

"She's talking about Comic-Con," says Martín. "It's not even time for that, anyway."

"Let him answer," Isabella says.

"Chill out," Martín says. "I wasn't stopping him."

"Do you want to learn about the border or what?"

This is no longer mere conversation; it's an offer, maybe even a challenge. When he had first planned to come this way he'd been thinking of the border as a boundary, a line separating his world from a different one. But in Isabella's pointed question that line takes on its own vitality, giving sudden life to everything beyond it, and Gabriel sees now that he has arrived not at an edge but at the center of something. In this growing realization he can sense Lenore. Why? Isabella waits for his response, her eyes narrow and her hand on her hip. She's someone's little sister, too. Maybe she knows about these things.

Gabriel nods. "Yes, I do."

"Meet me here at eleven tonight, then."

Gabriel's eyes flick to Martín's, who shrugs and grins. "Hey man, I wasn't going to be able to hang with you anyway. I've got a date with this girl I've been trying to hook up with for months, and I'm not breaking that for nothing. I'm off tomorrow though!"

Gabriel turns back to Isabella. "Okay. Eleven o'clock, then."

"Try to get some sleep this afternoon," she says, eyeing the wreckage of empty plates before him. She turns and heads back for the kitchen.

"Dessert, *cabrón*. I'll be right back," Martín says, following her.

Chapter 48

Leonardo rises, trying to discard the dream that has held him, submerged and spinning, the way an alligator kills its prey. He plants his feet on the floor and sits on the edge of the couch and though the spinning slows it does not stop completely. He stands and stretches but the floor feels uneven and slanted, a phenomenon he attributes to a cramped night on the lumpy, too-small couch. He plants his feet wide, as if on a ship's deck, and takes deep breaths while stretching his arms up and then out to his sides. The dregs of his dream and his sleep fall away. The room settles around him and the previous day's events come back: the discovery of the neighborhood down the hill, the bear's incursion, and his forty-five-minute struggle to drag the couch up the stairs and into the bedroom, whose intact door would at least protect him from marauding skunks and raccoons. He steps toward the window to check on his food, which is now hanging from a high cedar branch at the edge of the clearing, but he stubs his toe on a rock and yells out. He'd made a pile of them, fist-sized stones, two dozen of them, as a last line of defense if the bear decided to come back upstairs again.

He flexes the injured toe, stretches it against the floor, and continues on his way across the room. His bag of food looks unmolested.

After dragging the couch up the stairs he'd spent the rest of his day-light hours knifing the mangled mattress cover to shreds and weaving the strips into a rope. He'd fashioned a spring into a hook and after a dinner of canned chili mixed with canned corn he'd tossed the rope over the branch and hoisted his remaining supplies ten feet into the air, a bit of triumph pushing back against the despair.

The window sill feels like it's tilting now beneath his leaning arms; it is strange that his equilibrium has not come back to him. Light flickers on the edge of his vision, where there are no lights to flicker. He squeezes his eyes shut and presses his fingertips into them; lights and colors flare and flower. His palms are sweating now, and a sudden heat comes over him. The room feels stuffy even though he's standing at the wide-open window, with a morning breeze pushing through. Maybe he just needs some water. He pushes through the bedroom door and heads downstairs, steadying himself with a slick hand heavy on the railing.

Chapter 49

Vasco pauses outside the door to the interrogation room to take a deep breath and check his heart rate. It's a little higher than he'd like, but this is a huge break, the first big opportunity he's had in this whole strange Percival case. He needs to wrestle some solid clues out of this, or else he goes back to sitting and waiting.

He pushes through the door and sits down across from Bryce Sorenson. The UCSD junior has big blue eyes and long, chlorine-tinged surfer-boy blond curls. He's tall, easily six-foot-two, and Vasco imagines the privileged cockiness this kid must carry through his daily life. Instead of flirting with sorority girls or captaining his water polo team, however, Bryce is clad in county-issued blues, and looking like he hasn't been sleeping great.

"Good morning, Bryce," Vasco says. "My name is Francisco." He slides a fat manila folder onto the table and takes a seat. "I appreciate you sharing your time with me here today." Bryce provides a small nod. His eyes flash between Vasco and the file as he tries to figure out what's going on. "How are the days going?"

Bryce is here in the San Diego county jail due to the law-enforcement equivalent of celestial alignment. When the blissed-out, pajama-clad kids had taken to the streets surrounding UC San Diego a couple days back, in a reenactment of the produce raid up in Sonoma County, one patrolman, a certain Officer Salinas, had been on duty in the area. This Officer Salinas, whose teenage daughter's friend had recently been caught with a small amount of molly, had taken a personal interest in the story out of Sonoma State, so when Bryce, who was navigating a suddenly busy sidewalk, had stepped off the curb to circle a parked car, causing a passing delivery truck to veer just slightly, Officer Salinas decided to write him up for jaywalking. An ID check revealed a misdemeanor for driving on a suspended license, a five-day jail sentence, and a failure to appear to his turn-in date. Bryce's name had come across the wire to Vasco, and a few phone calls and a quick flight and here they are, elevated heart rates all around.

"It's okay, I guess," Bryce says.

"Day three now, is it?"

"I think so."

"Already losing track?" Vasco says, with a friendly smile. He raps on the file with his knuckles before Bryce can answer. In the folder is a printout of an Ikea instruction manual for a king-sized bed called "Brimnes." He'd asked one of the department's junior officers to print it for him, because the printer would shuffle the pages and make the fake report look authentic. "So listen," he says. "A conviction can be a real pain in the ass, right? Job applications, background checks, all that. What kind of work are you thinking of going into after college?"

Bryce shrugs. "Maybe business school."

"Yes, good. But then the best jobs are high-profile, and public scrutiny comes. People start digging into records, and things get messy. But listen. You're young, and this is a first-time offense. I can get this off your record, but I need a little bit of help. I have some important questions."

Bryce's eyes widen; his poker face is nonexistent. "What?" he says.

Good, Vasco thinks. This will be easy. "The night you got arrested. You were out with some friends. I need to know about the party."

A ripple of tension reveals some new conflict in Bryce. "I was just hanging out with some friends," he says, failing in his attempt at nonchalance.

"Yeah? How was it?"

"It was fine."

Vasco tilts the file away from Bryce, opens the cover, and flips through the first few pages. "Here's the thing, though," he says. He looks up and makes a show of scrutinizing the student. "You're what, about five-eleven? A hundred and ninety pounds or so?" Deliberately underestimating.

"Six two, two-ten," Bryce says.

"Swimmer?"

"Water polo."

"You're a healthy, strong kid. So for you, yes, maybe you had a good night." Bryce waits. Vasco leans back and flips to the center of the file, which details headboard construction. "Not everybody is built like you, though," he says. "We're pretty worried about kids with . . . lesser constitutions. You know about the kid in the coma?" The cement planter box is an inconvenient detail that needn't enter the story.

Bryce's forehead folds into wrinkles. He shakes his head.

"They didn't mention it?" Vasco says.

He continues shaking, the wrinkles deepening.

"And the girl? How's she holding up?" He closes the folder, sets it back on the table, and leans forward, planting his elbows on the table. There's been nothing solid linking the Percivals to these roaming groups of blissed-out collegiates, but after the coincidences at Sonoma State and the subtext of his short conversation with Peoria that day on her doorstep, he'd be shocked if these were two separate narratives.

A tightening comes across Bryce's face, and Vasco takes that as all the confirmation he needs. He leans in another inch. "She's the subject of a missing-persons investigation in Berkeley. Did you know that? Did they tell you that?"

Bryce doesn't move.

"You know what Megan's Law is, right? The sex offender registry? All the neighbors you'll ever have can search a website and see your face and your address and what you got convicted for. Here, let me show you." Vasco reaches for his phone, but Bryce is shaking his head frantically now.

"It's nothing like that at all, man!" he yells. "That's not . . . it isn't . . . " A bright shade of pink has climbed into his face; he looks somewhere between passing out and crying. He falls back in his chair, his shoulders drooping. "It isn't like that," he says, barely audible.

"Well, good. Her family will be relieved." Bryce nods, his eyes unfocused. Vasco uncaps a pen. "So what's it like, then, Bryce?"

Chapter 50

Far away, the sun drops into the ocean. On the grass in front of me soccer players shout at each other in a different language. I've heard it before but can't think of what it's called. Moms and babies on spread-out blankets. Across the lawn kids shout on the playground. Behind me in a mess of strip malls and gas stations is our motel. It's pink, with noisy air conditioners, but it's nice not having to sleep in the camper again. I took a half-hour shower this morning. It helped a little. Sitting on this bench behind dark sunglasses I could be fast asleep and no one would know. It's hot but now it's getting late in the day and there's an ocean wind. I can taste the salt.

Twelve more last night. The dregs of their stories are still tumbling in my bloodstream. They feel warm and heavy, dense. Like a sweater that's too tight and too hot. Maybe this is just part of it? My grandfather didn't write about this in his notebooks—not the ones he told me to get, at least.

Forrest is jogging on the footpath that winds through the park. Every few minutes he passes, pretending he isn't checking up on me. Somewhere in the city spread out below, the van is parked at a garage, waiting for a new part. They told me what it was but I don't remember. Repeater? Switcher? It doesn't matter. We were supposed to be on the road today, but I'm glad we're not. I need a night off. My head feels foggy. The worlds are getting mixed up. Did we eat dinner yet? I hope so. I need some sleep.

A family arrives and takes up a spot in the grass just across the footpath. A dad and a mom, two brothers with toy trucks, a baby sister in one of those seats with wheels. The boys head for the sandbox and the mom and dad spread out a blanket and get the little girl out. She scans the park on all fours, her face open, searching. Maybe she looks at me or maybe she looks past me. She sees her brothers playing in the dirt. Her whole face smiles and she begins to crawl toward them. Her mother's on her phone. She says something without looking up, and the little girl stops. Right before the edge of the blanket. Go, I want to say to her. Go. I am you and you are me.

Forrest is here again, panting, looking at his watch. His hair streaked with sweat. He sits down. "You good, Lenny?" he asks.

"Yeah. Where are we going next?"

"Berkeley."

"Home?"

"Kind of. Not really. We're not going to be in our own beds, if that's what you mean."

"What about after that?" He holds up a finger and takes a deep breath, and then another. I wait. The baby girl is patting the grass blades; I can feel the prickles on my palms.

"I'm not sure, actually," Forrest says. "There's some disagreement there."

"About what?"

He's staring into the distance, leaning, his elbows planted on his knees. "Going farther. Out of state."

"Fine with me. We were clear up by Oregon. That's farther from home than Reno. And here." She points at the city below them. "Where are we again?"

"San Diego. There are other problems besides distance though. But don't worry about it. We'll get it figured out."

San Diego. My grandfather. The desert. The baby girl is tugging at the grass, as if to drag her brothers back to her. "I need you to take me somewhere in the morning," I say to Forrest.

Chapter 51

I t's a gorgeous Friday night in Hillcrest and the boys are out in droves. The Blue Lotus has been remodeled since Vasco was here last—it was once a small neighborhood restaurant, but it has taken over a boutique next door, added a large bar area, and updated its design. Men crowd the entire length of its horseshoe shape, three deep; five sweating bartenders with tight black t-shirts and impeccable hair work to meet the demand. No more than a dozen women are scattered among the clientele, either at the bar or the tables in the outlying dining room. The lurid murals of temples and old kings are gone, replaced with collages of a vaguely Buddhist bent, epoxied onto what looks like brushed aluminum—the work of a local artist who goes by one name and lists each piece at five grand. Vasco wonders if the dishes will be any more familiar than their surroundings. But can he even trust his memory? He might fail to recognize his own image in a mirror amid the weight of unfamiliarity this day continues to press upon him.

At least his dining companion hasn't changed. Clay Usinger, a friend from their years together as CBP agents, sits across the table sipping beer and watching Vasco, who now pours the bottom third of a tall bottle of Singha into his glass. Clay had suggested they try some new place in the Gaslamp Quarter, with "neo-fusion" cuisine, whatever that is, but Vasco had insisted on visiting The Blue Lotus, hoping his favorite San Diego restaurant would serve as a touchstone of sorts. His interview with Bryce Sorenson had provided him with more than enough novelty for the day.

"So this kid really threw you for a loop, huh?" Clay says, reading Vasco's thoughts.

"It's not what I expected. I mean it is, but also it isn't." A group of men sweep past the table, talking and laughing, trailing aftershave and cheer. One of them—overtanned, silver jewelry, white blazer—catches Vasco's eye and winks.

"Druggie nonsense," Clay says with a shrug. "You must have heard some version of this a couple thousand times by now, right?"

Vasco shakes his head. "I barely deal with the end user. And the drugs themselves barely matter; it's all just merchandise and cargo. My job is supply chains." He drains the rest of his Singha and wonders what his chances are of getting another one anytime soon. "This is something new, though."

"Like a designer cocktail? I hear they're always mixing things up now. Start with some codeine, add a dash of fentanyl, a sprinkle of meth, top it with some whipped ketamine, maraschino molly on top. Or whatever. So what's this one?"

"No, new as in brand new. Some kind of . . . I don't even know what the hell to call it. More of a psychedelic. It's not like anything I've ever come across." Vasco feels like it's his first day on the force—all guesswork and bumbling, shaky conclusions just waiting for someone with more experience to come along and knock them apart and set him straight. Nobody's coming along this time, though. Nobody's heard of this.

"And there's a missing girl?" Clay asks. "What's she got to do with all this?"

"Teenage shaman high priestess, if we are to believe this guy." He thinks back to his conversation with Peoria and her reference to the home-brewed folk medicines they'd grown up with. But those were for congestion, fever. This was very different. What had Bryce called it? *El regreso.* The return. An hour-long voyage beyond words. He had spoken quickly for a few minutes, adrenalized as he was by fear, but then seemed to remember himself, and shut up. The brief story he'd told was about a tea made with the dried parts of a desert flower and a girl who walked you up to the edge of language and then sent you outside it, beyond the reach of your own vocabulary.

"The hell does that mean?" Clay asks.

"No idea."

Food arrives: tom yum goong, grilled pork, pad thai, and chicken panang. Vasco is relieved to see the dishes, at least, look and smell as he remembers. He orders more beer.

"Sounds like you've got a fun one on your hands, partner," Clay says. "And no word on where these kids are headed next, I assume?"

"One of the many things Bryce claimed not to know. We shall see." The jazz that was playing earlier has become techno and gained a few decibels and a small cluster of men is dancing in a spot not meant for dancing. Vasco saws off a chunk of pork, dips it in sauce, closes his eyes, pops it in his mouth. It's better than he remembers. Maybe not worthy of its seven-dollar price hike, but close.

"Well, give me a holler if I can help you out," Clay says. "When are you heading back north?"

"I don't know." This is all pushing him somewhere. It feels like a force amassing behind him, propelling him into a future he cannot yet see.

Chapter 52

Miguel's dusty Bronco bears the scars of a long and storied history—dents, a thick layer of dust, a window crack held together with duct tape, torn headliner, ripped upholstery—but someone has been looking after the engine, and it surges up the highway with a rumble that somehow feels both violent and soothing. Miguel's build is much like his truck's—square-jawed, with a firm but restrained handshake and a smile that misses most of his face. Isabella sits next to him in the passenger seat, answering texts. The name of Gabriel's backseat companion is a mystery—he'd introduced himself as one thing but Miguel and Isabella have each called him different things. He's restless, fidgety. There's punk rock playing, but it's quiet, as if someone turned it down to make a phone call and then forgot to turn it back up. The back of the Bronco is full of gallon jugs of water and protein bars and dried fruit. They're passing through a district of warehouses now; it feels to Gabriel like the city's edge.

Isabella shuts her phone off and then pivots in her seat, looking back at Gabriel. "Okay," she says. "I give you credit for coming out. I didn't actually think you would. Most people wouldn't expend the effort, you know?" She kills the music and then turns back to him. "So here's how it works. There are thousands of people out here every night, all along the border, hidden in the desert, trying to find their way in. Thousands. And whatever you think about whether they should or shouldn't be there, or what should happen to them after they make it, or after they get caught, they're people, and they're desperate. They're the victims of everything you can fucking imagine. So we have these caches of food and water spread out as far as we can to resupply them. Basic human decency, right? But there are these other groups out there, these incel wannabe militia motherfuckers, who go out and look for them and destroy them. Steal the food, dump the water out. One time they unwrapped all the food, shit all over it, and left it there. So someone on our side has to be out here all the time, refilling the caches, moving them around, re-hiding them. And then we have to try to communicate where they are, and by that time these other *pendejos* might have already found it."

She turns back around. Gabriel can only see the dark shape of the back of her head but he can feel the heat of her glare.

"It's the deadliest land migration route in the world," Miguel says. "People are out here dying every single day. Multiple people. Everybody talks about drugs moving across the border, and yeah, that's a problem. But they want you to focus on the drugs so you don't have to face the moral complexity of thinking about everyone else out here. Kids, grandparents. Babies. The vulnerable. And these punk-ass bitches are out here dumping the water that could save a kid's life."

The Bronco emerges from the electrified dome of San Diego's metropolitan glow and plunges into a desert that lies black and shrouded beneath the summer stars. There is steady traffic in both directions; they crest a ridge and the parallel strings of white and red lights describe the shape of the road across the next valley for miles.

Isabella continues. "And that's not all that's happening out here. It used to be that those who could get across the border would make contact with Border Patrol and then they'd get taken in and processed, and they'd get a court date for their amnesty hearing. But now, since the election, everything's different. These fucking cops down here are scary now. So it's harder."

Miguel picks up the story from there. "And then you get these militia groups out here, helping them. They get set up with their night vision and their radios, and they call in Border Patrol when they find people. So we've got other people out here, just searching for those assholes, and we've got spotlights and loud-ass stereo systems, and when we find them we crank up the lights and music to spoil their hiding places and let everyone know within miles to head the other direction, or wait it out. And then they go somewhere else and we try to find them again, and on and on." He points outside. "You can drive through here during the day and look out your window and it all just looks like desert. Empty space. But out here there's shit popping off all the time."

"And the whole fucking thing, all of it, is run by the cartel," Isabella says.

Gabriel squints through the window, as if to see what Miguel's describing. They fall into silence. Occasional lights stand out here and there, too weak or too distant for him to see what they illuminate. The road rises and dips, weaving its way over low ridges and falling flat and straight across wide valleys.

When they've been driving for an hour and a half, things suddenly change. Miguel steers the Bronco onto a side road. "Guillermo, let me get that GPS now please."

Gabriel's backseat companion, who now has a name, reaches into a bag and pulls out a tablet computer, a fistful of cords, and a box that must serve as a WiFi hotspot. Soon his screen is glowing with a scrolling topographic map, columns of numbers ticking off the coordinates. Miguel takes them onto a dirt road, and then turns off that one onto another. Gabriel watches the screen; outside the windows there is nothing to see but a dusty road. Guillermo sees him looking and turns the screen to give him a better view. They are running just along the border, within a network of narrow roads that branch across the hills like veins. Gabriel's attention goes back and forth from the computer screen to the windshield and in this way they move through a mile of the desert, and then another, and then Miguel slows and pulls off the road entirely. He switches to running lights, and with the light of the climbing half-moon they can see just well enough to crawl through the open scrubland. In a hundred yards they reach a jumbled mound of stone, twenty feet high, where they stop. Miguel kills the engine and the lights and they step into the quiet night.

Isabella switches on a headlamp and pulls the tailgate open. "Grab four gallons," she says to Gabriel, filling her own arms with boxes of food. Against a boulder there sits an open plastic crate, its cast-off lid lying atop a crumpled brown tarp. She peers in. "Everything's gone," she says, "but I don't see any damage. I think it just got eaten." She stacks her boxes in the crate and extracts a pair of empty gallon jugs, and then another pair. Just as Gabriel is stepping forward to replace them she whirls and freezes, the beam of her headlamp straining into the speckled darkness behind a cluster of scraggly bushes. "*¿Hay alguien allí?*" she calls into the night.

There's a rustling, and then the sound of a voice, an unintelligible word or two. Gabriel is riveted, seventeen pounds of water in each hand forgotten.

"*¡Vengan!*" Isabella says. "*Tenemos agua y comida. Somos amigos.*" She comes to Gabriel, takes one of the gallon jugs, and she's unscrewing the cap when a man and a woman emerge from the darkness. They're about Gabriel's age and they're dirty, drawn, and exhausted. The man has blood on his shirt. Gabriel sets two of the jugs in the crate, opens the other, and takes it to the man. Nobody speaks while they drink. Gabriel tries not to stare, but his eyes keep finding their way back to the couple. He has never known this kind of thirst, and probably never will.

"There's a house nearby we can get them to," Isabella tells him. "Other people will help from there." She turns to Miguel and Guillermo, who are working in the light of their own headlamps to stretch the tarp over the sealed crate, going about their business as if there's nothing out of the ordinary. "Memo, get in the back, yeah?" she says. He grunts, nods.

They give Gustabo the passenger seat and Susana sits behind him, each of them with a lapful of protein bars and dried fruit, which they both tear into before the engine comes back to life. Miguel drives on-ward, deeper into the desert. When Susana has finished eating, Isabella takes her by the hand and gives her arm a squeeze. There is a small sound Gabriel cannot interpret, and then a soft gasp, and he realizes Susana is sobbing. Isabella holds tight to her arm, and does not let go.

After twenty minutes on dirt roads they rejoin the highway, head-ing farther east. Now that he has food in his stomach, Gustabo relays their story. Gabriel's Spanish is rudimentary but he picks up broad strokes: from El Salvador, thousands paid to the cartel for the trip through Guatemala, up Mexico, and across the border. The car that was supposed to meet them on the U.S. side had arrived, but instead of collecting them, two men had jumped out. One attacked Gustabo with some sort of club and the other grabbed Susana and tried to force her into the car. Gustabo was a trained boxer, though, and he was able to avoid the initial blow and circle, and when his attacker lost his footing on the uneven ground, Gustabo closed the distance fast and dropped the man with a quick combination, breaking his nose. He yanked the club out of the man's hands, kicked him hard in the stomach, and then picked up a rock and hurled it, striking Susana's attacker just below the ear as he was shoving her through the door. Susana slammed a knee into the man's midsection, knocking him backwards and off-balance, and Gustabo closed in on him with the club. The two of them fled into the desert, where they'd been hiding all day without water, terrified, their phones dead.

The Bronco presses onward. Now Isabella is murmuring to Susana, explaining, reassuring. Gustabo and Miguel continue talking, their voices low. Gabriel listens to the sounds of their voices, the overlapping Spanish, trying to understand. He'd had his feet in the desert for all of thirty seconds before Gustabo and Susana had appeared. How much happens out here in the course of a week, a month?

After a half hour a dim glow on the horizon appears, and the edge of a small town comes into view. Miguel pulls the Bronco into a quiet lane right on the outskirts, with dusty houses lined up along one side of the street and open desert on the other. He parks in front of a small white home with drawn curtains and turns to his passengers. "*Vengan*," he says. "*Estan seguros.*"

He and Guillermo accompany Susana and Gustabo to the door, but Isabella steps out, walks fast across the street, and disappears into the darkness. They all seem to have forgotten about Gabriel. He slips over the backseat, climbs out of the car, and follows Isabella.

When he's across the street and back in the dirt the streetlights fade and the wide dark desert takes him into itself. It takes a moment before he can find Isabella—she's sitting on the ground, her arms around her knees. Gabriel takes a seat beside her. She doesn't look over. His eyes adjust to the night. Contours in the land appear; the sand lightens and separates from the black silhouettes of small bushes. The moon hangs directly overhead now.

"So was this what you expected?" she asks.

"I didn't know what to expect."

"I've been doing this for years," she says, "and I never know what to expect. Except that it'll be fucked up." She picks up a stone and hurls it into the darkness. "Those two got set up. They paid the wrong people.

Whoever came to pick them up, they were probably supposed to bring more help. But they didn't, and they underestimated Gustabo. If shit had gone according to their plan, he'd be lying in the dirt with broken bones and she'd be getting raped right now, before getting trafficked to fuck knows where, where she'd get raped some more. They'd never see each other again. They got lucky, but most people in their situation don't." She points, a gesture that includes the border, the lawless spaces that flank them, the abuses they hide. "So many people just vanish. The official numbers average about five hundred a year, dead or missing. But those are only the bodies they find, the reports they're able to collect. And then there's the extortion, the robberies, the rapes and assaults, the kidnappings that nobody reports."

Her profile radiates heat and fury. Gabriel imagines she can see through the dark, into all the lives hiding among the sand and stone. His eyes continue to adjust; now he can make out more of the landscape. The shapes of hills fall into place, distances become clearer. Maybe his eyes are playing tricks on him, but there seems to be movement everywhere.

"Does anyone give a shit?" Isabella asks. "No, they don't. If Susana had been taken, nobody would ever hear about it. Nobody would do shit. But one white girl gets picked up by the wrong parent from pre-school and it's amber alerts all the way up to Oregon. Because fuck brown people, right?"

Now Gabriel is sure of it—the desert is alive and crawling, if only with ghosts, or with someone else's memories. He feels tiny.

"This shit gets in your bones," she says. "This injustice, this anger. It gets deep in there, and every new cell you make includes it. It's who I am now. I dream about them. These hills. These hills, with no fucking shade in the day, no shelter at night, thieves and killers and kidnappers everywhere, preying on people who are already victims, and through it all, families just trying to get their kids to safety." She unwraps her arms from her legs, kicks a rock. "We've put a good team together," she continues, with a glance over her shoulder, back toward the others, the house and the Bronco. "Miguel is incredible. His connections, his ability to pull things together, recruit, find resources. Hangs sheetrock all day, taking shit from his *gringo* boss, but at night, he's a fucking general in this war. Guillermo is smart, dedicated. But me? I leave the thinking to the others. I'm too mad to think. I am the heart and the spirit and the rage. Reach down, feel my ankle."

Gabriel is not sure he has heard right. The heat from Isabella has intensified; she is a fire beside him. "Your ankle?" he asks. She scoots her foot toward him. He feels through the fabric of her loose jeans and finds the unmistakable shape of a small pistol's handle.

"The others don't even know I carry it," she says, quieter now. "But there's too much bad shit that can happen down here. Too many people who have no regard for the value of life. But I'm not going to let anything happen to me, and if I'm in a position to stop something from happening to someone else . . ."

She trails off, leaving Gabriel to imagine the rest of the scenario. "Thank you," is all he can think of to say. "Thank you for all you're doing here."

"Remember it, okay? Talk about it. Tell people. Okay?"

"I will."

Behind them Miguel fires up the Bronco and they rise, brush the dirt off, and start walking. "What are you doing here, really?" Isabella asks.

"Looking for my sister." After staring into the dark, he has to squint into the approaching streetlights.

"And you think she's here?"

"I'm following a path. It led me here."

He can feel her nodding in the darkness. "That makes sense. This is the land of the missing, after all." Here the ground is dust; their footfalls are silent as they climb the gentle rise to the road. "I hope you find her," she says. "It's a disaster not to be found."

Chapter 53

I t is four in the morning and Special Agent Velasquez has given up on sleep. He did not accompany his dinnertime beers with enough water and he'd awakened after a too-brief sleep feeling dried out, and after a spell of hotel-induced disorientation, his mind had awakened and begun running through a thousand different questions. He tried for an hour to get back to sleep but now he's sitting up, staring in the approximate direction of the television, where CNN is covering a series of tornadoes in Ohio.

He'd come to San Diego expecting more of a sense of recognition. He'd spent years here, after all, working the desert and the border, dealing with the brass downtown, and living his life through all the spaces between. He thought he'd had the place figured out: the surfers; the Marines; the ex-Marines; the sunburned professionals in their convertibles; the tourists, who were always either on their way to or from the zoo. And the hordes of border crossers, legal and otherwise.

He'd had his struggles working in Border Patrol—he'd been called a traitor, *un pocho*, but he believed in what he was doing and he believed, at the time, that this was where he could serve best, so he'd made his peace with his role, and suffered the accusatory glares of the migrants, every one of whom reminded him in some way of a *primo*, a *tío* or a *tía*, back up in Roseville. He'd found ways to keep himself on track when his belief wavered, or when the politicians meddled with their funding, or when the press beat up on them.

He has his own ancestral connections to this part of the world, as well, but these belong to a fuzzy and ancient history that is so intertwined with myth he no longer bothers to try to disentangle them. His grandfather Humberto, as a young man, or maybe still just a teenager, had left his parents and a sister and departed Sonora on a fruit truck, or a freight train. He'd made his way through the southlands over the next few years—his accounts of that time had him working on cars, stacking fruit in grocery stores, amateur prizefighting. No story was ever the same. He'd made his way eventually to Bakersfield and worked on a series of farms, his momentum still pulling him northward, until he'd ended up in Monterey, working the canneries, sharing meals and sleeping quarters with Steinbeck characters. As for Humberto's parents and his sister, back in Sonora, there was little known about them. He'd made it back only a couple of times, his parents aging in great ten-year leaps, steadily wrinkling beneath the perpetual sun that beat year-round upon their *pueblo*. When they died, he'd lost track of his sister.

That the mythic progenitors of his family tree had once haunted the other end of the same desert where he'd worked for those years at CBP had never held much significance for him. The intervening generations, the line of that border, and the changing sand hills had buried them and their *pueblo* like an ancient civilization, and now they belonged to an altogether different realm, more akin to the Aztec Empire than to him and his world of federal bureaucracy, internet dating, protein powder.

Somewhere between those two disparate realms there now arises a third, asking him to link it all together. A Berkeley high schooler, her mother's invocation of Vasco's own father's homemade *medicinas*,

Bryce's report about some flower that grows from the hearts of sand dunes, and its strange effects. There is some cord running through each of these, pulling them along, and now they seem to be falling in upon one another, converging as though drawn in by the gravity of—what? What lies at the center of all this?

He flicks through the channels and finds infomercials, chat line solicitations, the movie *Splash!*, which he leaves on, its volume too low for him to hear, until it, too, becomes commercials. He flicks back to SportsCenter where the same mid-summer baseball highlights he'd watched the previous evening are still playing out, all diving infielders and double plays and homeruns, and suddenly the city around him is too big and cluttered, too noisy, even in its sleep.

He remembers how the desert used to help him think, how on his drives out of the city the parking lots would fall away and the sky would open above him and the sand would pull him into itself and connections would appear; epiphanies would arise. With dawn nearly upon him he rises, dresses, and emerges from his room. He buys an apple and a mango yogurt and a large black coffee from a twenty-four-hour convenience store and drives along well-practiced routes toward the city's eastern edge, thinking hell, I might even run into Davenport out there, or Mendoza, or Perkins, or one of the others, out there in the sand.

Chapter 54

After dropping Gustabo and Susana off, the Bronco resumes its circuit. Gabriel and his companions replenish three more caches of food and water, one of which they relocate. Sometimes they see other vehicles in the distance, and once their headlights sweep across a trio of trucks, parked together with their lights off. Guillermo notes the coordinates and texts them to somebody. "We'll have somebody come fuck with those *culeros*," he explains.

Just before sunrise they pull into a clearing and park alongside another half-dozen trucks, all covered in dust. In the center of the clearing, fifteen or twenty members of *Las Salvavidas*, as they call themselves, stand in a loose group around a folding table, holding steaming paper cups of coffee. On the table, a battery-powered lantern spreads white light across a large worn topographical map. Gabriel meets a few of them, briefly—twenty- and thirtysomethings, tired, in ranch coats, from across the ethnic spectrum. A young Korean couple pulls up in an SUV and opens their liftgate to reveal hard-boiled eggs, boxes of *pan dulces*, and bunches of bananas.

The *Salvavidas* eat quickly as they file their reports. Gabriel stands on the periphery with his coffee, listening in. The map is dotted with small color-coded star-shaped stickers, like those that adorn completed grade school homework assignments: existing food caches, former and potential hiding places, militia encounters. Miguel recounts the story of Gustabo and Susana, and there are shouts and cheering when he describes the outcome of the fight. When all the reports are in and the updates to the map are complete, the meeting disbands. Nobody offers an assessment of the night's work; there are no concluding remarks, no words of encouragement, no references to the next time. The map and table are folded and stowed, banana peels collected, cold coffee dumped into the dust. They disband and their wheels kick up a single collective cloud of dust that drifts briefly toward the rising sun before sinking back to the ground.

Back on the highway, Guillermo falls asleep almost immediately. Miguel is stoic and steady, both hands on the wheel as he pilots them back toward San Diego. Isabella stares past him and through his window, watching the border, still on patrol. The rising sun casts rays through the dusty rear window, painting the Bronco's black interior a deep orange. Isabella turns in her seat, squinting against the sunlight, and glances at him and the sleeping Guillermo. "Thank you for your help," she says. "It was good of you to come. Not enough people know what goes on down here. The media only cares about immigration if politicians are arguing about it, and even then, they only focus on the politicians. They talk about migration without talking about migrants. It makes me sick."

Gabriel imagines her spitting on the ground. "You're welcome," he says. "Thanks for showing me all this." The land around them is alight now, a thousand shades of gold shot through with deep brown shadows.

"There's a lot to do, but we aren't the only ones out here working on this," Isabella continues, quietly. She points at the ridge running parallel to them to the north. "We have people up there, signaling. Other safe houses and lookouts all along this corridor. We'll never be able to do anything about the cartels or the corruption, and we can only help so many, but what happens to people like Gustabo and Susana if we're not out here?"

"There are good people all through this corridor," Miguel says. "A church group in a town back there with a shelter and supplies. And in this town up here, Ocotillo, there was a *viejito* who would walk the desert by himself and take care of the sick. First aid, medicine, stuff like that." He takes a hand from the wheel, crosses himself, and points to the sky.

Ocotillo. The name tumbles out of a corner in Gabriel's memory. And the description—a grandfather walking the desert by himself. "Why did you cross yourself?" Gabriel asks.

"He's been gone a year or so now. He's missed out here."

"A year and a half already," Isabella says. "It was last winter."

Last winter. Gabriel's eyes widen and his gaze leaps out to the passing hills. When Rogelio disappeared, Gabriel was sequestered in his San Quentin cell, disconnected from that whole stretch of his family's history, but the isolation was only part of it. It was almost as much a surprise to learn his grandfather lived right here in California as it was to learn he'd died.

Rogelio had always been a difficult man to track. Peoria herself was prone to mixing up his various posts as he toured the biology departments of the universities in Barcelona, Santiago, Buenos Aires, Lima. In the midst of his professorships he was also just as likely to be doing fieldwork or a fellowship on some other campus. Only once in Gabriel's childhood had they gone to visit him, in Mexico City. Typically, Rogelio had come to them instead, staying only a day or two each time, in accordance to no schedule whatsoever, and usually while on the way to some other place.

Only now that Gabriel accidentally finds himself in the landscape of his grandfather's final months does he wonder why Rogelio had chosen this place for the culmination of his prodigious career. As Gabriel studies the barren, jagged ridges, it strikes him that some unseen force has delivered him to this pocket of the desert.

"What was his name?" Gabriel asks.

Isabella's head twitches, just a bit. Miguel's eyes catch his in the rearview mirror. "Nobody knew," he says. "Everyone called him *el lagarto*. The Lizard."

"He worked with you?"

"Not exactly," Miguel says. "I mean, yes, in the sense that he was out here doing what's right. But he kept to himself. Some people said he was a *brujo*."

Isabella turns and studies Gabriel. "Why did you ask his name?"

"My grandfather lived out here somewhere, by himself. He died a year ago January. Seemed like the type of guy who would likely be roaming the desert, alone. His mom was a *curandera* in Sonora." He looks to the south, across the golden expanse. "Somewhere down there," he adds, speaking more to himself now.

An idea jolts him; electricity ripples through his spine. "Hey, Miguel," he says. "Where did you say Ocotillo is?"

Chapter 55

We drive through the darkness and the trees and houses shrink and get far apart and there's more dust and then it all dries up and it's just our car and the rocky hills and the rising sun. Dirt roads cross the sand. Wind turbines huddle in passes. Piles of stone.

I slept for eleven hours last night and I feel lighter, clearer. The road is empty and we're moving fast but my eyes catch all the details outside: shades of orange in the growing light, the small jagged leaves of small dull shrubs, cracks in the stone outcroppings. A thousand different shades in the lightening sky. There's a rhythm to its undulations, patterns in its patchwork of empty space, scrubland, ridges. The van will be fixed by this afternoon, and we'll drive through the night. Sleep in the camper has been weird lately, so it's good I got some decent rest last night.

I don't feel like I have the right to expect much. I don't know how this works. I just know that the one time I visited my grandfather's house, I somehow knew what to do. Maybe it will happen again. Sometimes I catch myself starting to think that he owes me something. A little help. But I don't want to think of my grandfather as the type of man who has to carry debts beyond his death. He left me a pile of mysteries, but I don't think he ever hurt anyone.

In Ocotillo there's only one exit. Atop the sign that points the way there sits a single black-and-white bird, like a sentry. There's only one road south. It curves around the base of a hill and takes us to the other side of the ridge. I've only been down this road once before, so why does it feel so familiar? In a couple of miles we reach the dirt road. Off the asphalt, the camper sways and creaks as we climb the gentle slope and turn into the clearing and my grandfather's home slides into view, looking dustier, more tired. The engine dies and a vast still silence closes in. The dust and sand catch and hold the sound of my feet as I walk. The key is still in its hiding place and the door creaks when I push it open. The desert has found cracks in the walls, and a layer of fine sand covers the tile floor. "I'll be a few minutes," I tell Forrest. He nods and takes a seat on the dusty couch.

More sand has blown under the back door. Here are tiny drifts, ridges like on the back of a hand. When I pull open the door a cloud of desert blows in. This time the trail up seems longer, steeper, rougher, and though it's just a few hundred yards, it feels like a mile. In the stone circle the *centella* is in full bloom, just as I'd envisioned it—a sea of sun-drenched red, streaked with black. The flowers sway and bend in a wind I can't feel. I sit down on the same rock where I sat before and take a deep breath. All right, *abuelito*. I'm here. Talk to me.

I take breaths, listen to the wind, to the sounds of a thousand small things moving in the dirt. I don't remember picking up this stick, but now I'm drawing in the sand at my feet, my arm moving by itself. A line that descends and branches and descends and splits again. It's the branching path, the taxonomy from my grandfather's drawing. I watch as the stick's tip traces the lines down to my feet, and then I set the stick aside and collect a handful of stones. Working from the top, I place them beneath a series of nodes, where the symbols are in the drawing. The last stone in my hand is not a stone but a large piece of amber quartz. I set it on the last remaining spot, and then my empty hands are mine again. I stare at the drawing, trying to remember the sequence of strokes, searching for meaning in the placement of rocks and quartz. It makes no more sense to me than the paper drawing. "What does it mean?" I ask aloud. I wait, but no response comes. I gather fistfuls of flowers from the circle's edge, reaching low to make sure I collect the roots. I scan the area one more time, and then climb back up to the trail.

Chapter 56

Unlike San Diego and the events it held for Vasco, the desert presents him with familiarity: the tans and roses of its sunrises, the taste of its air like eating a stone, that quality of stillness when every surface absorbs sound. During his years patrolling the border he'd seen it in all its temperaments—times of day, seasons, weather. It could be welcoming or foreboding, but there was a constancy to it, a deeper steadiness beneath the obvious changes of its sounds and colors, like a hum for which he has receptors not in his ears but in his bone marrow.

Although he's driven through this chain of hills countless times he's never stopped and hiked this particular trail, but the dust and sand are the same, the scrub, the light. Down to the east he can see Ocotillo, no more than a few sandy blocks' worth of buildings, a town he knows well. He wonders if Arturo still mans the short-order counter at the Cactus Market. He'll go see after his hike. Maybe he can talk his old friend into firing up the grill early. A morning like this calls for more than his usual fruit and yogurt.

Although the terrain is familiar there is novelty in his capacity here—it's strange to be a mere hiker, essentially a tourist. On all his previous trips he'd been in uniform, with his partner and his service weapon, in a four-wheel drive decked out with searchlights, radios, computers, rifles. He'd seen the hills not for their shapes or the shadows they cast but for the hiding places they provided, for the tactical advantages and disadvantages they might confer. It had been a battleground, and as he scales the ridge, rising like the sun, the memories of his battles come back, crawling to him through the sand like hungry coyotes on the scent. Pursuits, captures, evasions, hiding places. Men, women, and children; determination, despair, and resignation; criminals and innocents. Victims of the heat, of their guides, of each other. And it isn't just the sense of these memories that returns to him—it's the specific details themselves, the individuals, as vivid as if they'd been waiting here for him all this time. An *abuela* with no teeth in a purple serape, a *vaquero* with one boot and the other foot wrapped in duct tape, a hundred fathers trying to make the crossing while carrying crippled children, and a thousand other desperate souls come to him in such a horde that they push Lenore from his mind, along with that college kid from San Diego whose name he cannot even remember now. So much for the desert helping him think.

He takes a deep breath and tries to bring himself back into the present, to center himself in his body, but when he sends his mind on a tour of his senses he gets stuck on his empty stomach. A minute later he attains the summit of a small hill and decides he's had enough of this. He'll head to Arturo's, catch up with his old friend, and then he'll find someplace else to think.

Chapter 57

Gabriel awakens to the sound of a car door slamming and opens his eyes to find himself under scrutiny. A dusty Ford pickup sits in the dirt outside the Cactus Market, its motor ticking. The ostensible owner of both truck and market is on his way from one to the other, in no hurry, his boots kicking up clouds of dust. He is nearly as tall as the doorway, or perhaps it is his oversized cowboy hat that makes him seem so. Beneath the hat is a black buttoned shirt and blue jeans, worn but clean. A thick blond mustache curls over the ends of his mouth and terminates on either side of his chin. His eyes are bright, even under the shade of his wide brim, and he does not remove them from Gabriel as he unlocks the door.

Gabriel sits up and gets his feet under himself, but does not stand yet. He brushes imaginary wrinkles from his thighs, stretches his arms, and nods at the shopkeeper.

"Good morning, young man," says the shopkeeper, with a voice that sounds like cigarette smoke and dust.

"Good morning," Gabriel says.

"Are you looking to do some shopping?"

"Yes, sir."

"Well come on in then, my friend," he says, holding the door open. "I'm Arturo."

"I'm Gabriel. You've got a comfortable bench here." He'd walked the two blocks up from the highway, passing an off-road rental store, a laundromat, a post office, and fire station, all loosely arranged along a strip of asphalt that was losing its battle to stay above the sand. He found the Cactus Market had not yet opened, but it offered a stout wooden bench, protected by an awning from the climbing sun. He sat, leaned his head against the wall, and immediately fell asleep.

The shopkeeper points at the sky to the west. "You should try it around sunset sometime."

"I just might," Gabriel says, rising and shouldering his backpack. The shop's interior is clean and orderly but small, with a lot of empty space on the shelves. A lunch counter in the back suggests options for travelers with different timing, but he'll make do.

"You look like you could use some coffee," Arturo says. He points to the corner of the market, where a collection of iron tables and chairs cluster together. "I'll be right back." He heads for the back of the market and a coffee grinder's whine echoes off the market's plywood ceiling.

Gabriel drops his backpack on a table and circles the store, selecting a small box of Ritz crackers, a package of a dozen squares of American cheese, some salami, the last browning banana in a hanging basket, and a carton of orange juice. He arranges them on the counter and then returns to the tables, weaving to the backmost chair where he can sit and rest his head against the wall. The weariness from his circuit through the desert weighs on him. He wonders where he'll sleep that night.

The shop's front wall is a floor-to-ceiling window, tinted against the desert's glare and coated with an even sheen of dust. An old red truck drifts up the street at perhaps fifteen miles an hour. After a two-block stretch, the town gives way to the desert. It feels like the sort of place where everyone knows everyone else, and where they live. Or lived.

Arturo emerges from the back with a tall plastic cup of ice water. He briefly eyes the groceries on the counter before approaching. "Put that shit back," he says. "I'll make you some eggs."

"You don't have to do that, sir. I mean, is that what you'd normally do?"

Arturo studies Gabriel for a beat before turning on the flat-top grill. There are clicks and a whoosh as the burners ignite. "Where do you call home, son?"

"Berkeley," Gabriel, says, rising to retrieve the groceries.

"Well, in a place like this, 'normal' is whatever a situation calls for."

"Thank you. Eggs sound great."

"Berkeley has hills, does it not?"

"Yes, sir."

Arturo stoops, pulls open a refrigerator, and pulls out a pound of bacon. "Do you always find them where you left them?" he asks.

"What do you mean?"

Arturo straightens and the doors swing shut. "Do they stay put, son? Can you climb one, and come back to the same place the next day, and climb it again?"

"Sure."

"Well, that's another difference between here and there." He squirts oil on the center of the cooktop. "Our hills don't sit still." He points to the horizon with his spatula. "You see those three peaks there, in a little group? The ones that ascend, left to right, one-two-three?"

"Yes."

"The highest one used to be in the middle. Do you see the one about a quarter-mile to their left? Steep on the south side, gradual slope on the right?"

"Yes."

"That one used to be on the north side of town." The spatula swings ninety degrees, pointing to a flat spot perhaps ten miles from the peak in question. Gabriel imagines the hill pulling up its skirt and running across the sand. Arturo transfers bacon and shredded hash browns onto the cooktop and they start sizzling. The smell of coffee. "Land is not a place," Arturo says, his eyes on the grill as he situates its contents. "It's a process. Islands rise and fall; mountains do too. We usually don't notice it, because we move so much faster than it does. Usually." He sets his spatula down and vanishes behind the curtain, returning with a full pot of coffee and a mug, both of which he places on the counter. "Out here," he continues, pointing at the mug and nodding at Gabriel, "the land can move faster than we do. Makes it hard to find things sometimes." He turns back to the grill. "Speaking of which, what brings you to Ocotillo? It's not the sort of place people pass through on foot."

Gabriel gratefully fills the mug and lifts it to his nose, inhaling deeply before taking a sip. The rich heat floods across his chest. He takes another sip before responding. "I'm looking for somebody."

Arturo cracks an egg, one-handed, onto the grill, and reaches for a second. "You sure you're in the right place?" he says. "Not a whole lot of people to find down here."

"Rogelio Gonzalez. Any chance you knew him?"

Arturo cracks the second egg, and then a third, before slowly turning around. He studies Gabriel's face while breakfast sizzles. "You're his grandson," he says, at length. "The older one or the younger?"

"I'm the middle child."

Arturo nods, as if this confirms his suspicions. He walks to the counter, folds his hands in front of himself, and regards Gabriel. "Son, I'm sorry, but your grandfather died last year. Did you not know this?"

"I knew. I'm looking for him anyway."

"Well, then you're in the right place. Your grandfather was a close friend of mine. You might be interested to know you picked his favorite seat. And I gave you his favorite mug." He nods back toward the grill. "I don't want to ruin your breakfast. Let me finish up here and you can eat in peace and then we'll chat."

Gabriel thanks him and returns to his seat—his grandfather's seat—with the coffee, seeing the market with new eyes. A sudden longing for his mom comes over him. He wishes she was here with him now, waiting for food, this woman who links him to the past, to a sprawling, murky web of ancestors. What does she know, that she has not yet shared with him?

A camper pulls into the dirt parking lot in front of the market and falls quiet, and a young man emerges, looking disheveled and road-weary. He comes inside and hurries to the refrigerator, where he pulls out a bottle of Gatorade and a carton of orange juice. He eyes the banana Gabriel has just replaced, decides against it, and heads to the register. The transaction complete, he pulls the orange juice from the bag, opens it, and takes a big sip as he turns to head for the door. Something in the back corner of the market catches his eye, though, and he diverts his course and heads toward Gabriel, stopping at a revolving display of phone chargers and other cheap car accessories. Gabriel lifts his mug; the young man lifts his carton of juice. Their eyes meet and everything goes still. On the wrist of the man's upraised arm, there's a small tattoo—an origami antelope. Gabriel's fish tattoo is similarly on display, just beneath his own mug. Gabriel starts, nearly choking on his coffee.

With a shout, the young man launches his open juice carton, and Gabriel barely has time to spit out his coffee before the cold juice hits him in the face, blinding him. There's a sound like a car crash, and Arturo is roaring words that Gabriel can't understand. Still unseeing, Gabriel lunges toward the space where the man had been standing, but stumbles over a toppled pile of tables and chairs, going down hard on his elbow and wrist. By the time he regains his feet and clears the stinging juice from his eyes, the camper is pulling away.

Chapter 58

The smells of bacon and coffee greet Vasco as he steps through the door of the Cactus Market, and he's already feeling better. Arturo is not behind the counter, but he catches movement in the back corner near the tables, and he proceeds down the aisle to find his old friend mopping the floor. In a chair sits a young man who looks like he's just stepped out of a swimming pool—his hair is shining with water, and a towel hangs from his neck. His white shirt is splattered with orange, and he's holding a bag of ice on his wrist. Vasco catches the smell of oranges mixed with the floor soap. Arturo looks up and smiles, his mustache stretching itself well out of shape.

"Well, look what we have here," Arturo says. "As usual, five minutes too late to the scene of the crime."

Vasco takes in the scenario again: orange juice and floor soap, a bewildered and waterlogged twentysomething who looks like he might have picked up some gringo blood somewhere along the line. "I'm a little out of practice on my forensics," Vasco says, "but it looks like you might have swapped out the Mossberg in favor of Minute Maid? The boys in Sacramento would be proud of you. Non-lethal weaponry is the way of the future."

Arturo chuckles. "Lulu is still in her spot behind the counter," he says, turning toward the man sitting in the corner. "I don't consider myself a nosy man, but I was just about to start asking questions, too."

"This wasn't your doing?" Vasco asks.

"Does this look like my style?"

They turn to the young man in the chair, who looks like he has no idea what to do with himself. Vasco sees a weariness in him, the weariness that comes from wandering this desert for too long, looking for things that don't exist.

"*¿Como se llama, amigo?*" Vasco asks.

Arturo chuckles again.

"What's so funny?" Vasco asks.

It turns out the kid, who hitched a ride here to visit the town where his grandfather lived, is from Berkeley. His name is Gabriel. They sit and talk while they wait for their food—Arturo's first attempt to feed his customer had been interrupted, so he's back at the grill, cooking now for three. The kid is quiet, distracted, exhausted, or maybe all three. Vasco asks him about the juice shower, and Gabriel mumbles something about the guy mistaking him for someone else. It's a lie, but Vasco doesn't press. It's bad form to badger someone before breakfast, and besides, it's none of his business. Arturo returns with a bowl of scrambled eggs, a plate full of bacon, sourdough toast, mounds of home fries, slices of avocado, two different bottles of hot sauce. He sets the food down and retrieves a pot of coffee and the three men sit together, each at their own little table. The familiarity is every bit as welcome as the sustenance. The Cactus Market had been a regular outpost for Vasco during his years of patrolling the desert, and Arturo, twenty years Vasco's senior, had always had an ear to lend, sage advice to dispense, and a hot grill. The kid's attention is split between his food and whatever life development he'd just experienced, so Vasco is able to catch up with his old friend while they work their way through the

233

platters. When they're slowing down, Gabriel turns toward them and gestures to Arturo. "So," he says, "do you happen to know where my grandfather used to live?"

Arturo nods. "I do. It's about a forty-minute walk from here, and with the sun that'll feel more like a hundred and forty." He points to the empty space behind the counter. "I'd drive you over there but I've got no help here today."

"I can take you by," Vasco says. "You meeting someone out there?"

"No, the house is supposed to be empty."

"Well, I wouldn't want to dump you in the middle of nowhere on a day that's heading for triple figures. How long are you planning on being out there?"

Gabriel shrugs. "Not long. I just wanted to take a quick look."

"And then what?"

"Hop on a bus, I guess," he says. His eyes are back on his plate, where he's sweeping together the last bits of his food with a scrap of toast.

"San Diego?" Vasco asks.

Gabriel nods.

"I can get you there, too," Vasco says. "I don't think there's a whole lot of bus service out here. Sounds like you've got some family roots here?"

"I don't know very much," Gabriel says. He's looking outside now, through the windows and far away. "Not yet, anyway."

Vasco nods. The market's air conditioning kicks on, already working against the day's rising heat. He takes a final sip of coffee and then rises and gathers dishes.

Chapter 59

G abriel feels centerless, scattered, straining in a dozen different directions, going nowhere. It's astounding that his path
has led him to this encounter, to this wrist tattoo, and it's
equally astounding how completely he botched it. The exhaustion
from his night and his full stomach want to pull him into sleep, right
there in the passenger seat, but there's an undercurrent of adrenaline
coursing through it all—perhaps his sister, and those she's traveling
with, will be at his grandfather's house. His chauffeur and benefactor is
about mid-thirties, well-built, with the air of confidence that comes in
a man who knows how to handle himself. He could prove to be a helpful companion. It's hard to hit two faces with juice at the same time.
Gabriel debates telling the man—was his name Francisco?—about the
possibilities before them. The car carries them southward, back toward
the freeway and then under it, and as a pitted road half-covered with
dust and sand carries them toward a low line of hills, he decides to let
things play out.

Arturo's directions keep them on this road until it sweeps in a
broad arc around the base of the hills, heading toward a distant gap
in the terrain. The land shines in the blaze of the morning sun now—
browns and tans that stretch and ripple out all around, coming to an

end at low hills and ridges, or vanishing in the distance against the sky's pale blue fringes. Scattered across the land are occasional homes, some of them little more than trailers, all of them dusty, sun-beaten, doomed to fail in their efforts to remain intact and standing in the unforgiving environment. He wonders what else is hiding out there.

What had been here for a man like Rogelio? Gabriel hadn't actually known anything about his grandfather beyond a handful of interactions, beyond the résumé highlights: botanist, professor, researcher, department chair, international. His only real feel for his grandfather had come from Peoria. It was a process of inference, of reverse engineering. Who was the man who had produced and raised someone like her? How could such a man find enough out here to occupy him?

The road bends and bends again, just as Arturo described it, and a dirt road appears on the left. He and Francisco exchange a glance and a nod, and Francisco slows.

"Thanks again for this," Gabriel says.

"Happy to help," Francisco says. "History is important."

They rumble over the dirt road for a few minutes, and when they reach the chain roadblock Arturo had described, Gabriel sees recent tire tracks in the dirt beside the gravel road. He sits forward, trying to see around the upcoming curve. They circle the base of a hill to find a small house standing there in a small hollow, a container shed behind it showing just over its shoulder. In a clearing before the house sits an old pickup truck, its windshield opaque with dust. No other vehicles. Behind the property the hills climb up fifty feet to a ridge, cutting off the view of the bright expanses around them.

Francisco stops the car some way from the house, kills the motor, and the two men step out. "Someone's been here," Francisco says, pointing at the ground. "Very recently."

Gabriel imagines Lenore inside the house doing . . . what? Had she come to collect something? Leave something? Or simply to pay homage? Francisco squats to examine the ground while Gabriel steps up to the door. It's locked, but he pulls back the corner of the doormat and finds the key there. He pushes the door open to find a fine layer of sand across the tiles, just thick enough to show fresh footprints.

Chapter 60

Vasco hadn't been looking for further intrigue but here he is, examining footprints in a dead man's living room in the middle of the desert, with a companion who will not say why he smells like orange juice. Gabriel is somewhere in the back of the house now; the sounds of doors opening and closing echo off the stucco walls and the tile floors.

"Were you expecting anyone else to be here?" Vasco calls.

"I wasn't expecting anything."

It's stunning that there are only these few sets of footprints here, actually—in a house that's been empty for eighteen months, in the midst of a desert crawling with people seeking shelter, he'd expect the place to have been destroyed twenty times over. Nobody seems to have found this little hollow in the hills, though. Not until recently.

Another door opens and closes, and then silence takes over the house—Gabriel must have slipped out a back door. Vasco follows the footprints to the far side of the living room, but hesitates to plunge any farther into the house. It's not his business. But as he's standing there a thirst hits him and moves him into the kitchen. He's got a bottle of tepid water in the car, but maybe the water is still on here. In the kitchen's corner stands the back door, with tracks leading to and from it. There's a window over the sink, and through the pane he can see Gabriel, making his way up a path to the ridge, with his head full of secrets. The faucet yields nothing, so Vasco turns to head back to the living room. A slip of paper on the refrigerator catches his eye. It's the only thing there, a handwritten note on a piece of graph paper, held in place by simple magnets. He crosses the room and sees it's a recipe of sorts, in Spanish, for something called *centella*. It's a dish he doesn't recognize. The recipe bears a record of experimentation. Quantities and durations are marked, crossed out, modified. He scans it, looking for ingredients, but all he sees are *tallos*, *pétalos*, and *raíces*. Stems, petals, and roots. *Centella*. It means "spark." It's not a dish—it's tea. *Medicina*. His conversation with Bryce crashes back to him then, about the psychoactive tea made of desert flowers, and the girl from up north who knows how to make it.

Vasco's pulse leaps and hits him in the back of his eyeballs. He takes a step back, his hands tingling, his legs ready to pounce, thoughts flying as he tries to calculate the new parameters of his situation. Whose house is this, and who the hell is this Gabriel? He moves back into the living room, searching for . . . what? He stops before a small bookshelf, where a half-dozen framed photographs stand shoulder-to-shoulder. Here's an image of three kids—two boys and their little sister. Gabriel could be either of the boys. And the girl—Lenore? Had he actually stumbled upon Lenore's brother? Leonardo—that's the one who'd tangled with Yeager's kid. Leonardo and Gabriel, the artist and the angel. He scans the rest of the photographs: a man in his fifties or sixties with a young couple; older scenes, their colors washed out and faded, from somewhere in Mexico, including a shot of an extended family with maybe a dozen members. This one he picks up, scanning its faces, trying to make connections across the years to the people in the other shots. An elderly woman stands in the center of the group, wrapped in bright fabrics, her hands on her hips, silver teeth showing through a wide smile. Her family clusters around her: a husband behind her shoulder, younger couples, a pair of teenagers. Vasco's eye tracks to a couple in the bottom corner of the photo, just inside the frame, and when their faces come into focus, he gasps. His own parents smile back at him, from across a thirty-five-year span. In his mother's arms rests a colorful bundle, with his own small, sleeping face just barely visible amid the folds of bright fabric.

Chapter 61

The tracks inside the house don't lead anywhere in particular, but Gabriel finds a set that leads to a back door. He follows them up the hillside and to the ridge. In the glare of the rising day the terrain's inhospitality becomes stark—there's no shade, no easy paths.

Cliff faces and jagged outcroppings fracture the hills. As he gains elevation the desert opens around him, and its vast spaces ring with the sound of his failure.

He imagines his grandfather moving along this path, with a broad-brimmed hat to protect him from the sun, pruning shears and collection bags, bottles of water. Why had Lenore come? It's not an easy place to get to. It's not on the way to anything. What had she remembered, from her trip two winters ago? Who is she with, and why? So many things happened in the world while Gabriel had been sitting in that prison cell.

He crests a small rise in the ridge and a strange patch of red appears on the slope beneath him. It takes him another minute or two of walking before he arrives at the edge of the crater and the flowers come into view. They're shifting in the slight breeze, petals rippling from one edge to the other, waves of red shades swirling around in the crater, shot through with flecks of black and the pale sage green of their stems. Right beneath his feet on the edge of the circle is a patch where several plants are missing, the dirt freshly disturbed. Gabriel squats, imagining Lenore here, her hands in the soil, just as they had so often found their mom. The tracks lead also toward a low nearby rock—he follows them and finds a drawing in the dirt, a branching pathway that runs and spreads through a series of rocks. A hunk of amber quartz sits among them, and he picks it up and turns it in the light, examining its facets, the way it catches and reflects light. He has lost track of all his questions; they've overflowed his mind and spilled everywhere. After replacing the quartz, he plucks one of the flowers and then returns to the house, studying the small dusty bloom as he walks.

Back in the house he finds Francisco standing in the living room before a bookcase, holding a small framed photograph. He looks as if he's been struck by lightning. He looks Gabriel in the eyes, so much intensity across his brow that Gabriel stops where he is, pinned into stillness.

Francisco mutters words that make no sense.

"What?" Gabriel says.

"I think I'm your uncle."

Chapter 62

The fever rips back into Leonardo that morning and when he awakens he finds the house has broken into a dozen pieces, each one flying around him in its own erratic orbit. He knows he needs water so he crawls down the stairs, backwards, battling vertigo all the way. Once he reaches the kitchen floor it is some time before he can find the strength to sit up and reach for a bottle. The act of uncapping it is equally demanding. The bottom half of his face is numb; he tips the bottle over what he thinks is his mouth and hopes for the best.

The house won't stop spinning. When he closes his eyes it gets a little better, but then it gets a little worse. He goes back and forth like this for several hours: attempting to stay hydrated; seeking out the more stationary parts of the house, freezing and burning.

That afternoon, after a nap full of monstrous dreams, the house finally stops its revolutions and settles back onto its foundations. He sits on the cushion-less couch in the living room, the door open, layers of dried sweat across his brow, streaks of salt running down his temples where he has poured water. His mind is the sort of blank that threatens to remain blank forever, an expanse of emptiness like an ice sheet upon which it is impossible to imagine any structure, any color.

He dozes through the afternoon, moving little, and when day is fading he returns to the kitchen, grateful to find the floor holding steady. It takes some time, but he's able to get down a few crackers and some more water. The flashlight batteries are nearly dead, so he lights a candle and struggles back upstairs, panting by the time he reaches the top. He sets the candle on the sill and collapses onto the sofa cushions. If things get bad again, he is going to need some help. But where will that help come from?

The warm light awakens him. There's a sense of relaxation flowing through him, an ease he has not felt since the fever began. The flames are beautiful, the rising flight of a thousand orange angels soaring up the wall and across the ceiling. They are singing to him. They are nearly to the doorway when Leonardo registers the importance of beating them out.

Part III: Converge

Chapter 63

Garza is hardly ever quiet or still, and right now he's both. It's putting the whole team—Moriarty, Phillips, Johnson, and Vasco himself—on edge. Garza sits in his chair, his arms folded on the blotter, a mermaid in a sailor's uniform smiling at the proceedings from her spot on his right flexor. He's looking back and forth from Vasco to Johnson, who are seated across from him, contemplating what he has just heard. Phillips leans against the side of a file cabinet, chewing his gum in slow motion, a small grin on his face.

Garza unfolds his arms, leans forward, weaves his fingers together. "You're telling me the girl is your goshdarn cousin?" he says.

"Second cousin, once removed, to be exact."

"What the heck does that mean?"

"Her mom? The piano player?"

Garza nods.

"Her grandmother was my grandfather's older sister."

"Mind if I say something?" Phillips says.

"Is it about how he's Mexican, and the chances of this were actually about fifty-fifty?" Garza says.

"Yes, sir."

"The US government has no tolerance for racial discrimination, Special Agent Phillips."

"Somebody had to say it," Phillips says, still grinning. "Otherwise, the bad guys win."

"Well, we wouldn't want that," Garza says. "So now what?" he asks Vasco.

"I'm not sure." It's the most truthful response he can offer. He's still trying to collect himself, a full day after the discovery of the photograph. Gabriel had not seemed nearly as surprised as Vasco expected him to be, at least not at first. It was only when Vasco explained who he was, and how he'd happened to be in the area on this particular day, that the infinitesimal odds became clear. They stood together there in Rogelio's living room, studying the photograph, discussing the connections, while the sun climbed to its zenith. All the while Gabriel held the stem of a flower—small red petals, flecked with black.

They climbed back into the car and Vasco wanted to ask a thousand questions, but his professional duties and his personal curiosity were all mixed up and he didn't know how to start asking, but it turned out not to matter anyway. Gabriel was fast asleep before they made it back to the freeway. They parted ways in San Diego, each knowing they'd see each other again soon, and Vasco headed to the airport. He drove without seeing, without hearing, lost in his amazement at the appearance of an entire branch of his family tree. And this wasn't just some enclave of distant cousins, but the entire, intact lineage of his grandfather's enigmatic sister, who until that morning had been little more to him than a historic phantom on the fringes of his family's lore, a specter on the remote edge of a foreign desert. *La urraca*, Gabriel had called her, and though Vasco has no conscious recollection of the name, the sound of it is familiar. "The Magpie" is no phantom anymore—Vasco has a photograph of her now, tucked in his glovebox. The convergence of faces in that image is miraculous, a coincidence so unlikely that a large part of his brain still resists its reality. But there are no other explanations. This is his *familia.*

It is strange, the sense of intimacy he already feels for all of them: his great aunt the *curandera,* her son the botanist and his abandoned laboratory home, his daughter the pianist, and her own three children, around whom his life had already fallen into orbit. And it is not just their present versions that intrigue him, these three young adults and their parents, but all their past versions, too. His cousin, Peoria: Who is she, and who was she ten years before that, and ten years before that? Who was she as a girl, as a young woman; who was she when she fell in love with her husband, and who was he? Lenore had been a baby not too long ago; Vasco wonders where he'd been when his baby niece had been born. He's never held a baby whose parents he and his team were not in the process of detaining. It staggers him to consider the sheer volume of humanity contained in this new branch of his family. Their renown and their accomplishments, their migrations, their flaws and transgressions, their science and prison time and math and music and birds. Their past, present, and future. He wants to ask them each a thousand questions.

They seem so sprawling and wild compared to his own parents. His own grandfather, Humberto, had left Sonora alone for *el norte,* and landed finally in Northern California where he'd married the daughter of a minister and a nurse. Together they had a single child, a son they named Javier, who grew up to be quiet, contemplative, more interested in working on cars than carousing with his friends or meeting women. Vasco's mother Sandra was an avid reader and a weaver whose thoughtfulness and dexterity captivated Javier, as did her sprawling clan of siblings and cousins, aunts and uncles. He married her, and they'd set about building a life together.

Vasco sees them often, even attends Mass with them on occasion, and not just on holidays. They're good, peaceful people: his mom with her books and her *novelas* and her work with her friends at the church; his dad with his nickel card games with the other guys from the body shop, his front-porch lemonade breaks, his ongoing pursuit of the perfect carne asada, which he'd perfected long ago. They both still call him *mijo*. Together they are a cozy unit, but quiet, contained, and it has been a couple of years now since his mom last asked him about settling down and making her an *abuela*. Vasco's own persistent bachelorhood had seemed to portend the end of his father's family line, but now, through the chance discovery of a photograph on a bookshelf in an empty home in the borderlands, the story of their lineage is evolving.

Flying north the previous day, he'd closed his eyes and seen flashes of details from the little home in the desert: the photos, the view out the back window, the laboratory, the space on the shelf, clearly labeled *centella de las arenas*, with its missing jar. He saw the mess in the Cactus Market, the first glimpse of his befuddled nephew. And he saw the desert encompassing all of them, a great hot circle holding these two countries together like a clasp, a singular geography far greater than the attempts to draw a line, a fence, a wall, through its midsection. He thought of the way the desert had awakened him early that morning and drawn him into itself, as if calling him to a reunion, a homecoming, and the way its sands had parted to reveal a hidden building of secrets, where the image of his own face had a home.

But to what end? He is a federal agent, and they are the targets of his investigation. There's a young man in a coma. Leonardo is a fugitive and Lenore is missing, ostensibly peddling some unheard-of psychoactive intoxicant up and down the state. In his glovebox, alongside the miraculous photo, is the strange flower, secure in an evidence bag. It had fallen to the floorboards of his rental car at some point during their drive back to San Diego, when Gabriel had dozed off. Vasco really should send it to the lab later, for identification and analysis. He thinks again of his own father's homemade cures for ailments, the stories of his great aunt's powerful *curanderismo*, the link Peoria had pointed out with her comment about *medicina*. So now what is he supposed to do?

Garza sits back and clasps his hands behind his head. "Do you have any concerns that your newfound cousinhood will prevent you from discharging your duties in a coolheaded and professional manner?"

"I thought it might bear discussion."

"Okay," Garza says. "Let's discuss it then. What's our worst-case scenario?"

"Same as always," Phillips says. "Vasco here gets his head chopped off and dumped into a barrel full of lye in the basement of a meth lab in Chihuahua."

"Right," Garza says, "but I don't really get a decapitation vibe from the trajectory in this particular case. Second worst?"

Phillips pops a purple chewing-gum bubble. "Considering that Vasco here has been traipsing all over the state, I'd say he dies in an avalanche of paperwork."

"Always a consideration in this line of work," Garza says. "What else?"

"Waco."

Garza looks Vasco in the eye. "Given what you know now, and your considerable instincts, how likely is this to end with a botched raid on national television?"

"You never know," Vasco says.

"Isn't that the truth," Garza says. He sits back in his chair. "Look, we could discuss possibilities all day, but out of respect for the taxpayers' hard-earned dime, let's take a step back. Aside from the situation with the brother and Yeager's kid, which is feeling more and more like a fluke occurrence, nobody's getting hurt here. For all we know, this crew is nothing more than a roving vegan tea party." Phillips leans forward to protest but Garza holds up a hand, keeping his eyes on Vasco. "Our guts are telling us there's more to it than that, of course, which is why you'll continue your investigation. If and when you find yourself at a conflict of interest, or you get a whiff of some actual narcotics, you'll let me know and we'll reassess. Yes?" Vasco nods, thinking of the flower in its plastic bag, hiding away.

Chapter 64

When Yvette first sees the line of yellow caution tape stretching from tree trunk to tree trunk across the end of the gravel road, she thinks it is a glare from the sun across her windshield. But instead of shifting away with the rest of the light and shadows it stays put, obstinately clinging to its place in the world, and just as she registers what it is the burned house beyond it comes into view. She slams on the brakes, as if by stopping the car she can reverse her discovery. She oscillates from incredulity to terror and then back again and then she jams her foot onto the accelerator and the car surges forward through the gravel, spraying rocks and ripping through the tape. She jumps out and approaches the edge of the wreckage.

Some part of her is braced for the sight of Leonardo's charred body, though somewhere else inside her she knows the yellow tape means people have been here and if Leo had met his end in the fire, his body wouldn't be lying here. But the vision presents itself to her anyway, seizing upon her fear, ignoring her reason. His corpse rises out of the rubble, fifty feet tall, staring at her as if to say, Look what happened to me. Why didn't you come earlier? She closes her eyes and takes three deep breaths. If he's dead, she tells herself, there will be plenty of time to think about it later. The task at hand is to figure out what the new problem is.

She takes another three breaths, slower this time. The taste of wet burned wood hangs in the air. Her eyes re-open and she approaches the house's foundation, studying the rubble. It's still sopping wet— wisps of steam like little ghosts rise from the pile. It must have just happened. Last night, maybe. So he could still be out here somewhere.

From the edge of the clearing she peers into the forest, and she sees nothing. She walks around the perimeter, her heart leaping at every little movement, willing a voice to come from out of the undergrowth, carrying her name. When she has nearly completed her circuit she discovers a bag hanging in a tree with a rope that looks as if it's made of torn fabric. She pulls it down, looks inside, and recognizes some of the food she brought him. She stares into it a long time, thinking. There had been bears, apparently, before the fire. Maybe he'd been chased from the house days prior. But where would he have gone? She calls out his name once, and then again, louder. After another useless scan of the clearing's edges she releases the bag and walks slowly back to the car.

Chapter 65

Ayla's door is ajar, so Gabriel pushes through it and steps into the entryway and finds the home every bit as sparse as it was the last time he was here. The back windows are still wide open so the air is fresh, but there is a sense of abandonment to it, like dust, like an old silence. Not wishing to violate it he refrains from calling out and instead walks to the couch. He sets his backpack on the floor and sinks onto the middle cushion. If she is here, she will materialize.

He'd considered flying home from San Diego, but there was nothing to rush back to, so he'd purchased a ticket for the twenty-hour-long Greyhound bus ride back to Oakland, figuring he could use the time to think. He'd boarded the empty bus, found a window seat halfway back, and settled in. There was an electric outlet in his armrest; when his phone regained its life it convulsed with notifications for voicemails and texts, all of them from home, or somewhere near it.

Nobody knew where he was. Lenore was still missing. And bizarrely, Leonardo was a wanted man, a development nobody had bothered to tell him about until the previous day. Incredulous, Gabriel read a half-dozen articles on the incident and the aftermath, trying to figure out why it had happened, and where Leo might have gone, but there was no sense to make of any of it.

When the adrenaline wore off, weariness rose up and took hold of him. He dozed. Sometime later he awakened to find that an assortment of other passengers had boarded. Scraps of words from their murmured conversations came to him, drifting over the constant whine of the air conditioning. Gabriel's mind circled back to the hugely unlikely events that had befallen him that morning. Circumstance had carried him to a desert outpost where he'd found the object of his search, lost it all over again, and then found before him a long-lost uncle. It was like getting struck by lightning and bitten by a shark and winning the lottery, all in the same day. But even that would have to happen to somebody, sometime, he realized. With the countless experiences that befall every single one of the billions of lives in the course of humanity, all things must occur, eventually. Everything, no matter how implausible, was inevitable.

Fatigue resurged and he fell back asleep. Strange and vivid dreams waited for him this time, where the lines between things were blurred. He dreamed of seeing himself from the outside. He dreamed he was his newfound uncle, the DEA agent. He dreamed of his sister and his brother and his parents and of his grandfather, who had dissipated into the desert, transmuting into a thousand small lizards. Everybody cycled around and through one another, clambering from one layer of his dreams into the next, dividing and reuniting. In the first seconds of awakening, just before the last of his sleep released him, there were moments when it seemed there were no spaces, no interstices at all between Gabriel and anybody else. He and his brother and his sister, his mother and Francisco, the people they used to be and the people they were now—perhaps they were all one and the same thing.

He floated in and out of sleep, cycling between his dreams and the dark upholstery of his seat while the bus rumbled up Highway 101, pulling in and out of stops as the summer light drained from the sky and night moved in. They made it to Oakland early the next afternoon and Gabriel came straight to Ayla's, where her couch now cradles him as he waits for her to reappear. He pulls his shoes from his feet and lets himself tip over, realizing that he hasn't actually lain down in three days.

Chapter 66

After the San Diego revelations, it's hard for Vasco to focus on his desk. There's the promised mountain of paperwork to reward him for his initiative, a clogged-up inbox, and updates on the other cases he's working on, which are struggling to hold his interest.

Now that he has briefed Garza, his thoughts keep returning to a woman in the hills, sitting at her piano. A woman born to Rogelio Gonzalez, who himself was the son of Maria Gonzalez, born Maria Velasquez, the elder sister of Vasco's own grandfather, Humberto Velasquez. A woman with a daughter who is tearing around the state administering psychedelics and a pair of wayward sons, one of whom is wanted in an assault case. Vasco wants his phone to buzz. He wants her to get up and go to the refrigerator or the junk drawer or wherever she put his card and he wants a text that says *Hey primo, let's talk.*

He plows through another five minutes of busy work and then he checks his ringer and the reception. Neither are at fault for his phone's silence. Maybe she emailed? After his days on the road his inbox is a disaster zone, but a quick scan through it does not uncover her name. Is it possible Gabriel hasn't told her the news yet? He did seem a little . . . "unreliable" isn't exactly the word Vasco's looking for.

After all, he'd come across the guy in the aftermath of an altercation, which itself had followed a sleepless night. He'd been alone, on foot, in the middle of the desert, with nothing but a backpack and a dead phone. The man—his nephew!—had hardly been at his best. Maybe it's unreasonable to think that Gabriel would have reached out to his mom right away. For all Vasco knows, Gabriel could still be fast asleep in a San Diego motel room, his phone still dead.

Vasco deletes an assortment of useless emails, glad for even that small of an accomplishment, and then picks his phone back up. He stares at it for a minute, and then he punches in Peoria's number and tries to compose a text. *Hello, this is Special Agent Velasquez*, he types, but that's too official. He can just be "Francisco." He deletes and starts again. *Hello, this is Francisco Velasquez with the DEA.* No, too aggressive. *Hello, this is Francisco Velasquez (with the DEA).* Yes, that's better. *I would like to talk—it's related more to family than to the case. Is there a time we could meet?* He hopes it won't come across as coy, but this is a conversation he needs to have in person.

Her response comes back quickly. *Whose family?*

That's what I'd like to talk to you about, he types.

There's an uncomfortable delay before she writes back. *You have our lawyer's number, yes?*

I met your son, Gabriel, he writes. And then he adds: *In Ocotillo.*

An excruciating minute passes, and then another before Vasco tells himself to breathe. He puts his phone down and wills his heart rate downward, his attention back to the contents of his desk and his inbox. An email arrives just then from a CSU address—it's his contact at Sonoma State. Vasco opens the email to find with some excitement an attached video. It's a new angle on the confrontation between Percival—Leonardo, Vasco corrects himself—and Adam Yeager. Vasco skims the message: There had been a webcam rolling on the roof of the adjacent building as part of some research project. Vasco launches the video and finds the camera trained on a cluster of trees. Just next to them, he recognizes the first of the cement planters. Leonardo enters the picture, his phone extended, and meets the trio in the bottom corner of the frame. There's a ninety-degree difference between the mobile phone footage that had made the social media rounds and the webcam feed; Vasco's pulse thumps when he realizes it'll reveal the altercation from the side, with both of them in full view, small though they appear. The two flee, and then Leonardo engages Yeager. He pushes; they circle. The grab of the neck. Leonardo is shouting, furious, frantic. Yeager says something and then Leonardo spies the approaching rescuers. Vasco looks for the shove and is perplexed when it does not come. Instead, Leonardo recoils, withdrawing both of his arms as he spins away. Vasco rolls the video back and this time he's sure—the arms are pulling backward, not pushing forward. Adam twists, lurches, and then begins his fall. Why? Vasco leans forward, squints, and watches the video again. In turning, Adam had stumbled over his own feet. There was no push. Vasco watches the video again. No push. But is he just seeing what he wants to see? He watches twice more, and just as he's about to jump up to head to Garza's office his phone chimes. It's Peoria. *Café Strada, 3:00,* her text says.

Chapter 67

come through the door with Ayla and Forrest and Preston and by some miracle Gabo is here, stretched out on the couch, fast asleep, with a tattoo of an origami fish on the inside of his wrist. It feels like so long since I've last seen him. And so much has changed. "*La centella*," I whisper to Forrest, reaching for my backpack, my blood already churning with the anticipation.

Chapter 68

Yvette sits at a table in the middle of the Bootjack Coffee Shop with a barely touched plate of pancakes, a third cup of coffee, and a gas station romance novel before her. She chose the central table because it gives her the ability to eavesdrop on as much conversation as possible. She chose this restaurant because it's just around the corner from the headquarters of the Mount Shasta Police Department.

With her eyes on the book's open pages and cement in her stomach, she listens to her fellow diners discussing their families, the weather, local swimming holes, vacation rentals, and a dozen other civic concerns, but in the hour she's been here there has been no mention of a fire or a stranger in the mountains. Her time is running out. The pancakes, which she doesn't even like anyway, are cold. She's at her limit with coffee, and if she accidentally reads another pulpy passage in her book, she's going to vomit what little she did manage to eat. She'll have to shift to a more aggressive plan, so she takes another sip of lukewarm coffee and reviews the cover story she created for herself on the drive down out of the mountains.

She is not Yvette Cartwright but Marissa Martin, who has taken all of her vacation days from her job as an executive assistant to search the state for a warm, safe, quiet town where her dear father can retire and take care of her dear mother, who is now confined to a wheelchair, but just as spunky as ever. The requirements for their new hometown are a nice little café with really good soup, a decent hardware store, a good hospital, not too many hills, because of the wheelchair, and super-friendly people. While on her trip, Marissa is feeding herself pancakes with whipped cream and strawberries and entertaining herself with romance novels, items for which Yvette has little tolerance. And with no audience to play to, and no clues anywhere about what might have befallen Leo, her patience for the book's maudlin heroine and for her stupid, cloying lunch is coming to an end. Just beneath the veneer of her made-up character is an ocean of panic and guilt.

She is just about to wave the waitress down for the check when a pair of patrolmen walk in, and with a mix of relief and hope she notes that the table just next to her is available. Sure enough, they head in her direction and settle in. She lets them order their lunches—BLTs and coffee—and then before they can return to their conversation she summons Marissa and pounces.

"Excuse me, gentlemen," she says. "I see you're on your lunch break and all, but I'd be much obliged if you wouldn't mind answering a few business-related questions for me. It won't take more than a few minutes, promise. I know I'm interrupting, but I'd be more than happy to make up for it by having a couple slices of pie sent your way after you're done with those sandwiches. How about it?" She smiles and does a thing with the angle of her head and her eyelashes, but it isn't necessary. She's already won them over; they'd murder each other if she asked them to now.

"That's very kind of you, miss," says the older one, leaning back a bit and patting his paunch. A silver nametag above his pocket says he's Wilkins. "But a slice of pie at lunch and I'll be spending the afternoon napping instead of patrolling."

The other one, Higgins, a good deal younger than his partner but still a decade or two older than she is, gives her a broad smile. "I'll eat them both, then," he says, visibly straining to add a twinkle to his eye. "What can we do you for?"

She runs through Marissa's story and the patrolmen listen, nodding, eager to launch into proclamations of Mount Shasta City's suitability for a pair of aging parents. She hands the floor over to them just as their lunches arrive, and they take turns eating and talking about how perfect their town would be, and though she is dying to drive at the information she needs, she hears them out.

"How about crime?" she asks, when they've had their say, and are shifting their attention to the second halves of their sandwiches. "What's it like here?"

They give the answer she knew they would—a few folks get rowdy from time to time, like anywhere else, and sometimes when folks are out of work and in need of things they can't pay for, there can be problems, and, well, the drug thing is a nationwide plague, but all in all it's the sort of place where kids can play in the streets all day without their parents worrying. She lets her smile fade a bit and makes a show of appearing thoughtful. Marissa would play with her hair when she's thinking, Yvette realizes, so she curls a strand around her finger.

"I totally believe you and all," she says when they're finished, "and it sounds real great, but honestly, I've heard that a half-dozen times now." She uncurls, curls the other way, uncurls, repeats. They wait, scared they're blowing it, watching her, and then she pantomimes the arrival of a great idea, brightening and pointing to the spot above her head where a light bulb would appear if this were a comic strip. "I know!" she says. "Tell me about the last, oh, I don't know, the last week or so." She snaps her fingers. "That's it. Give me the whaddya call it. The blotter."

Wilkins relaxes, wipes his mouth, puts his napkin down. "Let's see, what have we had, Joe? Narcotics, like any little American town. Real easy for folks like your parents to steer clear of, though, of course. A couple of domestic disturbances. Some broken car windows, with a few things missing. Bored kids, probably."

"There was that fire," Higgins says. "Yesterday, up on the mountain. A house."

"A fire?" Marissa/Yvette says, trying to contain the sudden jack-hammering of her heart. "Like arson?"

"No, no evidence of anything like that," Wilkins says. "It gets dry up here, and accidents happen."

"Anybody hurt?" It takes all her effort to pantomime innocent curiosity.

"No, fortunately. We think it's a house that's been empty for a while. Way up there." He nods in the direction of the peak. "No neighbors for quite some way, and nobody in the area knew much of anything."

"And there was that John Doe," says Higgins, between bites.

"Oh right," Wilkins says. "This fella, real sick, up on the mountain just a few hours later. Might've been related; we're not sure. He collapsed on someone's lawn and the homeowner drove the guy right down here in his truck. Probably not a crime story. More like folks helping each other, but that's how it goes around here."

Yvette's mind goes fuzzy. Sick? Collapsing? She tries to draw a deep breath through a constricted chest, fighting to stay in character.

"My goodness," she finally manages. "John Doe, like in the movies?" She's overdoing the naïveté, but it doesn't matter anymore. Her business is elsewhere and she just has to figure out where. "Sick like with malaria or something?"

"No ma'am, I think that's just in the tropics," Higgins says. He looks at his partner. "What'd they say? Some kind of fungus thing?"

"Allergic reaction, the kind you might see from black mold," Wilkins says. "Real rare, from what I hear." He chuckles. "Maybe the Lemurians had something to do with it," he says. "Have you heard of them?"

"I think so," she says, "but is the guy okay?"

"Sure," Wilkins says, "but he's still pretty out of it. It's been since last night and we're still trying to get an ID on him. Until then, he'll just be John Doe."

"It's a good thing there were folks around to help out," Marissa says, everything inside of her wheeling and surging. "And it's a decent hospital you've got here?" she asks. "That would be good for my folks. Elderly and all."

"Sure," Wilkins says. "Mercy's the best hospital in the area. Gets pretty busy there, so they need to know what they're doing."

It's all she can do not to sprint out. Higgins is back on the Lemurians, though, so she sits and listens for as long as she can bear it. She thanks them and rises and heads to the register, adds two slices of cherry pie to her order, and heads outside.

Chapter 69

Gabriel awakens to find himself at the focus of a semicircle. He starts, braces himself, but nobody moves. He sits up quickly, scanning, trying to figure out options. There are six of them. One he recognizes from the encounter at the Cactus Market, and another is the blond who'd questioned him in the van. What was his name? Emilio? Eddie the driver must be among them as well. They all have tattoos on their wrists. Through the phalanx he can see into the kitchen, where Ayla sits at the island, a Thermos in front of her. She gives him a slight nod and a look he cannot decipher.

"Where's my sister?" Gabriel asks her.

"She's fine," says Emilio, who stands at the center of the phalanx. "She's safe."

"That's not what I asked."

"That's what we're prepared to share right now."

"Who the fuck are you people, and what is this?" he asks.

No response comes. Gabriel searches their faces and finds there is little confrontation in them. There's weariness around their eyes and most do not meet his stare but in their stances there is resolution. Ayla continues to watch him from the kitchen, her gaze unwavering, her expression blank.

"Why did your brother attack that kid at Sonoma State?" their spokesman finally says. He's in a t-shirt that has gone from black to gray at some point. Brown hair, stubble from his temples to his throat, glasses that will need to be replaced soon.

Heat flashes inside Gabriel. Where is this going? "I don't know," he says. "I don't know anything about that. What does that have to do with this?"

"Why were you in Ocotillo?"

"It's none of your fucking business," Gabriel says, folding his arms. "What are we doing here?"

"You make a choice."

"A choice?"

"You can leave. You can get up and walk out of here. We have your phone, because we can't have you calling anyone to let them know we're here, but you can come back in a couple hours and get it. We'll be long gone by then, of course."

"Or?"

"You can drink a cup of tea, and then we'll answer all your questions."

Gabriel thinks of the flower he'd plucked from the caldera behind his grandfather's place in the desert, the laboratory with its jars of herbs and tinctures, the recipe on the refrigerator, all of which he'd discovered with Francisco after the revelations of the photograph. What piece of his grandfather's work had fallen to these people? To Lenore? His mind travels to the bedrooms in the house's rear. She must be here. "Lenore!" he yells. "Lenore! Are you here?"

The semicircle still does not react. There is no attempt to quiet him, no statement that his shouting is in vain. They meet him with complete impassivity. "What'll it be, then?" Emilio asks, his voice even and quiet.

In Gabriel's thoughts the specter of his legendary great-grand-mother appears, the one they called *La urraca*. His mom had only shared a little about her *abuela*, who could float high above the desert, who could speak to animals, and who knew the language of the plants. Gabriel thinks also of his grandfather, cloistered in his laboratory, and of his own mother and the music that surrounds her perpetually, hiding her like clouds around a mountain peak. This is his own lineage, a trajectory that has arched through a century and across a desert and up the length of California to lead to . . . what? As he considers this heritage, the group before him transforms. He wasn't sure what to make of them before, but now he sees them for who they are—assistants who have somehow been enlisted in the family business. *His* family's business.

"Fine," Gabriel says. "The tea, then."

There is a barely perceptible shift within the semicircle, a slight loosening. In the kitchen, Ayla rises, takes a shot glass down from a cabinet, and unscrews the Thermos's cap.

"What does it do?" Gabriel asks.

"It's medicine," the man says.

"For what?" Gabriel says.

"There's no way to describe it. You'll just have to see."

Ayla enters the living room, cupping the glass and its golden liquid in her hands. The semicircle parts and allows her to enter. Gabriel reaches for the glass but instead of handing it to him she steps forward and swings a leg across his lap and encircles his head with her free arm so that she is straddling him, her warm body engulfing him from his thighs to the top of his head. She's holding the warm glass against the side of his head. He can smell it now, or some combination of it and her. It smells like rain in the desert, flowers and salt.

"Focus," she whispers, so quietly he's not even sure she is speaking at first. "If she can control it, so can you." She grabs a handful of his hair, tilts his head back, and pours the tea into him. There is a spice to it, and a flavor that reminds him of a lightning storm. Heat radiates from his throat. Once he swallows she leans down and presses her lips into his like she's trying to follow the tea.

And then she is gone, and they are guiding him to lie down on the couch and close his eyes and take deep breaths. Once he's supine the heat spreads, reaching into his fingers and toes, and then his thoughts slow down and his mind becomes slippery. A parade of memories arises, scattered moments he has not thought of in years: a box of green toy soldiers, dirt caked into their folds, softened from a summer of sun; a spot of blood on the thumb of an uncle who'd reached right in front of him as Gabe was loading a knife into the dishwasher; a girl in high school who'd asked him to the turnabout dance, to whom he'd said no, and later could not figure out why. With the memories come hopes, random thoughts, visions. Though each one brings a constellation of stories and a burst of emotions, they move through him easily, each one fading to leave room for the next.

As they continue to cycle past, they start to lose their structure. The names of people and places detach and drift off; the stories fall away. Wide empty spaces appear in what remains of his vocabulary— he cannot bring his words together to say where he is, or why he's here. Without the usual clamor of language cluttering his mind, sounds and images and textures and raw emotions rise and swell and whirl. The last of his words vanish, carrying away even his name. All of his thoughts are churning and breaking over him now, like storm-driven waves, and just as panic threatens to overtake him, he hears a song, a lone, familiar voice that falls from the sky. He reaches out and catches it and it pulls him forward, carrying him across the entire breadth of his life with new eyes.

Chapter 70

I n her borrowed car outside of Mercy Medical Center, Yvette takes a final pause to review her plan. Is it illegal to sneak somebody out of a hospital? Probably, but no more illegal than harboring a fugitive. And she is not one for half-measures—if she is going to harbor Leonardo, she is going to harbor the fuck out of him, whatever the obstacles. Her task here is incomplete.

She checks herself in the mirror, grimacing at her makeup job—eyeliner to change the shape of her eyes, heavy rouge, hair in a tight braid. She pulls the brim of her ball cap lower and climbs out. The hospital is exactly what she hoped for: medium-sized and busy. A harried receptionist sits behind a desk, clearly aggravated at the young couple across from her. A dozen people are splayed on chairs around the waiting room; kids are playing on the floor and a baby is crying. Orderlies and nurses come and go through wide swinging doors, rushing from one wing of the building to another.

She takes a seat with a good view, picks up a copy of *People* magazine, and continues her observations. A system of stickers marked with illegible Sharpie squiggles gives visitors the right to pass through the doorways and into the back rooms. It's all cursory, though—nobody is checking the stickers, and she can see through the doors' plexiglass windows into another room where there is an equal degree of disorder.

Near the main doors stands a trash can where many of these stickers ultimately end up, deposited by exiting visitors. Yvette pulls a stick of gum out of her purse, pops it into her mouth, walks to the trash can with the wrapper, and returns with a sticker hidden in her hand.

She waits, watching. A few minutes later the chaos at reception intensifies. A woman approaches with a teenage boy, who is clutching his arm and looking pale, and tries to shove past the couple at the window. The receptionist raises a hand to stop her while yelling for help from her supervisor. Yvette slaps the sticker on her shirt, takes a few purposeful strides, and shoves through the swinging doors into a different variety of chaos. An overcrowded nurses' station stands in the middle of an open area where a cluster of scrubs-clad staffers are attempting to work. Lining the walls are triage rooms, and occupied gurneys stand against the walls in places. A smattering of unhurried paramedics mingle among the disorder, looking at their phones or vying for the attention of some of the younger nurses.

Beyond the station, a pair of long hallways, one to her left and one straight ahead, lead into the hospital's wings. At each doorway stands a uniformed security guard. The left-side hallway is guarded by a surly-looking woman about Yvette's age, who looks like she spends her free time chopping wood. The other guard is a chubby, elderly man who could easily work as a department store Santa with the right fake beard. She chooses him and picks out a route through the disarray.

He glances at the sticker on her shirt as she approaches and gives her a smile and a nod. "Good afternoon, Miss," he says. "About a half-hour left for visiting."

"Thank you," she says, and plunges into the calm of the hallway beyond. Closed doors line both sides of the hall; whiteboards beside each one list patients' names. A dozen of the wrong ones bounce past and then finally she finds him in the last room. Doe, J., says the whiteboard.

Everything inside her twists and crumbles when Leo comes into view. He's gaunt and the patches of skin that show through his new clumps of facial hair are the wrong color, the wrong texture. He's asleep, and Yvette is almost glad she can't see his eyes. A pair of IVs drip into his arm. She allows herself only a second to take all this in. Later, when there's time, she'll eviscerate herself properly over what she allowed to happen here. But then a wave of doubt crashes over her. He's truly sick, after all—maybe this is where he needs to be. She checks the IV bags, and sees that one is saline and the other is ibuprofen. Gatorade and Advil. Nothing she can't handle herself. She marches to the far side of the room where a sliding glass door opens out onto a small patio, which is bounded by a waist-high brick wall. Two plastic chairs sit in its center. She unlocks the door, draws it open, steps outside, glances around, and then returns to Leo's bedside.

"Leo, sweetie," she says, placing a palm on his cheek and massaging. He stirs and mumbles but does not awaken. She gives him a light slap; the massage becomes a shake. "Honey," she says, louder now. "Wake up."

Leo's eyes, rimmed in red and purple, open slowly, as if each one is fighting a weight, and he looks up at her. His mumbled words are unintelligible, but there is no mistaking the flicker of recognition.

"Baby, can you sit up? We need to get you home."

He nods, robotically, as if in a dream, but he does not take his eyes off her. He pushes himself onto his elbows.

"Good, baby," she says, her heart rising. "That's really good. Can you swing your legs off the side?"

He nods again, and complies. He mutters something about a fire.

"I know, honey," she says. "You did real good. Let's get some fresh air."

Leaning upon her shoulder and dragging the rolling IV stand, he allows her to lead him to the patio, where she guides him to one of the plastic chairs. He sinks down and takes a deep breath. There are people in the parking lot, but no one is paying them any attention. She cups his cheek in her hand.

"I'm going to grab the car, baby," she says. She pulls the bags of solution off the stand and puts them in his lap. "Think you'll let me help you step over that wall?"

He nods through heavy eyes, confused but trusting. She vaults into the parking lot and runs to her car. It's a struggle helping him up and over the low wall, but soon they are heading for the exit, with Leonardo reclining all the way back in the passenger seat. She drives at the speed limit, along roads she hopes will take her inland, away from the interstate.

Chapter 71

Peoria and her cappuccino claim a table on the patio, where she has ten minutes to wait for her appointment with Special Agent Francisco Velasquez. With just one day to go before the performance, she's in Berkeley for a full rehearsal. Benicio has done outstanding work preparing his orchestra, which is all the more remarkable because of this particular program, which requires exemplary fortitude. At their last rehearsal, even the flutists were sweating. They'd played with absolute virtuosity, these one hundred incredible musicians, each of whom had dedicated tens of thousands of hours of practice to arrive here in these chairs, in supporting roles for the biggest night of her career. Hundreds of thousands of hours of sacrifice, and she would waste them all if this meeting doesn't restore her ability to concentrate.

What the hell had this guy been doing in Ocotillo? What had Gabriel been doing there? This concurrence must mean something. She senses Lenore somewhere among these improbabilities, but she can't tell where. She closes her eyes against the swirl and chatter around her. The students are in the midst of finals; she'd been lucky to find an empty table. To her right, a lanky kid in a ripped t-shirt is exasperated over his tablemate's math errors. To her left, a girl in

275

oversized headphones is staring at a laptop, looking stricken. Peoria might have chosen a quieter spot but she knew she'd need the caffeine, and wherever there was caffeine there would be crowds. Not that any of it makes any difference, not in light of the questions she has for this Francisco.

She has not had time for a second sip before he is there, sinking into the chair across from her, a look on his face of such intensity that her breathing falters. He slides across the table a photograph and a plastic bag with a small black-and-red flower in it. The flower has no meaning to her, but the photograph does. There's a ten-year-old version of herself in it, along with her father and her *abuelita* and another eight or nine aunts, uncles, and cousins. She'd seen it in Rogelio's cabinet, and it was supposed to be there still, waiting for her to come collect it.

"I wasn't looking for Gabriel," Francisco says. "I ran into him at the Cactus Market in Ocotillo, a place I used to go pretty often when I worked down there." She can't read his tone. It sounds almost pleading, but that makes no sense.

"Why the hell do you have this?" she asks him.

He extends a finger and points to a trio in the corner of the photo. It's her dad's cousin, his wife, and their baby, a tiny little bundle that couldn't be more than a few months old. She can't remember their names—there's a hand-drawn family tree somewhere, folded up among her things. Was that baby a boy or a girl? And why does any of this matter right now? The tip of his finger lands on the baby in its mother's arms.

"That's me," he says.

"What does that mean?" she asks. "That's my dad's cousin and his family."

"Yes," he says, his voice barely rising above the café's din. "That is also true." He goes on to explain, his eyes wide, his voice slow, that his grandfather, Humberto, had left Sonora behind, saying goodbye to his parents and his older sister Maria, and had come to California. Humberto had died not long after their one and only trip back to Mexico, when the photograph had been taken, and Javier had not maintained the connections.

As he talks, Peoria sits very still. She searches his face and finds her father, her grandmother, her own children, herself. Her cappuccino goes cold. Francisco is talking now about how he'd come across Gabriel in the Cactus Market in Ocotillo but she can't make all the pieces fit together, can't figure out why Gabriel was in the middle of the desert without a car, where he had come from or where he was going, or what any of these things had to do with one another. And this flower before her, contained in its baggie—why is it here?

Seeing her gaze, Francisco points at the little bloom. "Do you recognize this?"

It takes her a moment to understand he's asking her a question. She holds the bag in front of her eyes and studies the flattened petals. "No," she says. "Why?" Her fingers pry the seal open and she sniffs, expecting nothing, but the aroma that comes to her is surprisingly clear, and makes her think immediately of her father. Francisco sees her react, but he doesn't press her.

"There's something else," he says, and she can barely imagine what more there could be to this, but then he's explaining that a new video surfaced of Leo, at Sonoma State. He hadn't pushed the kid, after all. They were still going to want to talk to him, but it changed the case considerably.

His bulletin complete, Francisco—her *primo*—sits back in his chair and folds his hands in his lap. It's her turn to talk, but she feels like she has just emerged from a hurricane. "Come hear me play tomorrow," she hears herself say. "We'll talk more afterward." He nods, puts the flower back in his own pocket, and slides the photo over to her.

Chapter 72

Vasco climbs into his car and drops the flower on the passenger seat. He hits the ignition and rolls the windows down but then sits back, the car still in park, his seat belt still unbuckled, unsure where to go next.

Two days earlier he felt he had a clear grasp on the parameters of his life. There had been a sense of order and predictability, routines. A clear division between the things he was responsible for and the things he was not. But now he has somehow landed in the center of this sprawling family story, this wilderness of relationships that has sprung up all around him. His thoughts veer from there to Nicole and the promise he made to call her. Two days ago? Maybe three? He takes out his phone and sees that it's been five. Of course. Days before San Diego. He calls, and after four rings he's trying to figure out what to say on her voicemail, but then she answers.

"Well, hello there," she says, with what might be some cheer in her voice.

"Hey, hi. I know this is sudden and maybe a little outside normal, but something kind of time-sensitive came up, and I was hoping to talk to you about it in person. Are you available for ten minutes sometime today? I'll come to wherever you are."

"Yeah, outside normal is right," she says. "Sounds like you're not planning to give me a preview of this burning issue?"

"I think I'm going to be able to explain it better in person. Name the time and place."

"Well, now you've got me all curious. I'm having dinner tonight with some friends on Shattuck, but Liz has to leave at eight to get back to her kids. I'll be at Shattuck and Center, 8:05. Bring me some Red Vines."

"Red Vines?"

"Yes. Not the black ones. You bring me the black ones, and this conversation, whatever it is, will not be going as planned. Clear?"

Chapter 73

Yvette keeps the car moving, away from the hospital, heading vaguely north, maybe a bit east. It's the opposite direction from home, but I-5 is the only real way back out of town, and if anybody has seen her car, or caught it on surveillance video, it would take little effort for the police to find her.

In her haste to put together a disguise and get to the hospital she had tried to look at a map, but her reception had been shitty, and the image hadn't resolved, other than to show this highway—State Route Thirty-something—heading along the base of the mountain. There was a faded map on the wall outside the gas station restroom, but an inset featuring some rafters in whitewater blocked the region in question. The only turn-offs she has seen in twenty minutes of just-slightly-over-the-speed-limit driving are dirt roads, plunging into the woods. But she knows enough about this area to suspect it won't be long before the Oregon border appears, which will force a decision out of her. With her ability to claim ignorance long gone, and with her image on who knew how many CCTV feeds, crossing state lines might just be her last and worst decision of all.

Either an outlet will present itself or she will have to turn back and risk going down I-5. Once at the border she might be able to cut back over to the coast and head south that way, but she'd probably still have to go back through Mount Shasta City, and for all she knows, they have figured out who John Doe is by now, and who she is, and the whole area is one big trap. "Why the fuck did I just do that?" she asks herself, in a whisper. What has she actually changed? She could have let things run their course. Leo would have been taken into custody sooner or later, regardless. In this scenario, she is neck-deep in it with him. In the other scenario she is back at home, uninvolved, the caring, innocent girlfriend, and his fate is not much different either way. In fact, it might have even been better to just let him get identified at the hospital. This whole time she had been trying to create a narrative of sympathy for him, and what the hell could have possibly been more sympathetic than this pitiful creature, undernourished, feverish, fleeing a fire, crawling out of the wilderness and collapsing in someone's yard? Maybe all she's doing is fucking things up for both of them. Leo groans and shifts in his seat. He babbles a few words and emits a little laugh and falls back into stillness and her heart rises a little and warms. She allows herself to study him as much as the windy two-lane highway will allow her to. Sleeping in her reclined passenger seat, a blanket over him, the IV bag hanging from the visor, Professor Percival—or Professor Precocious, as she sometimes calls him—is the picture of helplessness. And he is entirely her responsibility.

That's why she went back for him. He had trusted her to leave him in the middle of absolutely nowhere, with no contact to the world but for her, utterly reliant on her for every bite he ate, every sip of water, and she had failed him. She had miscalculated, spent too much time letting things develop, or blow over, or do whatever the hell they were doing, and this is what happened. God only knows how close he might have come to death. At least he wasn't burned. If she had come up here to find him in the burn ward she would have died. She put him in this position, and regardless of what it means in the eyes of the law, she is going to carry out her responsibilities.

And when it does come to a close, what will these weeks mean for their future together? From where she sits now, flying north along a two-lane road through the woods with the light of a summer day weakening around them, it all seems just as likely to bind them together forever as it does to drive them apart. If they don't make it, though, one thing is for sure. He'll never find another woman like her. Nobody else will ever do this kind of shit for him. He'll remember it, too, and if in a dozen years he finds himself eating an underseasoned chicken breast with a wife named Jessica or Allison and a couple of boring kids he will always be wondering if Jessica or Allison would hide him from the cops and then bust him out of a hospital. She allows herself a wry smile and a glance at her unconscious passenger.

Another fifteen minutes go by without a single major intersection. The road cuts a canyon through the pines and firs, which soar up on either side of them, their branches knitting into impenetrable walls. After a bend a road sign appears, announcing the Oregon border in thirty miles. Her phone still shows no reception. Leonardo sleeps, oblivious to her deliberations and the approaching crossroads.

Chapter 74

When language returns to Gabriel's brain it comes first in basic colors: white, brown, red. The room comes back into focus—not that he couldn't see it before, but it had lacked order, meaning. Nouns come next—couch, wall, chair, table—and as the names of things return, so does his memory of their functions. Wood, leather, sunlight, girl. In a rush now comes description, back all at once. *Ajar*: the front door, halfway open. *The golden hour*: the angle and color of the day's waning sunlight. And *Ayla*: the girl watching him from a chair at the kitchen table.

"Your body needs sustenance," she says. "Come here."

He understands her words, but can't remember how to reply to her. There is a name for the tone in her voice, but it hasn't come back to him yet. But she's right. A sudden hunger fills him, a strange craving for plants, for the earth. He rises to his feet, feeling the strange contrast of a heaviness in his limbs and a weightlessness in his chest and throat.

There is a huge salad on the table, topped with nuts and slices of pear. In other dishes are slices of cucumber, carrots, celery. There is a full pint glass of thick green juice. He gives Ayla a look of surprise and she responds with a small nod. "Sit and eat," she says.

When he bites down on the first forkful of salad it is as if he's never eaten before. He can feel the sunlight in each leaf, nut, and slice of fruit as its cells dissipate, sending nutrients and minerals and elements he cannot name plunging happily into his body. The flavors trigger sensations in his toes, in his fingertips, the back of his head. Ayla sits quietly, sipping her tea, watching the steam rise. She isn't looking at him but somehow he can feel her attention upon him, and it, too, feels like warmth and vitality, like sunlight. The past tense trickles back into his brain, bringing with it the memory of who she is, and how this braid of lives formed when Ayla and Lenore became friends, all those years ago. He sees, perceiving with a mind that feels not fully his own, the net that holds them together.

Ayla allows Gabriel several minutes of silence while he works through one dish after another. When he is nearly finished, she sighs and tilts her head. "I hate to wreck your buzz, but we have to talk about a few things," she says. "First, I'm sorry I kissed you. I needed to get you a message, and I wasn't sure how to do it. I figured if I had only whispered in your ear, they would have noticed, and been suspicious. So I added the kiss to throw them off."

With that, his search for Lenore comes back to him. And more memories: the tea, a hand on his forehead, a song. "Wait," he says, finding it takes all of his concentration to choose and form his words. "What happened, exactly?"

"It's all about language. When we put a name on a thing, an action, a concept, we pin it down. We restrain it, kill its vitality. It's the same thing with the stories we tell ourselves. We encapsulate our experiences in short stories, and then we try to remember the stories. But actually, we can barely remember anything at all. What we're really remembering is the last time we made the memory, not the event itself. We make imperfect recordings of imperfect recordings, and everything just gets more and more calcified and brittle. The tea—it takes all that away.

All the words, all the stories. Everything can move and breathe again. And now, as things come back to you, you can reconsider where they belong." She points to his forehead and draws a little circle in the air. "You can tell yourself new stories."

Gabriel is barely keeping up with her words. With a monumental effort, he returns his focus to his search. "Lenore," he says. "She was here."

"Yes. She's the one who figured this all out. But you're going to have to get that story a different time." He tries to get the memories to hold still, but they float like vapor and vanish whenever he reaches for them. Ayla is watching him, the steam gone from her tea. "It can take a while for it all to come back," she says, seeing his confusion. She lifts her mug and sets it down with a thump, like she's gaveling a meeting to order. "But unfortunately, we don't have a while."

"For what?"

"I'm supposed to tell you to meet them in Seattle. In two days."

He grabs a hold of the edge of the table. "Why?"

"Either you passed the initiation and now you're part of the club, and they want you to join them on the northwest leg of their tour. Or they're trying to get rid of you."

"Why don't you know?" He turns and gestures toward the open front door, in the direction of whoever they are, wherever they went. "Aren't you in the middle of it?" The words are getting easier to produce, but his ideas are still not coming together. It's like he can't remember how to think.

"I've been deposed, Gabriel. They don't trust me anymore."

"What happened?"

"What happened? You happened. You and your brother."

She reaches across the table and takes his hand, runs her fingers over the healing tattoo. "These were an identification system. One of them, I don't know who, came up with it, along with some tattooer they knew. I thought it was all kind of elaborate and silly, but I wasn't on the road, taking the risks, so I went along with it. Fine." She releases his hand and sits back. "But almost as soon as they left, I got a bad feeling. The whole thing took on a life of its own fast, with all these other people involved. And that guy, Emilio, who's like their leader. I worried that Lenore was going to be able to stay in control of it. So when you showed up, I decided to send you after her. There was a mechanism for that—members of the group coming and going, cycling in and out, spelling each other, coordinated by me and my uncle with the help of the tattooer. But then that shit went down with Leo, and as soon as they learned about that, you appeared. But you hadn't experienced *el regreso* yet, and they were beyond paranoid at that point, so they tossed you out on the street and they closed ranks." She points to his wrist, where the carp sits between them, still, as though listening. "Your passport expired before it scabbed up," she says. "But at least it's pretty."

"So now what?"

"I know you don't really remember seeing her," she concludes, "because of how the *centella* messes with your memory. But I don't think she's doing okay. This isn't on her terms anymore. She's altered all the time now, and what did we learn in sex ed? If you're fucked up, you can't give consent. But they're not going to stop. They've seen what she can do, and they've built up this momentum and word is circulating. They're looking to get her out of the state next. It's too much for her, though. And I think they might be trying to steal the information, and maybe even the *centella* itself."

"Does she really own it, though?"

"That's not for me to decide, or them. It's your family's. It's powerful—you've only experienced the first part of it. As time goes by you'll come to see how it's changed you. If you want to give it to the world, that's up to you." She points to the door. "But these random dudes don't get to decide that, no matter how much my uncle vouches for them."

"Your uncle?"

"It doesn't matter. What you need to decide right now is if you're going to Seattle or not."

The table and the dishes, the girl and the kitchen vanish as Gabriel's mind twists to take this all in, to assimilate this new version of his little sister. He'd always known her to be unique, extraordinary, precocious, but now Ayla's revelations have made her nearly unrecognizable. He closes his eyes and fixes her face in his mind, just as he'd done countless times back in prison, when he'd wanted to conjure a sense of her presence. He forces himself to take a deep breath, to study the image of her face, to think about the shape of her life. Why shouldn't this be her? Is there anything about her that precludes a capacity for any of this? Why shouldn't she be the heir of their strange lineage, the spiritual descendent of a flying *curandera*, a mad scientist grandfather, an otherworldly pianist? And where did he come in?

He brings his focus back to Ayla. "So what's in Seattle?" he says.

"A wild goose chase, if you ask me," she says. "I think it's a ploy to get rid of you. They don't trust anybody outside their little group. What I believe is that she communicated something to you, in the midst of your journey. It won't be in words, so don't try to remember words. A shape, an image, a feeling that will point you somewhere. Somewhere nearby, where she'll be. A place you have to go to get her."

Gabriel folds his hands and looks toward the west-facing windows, where the sun is sinking toward the bay. He tries to get a fix on the images he'd seen while under the flowers' influence, but there had been thousands of them, and each one is dim and faint, like the substance of a long-ago dream.

"It's dangerous for them to be here in Berkeley," Ayla says, "but there's a journey planned for tomorrow night. I don't know where. And I'm guessing they'll be gone by the following morning. So remember fast."

Chapter 75

The world comes back to Leonardo in fragments, small bits of sensation that lack meaning, disconnected from each other, each one like the contents of a flash card briefly shown to him by some erratic and half-interested inquisitor. Smell comes first: the scent of pines and warm dirt, a floral spice that brings him comfort though he can't name it. And then touch: vibrations, an alternation of heat and cold that he feels not on his skin but in his bones, a rocking like a boat's, a thirst that comes and goes of its own accord. Next, sounds: a hum, wheels on a road, quiet radio voices, somebody breathing. Images arrive last. Yvette is here, driving him somewhere. Their headlights illuminate the road up to the next rise; beyond that and on either side of them rise black walls of trees. A purple tinge in the sky signals either the end or the beginning of a day.

"Hey there," she says. "Leo." There is emotion in her voice, but he can't tell what kind. When did they leave for a drive? What is this forest? She puts her hand on his leg, rubs a few small circles, gives his thigh a pat. "How are you?" she asks. "How are you feeling?"

He thinks, but he does not think about how he feels. Instead he thinks of the dream he was having. He'd been in a cabin somewhere and then there was a fire, a fire that nearly engulfed him, and then a dark sloping forest. He stares through the window, trying to finish waking up. It's much harder than usual, for some reason. He tries to stretch out, to coax feeling through his limbs, but his feet feel like they're a thousand miles away, and his fingers belong to someone else.

"Where are we?"

"Pretty well up north. But we're heading home. We have to get you some clothes first, though."

He looks down and finds himself covered by a cheap, unfamiliar blanket. He peeks underneath and sees a hospital gown, an IV line stuck in his forearm.

A flash of heat sweeps over him, starting in his brow and sinking quickly to his toes, twisting his gut as it descends. "What the fuck?" he says.

Yvette is chuckling for some reason. "It's a long story," she says. She points to the road ahead, which stretches out before them, black and empty, through the endless forest. "But it looks like we'll have time."

Chapter 76

The sun is setting as Gabriel reaches the driveway that leads to the door of his childhood home. Upstairs the light is on in his father's office, pressing through the open window as if to meet the coming darkness. Ahead, his mother is elbow-deep in her flower garden, her burnt orange shirt glowing and twisting like a flame with her movements. Her presence there means she's ready. Returning herself to *la tierra*, as she once told him, is a critical part of her process. A cleanse. "After all those hours in the company of dead European men, I have to remind myself who I am," she'd said in an interview once, a quotation that traveled well beyond the usual publications of the classical music world. She notices her son's approach and she stands to meet him.

"*Hola, mijo*," she says. "Welcome back." She leans in and kisses him on the cheek. "You went to find a sister and found an uncle instead. Serendipitous."

"I'm not done yet," he tells her, looking up at the darkening house as if it might impart a direction, a clue, an idea.

"Don't worry," Peoria says. "She'll be home soon."

"You heard from her?"

"No. Just a feeling."

"Okay," he says, but he has begun listening for other things: the echoes of his family's long-ago voices as they spill through the windows and the open doorway, the various rhythms of their footfalls upon the hardwood floors.

"Go in," she says, turning back to her flowers. "Get something to eat."

He heads down the hallway and into the kitchen and sees that everything is a little too clean, a little too orderly. This is his father's influence. With his sons out of the house and Lenore's absence, Redland would have been channeling his anxiety into organizing, cleaning, expunging. There's a sense of precariousness to the tidiness, though. Entropy is never denied, especially in the vicinity of *la familia Gonzalez.*

It was always difficult for Gabriel to find a home for himself between these two poles. On the one hand, here was his father, the James Fife Endowed Chair of one of the most esteemed mechanical engineering programs in the country, whose methodical quest for sparse efficiency had carried him to the top of his field. And on the other hand, here was his mother, who seemed perpetually to be under the spell of some force trying to pull her right out of this reality. He had to wonder where she'd be if it weren't for her music, for the massive piano downstairs that anchored her to the planet. Of the three siblings, he'd always felt like he was the only one who hadn't been able to figure out how to achieve some functional combination of these opposing examples. Leonardo had taken after Redland in terms of his schooling and his career, but he carried Peoria's unpredictability as a rakish charm that brought him interesting friends and exotic girlfriends. Lenore had inherited her mother's ease with the arts—throughout her childhood she had experimented with drawing, sculpting, painting, ceramics, music, dancing, and who knew what else, and in each discipline had exhibited an immediate competence that pointed to limitless potential.

She carried just enough of her father's reason to stay out of trouble and maintain her grades and to steer clear of the traps that adolescence often held for those with unconventional intelligences. Gabriel, on the other hand, had stumbled in and out of trouble, struggled with grades, and only delved into the arts when he was bored and there were materials in arm's reach. He alone, it seemed, had failed to seize upon either of his parents' gifts, to take a single significant step in any direction despite the endless range of possibilities they modeled.

But now, as he shuffles out of the kitchen and back into the hallway, heading for the stairs, it's clear that he was wrong. He isn't the only one struggling to reconcile these disparate entities, after all. On the contrary—he had been ahead of the curve, the first of the three of them to figure out that there is actually no way in hell to gracefully balance these opposing forces. He and Leo, and Lenore—their respective attempts had all led to strangeness, unpredictability, disarray. Disappearance. The best any of them can hope for, he realizes, is to simply contain those forces, to stay intact as the factions warred inside them, pulling them first one way and then the other.

He heads up the stairs, still searching the air for a sense of his sister. The sparseness of Lenore's room startles Gabriel anew—he'd forgotten that she had packed up all of her things. He walks to her dresser, where her two-word note still remains. He places a hand on either side of the note, his palms pressed against the dresser's surface as if to draw out any secrets contained inside it. When none emerge he moves a hand to the wall and walks over to her closet, sliding his fingers across the wall's surface, unwilling to break contact. Inside the closet are stacks of banker's boxes. He lifts the lid from one and finds boxes within boxes, all labeled in precise handwriting. Gabriel closes the box, shuts the closet door, and returns to the dresser, this time with his other hand on the wall. He takes the note from the top of the dresser and crosses over to her bed, where he sits down. He makes a bowl with his hands in his lap—palms up, one hand over the other—and holds the note inside it, where he can study it. But nothing in the ink or the paper speaks to him, and after a time a sudden weariness overtakes him. He kicks his shoes off and lies down on his back, the note contained in a closed fist over his heart, and immediately falls asleep.

Chapter 77

Vasco is at the appointed intersection at the appointed time, a box of Red Vines protruding from his coat pocket. It's a Friday night in downtown Berkeley—in the fall the bars and restaurants here would be overflowing, the sidewalks knotted with undergrads, but most of them have scattered back home for the summer, leaving the streets to couples, families, and small clusters of grad students. Vasco's nerves are getting to him a little bit. It's been a long time since he allowed himself to want anything from a woman, and it's a foreign feeling. He's not sure he likes it much, but nonetheless, here he is. And he'd even had to talk himself out of buying her the giant tub of Red Vines, the one that's the size of a spare tire.

Nicole appears right on time. She's wearing a red sweater over a black dress, with her hair in a neat bun, and strands framing her face. Droplets of silver hang from her ears. There's a smell around her, like jasmine mixed with oranges. She steps right up to him, as if to give him a kiss, but then reaches out and pulls the Red Vines out of his pocket. "Why, thank you," she says, ripping into the packet. "Let's walk up the creek a bit, shall we?"

He nods. "How was dinner?"

They head toward the edge of campus, where Strawberry Creek winds through a grove of redwoods and eucalyptuses before diving underground. "It was lovely, thank you. But you didn't come here to ask me about food." She hands him a couple of pieces of licorice.

"No, I did not." He accepts the candy and takes a breath. "A couple of days ago I found out I have a cousin in the area, someone I never knew existed. I met her for the first time yesterday. Well, that's not entirely true. I met her yesterday for the first time knowing she was my cousin. But anyway, it turns out she's one of the top classical pianists in the world. And the new arts center?" He points up the hill, where the newly reconstructed concert hall stands, just a quarter-mile away. "The grand opening is tomorrow. She's performing."

They stop at the corner to wait for the light, and he steals a glance at Nicole. She's chewing slowly, looking puzzled. A fair reaction. "She invited me," Vasco says, "and I wondered if you might be interested in coming with me." Her puzzlement remains in place, but there's a tinge of a smile in it. The light changes, and they step into the crosswalk. "If you're free, of course," he adds, and then wishes he hadn't.

Instead of answering him, she hands him another pair of Red Vines, and then takes a bite of her own. On the other side of the street they step onto campus, and into the darkness of the grove. "I have some questions," she says. "It's not normally my style to pry, but you just asked me to a black-tie affair with your family as a first date. You know that's like a year-two kind of thing, right?"

"Yeah, that's why I wanted—"

She cuts him off with a wave of her licorice stub. "It's fine. I'm tired of coffee dates and walks around the marina anyway. But you've also given me less than twenty-four hours' notice, and I want to know what I'm getting myself into here. Deal?"

"Deal."

"Good. First—you just discovered a cousin? How does that happen?"

"A cousin, her husband, and three kids. Two nephews and a niece I never knew I had." They leave the sidewalk for the cobblestone path, which runs through pools of lamplight along the creek. Above them, the day's last light is disappearing. "It was through work, actually," he says. "In a way. Kind of."

"Okay. So what kind of work leads a man to long-lost family?"

"Law enforcement," he says. "I'm with the DEA."

"What does the DEA have to do with your famous musician cousin?"

Vasco wasn't expecting this line of questioning, and he isn't sure what to say. When people find out what he does for a living, they're usually so intrigued that they forget what they'd been talking about before. She hadn't even blinked.

"It's kind of a long story," he says.

"So give me the short version."

"I'm not sure I have a short version."

"Well, is she a good guy or a bad guy?"

"It's not exactly like that."

"Okay. So tell me what it's like."

"It's complicated. She's . . ." He trails off, unsure if there's any way he can possibly convey a sense of his last couple of weeks. Maybe it had been a mistake to reach out to Nicole. Why had he asked her to step into all this chaos?

"You want me to jump right into the middle of this thing with your cousin, but you're not able to tell me a thing about her? Is it classified?"

"No, nothing like that."

She stops walking, and this time when she bites off a chunk of licorice it reminds him of a wolf severing sinew. Vasco stops and waits, trying to figure out when this conversation went off the rails. She chews, studying his face, and then levels the candy box at his chest. "So you're the big, strong, independent cop, and I'm the girl whose sensitivities are just too delicate to handle the emotional and psychological complexities of your important job. Is that about right?"

Long ago, Vasco learned that if he didn't have a good response, then he should just shut up. Nicole resumes walking, a little faster than before, and he remembers why he spends so little time dating.

"You don't imagine that I pay Bay Area rent with occasional bouldering lessons, do you? Would you like to know what I do for a living?"

"Yes," he says, a little more quietly than he'd intended.

"I'm a lieutenant in the Richmond Fire Department. I learned emergency medicine from the US Army, and I did tours as a combat medic in Iraq and Afghanistan." Without slowing down, she pulls up the sleeve of her sweater and shows him her forearm. The lamplight illuminates a constellation of small scars. How had he missed those when they were climbing? "Shrapnel," she says. "IED. The soldier next to me lost his leg."

They reach the bridge and she stops at the edge and looks down at the water. California is drying out, like it does every spring, and there is only a trickle. It's stunning to Vasco, the degree to which he'd underestimated her, without ever having made a single conscious assumption. It hadn't been deliberate—he just hadn't taken the time to think about who she might actually be, what worlds she might be hiding within herself. How many times has he done this to others? He'd let his career grow to be so all-encompassing that human relationships outside the agency had become speed bumps. The discovery of Peoria and her family had shown him something new, though. Their appearance was like a glimpse through an open doorway into a warm, bright home when he'd been wandering outside. And now he'd come across Nicole, who not only sees right into him, but also has the words to dismantle him entirely in less time than it takes to eat a three-dollar pack of licorice.

She turns to him and taps him in the chest with the empty candy box. "I do happen to be free tomorrow, and I accept your invitation," she says. "It sounds wonderful. Thank you. And I suppose there should also be a part of this conversation where you tell me that you might get yanked away from our date, or any other date, at any time, right?"

"Pretty much."

"Not if I get yanked away first," she says.

Vasco can't do anything but nod. He's not sure which of Nicole's revelations have him reeling the most. She tucks the empty box into his pocket, takes him by the arm, and leads him back the way they'd come. "Whatever happens," she says, "don't forget—you're the one who decided to kick this off at a hundred miles an hour."

He smiles. "I guess I did."

"Good. I'm glad we're in agreement there. Now go and get yourself ready, because I'm going to look fucking stunning tomorrow."

Chapter 78

On her way up the stairs, Peoria examines the dirt on her hands: reds, browns, blacks. After weeks of the black-and-white, ordered worlds of musical charts and her piano keyboard, it feels glorious to have been able to plunge her hands into the earth's wildness, to feel the warmth and movement of microbes, insects, worms, weeds. She puts a fingertip into her mouth and sucks the dirt off of it, cleaning out the underside of her fingernail with the corner of a tooth. She feels the grit of tiny pebbles across her teeth and tastes the chalk and the minerals, the forests and mountains and deserts. When she swallows it she imagines the sunlight it contains shining out of her throat.

Lenore's door is ajar, so she pushes it open and finds Gabriel asleep on her bed, his hands clasped over his heart as in the stone carving atop a knight's sarcophagus. She stands in the doorway for a time, watching his arms rise and fall with the breath in his chest, and then she enters the room and very slowly, very carefully, she lies down next to him, on her side. She places her hand over his, nestles her forehead against his temple, synchronizes her breathing with his, and within minutes, she, too, is asleep.

Chapter 79

've been asleep and now it's night. In this bed I feel weightless, numb. I think I'm on my side. There's a smudged glass door, a courtyard, two palm trees, and a patch of grass in floodlights. I can't stay at Ayla's—it's too close to home. So we're here, somewhere else in town. I'm not sure where. I wasn't paying attention when we came. It doesn't matter though. We won't be here long. Another journey tomorrow and then we'll be moving on. I feel like there's something I'm supposed to be thinking about, but I can't remember what it is. There are too many places to be at once. I do know Gabo was here. Sometimes I could hear him humming. I wonder where he is now. I wonder when I'll be able to talk to him. And Leo.

Between the palms is a small cactus, lobes stacked upon lobes, and that's when I realize it: My grandfather's drawing is not a taxonomy but a family tree. Ours. The dark line, and the string of stones—they run through my great-grandmother, my grandfather, my mother, me and my brothers, and down through children who do not yet exist. The quartz—that's me. What does it mean? The darker lines, the symbols? Who are we?

The lights switch off; the cactus disappears.

Chapter 80

The beginning of Gabriel's dream contains no light—just a feeling of tight closeness and the smell of the earth. The darkness lightens to brown, and then red and then yellow, and he emerges from the sands of a bright and endless desert. He grows and blooms into a red flower, flecked with black spots, and then he comes loose and rises. Now he's flying, with the sun at his back. He soars over dunes and scrub. Small pueblos appear, clusters of huts huddled around church plazas, bound to one another in a web of dirt roads. He crosses plains and ridges and valleys and then the ocean appears, far off to his left, blue and glittering.

A flash of color at the edge of his vision causes him to look down at himself and he finds he's wearing voluminous skirts, every color imaginable layered over one another, all of them flapping and curling in the rushing wind. There's a pocket hidden in one of their folds, and from it he produces a small painted flute. The flute rises to his lips and he plays a melody, a short phrase that makes him think of the rising sun. He repeats it, once and then again, and though he returns the flute to its secret pocket the song remains in the air, flying along with him.

A sprawling city appears now, perched on the edge of the land, and Gabriel recognizes San Diego. Los Angeles glides past next, and before long the southern edge of the San Francisco Bay slides into place beneath him. He soars up its eastern shore, heading for his hometown and back to his sleeping self, but instead of angling toward the house on the hill he soars down over the flats until he's just above a large, multi-storied, wood-shingled building just off the Berkeley campus. His feet touch down in a patch of long grass in a courtyard, just between two palms, right next to a cactus. He needs to go inside the building—there are tasks waiting for him but he can't move, for his feet have taken root. The skirts are gone; his legs have become a single sage-green stem, his arms black and red petals. The petals shrink and withdraw, collapsing into a bud, and then the stem collapses, pulling him underground as he becomes a seed again.

Chapter 81

In the darkness of her daughter's bedroom, Peoria jolts awake. She gasps, her eyes wide. The song—her grandmother's song—is suddenly there, filling her ears, rippling across her skin, vibrating in her marrow, every note clear and pure. She leaps up and runs downstairs to her piano.

Chapter 82

Gabriel awakens with the clarity and urgency of his dream still intact. He knows the building and its courtyard—it's Longford Hall, a student housing co-op with a notorious history. He and his high school friends had developed a knack for infiltrating parties there, coming away with stories to astonish their less ambitious classmates. But this hadn't been a nostalgia dream, some random neurological replay. This had been about the future.

As soon as it's light, Gabriel sets out. Peoria is already at her piano downstairs. The melody rising through the floorboards is familiar, but he can't place it. Outside, the cold, quiet dawn opens up all around him.

He approaches Longford Hall slowly, the brim of a ball cap pulled low over his face, and is happy to find the residence hall in an end-of-year state of chaos. The front door stands wide, propped open by a cinder block, and a line of minivans, station wagons, and moving vans are double-parked outside it. A trio of women carrying a futon frame emerges from the doorway and heads for one of the moving vans. Gabriel slips inside and quickly scans the entryway, trying to remember the array of faces that had confronted him at Ayla's. He has to find them without being seen—if one of them recognizes him the whole opportunity could be lost, so he needs to find a way to blend into the wallpaper, the battered wood trim. He needs to be a phantom.

The halls smell like a thousand lives, old furniture, the spills of last night's beers beneath lemon wood polish. He'd always been here at night and in thick crowds, but his memory of the layout serves him well, and he formulates a plan to begin on the top floor and work his way downward. On the stairway he climbs quickly, reaching the top with a thudding heart. The top three floors reveal nothing, and as he picks his way through the larger ground floor he begins to doubt himself but then in the back corner of a common room, he finds what he's looking for—the man he'd encountered at the Cactus Market, arguing with two of the others he'd seen at Ayla's. He turns and heads for the door, keeping his face hidden.

Once he's clear of Longford Hall he slows and peels off his sweatshirt. He'd begun to sweat, and the morning air is an instantaneous balm. He adjusts his cap and wonders at everything the last few days have sent hurtling toward him: his grandfather's house, a long-lost uncle, the *centella* journey, the dream and its song, and now—his sister. He's a spider in the center of a web, a hundred filaments converging in his abdomen. Everything is in his hands now; he just has to figure out what to do with it.

He tells himself to think. What he really wants to do is to call his brother. Not the version of him who had become too preoccupied and too busy for everyone else, but the version Gabriel had known when they were kids—the Leonardo who always had a plan, who seemed to know his way in and out of every situation. He'd been the one to show Gabriel how to sneak into Longford Hall parties in the first place.

Where Leonardo should have been, this Francisco has appeared. Is he the trade? Had the vacuum left by the disappearances of his siblings somehow pulled this uncle into being? But he is not just an uncle, Gabriel reminds himself, as he crosses Bancroft Way and walks onto campus. He is also a federal investigator who got wind of the *centella* and his job is to put people in prison.

But there's nobody else. There's nobody else to help, and if he cannot get to her tonight, she could disappear again. Could Francisco help? Would he? He takes out his phone, pulls up Francisco's information, and taps out a text: *How soon can you meet me? Sproul Plaza.* No sooner does he send it then his phone buzzes with an incoming text. It's from Yvette: *I need to talk to you in person ASAP.* He takes a seat on the steps and taps out a response, telling her where he is.

Chapter 83

Vasco walks into Sproul Plaza, coffee in hand, unsure what to expect from Gabriel. Sudden text requests for in-person meetings are always cause to be on high alert. And in this case, the timing is strange, as well—he would be seeing Gabriel that evening, at Peoria's performance.

Finals must be just about over. There are no more than a dozen, unhurried students scattered through the whole plaza. Pigeons cluster, lamenting the lack of scavenging opportunities in the quiet season. A single toll from the bell tower announces the bottom of the hour. Gabriel is sitting on the steps of Sproul Hall, alone and empty-handed. Vasco recognizes him from afar—there's something familiar in his posture, his body language. Gabriel sees Vasco coming, too, and he nods without rising. Vasco closes the distance and sits down.

"She's here," Gabriel says. His voice is low and even.

"Home?"

"Not yet."

"Okay. So let's get her there."

Gabriel nods and looks up, but not at Vasco. Out toward the street. "Yeah, that's the plan," he says, almost to himself.

Vasco waits, but Gabriel doesn't elaborate. A beat passes, and then another. "So why are we still sitting here?" Vasco says.

"It isn't time yet," Gabriel says. He reaches down and rubs his thumb across his wrist tattoo a few times, then shoots another glance toward the street. "You'll be around tonight?"

"Why isn't it time?" This isn't making sense. Gabriel's message, his weirdly calm demeanor, his preoccupation with the foot traffic along Bancroft—it isn't coming together. Vasco sets his coffee down. He likes to have his hands free when he doesn't know what's going on.

"Can you back me up?" Gabriel asks.

"What does that mean?"

"I just want to know if you'll be around, and if you can back me up."

"What would I be backing up, exactly?"

"I'm not sure yet."

Vasco takes a few seconds to try to understand what Gabriel might be considering. None of the outcomes he imagines end well. Gabriel doesn't look remotely worried, though. "We're two people," Vasco says. "And they're at least, what? Seven? Eight?" Gabriel shrugs. Vasco still doesn't know what's going on, but he picks his coffee back up anyway. "Gabriel, let's get your sister home safely. I do this kind of thing for a living, okay? Situations like this—they can go sideways in a heartbeat. You don't want to be responsible for endangering Lenore."

"Situations like what?" It sounds like it might be a challenge, but Gabriel's tone is calm, almost sleepy.

"Where there are drugs, there are guns, Gabriel. You're planning to walk into an unknown situation and you want me to back you up, alone, with no intel at all? I couldn't do that if I wanted to."

"I haven't seen any drugs. Have you?"

"You don't know what these people are up to. Your sister is involved, and your care for her means you can't evaluate the situation objectively. You're too close."

"I took it yesterday."

"Took what?"

"The *centella*."

The steps disappear from under Vasco. His equilibrium slips away; he has to plant his elbows on his knees to steady himself. A squirrel darts over from the lawn, rears up and looks at them, and then darts away.

"They were all there," Gabriel says. "They gave it to me. Lenore."

Vasco wants to ask what it was like, what it does. He wants to ask why, and how, and where, not because it matters to his case, but for some other reason he can't quite identify. He turns and looks hard at Gabriel, whose face remains beatific. "What now, then?" he asks.

"Now I want to have a word with my sister."

Vasco tells himself to refocus on the task at hand—the missing girl, his training, his reasons for investigating all this. But his grandfather had never told Vasco much about his childhood. He had come north, a branch falling from the family tree, and all the stories Vasco knew about his lineage began with that trip across the border and up the fertile valleys of California. They had all gone back to Sonora just that one time, when Vasco was a baby, and then never again. Why had he never wondered about all that had been left behind? What else had been lost in that schism?

"I suppose this all looks pretty different to you now, then," Vasco says, trying to get a foothold on the shifting ground. Gabriel doesn't respond. He's tracking someone on the other side of the plaza now—Vasco follows his gaze and notes a woman, walking quickly, her long red ponytail swaying. Gabriel's eyes dart away from her and back, and then again. He's trying to make it seem like he's not watching her as she takes a seat at a table on the patio of the café across the plaza, pulls out her phone, and crosses her legs. Vasco is doing everything he can to find his way back to center, and Gabriel is calmly checking out women. The contrast only adds to Vasco's confusion. "Gabriel, try to see this from where I'm sitting. You tell me you want to talk to your sister, but you also say you want back-up. I don't understand if you're looking for an uncle or the police."

Gabriel doesn't respond. A cluster of students walk past, laughing. The pigeons scatter before them and then come back together in their wake. And then Vasco recognizes her. Yvette Cartwright, Leonardo's girlfriend and spokesperson, here for an in-person with Gabriel of her own. A jolt of heat pierces Vasco's chest, launched by one of the many questions swirling in his head now. He's not sure which.

"I might be able to help you," he says, "but I'd need to know some things first." He rises to his feet and collects his paper cup. "If you remember anything helpful after you're done chatting with Yvette, give me a call." He walks away without a glance back at either of them.

Chapter 84

Yvette spies Gabriel on the steps of Sproul Hall. He's mid-conversation with someone else, so she veers to the opposite side of the plaza, heading for the café just beyond the fountain. The guy he's talking to looks like a Mexican pop star who's about ten years past his prime. He looks confused, and Gabriel is as calm as he can be. Is he high? What now, with this family? She didn't know she was going to have to wait in line here.

She takes a seat at the corner table on the café's patio, angling herself toward the clock tower, and then lets out a big breath. Weariness comes over her; it begins at her crown and then drops down through her eyes and lungs. She clamps her eyes shut, breathes in, and tells herself there can't be much left of this saga. Not for her, anyway.

She and Leonardo made it back to town a little after two in the morning. The drive southward had been painful. She'd kept to the highlands for as long as she could stand it, winding through the forest for hours, past innumerable clusters of run-down cabins, weathered motels, the occasional two-block town. When the adrenaline finally washed away it left her depleted but she drove on, feeling her way southward, her mind too weary to do anything but wonder, over and over, how much she'd fucked everything up. Finally she'd dared to turn west, tumbling out of the mountains into Oroville, which stood on the edge of the valley where flat, straight roads would guide her back toward the Bay Area. If she could stay awake, that is. If not, they'd fly off the shoulder and die together in a ditch at the edge of some farmer's orchard.

Leonardo seemed to have been improving as they continued their drive. He stayed awake for longer and longer intervals, each time seeming more and more like himself. His memories of the fire and what happened afterward were spotty, but he told her about the days prior, and he even cracked a couple of jokes, his laugh splintering into shallow coughs. The slow inhalation he took to catch his breath sent such a flush of soft warmth through her she worried she might start crying, right there in the fast lane.

With the help of some drive-thru coffee she made it home, where she'd quickly ushered him into her house, fed him some leftover enchiladas, and put him to bed, where he instantly resumed his sleep. He was home and healthy, but now she had a fugitive on her couch, and Lenore was still nowhere to be found. She wanted to help—she'd done everything she could do to mitigate Leonardo's wayward direction in all this, and to navigate the detour the mountain had thrown at them, but she's running out of time, space, ideas, and energy. She needs someone else to step up and take charge of this man, someone who shares his blood and his name.

It is strange to know so little about his brother. Her understanding of him has been pieced together entirely from his family's stories, from the photos hanging on the walls at his parents' house, from the shapes of the empty spaces where he used to be. She'd gone once with Leo to visit him in prison. Leo hadn't wanted her to, but she'd insisted, for reasons she still doesn't understand. She'd gone in expecting to feel something powerful—anger, sadness, maybe sympathy. Other than the novelty of the steel and the cement and the procedures, though, it had been almost forgettable. She found Gabriel to be warm but distant, strangely calm given the surroundings, like the quiet neighbor you're friendly with but know nothing about. She saw him a couple of times after his release, each time at the Percival home, where she'd been preoccupied with studying the shift from the balanced symmetry of a family of four to the sprawl of five. The middle child, returned. And then everyone's life, her own included, had taken a sharp turn.

She grimaces and reminds herself that it's okay to pull a bit of herself back from these people. That morning, Gabriel had texted her right back, fortunately—with a fugitive in uncertain medical condition stashed away in her house, she didn't have the patience to sit around waiting for things to happen. It was also fortunate that he was right on campus. She could walk there in ten minutes.

Now she's sitting at a little cafe just across from them, on a plastic chair warmed by the sun, pretending to study her phone while she wonders who the hell Gabriel is talking to, and why. She doesn't trust this guy—he's got a cop vibe. A probation officer? This doesn't seem very official, though—street clothes on the steps of Sproul on a Saturday morning. This goddamn family, she thinks. She herself, the only child of a single mom with two jobs, had been raised by the television, with occasional check-ins from the neighbors. There is much she admires about these Percivals, but right now she needs a fucking break from their expanding weirdness.

Gabriel's not even talking anymore. The guy says a couple of things, but there's no response. For a time they stop talking altogether, and they go so still that she has to glance over at the pigeons to make sure the world is still in motion. And then the guy stands, delivers a final comment, and walks away. She slips her phone back into her purse, stands, and stalks across the plaza.

Chapter 85

The world comes back to Leonardo in sudden, blinding bursts, as if someone is letting light into a house not by pulling open curtains but by knocking down walls. First his awareness is entirely occupied by the experience of his recovering body. His limbs, which for days have felt like bags of broken glass, are regaining their feeling, their capacity to obey him. Then the nausea lifts enough to allow for some hunger, and the vague, familiar sense that he has important things to do. He can't remember what they are though.

Another wall falls down and the weeks come crashing back in. The wreck of his career, his missing sister, the kid at Sonoma State, Chico, the house on Mount Shasta's flank. There's a gap in his memory, a recent segment where he can make out only vague colors and shapes and sensations, like the contents in the warped frames of a half-molten film strip. A fire, a forest, Yvette at the wheel. He sits up and finds himself on her couch, in a hospital gown. Nausea comes over him. A wave of fuzz pushes into his skull. He reaches up to rub his eyes and finds his arms so heavy and clumsy that he hits himself in the nose, which sends the world into a spin. His equilibrium returns after a few deep breaths, and then he remembers the condor.

Had that been real? He wills his head to clear, bringing his hands to his head as if the pressure will help the memories to coalesce. A night on the mountain, a black shape in the trees. Those splayed primaries and those white underwing streaks, soaring through the morning sunlight. The condor in its ancestral homelands. He didn't know what he'd be able to do about his missing data and Clifford's sabotage, if anything, but this discovery is a consolation, a reminder of the might of his field, and of the many things greater than any one researcher's dataset. And if the condor could return to the north, then he could sure as hell get his ass off this couch.

"Hon?" he calls.

There's no response. On the coffee table before him sits a pint of pecan praline ice cream, half of it remaining, and now completely thawed. He'd been in her bed sometime earlier, and hunger had set in. This must have been his solution. Where's Yvette?

Leo sits up a little higher, takes another look at himself. "For fuck's sake, man," he mutters. He isn't sure what he's supposed to do next, but he knows where he needs to go. There's only one person to whom he can present the wreck he has become. He stands, and when the next wave of nausea and lightheadedness passes, he sheds the gown and tracks down the only clothes he keeps there—some pajama pants and an old t-shirt. He forces his feet into a pair of her flip-flops and borrows a ball cap, pulling the brim down low. After dumping the melted ice cream down the drain he tosses the carton and stumbles out the door, heading for his brother's apartment.

Chapter 86

Gabriel follows Yvette back to her apartment, his amazement growing with each development as she tells the story of their course through Chico to Mount Shasta and the empty cabin, and then the cinders, her detective work, and the escape from the hospital. It is not a big surprise for him to learn that Leonardo is back in town—as soon as she reached out to him he figured a reunion was imminent, and in light of the way that everything else has been spiraling in toward him, this all seems logical. What he could not have anticipated, though, was Leo's state, or the events that had led to it.

She finishes her account and then loops an arm through his. "I've done just about everything I can do," she says, "and now I'm just really tired and I need to catch up on the parts of my life that don't include your brother. So it's your turn now." She gives his arm a squeeze before releasing it, and then she turns and walks up the stoop of a small duplex.

Gabriel follows her, wondering exactly how he's supposed to pull off the rescue of not one but both of his siblings. She unlocks the door and he follows her into an empty living room. "Hang on a sec," she says, and disappears into the back of the house. But a moment later she's back, with a look on her face like she just got punched. "He's not fucking here," she says. She gestures back toward the empty bedroom, the bathroom. "He's gone."

"You said he could barely walk," Gabriel says, surprised at how thin his voice sounds.

"Yes, that's what I said. So he barely walked somewhere, then."

"Well, where do you think he went?"

"I don't fucking know, Gabriel. I have no idea. I've done everything humanly possible to try to help him, but now I need to stop thinking about him for a bit. I know you've got a missing sister, but what I need to hear is for you to tell me that you're on this," she says.

"I'm on it," he says, unsure if he's on anything.

"It's going to be okay," she says. Whether to him, or herself, he does not know.

He walks back toward his downtown apartment, scanning for his brother, for police activity, for anything that might give him a sense of direction, but he finds nothing out of the ordinary. In the walkway to the front door of his apartment building there's a gaunt man leaning heavily against the cinder block wall, in pajamas and pink flip-flops. The streets of Berkeley are full of such characters, but this guy is a covered in a sheen of sweat and he's looking right at Gabriel, or something just behind Gabriel—the man's half-closed eyes are hidden in the shadow beneath the bill of his cap, and his focus is unreadable. Gabriel braces himself for a cloud of booze, or worse, and then the man nods, opens his mouth, and says, "Gabo."

Gabriel's stomach lurches sideways. "Holy fuck, Leo."

"Nice to see you too. You've heard I'm a wanted man?"

"Yeah."

"So let's minimize the outside time, okay?"

Gabriel unlocks the door and leads Leo through dark hallways to his dingy one-bedroom unit. Once inside, Leo drops heavily onto the futon couch and asks for water. Gabriel brings him a glass with ice and takes a seat in one of the two vinyl-covered chairs that flank a gray plastic table—the whole set a street find—and watches as his brother drinks and surveys the room through heavy eyelids. Gabriel owns virtually nothing. Beyond the futon, the table and chairs, there is a blue milk crate of assorted items. On the floor, leaning against the wall, sits a single framed 8 x 10 color photograph of himself and two high-school friends in front of a yellow tent in the Sierras. In the bedroom there is a mattress on the floor and a loose pile of clothes and a small upturned cardboard box he uses as his nightstand, a place to put his keys and wallet and phone when he comes home.

Gabriel waits in silence while Leo slowly finishes the water. When Leo is nearly done he licks his lips, grimaces, fixes a look on his face that makes Gabriel sit forward, and says, "I'm going to need your interior designer's number. I really like what she's done with the place."

Gabriel laughs. "You come in here wearing pink flip-flops, and talk shit about my style?"

Leo sits back, wincing. "Yeah, these things suck. They're killing my feet." He slips them off and flexes his toes. A couple of them crack. His forehead buckles suddenly and then he looks up with more uncertainty on his face than Gabriel has ever seen before. "Gabo, I think I'm going to be kinda fucked for a while here," he says.

Gabriel shrugs. "It's all relative, I suppose."

Leonardo looks around at Gabriel's musty apartment, his blank walls, the spaces where someone else would put furniture, or whatever people put in their apartments. "You been okay?" he asks.

"I've got a story to tell you about that," Gabriel says.

"Good," Leo says. His chin sinks halfway to his chest. Gabriel wonders if he's passed out, but then Leo takes a sudden sharp inhalation. "I want to hear it," Leo says. "But first, what's up with that sister of ours?"

"She's in the story, too."

Leo nods.

"She got a hold of some weird shit from Rogelio's lab."

"She okay?"

"Ayla doesn't think so. Francisco doesn't think so. I'm not sure though."

"Who's Francisco?"

"Mom's cousin. A DEA agent. I found him in Ocotillo."

Leonardo stares at him, a look on his face like a headache just set in. "What the fuck are you talking about, man?"

There's so much to tell. It's an endless tangle, and Gabriel can't find the end of any one thread, but they have some time, so he backs up all the way to the last time he and his brother were together—in their father's office in the hills, learning the news of their sister's departure—and then he describes his voyage inland and then south to the border. He tells Leonardo about his night on the border, and his morning at the Cactus Market, where he'd met their uncle. He describes their grandfather's house, the petals and colors of the *centella*, and the taste of its tea. He tells his brother of the journey and the ways his words had all left him and then slowly returned, and he tells him how he'd discovered Lenore's location in a dream, and then awakened with the dirt of their mother's garden smeared on his hands.

"Longford Hall? You dreamed it?"

Gabriel nods.

"*La urraca* would be proud of you," he says.

"You're the one who flew down a mountainside."

The brothers sit quietly, considering. From outside there's the ding of a distant bicycle bell, and then, closer, the laugh of someone who's had too many cigarettes. Leo's face crumples. Another flashing headache? Gabriel shifts in his chair, discovering how uncomfortable it is. He's never sat in it longer than the duration of a quick microwaved meal.

Leonardo takes a breath that lifts his shoulders halfway to his ears, and then another. "So who's in charge of this operation of hers?" he asks. "Is it her? Or someone else?"

"Let's find out."

Leonardo nods. Outside the voice laughs, curses, and then laughs again.

Chapter 87

Very little of Vasco's evening feels familiar. The coat and tie, which he was relieved to find still fit. The resplendence of the newly remodeled concert hall, which manages to combine an understated modernity with elegant classicism, according to a conversation he overhears in the lobby. The sconces, whatever those are, are particularly notable. For Vasco, the architecture is irrelevant—the evening's chief curiosity is the woman at his side. When she answered her door she was barely recognizable in a long silver gown, a jade pendant, and earrings, her hair swept up and held with silver pins that seemed to catch more than their share of light. His reaction had been visceral, warmth in a half-dozen places where he'd grown unaccustomed to warmth. Now as he follows her path through the crowded lobby he keeps looking at the curve of her neck as it descends from her hairline and sweeps toward her shoulder. It is the slight indentation made by the strap of her gown that captivates him the most. In that tiny phenomenon he reads pliancy, strength. He wants to move that strap aside and see her skin smooth itself out, change color. She's looking at him now, over that shoulder, with a look that says she might be reading his thoughts. He smiles and tries to remember where they're going.

Nicole is following Redland, who in turn is following the assistant director of something or other. Upon their arrival at the box office, he and Nicole had met Peoria's husband, who wore a navy suit that seemed tailored for an earlier, slightly larger version of himself. He'd greeted them with warmth, but Vasco could see the tightness at the edges of his eyes, the way his smile faltered just a little. Not far beneath the surface, a family in disarray. They'd only just had time to meet one another and enter when their exuberant host had appeared in his tuxedo, introduced himself as Carmichael, and bade them follow him. Now they're heading to a champagne reception somewhere. In the DEA there are very few champagne receptions. This building, this woman, these circumstances—they make Vasco feel as though he's occupying someone else's experience. More than once he catches himself looking down at his hands to make sure they are still his.

Beneath it all, though, is more familiar terrain: subterfuge, questions, blind spots. People in danger. That sense of things being just beyond his reach. According to the brief text exchange he'd had with Peoria that afternoon, she's expecting Gabriel to be here for the performance as well. Does she know about his other agenda, though? Perhaps he will arrive, and perhaps he won't. Perhaps he'll have information to share, and perhaps he won't. Perhaps a decision will present itself to Vasco. And then what? He pulls out his phone for a quick glance and sees no notifications. He slips it back into his pocket and looks up to find Nicole's head turned, her eyes on him. Is it the briefest flash of a scowl he sees, directed at his phone, before she smiles, and then turns back to follow Redland? He winces and tries to think about champagne receptions.

Carmichael leads them to an elevator. They ascend and then disembark in a hallway, whose wine-colored carpet leads them to a doorway where a smiling usher stands guard. He says nothing but beams at them as they pass. The reception hums with conversation and laughter. In the rear of the room, food covers a table that runs the full length of the wall. A white-gloved waiter immediately appears with a tray of champagne. Redland takes a glass and Nicole takes two, gives the waiter a tiny curtsy, and then turns to offer Vasco one.

"Here's to your cousin," Redland says, his glass extended in a toast.

"To your wife!" Nicole says.

The glasses clink. It's the best champagne Vasco has ever tasted. As soon as the sips go down, Redland is accosted by a series of well-wishers. He introduces them all; after the first dozen Vasco stops trying to keep them straight. The news of his cousinhood produces great excitement, even elation, as if their shared genes are a blessing on the reception. A half-hour later, he is deep in conversation with Nicole when the lights flicker. Redland materializes before them.

"Are you ready?" he asks.

Chapter 88

Peoria strides onto the stage in a simple black dress, a green and orange scarf around her neck. On her way up Bancroft to the hall her attention had fallen upon a cluster of redwoods and she'd veered from the sidewalk and walked into their midst. After gazing up at them she'd walked over to one and placed her hand upon it, and then rubbed it until its red tint marked her hand. She dug her fingernails into the soft bark, clawing fragments of its grain so that she could bring some of it with her. Her hands should not be too clean if all this is to unfold properly, after all. After continuing on her way she'd untied her bun and woven her hair into a pair of loose braids, black and silver. Just before the lights dimmed she'd also decided to leave her shoes in her dressing room, and her bare feet flatten and arch against the varnish of the brand-new parquet.

There is tentative applause, but it fades because she's heading not toward center stage, where the piano and her audience await, but toward the conductor's podium, where Benicio stands, his face revealing not a hint of the confusion he must be feeling. She places a hand on his back and cranes up toward his ear and he understands and stoops to listen.

"I'm sorry to do this to you," she whispers, "but I need five minutes. G major. You'll know when to join me."

This would have been the norm in a Harlem jazz club a hundred years ago but on a stage like this it's unthinkable. For a man who has just been broadsided, though, Benicio is unflappable. "*Claro, señora,*" he says. He has always struck her as a fellow revolutionary, and tonight she loves him for it.

She still does not walk toward her piano, but steps instead into the curve of space that separates the orchestra and their conductor. With her hands at her side she stands, her shoulders back, and makes eye contact with every single musician, holding it for a full second before moving on. "*Con ganas, compadres,*" she tells them, her voice a low exhortation, and only then does she turn toward the audience. She takes her seat and plunges into her grandmother's song, playing it into the building's every fiber, pressing it straight through the walls, hurling it in long glowing arcs deep into the falling night.

Chapter 89

Just before his brother returns a spike of heat hits Leonardo. It starts in his solar plexus and rushes outward, pushing sweat through his palms and forehead. He drags the sleeve of his Hawaiian shirt across his face. "Fuck," he says, his breath suddenly short and shallow. It is a warm evening and Gabriel's shitty apartment gets no circulation. With the sun now gone he's hoping it'll be a lot cooler outside, because he has to wrap himself up before they go out—in a too-large yellow windbreaker, high-top sneakers that Gabriel dug up from God knows where, some stupid gardener's hat with a brim big enough to cover his whole face. He is a wanted man, after all, and he's back in the one place in the world where he's most recognizable. This hodge-podge ensemble is exactly befitting of someone who's struggling to haul himself up a south Berkeley sidewalk, though, and no one will give him a second glance. He leans back on the futon and unbuttons the top few buttons of his shirt and fans the lapels, trying to coax air across his chest. He kicks the gigantic shoes off his suddenly too-hot feet and then the door swings open.

Gabriel comes in, looks over, and then squats so he's down at Leo's level. There's something in his face Leo hasn't seen before. It's true that he's still getting used to having his brother out and around, after he'd been hidden away these last few years, but it's more than just a few hard years' worth of aging. There's a different quality there, a shift in his eyes, his bearing. He doesn't look the part of a little brother anymore.

"You sure you're up for this?" Gabriel asks.

"I'm fine," Leo says. "You've been keeping an eye on the place?"

"Yeah. I think it's probably a good time to head on up."

Leo nods. "I wonder how Mom's doing."

"Outdoing herself, I would guess. Speaking of Mom, she texted me earlier. This cousin of hers, the cop—he found some new video of you and the kid at Sonoma State. It might show you didn't push him. I don't know. She hadn't seen it. That's what they told her."

Leonardo's chest loosens. He sits up a little straighter. "I didn't. I just let go and ran away."

"Sounds like it could be okay, then. But I think you should still cover up. We'll walk on separate sides of the street. I'll stay a few dozen yards back."

"Longford Hall, then?"

"Ground floor." Gabriel smiles and then Leonardo recognizes what he's seeing in his brother's face. It's in his eyes, and the patterns of wrinkles that extend from their outer edges. He's starting to look like their *abuelo*. Leonardo rises from the couch and the brothers head outside, where the day's light is gone, and cool air washes over them.

Chapter 90

From across the street and half a block back, Gabriel watches his brother lurch through town and in the midst of the chaos, the familiar streets carry him into a simple memory, one of his earliest. They were at Stinson Beach, on a perfect fogless day. Leo had been maybe nine, Gabriel about four. One or both of them had begun begging for ice cream, and their parents handed Leo some money and sent them away to the snack bar, which was on the other side of the dunes and across the parking lot, a distance that seemed a thousand miles away to Gabriel. He remembers his own trepidation about the parentless voyage, and then the feel of his brother's hand around his own. Leo held onto him the entire way and once they had their cones they didn't return, but instead sat down on a bench and ate right there, by themselves, two boys in a boundless world, who knew how to get what they wanted. When they finished, Leonardo wiped Gabriel's face and led him back across the busy parking lot, over the sand dunes, and along an unerring course through the crowds to where their parents were reclining on a green plaid blanket. Leonardo went from sibling to demigod that day. There was nothing his big brother could not accomplish, no situation he could not master. Even as they grew up and apart and came to share their home with a squalling baby girl, even as Leonardo's ego and sharpness began to eclipse his better qualities, Gabriel never lost that sense of faith in his brother's abilities. And now, watching Leonardo shuffle along, dressed like a lunatic, perhaps over-doing it a little on the stumbles, Gabriel has little doubt that they will once again find what they're looking for, and return to their respective green plaid blankets.

Taking out his phone he sends a text to Francisco: "Channing and College. I'll explain later." The intersection is one block removed from Longford Hall. It'll bring Francisco to the neighborhood, and then they can call him in if they need him. After thinking a minute, Gabriel sends a second text: "The uncle, not the cop."

Leonardo staggers and plants a hand on the window of a frozen yogurt shop to steady himself, attracting brief glances from nearby pe-destrians. This is definitely overkill now—on a quieter stretch Gabriel will cross the street and overtake him and tell him to go a little easier on the playacting. At the next street Leonardo slaps at the crossing signal button and leans heavily into the pole, his head sagging.

Gabriel accelerates and crosses the street. They climb a half-block and turn to circle the top of People's Park. Just inside the grove that lines the park's edge the encampment is busy with lanterns, camp stoves, marijuana smoke. Someone hidden among the tents plucks a banjo.

Leo pauses, leans against a tree, and fumbles with the front of his windbreaker. Inexplicably he takes his hat off and drops it to the sidewalk, attracting the attention of a young couple who is sitting on the ground just inside the tree line, playing cards on an upturned milk crate.

Gabriel reaches earshot range just in time to hear the man, a white kid in his twenties with an assortment of fabric scraps and silver pieces woven into his dreadlocks, ask Leonardo, "Hey man, are you okay?" He takes a joint from his mouth and passes it to his companion, who looks back and forth from her hand of cards to Leonardo. And then Leonardo crumples into the tree and slides to the ground, lands on his hands and knees, and falls to his side. Gabriel surges forward and the man rises; they reach Leo at the same time. Gabriel kneels and finishes unzipping the windbreaker. Inside it Leo is hot and sweaty but breathing easily. With panic surging from his stomach, Gabriel tries to shield the sight of the fallen body from passing cars, glancing up and down the street to see if anyone else has noticed.

"Third one this week," the kid says. "Babe, call 911. He breathing okay? Let's see those pupils."

"No," Gabriel says, scanning the street behind him. "He's breathing fine. This isn't an OD." Berkeley PD is omnipresent in this part of town. He grabs for his phone, but there's been no response from Francisco. He's got maybe three or four minutes to figure this out.

"Pretty sure it is. We see this all the time out here, man."

"I'm with him. He's my brother and he's getting over a sickness. He'll be okay." He looks up at the girl, still seated at the milk crate. "No need for 911. Thank you. Sorry." Gabriel pats Leo's cheek, willing him to stir. Leo remains utterly limp, though; Gabriel takes another scan for unwanted attention.

The young woman rises and approaches. She's pale, pink streaks in her long blond hair, a too-big camouflage coat hanging from her thin shoulders. "What is he sick with? Is it contagious?"

"No, it's not contagious. It's like an allergy. He'll be fine."

She doesn't respond, but she doesn't look convinced either. He searches their skeptical faces, sees their tent behind them, a lantern glowing inside it. They're Leo's only way out of this now. Gabriel holds out his arms, a supplicant. "Look, I need a huge favor. He's wanted by the police for some shit he absolutely did not do. I swear on my life. But I do need to hide him in your tent for just a few minutes. He'll come around, and then we'll be on our way. Please."

The woman takes a step back, but the man stays where he is. "What is he wanted for?" he says.

"Just questioning. Our little sister is with these people, and we're not sure if she's okay, and we're trying to get her back. The police think he's involved, but we're the ones trying to help her. We know where she is, and we need to go get her, right now, tonight, so we can bring her home, and then he's going to go deal with it. I really need your help. We all need your help."

"That's a nice story," the woman says. "How do we know it's true?"

"You can look it up. It was in the news. He's a professor. Leonardo Percival, biology. Please."

She looks down at Leo, disgust on her face. "A professor? How stupid do you think we are?"

At his feet, Leo lets out a light snore. Across the park, Gabriel sees the black and white of a police cruiser slowly glide into the glow of a streetlight. "Please," Gabriel says. "Look." He opens his phone's browser and searches for one of the more recent articles, one that will mention Lenore. He finds a link and loads the page, but she will not even look at it. "Theo can look at that if he wants," she says, "but I still say this is a bunch of bullshit."

Theo takes the phone and scans the article.

"It was a total accident," Gabriel explains. "The kid tripped and fell. There's new video."

Theo pokes at the screen a time or two, scans another paragraph.

"We know we need to deal with it, and we will. I just need to shelter him long enough to go find our sister. She's right up the hill."

The cruiser is making its way up the side of the park now, heading for the nearby intersection. Gabriel resists the urge to grab his phone and run. Finally Theo hands the phone back to Gabriel, nods, and then stoops down to work his arms beneath Leo's.

"You have to be kidding me," the woman says, backing up.

"I believe him," Theo says. "It's not like we had big plans for the night."

"Speak for yourself. I planned for nobody to die in my fucking tent."

"Jesus, what kind of thing is that to say?" Theo says.

"He's not going to die," Gabriel says. "I promise." He grabs Leonardo's pant legs and he and Theo lift and drag him toward the tent. Seconds later, Leo is hidden away. The cruiser drives past, within a few feet of where he'd been lying moments ago.

Theo darts away, disappears behind another tent, and returns with a cold dripping can of beer. "Cool him off," he says, handing Gabriel the can. Gabriel bends down, duck walks into the tent, and takes an awkward seat next to Leonardo. He holds the can against his brother's forehead and then touches it to each of his cheeks. Leonardo does not stir.

Gabriel checks his phone again. Still nothing from Francisco, and now he's running out of time. "You're not going to like this," Gabriel says, "but I have to go."

"The hell you do," says Laurel, peering in through the tent's opening. "You're not leaving us with this mess."

Theo's squatting next to her. "You told us a few minutes, man. We need a little more info."

"I know. I'm sorry. I was hoping he'd come back around. I have to get my sister. I'll call for his girlfriend to come get him, okay? Give me a half-hour. If she's not here by then, drag him back onto the sidewalk and call the police." He scrambles for the tent's opening. "I'm sorry," he says. "I just don't have a choice."

Laurel begins to raise another protest, but Theo cuts her off. "You're someone's little sister, too, right?"

She sighs but stays where she is, blocking Gabriel's exit. "Okay, but I need to know exactly what the fuck is wrong with him. What are you leaving us with?"

"He had an allergic reaction, and then barely escaped a house fire, and he was lost in the woods up north. He was dehydrated and malnourished and he picked up a fever at some point. His girlfriend snuck him out of the hospital so he wouldn't get arrested before we can get our sister back and I just need you to be his guardian angels for thirty minutes." Gabriel is on his knees, literally begging. "Please. Just thirty minutes. You can come crash in my apartment for a week, take two hot showers a day. You can have my bed; I'll take the couch. I'll make you pancakes every morning. Please."

"We like it out here, thank you very much," Laurel says.

Theo gently pulls her aside, clearing the entrance. "Go do what you got to do, man."

Gabriel crawls out and jumps to his feet. "Thank you. Thirty minutes." He turns, hurrying away. "I'll call his girlfriend now."

"Wait!" Laurel says. She squats, pulls something from a pocket on her backpack, and offers it to Gabriel. He extends a hand and a small wooden figure falls into it. "It's Pele," she says. "The fire goddess. My brother carved her for me, before Theo and I went on the road."

Gabriel nods and closes his hand around the talisman.

"I want it back," she says.

Chapter 91

Vasco is transfixed, and has been from the moment Peoria's hands first fell upon her keys. He can see the music flowing from her body and through her arms and hands, and as it pours from the piano he can feel it in his hair and eyebrows, inside his nose, in the center of each tooth. It's made not only of sound but also of temperature, of light and darkness, of scent. He can smell sunlight on dry fields of grain, ocean air, warm earth. Memories arise, some of them from long ago: sunlight falling into his childhood bedroom, the taste of his mom's pozole, the sound of horses running in the fields at the edge of their neighborhood. The images swell and churn, pushing all else to the furthest fringes of his mind.

Chapter 92

Leonardo wakes up to find himself looking at a canopy of stained orange canvas, unevenly lit, and with a young woman sitting next to him, sipping a can of beer. He has no idea where he is. Is this a dream? He decides to lie there, doing nothing, waiting for the world to make sense of itself.

"Hey man," the girl says. "You okay?" She turns her head and calls, "Theo, he's awake." She turns back to Leo and puts a hand on his chest. "How do you feel?"

"Okay I guess," he says. "Where am I? What happened?"

"You passed out on the sidewalk, bro," says a man's head, as it emerges through a slit in the canvas. There is the sound of a zipper and the rest of the man's body appears. "You're at People's Park. Your girlfriend is coming to get you."

"Yvette?"

"Do you have more than one girlfriend?"

Leonardo doesn't understand the question, but he answers it anyway. "No," he says.

"Then Yvette it is," Theo says, dropping into a squat.

"Where's my brother?" Leonardo asks. "Where's my sister? We were going to try to get her," he says.

"Your brother went to get her. We don't know much else," Theo says.

"Yeah," says his girlfriend. "We're just in it for the pancakes." She smiles.

"What pancakes?"

"Never mind," she says. "You should drink some water."

"I'm going back on lookout," Theo says. "Drink some water." He backs out and the flap falls back into place.

"Look out for what?" Leo asks, sitting up.

"Don't worry," she says. "Your girlfriend."

"Don't worry about what?"

She hands him a bottle of water. "About any of it," she says.

He accepts the bottle with a grateful nod and takes a long sip, and then another. After handing it back he pushes himself up and through the tent door. His equilibrium is still a little off, and he's just finding his balance when Yvette appears before him, confusion on her face.

"Jesus, baby," she says. "What the fuck are you wearing?"

"You don't like my new look?" He takes a short step, testing his balance. He takes a second step, a third, and just then a man comes rushing up to them.

"It's them!" the man says, pointing away, where traffic is flowing down the cross street. "The white van. It's her!" Only then does Leonardo recognize his brother. "We have to go right now," Gabriel says, seizing Leonardo by the arm and dragging him to the car. "We have to follow them." He turns to Theo and Laurel. "I meant what I said about the pancakes," he says. "I'll come back."

Yvette jumps ahead of him to pull the rear door open, and Leo ducks and tumbles into the backseat. Doors slam and the car lurches forward.

Chapter 93

Gabriel strains for a sight of the van as Yvette approaches the corner, but it's nowhere to be seen. "They must have turned on Telegraph," he says. He whirls to check on Leonardo, who is wriggling into an upright position and pulling his seatbelt across his chest. "You okay man?"

"So now we're in a freaking car chase?" Yvette says.

"They didn't see me," Gabriel says. "They don't know I'm here."

"So?"

"Yeah, I'm fine," Leonardo says. "I just got a bit lightheaded for a minute."

"Good," Gabriel says, and then turns back to Yvette. "So it's not a car chase," Gabriel says. "We're just tailing them."

"And then what?"

She has begun to turn onto Telegraph when down the block the van appears, in front of a moving truck. "There!" Gabriel shouts, pointing. Yvette accelerates and changes lanes. Leo emits an involuntary grunt from the backseat and Gabriel turns back around. Leo's eyes and color look better than they did before, but he's slumping deep in his seat. "You sure you're okay? You look pretty fucking slouchy."

"You're giving me shit about my posture? I said I was fine."

The van is a block down, a lane over. With a couple more quick lane changes she cuts the distance in half. The van turns left down Durant and there is a long minute of tense silence when it is out of their view, while they wait for a gap in the traffic to follow.

"And then what?" Yvette asks again, more pointedly.

"Depends on where they're going, I guess," Gabriel says. He checks his phone again; there is still no response from Francisco, so he composes another text: *Never mind.*

They follow the van's right turn through a green light and find it has gotten hung up behind a double-parked delivery truck, traffic flowing wide to circumvent the blockage. "Don't pass them!" Gabriel says. "I can't let them see me."

Yvette slows and waits for the van to pull around, and then squeezes her car into a gap two cars behind it. The van's course reveals no sense of alarm. It could be piloted by a tired plumber, done with a long day of work.

"So what about the cop?" she asks.

"Doesn't matter," he says. "This is on us."

They roll forward again. At University they just barely make the yellow light for their left turn and they descend the broad boulevard that runs through the flats of west Berkeley.

"What if she doesn't want to come with you?" Yvette asks. Her hands knead the steering wheel. Her eyes remain forward, locked on the van, which is still meandering down the road just ahead of them, unhurried.

"I think she will."

"But what if she doesn't?"

"I'll figure something out."

The van crosses San Pablo Avenue, the last of the major cross streets, eliminating a whole collection of possible local destinations. The next stop is I-80, which connects to San Francisco, Sacramento,

Nevada, Maryland, Mexico. They ascend the overpass, and Gabriel wonders whether it will be east or west for them. But the van opts for neither. Instead it descends to the four-way stop at the frontage road and then continues straight into the Berkeley Marina, from which there is no exit.

Gabriel leans forward. "Holy shit," he says. "We've got them."

Chapter 94

There is no intermission, no chance for Vasco to collect himself. He's barely breathing; several times he has to remind himself to inhale. Peoria is riveting throughout, guiding the breathless audience through a series of pieces that build upon one another, rising and falling, accelerating and slowing, telling a thousand stories at once.

Sometime in the second hour his buzzing phone finally breaks the spell. It's a text from Gabriel, on top of earlier messages he'd missed, somehow. Holding his phone down near his hip to minimize the glare of his screen, he opens his texts and reads. There's a message with the name of a Berkeley intersection, and another cancelling it. The most recent message reads: *Berkeley Marina. Slip G. Come soon.*

Nicole is watching him. "I'm going to have to go after all," he says into her ear. "I'm really sorry."

She leans in to him. "No apology needed. I'm coming with you."

"Okay. I'll get you a car."

"No. I mean I'm coming with you. Wherever you're going."

"There are a lot of unknowns in this situation," he says.

"Good," she says. "I love unknowns." She sits back and goes to work removing a silver earring.

"I'm really not sure—"

She drapes an arm around his shoulder and brings her lips right against his ear. The heat of her breath spills into him and sends a ripple down his spine. "I'm not ready for my night with you to be over. And you sound like you might be able to use a combat-trained paramedic." She sits back, pulls her other earring off, and drops it into her clutch. "So let's get going."

Chapter 95

From the driver's seat in her darkened cab, four spots down from the van, Yvette can see the locked metal gate, the branching dock beyond it, and the houseboat in question, the first on the left. That morning, all she wanted was some space for herself, but here she sits, her attention riveted on the door of some houseboat. With her focus entirely upon Leonardo and damage control these last couple of weeks, she'd failed to see the true center of this system, the star around which she and all these other people had been orbiting. She'd followed the van down here with some reluctance, out of a sense of duty that sat in her gut like a rock in a shoe. Fine. If she was going to keep paying for therapy, she might as well have something good to talk about. But once she saw Lenore climb out of the van, leaning heavily on one of her half-dozen companions, everything shifted. Some wonder lies at the heart of all this, and it's big enough to reduce Leo's story to a subplot, a footnote. Lenore's decision to walk out into the night had curved the fabric that held them all together, and there was nothing any of them could do to keep from tumbling into this new gravity well. Not the people with her in the houseboat, not her brothers, not Yvette. And now Yvette is here for herself—she wants to see where all this leads. She wants for there to be a time soon when she can pull Lenore aside and talk to her for five or six hours.

Leonardo is in the front seat now; Gabriel in the back. After they'd parked, Yvette had darted away just long enough to find some dusty vending machines and now they wait in the darkness, their windows down, fortifying themselves with peanut butter crackers, beef jerky, orange juice, and candy bars. Whatever had come over Leonardo earlier seems to have passed. A rest in someone's tent, a few snacks, and he's back together again, doing as well as he could be doing considering he'd been semiconscious in a hospital just two days earlier.

"What if they don't come out?" he asks.

"They will," Gabriel says.

They've been over this already. There can't possibly be enough room for the whole group to sleep on the houseboat. There probably aren't even enough places for them all to sit down. A majority of them will have to leave. Would Lenore be among them, or would she stay?

The night is still and the marina's waters are like glass, as if the bay has fallen into a slumber. Every few minutes a weak breath of wind passes through, just strong enough to elicit a halfhearted jingling from the sailboats' rigging. The smells of mud and seaweed rise up from the dark shoreline below. On the road behind them a car creeps past. The houseboat light stays on, flickering occasionally. Another breeze renews the marina's chiming, and then the door opens and a cluster of figures emerges. There's an argument in progress—unheard words and gestures fly through the open doorway, and at least one of the departing group seems to be leaving against his will.

"There's four of them," Gabriel whispers, leaning forward. They watch as the group approaches and spreads. Lenore isn't among them. In the car the members of the stakeout hunch down and hold their breath while the group emerges from the gate, climbs into the van, and drives away.

343

"So that leaves how many inside?" Leonardo asks.

"I guess we'll find out," Gabriel says, and the two brothers climb out of the car.

Watching them walk away, Yvette feels an unmistakable warmth, an affection for this whole scene and everyone involved, herself included. Whatever happens next, however this story should turn out, it will live in her bones for a very long time and leave her wondering what miracles might reside in every other car on the road, in each sidewalk passerby.

In the silence left by the brothers' departure the night takes on a strange remote quality, as though she is remembering it from the distant future. She knows what to do next, but does not understand how she knows. She turns the ignition on, rolls all the windows down, and pulls out of her spot without turning on the headlights. After backing into the loading zone just in front of the gate she climbs out, opens both passenger-side doors, and sits back down behind the wheel, the engine still running. With her eyes closed she can hear two sets of footfalls upon the wooden dock.

Chapter 96

Leonardo walks toward the gate, his eyes fixed on the houseboat door. Whatever it was that took him down at People's Park has passed entirely. For days now he has been helpless, hiding, running. No, not even running—it was Yvette who'd spirited him away, who'd fed him, who'd come for him. He'd kept himself alive somehow, though, and that was surely worth something. How he'd managed it, he isn't sure. There's a stretch of time—perhaps two days, perhaps three—when his memories are only a series of indistinct, washed-out still images. Flames climbing the bedroom wall. Tree branches scratching at his arms and face as he stumbled through the dark, letting gravity draw him down the gully, fighting to stay upright.

It must be that same sense of mission that now propels him down the ramp to where the locked gate stands. The houseboat is silent, dim light shining through its drawn curtains. Reaching the gate, he climbs down the side of the pier and finds footholds in the woodwork. He sidesteps under the chain-link fencing that extends from the side of the gate and climbs back up on the other side, Gabriel right behind him. They continue.

Over the span of three or four steps Leonardo's mind tracks back to the life he'd been living just a few weeks ago—a life that had been turned inside out in more ways than he could count. Back then, the trajectories of his life, and his brother's and sister's, had borne little relation to one another. His days revolved around his work and Yvette and somewhere on the distant periphery Lenore was finishing up high school and Gabriel was finishing up a prison sentence and neither affected his daily life much. But now they're here, two of them on this side of a doorway and one on the other, and whatever is to happen next will be a singularity that will draw them in and bring their previous lives to a close and send them each hurtling away in some new and unforeseen direction.

A sense of tranquility comes over him, as palpable as his resolution. It's a strange combination, especially considering he doesn't know exactly what he's going to do next. They reach the houseboat's corner and make the turn off the main dock.

"Follow my lead," Leonardo whispers.

Chapter 97

G abriel doesn't know what Leonardo has planned but he knows Lenore is inside the houseboat. He can feel her, the way a hand atop a breastbone feels the beating heart beneath it. Leonardo reaches out and jiggles the doorknob and Gabriel prepares himself for whatever is to come next. "It's me," Leonardo says, making no attempt to disguise his voice. "I left my jacket in there."

There is rustling inside, and then the door swings open. Before Gabriel can register who is on the other side of it, Leo throws a clumsy haymaker into the widening gap. There is a dull thud and a shout and Leo's momentum carries him through the doorway. Gabriel leaps in after him and sees Leo's surprised quarry on the floor, struggling to get off his back. Emilio is in a small galley kitchen, a wooden spoon in his hand and shock on his face, and Leo is lunging toward him, stepping on the fallen man's forearm as he passes, eliciting another shout. Emilio drops the spoon, yanks a saucepan from the stove, and hurls it at Leonardo. Hot liquid fills the air. The empty pan careens off of Leo but does nothing to slow him down—he barrels right into his second target, knocking him into the back of a bench seat, tipping him over so that his feet fly toward the ceiling. Someone is spluttering and someone is shouting; Gabriel can't tell who is making either sound.

347

A quick glance past the melee reveals an empty room, a closed door at its opposite end. The man at his feet is working to get his knees beneath him, but Gabriel plants a knee on his back and grabs him by the back of the collar. "Probably just stay down there," he says, surprised to hear the calmness in his own voice. He'd witnessed a handful of fights in San Quentin, and always had to wonder how he'd fare if he found himself in the middle of one.

"You guys have the wrong fucking idea!" the man beneath him shouts. He's tense, shaking, but he's not trying to stand up.

"And what idea would that be?" Gabriel says.

Up ahead, Leonardo is raining blows into the space on the other side of the bench seat and from the sounds of it, many of them are landing. It's an astonishing sight—his brother the professor, the leader of ice cream quests, throwing punch after punch with his yellow windbreaker whipping all around him, his eyes clamped shut. Gabriel notices then that Leonardo's face is bright red, and his hair and shirt are soaked. The smell hits him then—it's the tea, the same tea Ayla had poured down his throat the day before. A paroxysm of coughing comes over Leo, but it doesn't slow his punches.

"Hey, Leo?" Gabriel calls.

There is a louder thump, and Leo's blows stop. "Stay down there or I'll rip your fucking head off," Leonardo manages, between coughs, before turning back to where Gabriel is half-kneeling on his quarry. There's a foot sticking out from beneath the table.

"Did you swallow any of that stuff?" Gabriel asks.

The man at Gabriel's feet protests, but Leo strides back over and grabs a fistful of t-shirt. "Get under the table with your buddy," Leo says, "and shut the fuck up."

"You can't do this," says the man, although he complies with the command, half-crawling, half-sliding toward the table as Leo drags him. "It's med—"

With his free hand Leo slaps him across the face, silencing him, and then he stuffs him under the table with the other man, who is groaning, whimpering, and cursing, all at once.

Gabriel is on his feet now, following closely. "How much of that did you swallow?"

Another flurry of coughs comes over Leonardo. He's leaning heavily on the table with both arms, his legs wobbly. "A good mouthful. Good thing it wasn't boiling."

Gabriel spins and runs for the doorway in the back of the room. He's not going to be able to carry two people out of here. He barrels through the door and darkness enfolds him. After a second his eyes adjust and lumps appear on the bed, atop the covers.

With a trembling hand he combs his fingers across Lenore's scalp. It's hot. He continues, gently brushing the hair out of her face and tucking it behind her ear so he can look at her. She stirs and her eyes open.

"Gabo," she says.

"That rare and radiant maiden," he says, smiling.

"That's me," she says, slurring. "What's going on?"

He chuckles. "I don't know. You tell me."

"It's complicated."

"Yeah. Do you want to go home so we can talk about it?"

She closes her eyes.

Chapter 98

The applause is mighty, but Peoria barely hears it. She's in the spotlight on the edge of the stage, in the proper place to welcome the ovation, but she's thinking about the redwood bark that was beneath her fingernails, and wondering where it is now. Is it still there? Some of it must be. The rest of it must be smeared across the piano keys, particles of it sitting around on the stage beneath her stool, floating in a cloud behind her. She likes this thought—that the towering redwood could be a part of this performance, that it could lend some of its strength and grandeur to her. There's a sound like an ocean roaring now; she can smell the saltwater. Grains of sand in her mouth. Where did they come from? No matter. It's time for a prayer. With her head bowed she brings her hands together so that her thumbs are against her breastbone, the tips of her index fingers against her lips. Her grandmother's song rises in her again, and as she hums it she thinks of trees and the ocean and the desert. When she opens her hands to express her gratitude for it all a wave of heat rises from her palms, washes up over her face, and rises into the sky.

Chapter 99

The bedroom vanishes and I'm sitting on the couch in my grandfather's living room. It's his home in Ocotillo, but instead of his roof there is a thin layer of palm fronds that breaks the midday sun into shards. I hear the sound of a refrigerator door closing and then he walks in, holding two glasses of iced tea. He hands me one with a wink and then he sits down across from me in the easy chair.

"*Hola, nieta*," he says. "You found us." He takes a sip of his tea, and then nods at me to do the same. It's ice cold, with mango, and just a bit of sugar. I had a thousand questions for him, but now that he's here before me, I can't think of any of them. We say nothing as we sip our tea. A soft breeze rustles the fronds and makes the shadows dance. Grains of sand fall through the dappled light and come to rest on the wooden floor. My questions return then, bubbling up slowly, as if through mud.

"The drawings," I say. "It was a family tree, right?"

He nods, his whole face smiling with delight.

"And a map? What's it to?"

He responds with a head movement that is somewhere between a nod and a shake. Yes and no. "*Sí, es un mapa*," he says. "But it was for me, and my world. Your world is different. Smartphones, drones, cars that drive themselves." He shrugs. "You'll need to make your own maps."

"How do I do that?"

His smile returns. "There's someone else here who wants to talk to you about that."

"Someone else?" I hear footfalls in one of the other rooms, but then the whole house flickers and disappears, and Rogelio becomes translucent. "No!" I cry, and I rise to seize him, but find myself waist-deep in sand. It moves and flows all around me like water, washing one way and then another. My great-grandmother Maria stands in the golden currents before me, a colorful shawl draped over her shoulders. Her braids are twenty feet long, thick and black, with strands of silver woven through them, and they dance across the sand, curling and un-curling with its movement, twisting and pointing. She smiles at me, and her smile is beautiful. The grains and their heat swirl around my legs and press against my hips, but my feet and my spine are rooted to the bedrock. In all directions the desert flows out from us, blurring with heat on the periphery. The sun is not a sphere but a field of stripes. One of her braids wraps around me; I can feel its warmth and weight. It unwraps and drifts away.

"Should I grow my hair out?" I ask.

She laughs. "There are many different ways of navigating here," she says. "We all find our own way."

"What do I do next? What should I know?"

"Just keep listening."

"That's all?"

"Let's try it." She turns her face toward the sun and closes her eyes. A coyote traverses the hill's shoulder, shooting us wary glances as she passes. A pair of crows in swirling flight. There's a slight westerly breeze, and riding on its back a lone, faint voice, humming a song.

Maria cocks her head and points to the sky, beaming. "There, see? *Mi canción*. What a beautiful surprise." She looks at me and smiles. "You never know what you'll hear." I listen. The melody is familiar, but I don't know its name, and can't say how I know it. "We'll see you next time, *mija*," she says, and then she rises from the ground, trailing her braids and the colorful fabric of her endless skirts, which billow out from her hips and become the night sky. Planets, stars, whole spinning galaxies appear, shot through with comets and meteors. An object falls out of the darkness, flashing in the moonlight, and lands in my hands. It's a little clay flute.

Chapter 100

For just a second he wonders if she has fallen back asleep, but when Gabriel reaches down to give her shoulder a gentle shake her eyes shine again.

"Yes," she mumbles. "Home."

He slides his arms under her and helps her to her feet. She gropes for the backpack resting on the bed, so Gabriel snatches it and pulls it on, supporting her all the while. Keeping one arm wrapped around her back, he angles through the bedroom's narrow doorway, his shoulder bearing much of her weight. In the main cabin, Leo is leaning heavily on the table, blinking. Beneath it, his two captives are sitting so quietly that Gabriel wonders if they're still conscious. Leo turns when he hears them emerge, but his eyes do not focus.

"Go," Gabriel says.

But Leonardo does not remove his hands from the table. In the stillness a phone buzzes with an incoming text.

"Looks like the reinforcements are here," calls one of the men from beneath the table. "So you all enjoy your evening stroll."

Gabriel grabs the fistful of fabric between Leonardo's shoulder blades, pulls him upright, and pushes him to the door, praying his brother's legs do not buckle. They lurch to the door as one, their legs dangerously close to entangling, and push back out into the cool dark air.

Down the pier and up the ramp, where Leonardo and Lenore both grow heavier. A screech of tires cuts through the summer night, from perhaps two hundred yards away. Leonardo shoves the bar latch. The gate swings open with a loud clang and Gabriel drives upward, pushing his brother with one hand, pulling his sister with the other.

Yvette is waiting at the top of the ramp, both right-side doors wide open. The van's engine roars as it careens off the main road and into the parking lot, and then again as it turns parallel to the shoreline and bears down on them, cutting off their forward route and closing the distance quickly. Gabriel pushes Leonardo into the backseat first, and then shoves Lenore in after him. He leans down and with his shoulder he drives them both across the seat, gripping the door frame for more leverage. The van's tires screech again as it veers and comes to a stop in front of them, sideways, blocking their way. Its doors fly open.

Gabriel pulls his own legs in and Yvette accelerates in reverse, the hinges of the open doors groaning under the strain. She spins the wheel and the car careens backwards toward the street. Gabriel has just enough time to plant his feet and grab the headrest to stop the force from throwing them all out the open door. Something that sounds like glass breaks in the backpack. Yvette keeps the wide-open doors clear of the light poles that flank the parking lot's entrance as she flies out onto the main road. She spins the wheel the other way, yanks the car into drive, hits the gas, and the doors slam shut in unison.

Chapter 101

After a maddening stretch of city traffic, during which time Vasco fills Nicole in on the whole story, they reach the overpass and climb over the freeway. The four-way stop is empty and Vasco runs through it without stopping. They're approaching the T when a beat-up Nissan sedan comes flying into the roundabout and turns the wrong way. Fifty yards behind it a white van is in pursuit. The sedan weaves around the median, rejoins its lane, and roars up University. As it passes Vasco sees Yvette's grim face in the driver's seat, and a backseat full of people and motion.

"Cut if off," Nicole says, unbuckling her seat belt.

"What?"

"Block the van. Get in the roundabout and veer left. Make him go the long way." She twists in her seat and leaps into the backseat—Vasco can't figure out why until he speeds into the roundabout, just ahead of the approaching van, gets sideways, and comes to a stop. He's now blocking the route the sedan took, the right side of the car an empty buffer. The van has already begun its wrong-way approach, and its driver has to stomp the brakes to keep from plowing into Vasco. He stops just short of the passenger-side door, puts the van in reverse, backs up fifteen feet, turns the wheel. He's aiming to circle around the front of Vasco's car, but Vasco pushes forward, cutting him off again while leaning on the horn. The van swerves toward the roundabout's center and the driver has to brake again. He slams his hands on the wheel and shoots Vasco a glare. He's young, in his twenties, and looks like he hasn't seen a shower or a razor in some time. Vasco gives him a smile and a wave. The van reverses again, heading for the far side of the roundabout.

"They're gone," Nicole says, looking up University where the sedan has disappeared. "Nice work." She climbs back into the front seat. "Now what?"

Chapter 102

We untangle ourselves and settle into our seats. Our hearts are hammers in our chests. Up and across the overpass. I can't remember the name of this road, but we're heading home.

I fold my hands over my belly. With deep breaths I make them fall and rise, fall and rise. Our heartbeats are slowing now.

Fall and rise. Our breaths slow.

Fall and rise. The *centella* is tumbling through Leo's blood now, too. I can hear his part of the chord. When did he have the tea?

Fall and rise. I spin in my seat and wrap an arm around each of my brothers and squeeze. Song rises from my throat. A torrent of sand floods the car.

Acknowledgements

This story grew out of my love for Roseland, California, the neighborhood where I grew up, and for its many families, from all over the world, who welcomed me into their homes. Thank you to my parents, David and Jadyne, for planting me in such a vibrant environment, and to my sister Jennifer and my brother John for their own interpretations of what it meant to grow up there.

Many thanks to my tireless agent, Wendy Levinson, whose steadfast support and patience made this dream come true. Thank you to Joe Olshan, whose enthusiasm, generosity, and perspective were critical in shaping this story's final form. And thank you to Isaac Peterson and Jessica Hammerman, the Green City Books team, for their vision and for giving this collection of ideas a beautiful physical form.

To Nikki Van De Car, my mentor in editing, who helped me to see the bloody beating heart that lies in the center of this work, and who believed in me enough to introduce me to her friend Wendy.

Thank you to the men and women of the San Francisco Division of the DEA; to the instructors, students, and supporters of the East Bay Judo Institute; and to the University of San Francisco's pivotal MFA program.

To Ben LeRoy, who published my first book, and then became not only a dear friend and a comrade in letters but also a gateway to a thousand other wonderful people, like Jim Ruland, Pedro Hoffmeister, and Scott O'Connor, all of whom helped welcome this book into the world.

To Robyn Russell, whose energy, brilliance, and support inspire me every time I sit down to write. To Jennifer Reimer, whose early read helped to coax Lenore from the ether, and whose words have been a beacon all these years. To Kat Poster, another early reader, who helped fuel subsequent drafts, and whose belief and effusiveness keep me striving.

To Rachel McGraw, Hawthorn Buchholz, and Hazel Buchholz, for making imagination and creativity core household values. To Kelly Grayer, Gina Melton, and Jaime Lemus, whose care and encouragement have buoyed me for nearly four decades now. To Jonathan Heuer, for the inspiration of his own fearless pursuit of individual creativity, and his unflagging care and support. To Mike Lennox, Eric Berry, and Miguel Huerta, my fellow congregants in the cathedral that is the Northern California wilderness. To Gina Dauter, who brought me stories from the desert. And to Sunny Lee, for creating spaces for all of this.

About the Author

J ason Buchholz is the author of the novel *A Paper Son* (Tyrus Books, 2016), which *Publisher's Weekly* described as "a gripping debut" and *Booklist* described as "wonderfully imaginative." He is the co-founder of Collaborist, an editorial boutique that provides writing, editing, and educational services for aspiring and established authors. He was an editor and the art director of Achiote Press, and his poetry and short fiction have appeared in *Gobbledegook* and *Switchback*. He graduated from UC Berkeley and holds an MFA in creative writing from the University of San Francisco.

www.ingramcontent.com/pod-product-compliance
Lightning Source LLC
Jackson TN
JSHW021902160925
91133JS00006B/13